Watchers

Guardians of Freelandia

Watchers

Guardians of Freelandia

Kent Larson

Watchers: Guardians of Freelandia

Copyright 2013 by Kent Larson
Cover design and interior illustrations by Shelley Mordue

Library of Congress Control Number: 2013933099
ISBN Number: 978-1-939456-05-2

All images purchased and used by permission of photostock.com

Published by Search for the Truth Publications
3275 Monroe Rd.
Midland, MI 48642
www.searchforthetruth.net

Printed in the USA

A Note To Parents

The story of Freelandia is of course totally fictional and in no way is intended to bear any close resemblance to current or historical countries, people or events. That being said, the author invites you to imagine what it might be like to live in a country wholly founded upon Christian concepts, and which has stayed largely true to God throughout its history. Imagine a place under God's direct blessing and protection for hundreds of years, where the leadership all loved and served a God who in turn loved them and remained actively involved in their lives and in the direction of the country itself. Picture the latter part of King David's and the early part of King Solomon's reigns as recorded in the Bible: a time of peace and prosperity where Israel was a true light in a dark world.

What could be better besides Heaven itself? Ah, but there is one more thing, one more incredibly important thing that we believers today have but David and Solomon and all those who lived before the New Covenant and Pentecost could only dream of: a portion of God Himself dwelling within us and the Holy Spirit present to guide, direct, enlighten and empower our daily lives.

So now imagine this country living true to God and endowed with the miraculous spiritual gifts of the New Testament believers given after Pentecost. Holy Spirit power would be commonplace: expected, relied upon and rejoiced over. Read again I Corinthians chapters 12-14, where the greatest gift of love is perfectly sandwiched between exciting descriptions and proper administrations of a wide range of active spiritual gifts. That is the intended setting of the country of Freelandia. Imagine along with the author what it might be like to live in such a place, set perhaps a few hundred years in the past.

The story should be read with an open mind that this is indeed fiction, though with very real moral and ethical dilemmas the main characters must face and learn from. Two main themes are intertwined throughout the story. One is around the spiritual power of worship and music. The Bible tells us particularly in Revelation that heaven is filled with music and song. The largest book of the Bible is a hymnal. God created us to worship Him, and created in us a wonderful ability to express this with dance, music, singing and so many other forms of expression. It is hard-wired into us. Yet many have this short-circuited and have instead used these forms of expression in anything but godly ways. Scripture also supports the idea that God has used music as a powerful offensive weapon for His people to use against His enemies (recall the walls of Jericho falling after the trumpet blasts and shouts, and of the other instances where Israel's "marching band" led the way into battle).

Another theme involves scientific curiosity and inventiveness. Think of the creative inventions of Leonardo DaVinci, and the explosion of mechanical and scientific creativity that ushered in the Industrial Revolution. Couple that era of concentrated industrial progress with Holy Spirit guidance and direction, and you start to get another look at the setting that this story takes place in.

Finally, the story puts to paper various plots and vignettes the author has had rattling around in his imagination for a very many years. With encouragement from his family, he has finally put fingers to keyboard and tried to capture many of those thoughts and ideas into an integrated whole. The intended audience always had been his own family, and at the time of writing specifically for his middle school aged girls. However, the author found his older sons and wife also becoming fully absorbed by the adventure and hanging on every chapter as it was written. Many an evening was spent in the family room reading aloud the next installment, with every family member intently listening (there is something to be said about reading out loud a story to your family, where you can add inflection and watch the play of emotions on their faces as various events in the story unfold– and take time to discuss both the good and the bad characterized throughout the storyline). Laughter was commonplace and many chapter endings evoked "Dad … don't stop there and leave us hanging! Please write more … right now!" So perhaps more will enjoy the story besides just the younger children. It was meant as entertainment, but also as a reminder of God's power and love, of various events and texts from the Bible, and of how we should keep in awe, wonderment and awareness of the Holy Spirit within us.

You are invited to join in on an adventure. If you enjoy it, great! If you begin to wonder what such a Godly place might be like, even better. If you catch a spark of what living with Holy Spirit's power might be like, if it makes you give glory to our wonderful loving God in any way, then all of the efforts to write it and get it into your hands were well worthwhile. A tree is known by its fruit. May this story be known for any blessings it brings.

Kent Larson
Awestruck worshiper of the *Most High God*
2013

The Freelandia Trilogy:

Watchers

Guardians of Freelandia

Book 1 of the Freelandia Trilogy

Chapter 1

An angel's voice

She was going to be late, and all due to that strange reoccurring day-dream that seemed to spring unbidden into her mind at odd times when she was singing in her most special place. But she had no time to ponder about that now.

Maria scuttled along the well-traveled dirt road, trying to avoid the mud and wagon wheel pot holes, and especially the debris left by the horses. That was easy enough just by the smell. At times she had to pick her way more carefully, slowing her even further. She only stumbled twice before making it to the path that led to the backyard of Sam the baker. It was not much of a path, but was one quite familiar to her. In a moment her questing hands touched the broken down fence and she found she was already at the gap where a board had blown off in a windstorm a few months ago. It made a very convenient access point, and Maria only had to stoop slightly to make it through. She heard the noises of several little children playing and from here could begin to smell the wonderful aroma of freshly baked bread.

Maria hurried for the small pathway that meandered through the garden, catching the pleasant smells of various herbs and growing vegetables. She was almost to the house when a carelessly abandoned toy caught her foot and she nearly lost her balance. Gyrating her arms frantically to remain vertical, she spun before regaining solid footing, and for a moment she was disoriented.

"Over here, clumsy!" came the squeaky voice of a child a few years younger than Maria. She turned toward the small boy and somewhat gingerly stepped over to him in hopes of avoiding any further mishaps. "You look a mess!" Todd rudely stated as he gave her a once-over look. "Why do I always have to be the one to clean you up?" he grumbled. He disgustedly went in the back door and returned a moment later with a wet hand towel that was only marginally clean itself. He proceeded to roughly wipe at the various dirt stains on Maria's face and arms. "You have another tear in that shabby old dress".

Maria thought that Todd was being unusually cross today, but didn't dare say anything. She endured his harsh rubbing with the wet cloth patiently, knowing she had little recourse. He finished with an especially hard wipe to her arm that nearly pushed her off balance. "There. Your hair is filthy and you stink. Why do you keep coming here?" The words stung worse than the course rubbing and a tear formed in Maria's eye.

Todd turned and literally ran into his mother who was just coming through the door. "Todd, shame on you! That is not the way God wants us to treat those less fortunate than us. You apologize this instant!"

Todd mumbled out a barely discernable "I'm sorry" as he scurried back into the house.

"He doesn't mean it, Maria; he is just having a grumpy morning." Gracie, the baker's wife, came close to Maria. "Here, let me brush your hair" She worked on the worst of the snarls with the old brush she had tucked into her apron pocket an hour ago for just this purpose, though there was only so much she could do with hair that was rarely washed and only sporadically combed or brushed.

"You are a bit late today, or otherwise I might just pull out the tub and give you a full bath!" That had happened once, and Maria was not so sure she wanted to endure it again. The littlest children had all gathered around to "help" and tease, and afterwards Maria felt like she was disappointing Gracie when she returned with the dust and dirt that inevitably wound up all over her. But that was not the worst part, not by far. Maria involuntarily flinched as she remembered. The Greely boys had found her later that day, all clean and even rather nice smelling of the lavender soap Gracie had so kindly proffered for washing her hair. Those three brothers seemed to go out of their way to pick on her, reveling in saying they had to make sure she remembered her position in life. It was as though by attempting to make her life miserable they thought it would elevate their own shortcomings. Maria's steadfast refusal to be daunted, her indomitable hope and joy of her Creator, irritated the brothers to no end.

Maria shuddered at the remembrance and Gracie took it as a sign that the young girl wanted to get going. "Well, I guess that will have to do. You really would have such pretty hair, if it only was cleaned up and brushed out. You are growing up Maria. Soon you will need to find a real place to stay, and a real job. Maybe take on a position as a scrub maid at the hotel, or a cleaner at a store, or a …" Gracie let the sentence die out in the air. Who, after all, would hire Maria? "Well, maybe at the church there is some kind of more permanent work you could do?"

"Maybe. Thank you — you and Sam are always so very kind to me." Maria smiled and gave Gracie a genuine hug.

Gracie paused a moment, and then hugged back. "I wish … I wish we could do more, Maria."

Maria shrugged and, still smiling, turned to go out the gate that led from the backyard out to where the bakery had a storefront facing the main road. "You already do a lot — and I am very thankful. God has taken care of me so far, and I know He will keep taking care of me.

I suppose it is time for you to feed your crew, and time for me to earn my lunch! God bless!"

Gracie watched for a moment as the so very lean and frail looking girl picked her way carefully along the path and unerringly reached for the latch on the small gate leading to the road. It was amazing how well Maria could take care of herself, but she was growing older ... and that was a dangerous and extremely difficult setting for a young orphan girl, especially one with Maria's ... difficulties.

She gave a quick prayer and headed indoors to round up her large brood of children. For the hundredth time she wondered if she could just set one more plate, find one more corner for another child to sit. But they were barely making it themselves, she and Sam, and one more mouth to feed would mean that much less going to the stomachs of their own children. Sam had declared they just couldn't, even though he also was quite fond of Maria. Gracie wondered if she should stop by the church and talk again to the old priest who let Maria and a few other orphans sleep in the back room. But it was not like the church had any extra money either, being one of the poorest in a town that was hardly thriving.

Maria arrived at the rough hewn timber sidewalk and wiped a few tears that had slipped out. Gracie and Sam were indeed very generous, but she knew she would somehow have to find more permanent work. But who would take HER? She stopped for a moment and composed herself, remembering how thankful she was for what God had given to her, and that He was and always had been her provider and strong protector.

And she was certain God always would provide for her ... well, at least she felt that way most of the time. It was harder to hold onto that faith when the Greely brothers were after her, or when she had that ... daydream. Maria wondered what you called a nightmare that came to you during the day? It had several versions, but all seemed to come to the same point. It was as thought she could see herself out in front of a procession of others, seemingly compelled to go forward. Maria could not escape to the right or to the left, for the pathway seemed hedged in the brightest of white light imaginable. She could only go forward. A short ways ahead, just out of sight of those on the path, was an intense black maw of darkness that filled her with fear and dread. The darkness seethed with evil, with dark power rivulets coursing within and across its surface.

She tried to shout, to warn her dream-self of the imminent awful danger that seemed to direct itself right at her. But the other Maria marched on.

Maria shook her head forcibly. The dream was so strange and terrifying. But it was only a dream. God had always provided and been by her side through every tough time in her life, and He always would be. She just knew that she knew that she knew that.

She shook her head again to clear it. If God wanted her to understand the dream, then He would just have to explain it to her, sometime, somehow. Fortified by that truth — somehow whenever she thought about God she seemed to find extra strength — she consciously choose to smile and think upon the good things God had given to her as she moved down the sidewalk toward the bakery store entrance.

The intense odors of fresh pastries and bread overwhelmed her senses as she neared the doorway - a wonderful and true joy she savored. She could hear the sounds of a good lunch crowd inside, where Sam would be bagging bread and serving sandwiches and soup. She ran her hand along the doorframe as she solidified her bearings and took a step inside, then immediately shuffled to the right a few feet to get out of the way for any paying customers, as Sam had requested. She waited several seconds until he noticed her.

"Maria, I am glad to see you — I was wondering if you were coming! Make your way over to your normal spot as slowly as you need to. It is particularly busy today so watch your step." She did not see Sam grimace over his word choice. "I will be over to you in a moment."

Maria heard Sam slide a tray down onto a nearby table and converse politely with its occupants. She gingerly slid along the outer wall and then cautiously began to weave and wind through the tables to the spot on the far side of the room which Sam had graciously allotted for her. She slowly bumped along, excusing herself prolifically as she inadvertently touched a few patrons. Most ignored her completely, and few snarled out impatient warnings. A couple of regulars greeted her more graciously and those were rewarded by a genuine and somehow disarming smile.

She finally made it to the back and was rather taken by surprise to find that "her" table was occupied. The bakery must indeed be packed today, Maria thought. She mistakenly bumped rather forcefully into someone who was sitting in the chair she always used. "Oh, excuse me!" she immediately stammered.

"What is this, can't an old man have his lunch in peace? What do you want?" growled a gruff and grouchy man's voice.

"I'm …. I'm so sorry sir, please forgive me!" Maria hurriedly moved sideways to put some space between her and this rather touchy sounding older man. She moved so fast that she bumped into the second chair at the table and something fell to the floor with a loud wooden clatter and she heard it roll away from her.

"Now look what you've done!" The man used his words and tones like a whip to strike at her.

"I'll find it … sir." Maria whimpered just for a moment at the tongue lashing and she got down onto her hands and knees to feel around for the object. It could not be located immediately and the man grunted his disapproval as she searched in vain.

"You are quite the incompetent one — can't you see it is over there?" the man disdainfully pointed.

Just at that moment Sam came bustling up and retrieved the object. "Here you are sir, no harm done" he said soothingly. "Maria did not mean to cause you any problems." Sam helped Maria to her feet and guided her to an open spot along the wall a few feet away. She was nearly crying and trembled noticeably, but took a deep long breath to regain her composure. "Here … you can stand here. Just try not to bother the customers!" Sam said that softly but with a tinge of impatience himself — he was the only one running the shop and did not have time to make amends for Maria. Sam turned to the disgruntled patron. "Sir, please accept my apologies. Can I get you something else, maybe something 'on the house' to make up for your trouble?"

The old man grunted a slightly mollified "no" and his chair creaked as he sat back in it.

Sam turned again to Maria and placed a small bowl near her feet. "Do you have any seed money? No? Well, here are a few pennies; you can pay me back later." Sam dropped a few small coins into the bowl where they made a rather pleasing tinkling sound, pleasing at least to Maria's ears. She smiled and whispered thanks, nervously wiping her hands down her tattered dress to try to reduce her trembling. This had not started off so well today.

Sam cleared his throat loudly and in a voice that could just be heard over the noise of the eating and conversation said "Gentle-folk, today is Wednesday, and every Wednesday at lunchtime we have a guest to provide us with a wee bit of entertainment. You regulars know how well Maria here can sing. For our new guests, I hope you will enjoy. For the occasion I created some special frosted cakes and the tea is ready. Come see me at the counter if you want any — but I expect they will go fast!"

He turned and simply said "Maria" in a gentle directive voice and headed back to the counter at the front of the store.

Maria blushed slightly at the special attention, knowing that nearly everyone in the store would now be looking at her, and then began to sing a popular folk song. She had no accompaniment, and it started off haltingly until she settled down into the song. Everyone there had heard it many times before; so many times that one would have expected the chatter to continue unabated. However, within a few lines of verse the lunch crowd din had largely silenced. Several stopped with food or drink part way lifted to their mouths, while others just stared as this little wisp of dirty and bedraggled girl sang out with a voice incredibly pure and sweet.

But those present noticed there was something more to it — something deeper, sublime … something more felt inside than simply heard. It was somehow captivating, reaching out to grab people from their private reprieves to stop all other activities and just listen as the words and melody soaked into their minds and hearts.

The old man near her harrumphed under his breath at first — his day had already been going rather poorly and he had just wanted a quiet and peaceful lunch — and then he too was caught and silenced. His affected gruff demeanor faded and a wry smile flirted on the corners of his mouth, alternating with the practiced scowl when he realized his façade was slipping.

He had never heard such a voice. The tune was simple and the words did not have much depth, but regardless — it was mesmerizing. This girl — the shopkeeper had called her Maria? — seemed to put a palpable depth into her voice, as though it had multiple dimensions that allowed it to be experienced with more than just one's ears.

Despite his considerable self control he could not help but smile. He whispered a silent praise to God for such talent awarded to what was likely a poor scullery girl, for ears to hear the beauty found in the most unusual places, and for directing him to this particular place for his simple lunch.

The first song ended and for several seconds there were few noises in the shop, then first one and then several patrons began clapping and the bakery filled again with its normal lunch crowd sounds. Maria smiled, she could sense the people genuinely enjoyed her song, and perhaps they would be extra generous today. She sure hoped so, for she had a special purpose for the proceeds.

Maria readied herself for another song, licking her lips to moisten them and controlling her breathing. She was just taking a deep breath to start when a burly fellow at the table just in front of her loudly scraped back his chair, sneered sourly in her direction and spoke to his companions in a voice easily loud enough to be overheard.

"You'd think the baker would at least make the riff raff bathe before letting them in. And I came here to eat, not to be squeaked at by a mouse of a girl!" He laughed harshly at his own feeble joke and his table companions snickered. "If I have to put up with any more of that prattling noise I'll surely ..."

Tears began to well up and Maria took a short step further away with a tiny whimper of fear at the expectation of an imminent cuffing — she had had a few rough customer responses in the past before Sam could intervene on her behalf. Even as she was thinking that through she heard and felt a quick movement from the direction of the table she normally stood at. A whooshing sound of something moving through the air in front of her extremely rapidly startled her even further.

The big man was midway through his threatening comment when something blurred in motion directly in front of his face. He blinked and found himself staring at the end of a walking staff that had whistled through the air and come to a very sudden halt only a fraction of an inch away from his nose.

His words floundered and for a moment he was totally taken aback and did not know quite what to make of the sudden appearance of the hardened stick. Then his brow furrowed, his face became red with anger and he began to rise from his chair as his eyes traced the staff back to the arm that held it. He was about to curse the old man and punctuate his words with some rough action when he noticed the heavily scarred forearm. As his gaze progressed up the arm and shoulder and over to the seated man's head he stopped short at what he thought he saw. Narrowing his eyes, he tried to peer more closely at the man's face and in his peripheral vision he noticed some faded markings on the cowl of the man's outer coat. With an abrupt, shocked look the inconsiderate diner clamped down on the hard words that were about to spill out and sat heavily back down on his chair. "Oh, sorry ... I did not mean to offend" he lamely offered.

The old man sighed — the response told him his admittedly superficial cover had already been seen through — and the scowl came back on his facial features full force. "You surely did a superb job of it" he muttered in his characteristically gruff voice. "Now sit down and shut up: let the girl sing in peace". The staff returned to his side in a smooth arc. "Go ahead Maria" he said in a significantly softer and gentler voice.

She had lost much of her composure, and struggled to regain it. Without consciously choosing she began a song that had always worked well in the past to strengthen her and please the crowds. The words of *Freelandia*, the national anthem of their country, began to spill out and flow across the room. Again the crowd quieted.

The song spoke of the beauties of the country with its soaring mountain peaks to the north to its majestic large natural harbor. As Maria proceeded her voice grew in volume and power and even the hardened detractors at the nearby table ceased their conversation.

Her voice somehow seemed to capture the very countryside, painting an acoustic panorama that brought the audience along with her soaring words. More than a few eyes moistened as Maria poured out her voice and her heart into the highly patriotic melody. Her voice ascended into the finale with perfect purity of bell-tone notes and ended in a hushed dramatic whisper. Not a patron moved; even Sam had stopped slicing the loaf of bread before him in respectful stillness.

The silence in the room was profound as most of the people stared ahead of them with glazed eyes as the song and its meaning sank deeply into their minds and hearts. None had been touched by that song quite like this before; even Maria realized she had put an extra depth of feeling into it to oppose the hint of fear that had presented itself beforehand.

The old man was dumbstruck. He had never heard — or felt — anything like this, though he had heard the anthem sung hundreds of times before, and by some of the best local and international singers the Academy of Music offered. Who was this wisp with the voice of an angel? His curiosity was thoroughly aroused.

He mused over this as he slowly ate his lunch, enjoying the several more folk songs and simple ditties that made up the routine Maria had chosen for today's repertoire.

Maria finished with a light hearted and cheerful tune that ended brightly. As the last note faded she smiled at her audience but then could not help but slump against the wall at her back. She had sung with all her heart and it drained a considerable amount of energy out of her — not that she had much space in her very lean frame for any real reserves to start with.

A good many of the patrons came by and dropped a coin or two into her bowl, and she thanked each one graciously — it sounded like quite a good day's haul. The church bell rang in the distance, alerting all that lunchtime was over, and nearly all of the customers hurried out to get back to their workplaces and homes. After the last had paid for their meals, Sam came over and picked up the bowl, emptying its contents into a small leather pouch and handing it to Maria. She smiled at him as she hefted the little bag and then tilted her head to one side as a questioning look flitting across her small face.

With a laugh Sam answered her question even before she could ask it. "Yes, Maria … go ahead". Maria scurried over to the tables, and led by her nose she began to pick up any scraps of food left behind, which she hungrily wolfed down.

"So Maria, you had a very good take today — what will you do with it?" Sam was busily cleaning up the tables behind Maria, and she paused a moment between bites.

"It's Timmy's birthday — he is one of the little orphan boys at the church. We don't really know if it is truly his birthday, but I declared that it was and I want to get him something special!"

"Maria, you really should go and buy another dress from the second hand shop down the road. You have outgrown what you have, and it is getting quite tattered. While you are at it, you need another pair of shoes — yours have several holes already and they will only get worse."

"Oh, I can make due for awhile longer. God — and you — have been taking good care of me. Timmy has had nothing ever since he came to the orphanage. I so want to make him happy, at least once. Maybe next week I can get a different dress."

Sam smiled down on her in a very fatherly way. He so wished he could bring this gentle and kind soul into his household, but God had already blessed him with many children, and with the bakery he was just making it by to keep them fed and clothed.

"Ok Maria, but let me get something for you, and something for Timmy too." Sam walked over to the counter and Maria could hear him using his knife on a loaf. She next heard the sound of paper crinkling and Sam pushed a bag into her hand. "It is not much, but consider this as a gift for Timmy — but and make sure you get a slice too … promise?"

"Oh Sam, you are so special! God bless you."

"He does that each and every day, Maria. And I get a double dose on the days you sing."

"Oh Sam, you are sweet!"

"No Maria, you are sweet. I am more just … flour-y! No really, I get half again more lunch business on the days you sing. In fact, I was wondering if you would consider singing twice a week? Maybe both Wednesday and again on Saturday — that is my slowest day for lunches. It would bring in more business for both of us. What do you think?"

Maria smiled brightly and nodded. "I'll have to ask if I can do some of my chores at the church later on that day, but I think it would be alright. That would be marvelous Sam; of course I would help you even if there was nothing more in it for me."

"Good then. Let me consider the best schedule and talk it over with Gracie. Now it is time to clean up the lunch mess!" Sam turned away and was soon busily clearing more tables and carrying the dishes, glasses and utensils back to the kitchen area where one of his older daughters would clean them up for the next set of customers.

Maria moved to another table ahead of where Sam was picking up. There was a faint far away noise outside, one Sam did not even hear. Maria stiffened abruptly and under her breath let out a quiet yet very concerned "Oh no! They are too early today!"

She ceased her table scavenging and whisked toward the door with her bag, the small leather purse disappearing through a small slit in the side of her dress where a pocket may have once been but where now a small cloth sack could be just observed awkwardly tied to a cord around her waist. "Uh, I have to be going!" she stammered in a hurried — and to the ears of the old man, seriously distressed — quiet voice. Then she was flying out the door and moving down the sidewalk with her feet sliding forward, never overly far above the planks.

The old man stood and with surprising agility moved rapidly through the maze of tables and chairs toward the door with his walking staff in hand. He did not understand what had apparently frightened the little girl so considerably — frightened her enough to leave the partial sandwich which lay on one of the last tables. He sniffed and wrinkled his nose in distaste ... mustard and pastrami, not his favorite either, but he doubted Maria would have passed it by so readily.

No, something had seriously alarmed her. Now what would alarm such a delightful young gifted girl? He nearly bumped into a few chairs that had been inconsiderately left pulled out from tables and made his way to stand at the door.

Sam looked up, hoping he did not have to remind this somewhat odd customer to pay his bill before leaving. The old man just stood very still, head cocked slightly to one side, listening intently.

Chapter 2

Gaeten

Out on the sidewalk Maria shuffled along as fast as she dared, not wanting to take the chance on a spill that could cause her to lose some of the valuable coins she had tucked away, or drop the bread loaf or in any way call extra attention to herself. She was heading for a fork in the village road, where a few blocks down on the left the old run down church stood. She had already covered a surprising distance with her odd shuffling gait. If they had not spotted her … if she could just make it in time …

"Hey Maria, what's the hurry? Did you trick a good many of those sucker townsies out of their coins today at the bakery? Did they feel sorry for the poor orphan Maria?" The snarly voices of the Greely boys carried down the road as they rapidly closed in on her in a loping run.

"Hey, what do you have there?" One of the boys had snuck down and around a back alley and now jumped out unexpectedly in front of Maria, blocking her path. "Let's see what you have there in the bag, Maria. I'm sure you planned on sharing with us!" That was Jarl, the oldest and meanest of the three. He stepped in closer, blocking any hope she had of escaping.

"Leave me alone, Jarl!" Maria dodged to the side and though she knew it was pointless she tried anyway to get past Jake, whom she had heard come up on her right side while Brak jogged up quickly to close the loop around her.

"Hmm, what do we have here?" Jake snatched the bag right out of Maria's protective grip.

"Give it back!" Maria jabbed out with the short walking stick she had left just outside the bakery entrance and Jake did not dodge aside quite fast enough.

"Ouch! Oh, you're gonna pay for that one good." Maria slashed out again but this time Jake slipped away. "Mmm, I smell freshly baked bread — imagine that!" He fumbled with the bag and his hand dove in to retrieve the contents. "Mmm, it tastes good too" he said around a mouthful.

"Stop! That's for Timmy!"

Jarl laughed harshly and heartlessly. "That little lamely runt? He won't miss it. Now, let's see how much money you made." He grabbed at Maria, but she artfully dodged away from his grasp. That evoked another laugh, this time with a cruel promise implied.

The boys arranged themselves around her more closely, grabbing and shoving, circling around while they shoved and spun her until she was thoroughly disoriented and confused. Maria struck out this way and that with her the small tree branch staff, but the boys were practiced at this and her swings never scored any hits.

Brak kicked out from behind and tripped her, causing Maria to tumble heavily down into the dusty road. She tried to get to her feet again but a foot roughly shoved her back down and she cried out. Defeated, Maria cowered outwardly while inwardly crying out to God. The walking stick was ripped from her as rough hands tugged and tore until they had found and retrieved the money pouch.

"Ha, looks like you have plenty to 'share' with us Maria!" Jarl held the bag up in triumph. "But you really should not have poked Jake or fought with us. You obviously need to be taught another lesson in manners. Hold her fellas."

Maria felt hands grab her arms and legs and she whimpered but did not scream. She knew enough from past experiences not to scream. If one of them punched her face she might not be able to sing for a week until the swelling went down.

She tried to turn away as best she could and steeled herself for the inevitable kicks or slaps she knew were coming next. She heard Jarl come close. He used to just take her money, but lately he had been getting more violent, seeming to want to hurt her. She heard the movement of his arm rearing back but then heard a muffled sound of rapidly running feet coming near, unlike she had ever heard before. It was in fact the quietest running sound she recalled ever hearing.

Instead of the strike she expected, she heard Jarl grunt out in pain and fall heavily backwards. The hands gripping her arms unexpectedly loosed and what followed was a confusion of sounds.

She heard Brak yelp and then the sound of something heavy falling several yards away in a loud thud. Jake was next — he always seemed to be last at everything — and he too cried out in pain as his hands were torn from holding her ankles and by the sounds he must have went airborne backwards.

Jarl stood to his feet angrily and swung his meaty right fist at the mid-sized old man who had silently come and scattered them like twigs in a breeze. The blow sailed harmlessly through empty air where the man had just been and stiffened fingers drove upwards to strike into the soft underarm flesh. That arm flopped down numb at his side and Jarl grimaced in pain.

A smarter person might have stopped, but Jarl was not well known for his quick thinking. He tried to swing his numb right arm, but it would not respond. So instead he charged forward trying to simply bowl over the aged man with his greater size and bulk. Instead he was stopped abruptly in his tracks, running into what felt like an immovable steel fist positioned at stomach level. The air gushed out of him with a loud grunt and he dropped to the ground, writhing in pain.

By this time Brak and Jake had regained their footing and came running, and as best as Maria could determine, both left the ground again, this time at the same instant, and landed yards away. Neither immediately got back up.

Maria had become angry inside, but now as that anger faded the underlying fear welled up to fill the void and she began to sob loudly. Gentle strong hands lifted her up. She felt scarred wrists and calloused hands, and she smelled remnants of the bakery aroma on the man's cloak.

"There now, you are safe. Don't be afraid". There was no gruffness in the voice now, only calm strength and genuine caring. No one had stood up for her like that in a very long time, though Sam would put customers in their place that became too surly with her. It reminded Maria of her most cherished memories of climbing into her father's lap and being enclosed in a warm embrace where nothing bad could ever happen.

At that most comforting — and most painful — thought, all self composure left and she collapsed into the powerful arms and sobbed again, clinging to the man who had become her rescuer. He uncomfortably put his arms around her and rocked slowly to her sobs. Maria buried her head into his shoulder, not caring that she did not even know who this person was; just that he had cared enough to save her when she could not save herself. The sobs and shudders died off — an orphan in that town would not last long if they were not rather tough, and the softer cries and tears lessened and then stopped within a few moments.

Maria pulled away and tried to straighten what remained of her tattered clothing. "Thank you, sir. I don't know what I would have done, what would have happened to me …" A whimper started but she staved it off sharply and swallowed hard. "I don't even know your name, but God bless you for helping me."

The older man chuckled softly. "Gaeten. You can call me Gaeten, Maria."

Maria could hear the Greely boys stumbling to their feet and she held her breath for a moment wondering what they might try to do next, before hearing them shuffling off as fast as they could. It sounded like one was being half dragged. Maria shuddered. Then she remembered what they had taken and began to cry again. "It was for Timmy" she blurted. Just then another set of feet came running up, heavy falling footsteps announcing Sam.

"What happened ... are you alright Maria? Those boys ... I will put a stop to them!" Sam was breathing hard from the run, yet Maria realized that she could barely even hear Gaeten's breathing now, nor had she even when he had first suddenly appeared.

In a halting, quivering voice Maria answered. "No Sam, they would just hurt you, or get their gang to come and smash up your store! Let them alone; they won't bother you." Sam scowled and was obviously not convinced. "I am ok, I can take care of myself pretty well, and God has always provided for me." Maria stated this bravely, taking a step backwards and trying to arrange her badly torn dress to cover the greatest part of her dignity.

Sam was not quite done working through his own protective fatherly emotions. "But Maria — this is terrible! We cannot let those ruffians loose to terrorize you at will! What if some day they really hurt you? What if ..."

Though she worried about that too sometimes, Maria had an undefeatable resolve that she clung to. "Sam, I have heard Brother Rob say many times that God is always in charge, and that He will work ALL things out for the best — for His best — for those that love Him and follow His ways. God is going to work this out also for the best. I don't know what that will be, but just you watch and see."

Once again Sam marveled at the precocious faith bundled into this special little package. He wondered again if it took such seeming misfortune to nurture and grow such great trust in God. Maybe his life had really been too easy, leaving his own faith weaker. Then again, maybe faith can also come from learning from the examples of others ... even little orphan girls. He clung to that thought, not really wanting to contemplate the trade-offs of getting his own faith stretched by adversity.

Gaeten also was taken aback by the faithful statement he had just heard. There was much more to this child than might first come to mind. He turned toward the baker and asked "Sam, can you please find the coin purse? I think it is over that way." He pointed down the road a short distance.

Sam fetched the small pouch and put it into Maria's hand. "I think all the money is here, but I'm afraid the bag with the bread has been trampled up pretty badly."

"That's ok. I ...I really need to get to the church for lunch — we usually eat after the normal lunchtime bells." Maria gave the baker a sincere big hug and Sam could feel the trembles she was bravely trying to hide. She turned toward Gaeten. "Thank you sir, you were surely a Godsend. I will ask God to bless you for helping me." She turned and stumbled as she shuffled down the street toward the church a short distance away.

As she left, Gaeten turned toward Sam. "Can you please guide me back to the bakery?" Sam picked up the man's staff which lay close by on the ground and put his forearm in a place where the man could hold onto him. Sam had not been close enough to really see much of what had occurred, and Gaeten wanted to turn the baker's attention away from what might have happened on the street.

As they neared the bakery, Gaeten pulled out a large coin to pay for his lunch. "Sam, if you have some time, can you tell me more about Maria?"

Maria half ran, half stumbled up to the old church. She was shaken up a lot more than she would show to Sam or Mr. Gaeten. Now there was a puzzlement — who was this mysterious man who somehow showed up just when she needed help the most and who had somehow, in some nearly silently way subdued her three attackers? He didn't seem like any angel she recalled being told about, that was for sure. Nevertheless, he surely had been sent by God, and she humbly thanked Him for that provision.

Just before entering the back door Maria tried to smooth her hair, only to find it full of dust and straw. She already knew her old shabby dress was now torn beyond repair. It had not been in great shape before, and now it was essentially useless. Well, she might have enough money saved up to get a second hand replacement. She felt the door latch and let herself in.

All of the other six orphans were present; no one ever wanted to miss a meal, however meager it might be. The kindly priest offered bowls of thin potato soup and a few bread crusts, and Maria knew he was sharing from what little he had — he would eat a share with them, holding nothing back for himself. Maria did not know of anyone so self-less, but sharing equally with a very poor priest did not exactly fill any of their stomachs. Yet all were thankful.

After the blessing and eating, Maria asked to see Brother Rob privately. She fished out the small purse of money, though it felt lighter than before, probably having lost some of its contents in the scuffle. "Here Brother Rob, this is for you."

"Why thank you Maria. You know you do not have to give this to me — you earned it and it is yours." He pressed the small pouch back into her hands.

"No. I would have none of it without God's blessing … and His protection. It is His … and yours."

Brother Rob looked at her quizzically. "All right, Maria — I can hear your conviction and won't even try to talk you out of it. Now what should we do with this blessing?"

"Well ..." she had given up on the thought of a making a gift for Timmy, she was not skilled enough to make anything nice anyway, but if Brother Rob wanted to spend God's money that way ... "I thought Timmy could use a pair of shoes, his sandals have worn through and he is getting sores on his feet from walking. Maybe a newer pair would help him stand straighter too." Timmy had a hunched-over stance caused by a deformity he was born with, but Maria was always hopeful.

Brother Rob changed topics abruptly. "Maria, I see new bruises on your arms and legs ... where did they come from?"

"I ... ah ... I fell on my way here." She had actually fallen — after being roughly pushed.

"Is that all?"

"Does it need to be more than that?"

"Did anyone "help" you fall? Like maybe the Greely boys?"

"I ... I um ...." Her words failed and Maria stood silent and trembling. She had once told the priest about an instance of being picked on, and he had made a point to talk to the culprits. The next day they had found her and Maria had been repeatedly hit and told to never, ever tell on them again — or she would be very sorry she had.

Brother Rob meant well, but he could not handle the Greely boys and their tiny hamlet had no Warden to uphold the law and peace. She quickly changed subjects. "Is there enough now for Timmy's shoes?"

Brother Rob eyed her suspiciously but let drop a topic Maria obviously did not want to speak about. "Yes, I think so. And maybe a bit left over. I am thinking that we ought to pay a visit to the used clothing store down the road and see if they have anything that might fit Timmy ... and you. You are growing into a young woman, and it is getting rather ... inappropriate ... for you to be traipsing about in something with so many holes and tears. And you also could use some new sandals or shoes yourself."

"Oh, I am sure we don't have enough for that — and you really need some extra for food too. I get enough to eat at the bakery; perhaps you can give my part to the others."

"Oh Maria, you really are gracious and giving and a blessing from God to us. I don't know what we would do without you here."

Gaeten and Sam reentered the bakery. Gaeten feigned tiredness he did not feel and dropped heavily into one of the nearest chairs. Sam looked at him hard. He had noticed the unusual collar markings, but did not know what they stood for. He also had noticed the scars — they were hard to miss. "Ah, I don't mean to sound rude, but I am quite curious — how did you get such scars — what labor did you apprentice under or work at?"

The older man shrugged noncommittally. "I have picked up work where I could. It isn't easy to find work, being as I am." Sam pursed his lips and gathered up two tankards of tea and some biscuits. The coin the old man had given him had already paid for the lunch meal and these, with some to spare. "Now tell me about Maria."

"Well, I can't say I know everything, but I have talked both to her and to the priest at the church. It seems she arrived to Freelandia several years ago on a ship from Morgania. Her mother had died from some sickness that was spreading around the region ... sure glad we haven't been ravaged like that here! ... and after some time her father left with Maria to come to Freelandia to escape the illness, with hopes of setting up a small animal healing shop. He left with all he owned. A few days after they departed the sickness came over him.

The ship did not have much of a healer; it seems the captain was counting on her father's animal care skills for any needs of the other passengers and crew. Within a week her father was dead. That left a very young Maria at the hands of the ship's captain, who it sounds treated her like she was a nuisance. When they finally docked the captain put her off the boat with the few clothes she had, and confiscated all of her father's goods as fare for the journey, as her father had only paid part of the fee and planned on working off the rest along the way.

She found some shelter at the wharf church, but the priest there said she could not stay and took her to an orphanage out in Westnave not too far from here. They kept her for a few years, but the proprietors said they couldn't keep someone with her limitations. For the last three years she has been staying at the church here."

"How long has she been blind?" Gaeten asked that in a flat, very matter-of-fact voice.

"You noticed?"

"Yes. She shuffles a lot when she walks and bumps into many things."

"I suppose you might notice those things, wouldn't you? In answer to your question … I don't know. Maria has never told me." Sam finished his biscuit. "Well, I must get more bread baking for the evening customers." He pushed back his chair and stood. "Please excuse me, let me get your change."

Gaeten waved him off. "Keep the change — count it as a fee for useful information." He got up with feigned stiffness and moved toward the door. "I must get moving along too, it is a hike for me to get back to my lodging."

"Do you need a hand? I could get one of my children to help."

"No, not needed — but thanks anyway." With that the old man walked out of the bakery and down the plank sidewalk, shuffling a bit himself as he went.

"But how did you stop those ruffians who were going after Maria?" Sam yelled out through the open door, but the old man just kept walking. Sam figured, wrongly, that he probably had not even heard him.

Gaeten moved along rather quickly for the awkward looking steps he was taking. When he was further down the road he adopted a more normal gait, moving even more quickly. He headed toward the small lodge where the main thoroughfare passed by one end of the small town. He passed the smelly stables to his left and the clanging smith's shop to his right and then walked 50 paces further and turned. Three paces down a slightly sloped cobblestone path he came to steps —

four steps up, a step forward, then three more steps up and he came to the door of the Inn of Seven Steps.

Gaeten quietly swung open the door and stood silently in the threshold. In the open room off to one side the apprentice he had taken along for this trip dozed contentedly in the sunshine near a large window. Gaeten knew it was his apprentice Quentin ... he recognized the snoring.

Without making a single sound he crept up on the boy, moving as silently as a whiff of air. Quentin was a strapping lad of 16, and had advanced quite far under Gaeten's tutelage. The snoring continued unabated, a steady rhythmic sound of one fully into a restful sleep. Time to change that. Gaeten silently lifted his walking staff. He had not made a sound since entering the Inn, at least nothing that anyone without highly acute hearing — like himself — should have been able to hear. The staff slashed downward at the boy's stomach in a blow that would give pain without injury and that surely would provide a very shockingly rude end to his slumber.

Just as the blow was about to make contact with the invitingly soft tummy, Quentin's body erupted sideways from his position on the window ledge, falling toward the floor as the staff clattered harmlessly on the wooden boards above. Quentin rolled expertly forward and used his shoulders as a pivot point to launch his feet upward, precisely where the body that had swung the staff had to be.

But it wasn't. Quentin's feet met no resistance and he struggled to twist his body as he shoved off the floor with his arms. If no body was where he had expected, then it had to be ...he threw an arm in the direction he thought his master must be standing, and was pleased to connect with something made of flesh and blood. However, connecting and doing anything effectual were two very different circumstances. His arm was momentarily caught in a vise which caused his moving body to be yanked backwards and he landed awkwardly. As he came to a stop Quentin looked up to a stiffened palm strike fist inches from his face. He rolled his eyes and laughed. "I almost had you!"

"Almost! Almost! And you were almost really sleeping! Next time slow your breathing more, and tone down that snore. It was too obviously an exaggerated fake. Your roll was barely acceptable, and while you somehow managed to avoid my staff, that kick was terrible! If I had been more than just playing around ..." Gaeten's voice had his normal raspy gruffness, but Quentin knew that if he had really done poorly his master would be pronouncing extra exercises and work to give him added "incentive" to do better — and besides, he could see twinges of a smile peeking out of the affected frown. "Now hurry up, get a carriage and inquire about directions. I want to be at the region's Warden's yet this afternoon."

Chapter 3

Gaeten smells a Rat

Warden Harden came to the knock at his door. Well, it was really the fourth or fifth knock. He had held this minor position for many years and had grown rather comfortable, as well as rather rotund. He swung open his door suspiciously, peering out at the old man who stood before him and the younger man behind.

"Who … who are you?" Gaeten had washed up and had his clothing fluffed out and brushed. This was not, after all, an informal visit. He said nothing for a moment, giving the portly Warden a moment to take in the sight and to notice the markings that indicated Gaeten's position and rank. "Oh! Oh excuse me … please … please come in Grand Master."

Gaeten swept into the room rather imperiously and stiffly with a distinct frown. He could smell the man's sweat, and that along with the heavy tread gave him a strong clue as to the man's girth. "So you are the Warden of this district? For how long have you been favored with that position?" The emphasis on the word "favored" was a bit heavy and was not missed by Mr. Harden.

"I have dutifully held this position for 15 years, covering the 7 small towns and the many roads in district 17."

Gaeten sniffed disdainfully. "I've been spending a few days in your district. Tell me about Westhaven."

"Oh, well … Westhaven is one of the smallest and poorest of the towns, hardly worth the notice to someone of your position."

"I have noticed quite a lot. Where are your Watchers? I have not run across a single one yet."

"Ah, Watchers, right … my Watchers. Well, um …"

"You do have a contingent of Watchers — or at least apprentices — set up for each town and patrols for the main roads?" Gaeten said that much more like a statement than a question.

"Well, you know, times are tough … getting good Watchers is difficult in this district. The people are poor and every able bodied man is needed for the farms and shops."

"Are you telling me you have NO Watchers?" What about the stipend sent to your district each month by the Keep that is supposed to be exclusively for the salaries of Watchers and/or apprentices? Surely you send in requests for apprentice assignments?"

"Ah, well, you seem to have stopped by just … just when I was in-between hiring's. You realize of course that no one from the Watcher Compound at the Keep ever wants to come out here to work! The only Watchers that show any interest of working here are ready to retire, or have dropped out of active duty due to physical issues, or have left for other reasons. It is the same with apprentices. Often the best I have been able to do is hire locals as apprentices and train them myself. All my current Watchers are out on the … the northern roads … on a patrol!"

Gaeten sniffed loudly. "What about the gang of ruffians I have heard about around Westhaven? I personally had to stop a group robbing someone in broad daylight today!"

"Gang? I have not heard of any gang in Westhaven. I will check into it immediately! It must have just started up … or probably just moved in from District 18 to the north. You would not believe what goes on over there. Why just the other day I heard that …."

Gaeten interrupted. "It appears that this District has been over-due for an inspection by the Master Warden. I think I shall bring it up to him when I see him this weekend."

Quentin noticed that Warden Harden's face had paled significantly. "Oh, that is surely not needed! Why would the Master Warden want to come here? Certainly he has far more important duties than to spend time in this run down, derelict district. Now I'm sure that when my crack Watcher team gets back from the north road patrols they will straighten up Westhaven in no time at all. Tell you what, I will write up a full report on what they find and send it in to the Master Warden in, say, two or three weeks. How would that be?"

Gaeten was about to make a snide comment, but instead cleared his throat and proceeded along another tack. "Exactly how many Watchers and apprentices do you have?"

"Exactly? Well, that is hard to say, at the moment." Harden realized how lame that sounded and hurried on. "I have 5 solid men and several younger boys … er, young men … in apprentice. In fact, several are even from that dump Westhaven! I am working on their proper training myself."

"And what might their names be, these new recruits?"

"Uh … that is … one of my most senior Watchers takes care of such details."

Gaeten had several more questions, though he rather doubted he was going to get answers for them that would be any more satisfactory.

Maria curled up in her corner of the back room, feeling rather happy with the day. Her evening devotions were said with true thanksgiving as she recounted her day with her God. Brother Rob would take them down to the consignment shop tomorrow, and when Timmy had heard that he had literally jumped up and down with delight — as best his bent frame would allow — and had hugged Maria with all his little might.

Her new bruises were tender and hurt some. The pain reminded her of the altercation with the Greely boys, and she was apprehensive of how they may have taken their "thumping". And she was very puzzled over who the mysterious Gaeten could be. Perhaps she could ask Sam if he knew anything about him. She said a special prayer of thanks and blessing over her benefactor and drifted off into a contented sleep.

By the time Gaeten returned to the lodge the sun had set and darkness was overtaking the last vestiges of daylight. The sounds changed, with the night frogs and insects making their own distinct melody in the still air. Quentin helped to steady the carriage while Gaeten exited and both moved up the steps and into the Inn. They had a quiet dinner in the Great Room and Gaeten could sense the brooding anger in his young protégé. "Alright, out with it".

Quentin knew not to try to hide his thoughts. "That Warden was … was scandalous! Incompetent! Probably a thief himself! And a big fat liar! How could you let that go?"

Gaeten smiled, but it was not a particularly pleasant sight. "Patience, my young apprentice. I think we can clean up this entire District, and certainly Westhaven, if we play this well. In the early morning I want you to take a horse and ride immediately to the Master Warden. Tell him that I need a response team here by nightfall. There is very likely going to be some trouble. Tell him about Warden Harden. Oh, and tell him I want Ethan. He will surely put up a fuss, but say that I distinctly said I wanted Ethan to come along. He will surely want to discuss this with me in person, which is fine. Be back before the next nightfall and meet me here."

"You want to bring Ethan here? To Westhaven?"

Gaeten scowled darkly. "I will answer that to the Master Warden, not to the likes of you!"

Quentin swallowed hard, realizing he had overstepped the boundaries of his position. With little additional conversation they finished their meal and went to their room for the night.

Maria helped with breakfast dishes and tidied up the room. Not that there was all that much to clean. She did occasionally miss something or another, but having lived there for several years she had a very keen sense of where things were and when things were out of place. She also had very sharp hearing and sense of smell and had sensitive fingers, and so there were not too many chores that she could not accomplish, albeit somewhat slower than others might.

The younger orphans went out to tend the garden and the few animals the priest owned. They all looked up to Maria, as she was the oldest and as such was as much of a mother figure to them as they had. It put that much more responsibility onto her shoulders and it made her have to "grow up" much faster. Of course, being an orphan had that effect too.

Brother Rob had mentioned that they would head over to the consignment shop in the early afternoon. Maria was busy all morning washing the few clothes they had, cleaning up around the church and helping in the garden and small stable. The old mare the priest owned had developed a small sore where the saddle had chaffed, and Maria wanted to make an herb poultice that she vaguely remembered her father had used for similar problems. She recalled the various smells from each of the ingredients, and while she did not know the exact amounts he had used, she did recall the pungent odor of the mixture.

Most of the ingredients were to be found in their garden or in nearby fields, and she was especially cautious in going out today to collect what was needed, listening intently for the sounds of anyone who may be nearby. She was more than a bit nervous about the Greely boys. Jarl in particular had a real mean streak developing, and he would likely be furious both at the pummeling he and his brothers had gotten on the previous day and at the loss of the money sack they had dropped after stealing it from her. She worried that it was entirely possible they would want to exact their revenge out on her, being such an easy target to vent their anger on. At least they left the other orphans alone.

She could not bear the thought of them beating little Timmy. As they had slunk away yesterday, Maria thought she heard Jake say something about how someone named Ramsey was going to be very angry if they came back without their quota. She didn't really understand, but whatever it was, it did not sound pleasant.

Maria put it out of her mind as best she could as she ground up the various herbs and mixed in some water. The stable was only a short walk across the yard and the mare was whinnying as she approached. "There now, let's get this poultice spread on you proper" she cooed to the horse. Maria gently placed a thin bandage over the medicated sore and tied it loosely in place with long cloth strips. She heard Brother Rob call and hurried out of the stable, taking care to ensure the mare's stall was securely shut — that horse needed rest for a few more days to ensure good healing — and over to the back room of the church.

Jarl, Jake and Brak were very angry, and very sore. Like all the Rats, they had a daily amount of income they were supposed to bring back to the Rat's Nest, and each evening Ramsey demanded payment. Most of the Rats stole for their quota, and the older the boy, the more they were expected to get. Anyone bringing in extra could get a pass for a slow day, but anyone who came up short more than once was beaten, first by Ramsey and then each of the other Rats were expected to do their share to show the misbehaving member the group's displeasure.

Jarl had boasted loudly a few days back that he and his brothers were going to make a big and easy snatch. They had just recently discovered Maria's weekly schedule and Jarl had planned for them to watch the bakery each Wednesday to catch her as she left with her proceeds. This was to be their first weekly installment of the easy pickings.

Instead the three had dragged themselves back to the Nest, an old abandoned farm house on the outskirts of Westhaven, bruised and with empty pockets. When asked what had happened, Jarl fabricated a story that they had tried to rob the church, but the priest had caught them. Jarl's fabrication made Brother Rob sound like a burly prize-fighter who took their many punches and just would not stop coming, and who had finally overcome and beaten them mercilessly, even stealing what money they had already gathered to pay to the group.

The Nest leader Ramsey had listened with great skepticism, and cuffed each of the brothers roughly for their miserable failure — and then had each of the other Rats add their own blows. When the punishment had been administered and the Greely boys were covered with even more bruises turning an ugly blue-black color, Ramsey informed them he wished to pay a visit to that beefy priest. Only he, after all, was to be allowed to rough up the Rats.

Gaeten walked slowly around Westhaven, listening and getting a better feel of the place. Quentin had gotten off on an early start and it would be late afternoon or early evening until he could return. Gaeten was quite sure that James, the Master Warden, would do as he asked. He did not at all like the idea that some kind of criminal gang had formed here. The leaders of Freelandia took great care to prevent that sort of thing. Freelandia was well known for its rule of law and peacefulness. Yes, they did have some petty criminals as did all countries, but there was not a safer and more peaceful country in the entire world. The Watchers and Wardens had been established hundreds of years earlier to see to that, and they took their responsibilities very seriously … at least most did. Obviously their system of oversight on distant Wardens needed some review.

If he had the Greely boys figured out, they were likely back at whatever they called their gang hideout, licking their wounds, and had probably told a fanciful yarn of what had happened. One thing was for sure: they would not have told anyone that an old man had plastered them around the street. They would be quite angry, and that was not good for anyone they might meet.

However, Gaeten was not one to stir up a hornet's nest and then let them attack the nearest passerby's. He expected the leader of the gang would not take kindly indeed that some of his pack had been beaten. However the Greely boys had spun it, Gaeten was rather counting on meeting both those brothers and likely a few additional gang members quite soon, perhaps even today since they would not know when their assailant might leave the area. He had been trying to track down information on the rumored gang for several weeks, and this was the first solid lead he had found. A wry smile crossed his lips and his gait picked up. He heard the shrill cry of a bird of prey in the distance and he smiled again. Yes, this could be an interesting day indeed. Satisfied with his renewed familiarity of the small hamlet's layout, Gaeten headed back towards the only bakery in town, looking forward to a slice of fresh warm bread with butter and jam.

Brother Rob walked slowly, allowing Timmy and Maria to keep up. The priest was not as old as Gaeten, but years of poverty and the tireless helping of others had taken their toll on his lean frame. He was not a big man — hardly the image painted by Jarl — and one would be hard pressed to find a more gentle and kindly person. They reached the consignment shop without incident and excitedly went in. Once inside, the proprietress, whom everyone called Maggie, greeted them warmly. One look at Maria and Maggie knew at least one item that was needed. As Maria and Timmy began wandering through the store Brother Rob spread out the coins Maria had saved up, plus a few of his own that he had surreptitiously added. They both counted it out so they could know how much could be afforded.

Maggie was a kindly older widow with a heart of gold, and soon she was helping find Timmy a rather nice pair of walking shoes that were not overly worn and had only one buckle missing, but which would do quite nicely for his needs. The fit was not perfect, they were big — but he would grow into them and it meant he would not need another pair for at least awhile. Maria on the other hand was transitioning out of the children sizes and into women's clothing, which was both good and bad. Good in that there were more choices with brighter colors, ribbons and lace, bad in that they were generally more expensive. And the poor girl was in such tatters now!

After about 20 minutes of sorting and browsing through nearly the entire women's wardrobe selection they had narrowed the choices down to three. Timmy was getting impatient and even Brother Rob wondered why it took so very long for the two women to select a simple piece of clothing.

Maria tried them on. None fit perfectly on her overly thin frame, but then again she never expected that. She finally chose a hardy feeling broadcloth shift with sturdy and large pockets. Maggie held up one of the other top choices. "Are you sure you don't want this other one? Feel the lace at the collar and the fine buttons. It is so pretty too!"

Maria smiled, but knew she needed functional durability, not prettiness for clothing. She figured there was barely enough coin for one dress, and fancy lace would not likely hold up to the heavy chores around the church. "No, I like this one," she said, smoothing out the simple pleats.

Maggie smiled knowingly. Marie was not much to look at yet, but she had an inner beauty that was just barely hidden under the façade of dirt and grime and tattered clothing that indicated her poverty. And she was losing the gangling awkwardness of childhood and blossoming into what would likely be a rather pretty young woman — if her environment would every allow it. The fresh bruises about her face and arms attested to her very difficult life. Such might steal the outer beauty, but inner beauty was much more lasting and precious. If only she were not an orphan, if only she was not blind. Maggie could imagine Maria growing up in much kinder conditions and turning into a quite fair maiden.

She sighed and came out of her daydream. Life was usually not so kind, especially lately around these parts. She herself had been robbed several times over the last few months, not that she had much to be stolen. "Alright. I presume you will want to wear it now — and that I can, well, discard the old one you were wearing?"

"Oh my, yes — I never want to wear that old thing ever again! I don't even think it would make a very useful rag! But God let it last long enough. I am so very thankful we can get something else". Maria hugged Brother Rob as he paid for the items, and Maggie ensured there were a few small coins left over. She could only help a little, but the priest was doing so much good for those children that she tried to help out whenever they stopped by. She did not know how he could do it all alone, just by himself and those orphans.

Brother Rob smiled graciously at the storekeeper. "May God bless you richly, Maggie." He paused a moment in indecision and then stepped closer and gave her a grateful hug while whispering "Thank you!" Maggie held his hand for a moment. "Please let me know how I can help. I don't have much, and what little I had saved up was stolen last week. Perhaps I can stop by sometime and help you make a meal?"

"That would be extremely kind of you, Maggie. You are always welcome." They passed a warm smile between them, and Brother Rob swallowed hard, remembering his wife lost many years ago. As a tear formed in his eye he turned abruptly and addressed the children. "Let's go pick up a few things at the vegetable market with the coins we have left before we head home."

Jake was the front "man", walking down the sidewalk slowly, since he had the least visible bruises. A middle aged couple walked by, and as they passed Jake pretended to stumble, bumping into the woman. "Oh, sorry" he mumbled as he walked on, pocketing the gold chain that had been on the woman's wrist. Jake was not all that bright, but he was fairly good at pick-pocketing. It was likely only gold painted metal, but still worth a small amount and may at least pay for his quota that day. The others were back in the alleyways, staying in the shadows as they traversed the town.

He wondered if maybe they could break into one of the small shops and steal whatever was in the back room. Ramsey, however, had made it very clear that they had a specific mission that day, so Jake stayed on the look-out for the priest. Turning the next corner he spotted Brother Rob, along with a small boy and ... yes ... he thought it was Maria, though not in her usual torn rags. He snickered. Two for the price of one! If all went well the brothers could be vindicated of their defeat — Ramsey would never know the priest was not the culprit anyway — and they could get back at that dratted Maria. He motioned hurriedly to the others and scooted forward to see the threesome enter the vegetable shop.

Gaeten was finishing his bread at Sam's, giving the baker a handsome tip. He surely hoped he would meet up with the Greely boys before they caused too much trouble or hurt anyone else. He stepped out of the bakery and headed up the road. After a block or two he stopped, sniffing the air. From the south he could just detect a whiff of something that reminded him of one of the youths he had had a close encounter with the day before. He quickened his pace, but the city was still not that familiar to him and he could only go so fast. He strained his ears as he walked, and reached under his tunic to get a small metal tube he had hung on a light chain around his neck. Sasha was not too far away, and he thought he may want her services shortly.

Brother Rob carried the bag of groceries. It was not much, and most items were past their prime, but he was thankful for what they could afford. He held Timmy's hand as they walked out, laughing at how Timmy had made such a funny face when he looked at several of the oddly shaped fruits the store had just stocked. Maria walked on his other side, grateful that her singing had brought in enough money for the dress, shoes and even some extra food — a really bountiful blessing. It was not until they walked past an alley on their left that she heard quick movements and cried out. It was too late.

Jarl knew his only real hope of saving face with Ramsey would be for quick action that took the priest out before Ramsey could ever know for sure how "tough" the man of God was — or wasn't. He came out of the alley at a slow run, building speed quickly as he covered the short distance to his intended target. Maria's cry was far too late to stop him or really make any difference. The priest turned slightly to see the commotion just in time for Jarl's cudgel to strike him squarely to the side of his head. It made a sickening wet thud and the priest dropped like a rock and didn't move. The bag of groceries spilled out over the ground while Brak and Jake ran out and grabbed Maria and Timmy in fierce grips.

Ramsey came out more slowly. He has a lanky young man of perhaps 25, with a scar running down the side of one cheek that pulled one side of his lips into a permanent snarl. His greasy long hair hung down limply and he swept it aside as he strode out purposefully from the alley. "So this is the guy who took on all three of you? He does not seem like much." He kicked at the prone figure, which had not moved at all since falling. He looked over at the two children menacingly.

Jake's confidence had grown considerably with Jarl's successful attack and when the tall Ramsey was present. He twisted Maria's arm behind her back viscously and between the sounds of what had just happened, Timmy's cries and the sudden and unexpected sharp pain she lost her composure and screamed.

Brak immediately let go of one of Timmy's arms and slapped Maria hard across the face. That stopped the scream, and now Maria became angry. She knew she shouldn't be, such anger rarely accompanied godliness, but the anger rushed out hard and strong. She slammed her foot down onto the front shin of Jake behind her, skidding her foot downward with quite a bit of force and slamming it down onto the young man's foot. He was so startled he dropped her arm, and she swung her body and slapped at his head as hard as she could. Though small, she had quite a lot of determination behind that slap, and it made a very solid connection. Jake was knocked completely off his feet backwards.

"Oh ho, the mouse has claws!" Ramsey laughed. "And such a clean and pretty dress. It just does not become such a mousy beggar. You need a reminder of who you are — and that you will never rise above being a dirty little beggar!" He effortlessly shoved the off-balanced Maria, flinging her into a heap onto the dirty road. He began to kick dirt at her and the Greely boys joined in, splattering her with dirt, mud and mostly dried manure that spotted the road here and there. Humiliated she curled into as small of a ball as she could and whimpered in fear. Deep inside a part of her cried out to her Lord for help and mercy. She did not even hear the eerily high pitched sound that seemed to come from nowhere and everywhere all at the same time.

Gaeten was half-running but still too far away to stop the blow to the priest and was just nearing the group as the dust and dirt kicking became real kicking at Maria's prone and sobbing form. His blood ran

cold, his mind cleared and his breathing actually slowed. He nearly
did not remember to act his part — he wanted to dive into them and
instantly stop their actions, perhaps permanently. One riled a Grand
Master Watcher at very grave and great risk.

Yet a greater strategy demanded prudence. He slowed and affected
a wheezing old man's voice. "What, you couldn't get enough of me
the first time? Do you need to show how manly you are by beating
up a little girl? You bunch are quite pathetic! When I was your age I
knew how to respect others, I tell you." He had stopped a few yards
away. All four stopped instantly and swiveled around to face the new
threat. Jake, always the slow one, gasped, "It's him!" and took two
steps backwards.

Ramsey looked at Jake, then back at Gaeten, then back to Jake. "This
is the guy who sent the three of you scurrying back to the Nest with
your tails between your legs? You were beaten by an old blind man?"

Jarl looked very uncomfortable. "Well, he … he was with the priest
… maybe he had some part of it."

Ramsey looked Gaeten over, who had affected a stooped stance to
look even older and weaker. "Go away old man, unless you want to
get hurt too."

"My, my, such poor manners. One would think you could show
some respect for your elders. Maybe you need to be taught some
manners." Gaeten was mumbling the words as though he was getting
absent minded. "Yes, I rather think that would be appropriate. I can
hardly believe how kids these days act. Why, when I was growing
up, my pappy would have taken us back to the woodshed …" the
old man's voice muttered along at a dwindling volume that became
impossible to follow.

Ramsey was quite taken aback by this, figuring the old man who
must have come stumbling by at the wrong moment would have
turned away in fear by now. "I said to beat it!" With that he took the
two strides needed to reach Gaeten and gave him a shove he figured
was hard enough to more than bowl the old geezer over.

However, that did not happen. The shove had exactly zero effect. It was as if he had shoved a stone wall. Ramsey lost some of his bravado. He snarled and swung a fist at the old man's stomach and smiled as it connected. The smile rapidly transformed into a grimace of pain as the fist slammed into what might as well have been solid iron. The old man just stood there, grinning.

Meanwhile Jarl, Jake and Brak had begun to move around Gaeten in threatening postures, their feet making small shuffling noises in the dirt. He knew their bravado was really based on Ramsey being present — around him they felt stronger and secure. That was not what Gaeten wanted, not for his plan to succeed.

"You don't seem to have the strength of a horsefly young man! Maybe I can swat you like I do those pests!" With that Gaeten slapped at Ramsey, mimicking the flick would give to a bothersome insect. Ramsey just stood there, still rather dumbfounded over his completely ineffective punch, holding his injured hand with the other. And besides, the swat looked harmless enough. It was not swung with particular speed or seemingly much force. None saw how one finger bent stiffly inward at the last instant, and no one really noticed that this finger hit directly over the soft temple spot on Ramsey's head. The results however were decidedly singular. Ramsey snapped his head away from the strike and it took a few moments for the sharp pressure wave it created inside his skull to have full effect. He clumsily staggered a step away, then his eyes crossed and glazed over and he dropped to the ground unconscious.

"Maybe not even a horsefly! I think I must have squashed him! Ha ha! Let's see ..." the old man spun about as if searching for a new opponent. "Who's next?" Gaeten feigned a lurching step to his right, knowing full well where each of the Greely boys was standing from their heavy breathing. They looked at him, then down at the prostrate Ramsey, whose body was now quivering slightly in mini-convulsions. It had the desired effect. They panicked. The trick here was for them not to leave Ramsey. "Now where was that first oaf, the squashed housefly?" Gaeten took a step in the wrong direction and began feeling about with one foot. Jarl took the cue and grabbed one of Ramsey's arms and began dragging him away. Brak responded in a moment and the two of them began pulling the prostrate body of Ramsey. "Ho, what is that? Come back here and take your lickings!" Gaeten swung his walking staff ineffectively through the air as though he were trying to hit someone. That restored a mite of confidence back to the brothers and Jake grabbed at the cloth of their leader's trousers and they half carried, half dragged Ramsey off as fast as they could.

Gaeten dropped his pretensions as soon as they were well away and rushed first to the limp form of whom he guessed must be Brother Rob. He felt for a pulse and listened to the breathing. Timmy appeared totally unhurt, though he was sobbing loudly sitting on the ground next to the priest. Gaeten turned toward Maria, who was still curled into a tight ball with only muffled crying sounds coming out. That was not good. He needed her help. But first he lifted the odd little metal tube that hung on a cord around his neck and blew three short blasts. To Timmy, who was watching through his tears, nothing happened at all.

Gaeten reached over and tugged on Maria's arm. "Maria — its Gaeten — we need to get help for the priest!" But Maria was lost in her world of pain and fear, over-stressed to the point of blocking the outside world and trying to cling to the special place inside her mind where she always fled for safety, where only she and God could enter. She at first did not hear the voice, and then mistook it for one of her attackers. She struggled to get away, even though no danger was present.

Gaeten was familiar with fear. He took Maria's arm and pulled hard, hard enough to cause discomfort. "Maria — the priest needs your help!" That got a response, finally. She unwound from her ball of safety, needing a few moments to get oriented and introduced back into reality.

"Brother Rob? What happened?" Then it all came rushing back and threatened to engulf her again with fear. Gaeten had to get her attention back immediately. He shook her gently. "Maria, Brother Rob needs your help — right now!"

She shook herself, and then began to feel about to located the fallen priest. Gaeten helped; he could sense exactly where the body was. He lifted Maria to her feet. "We need help. Go get Sam the baker! I will stay here and do what I can. We need to get him to a healer as fast as we can!"

Maria still looked disoriented, but she cocked her head to one side to listen to the normal town sounds and began to recover her bearings, but the recent shocks to her system weren't helping, and she felt considerable pain in her leg that had received the most abuse from the kicks. Timmy's crying had subsided somewhat. She reached over to the young boy and took his hand. "Timmy, we need your help too — help me get to the baker's shop as fast as you can! Come on!" Timmy reluctantly stood, but then noticed how badly Maria was limping and that shook him out of his cry.

"Yes … yes Maria," he stammered and they both set off down the street.

Gaeten propped up Brother Rob's head and began to very gently probe the wound area, his hands getting sticky with the blood he could only too well smell. "If only I had been faster, had gotten here sooner! God, you are always with me. I need your help now — brother Rob needs your help now. Save this brother, your servant!" Gaeten felt spiritual power flow, as he often had in the past. He had no special gifting of healing, but he did have direct access to the Great Healer, and God had worked through him more than once before to keep someone alive. Gaeten waited, praying on.

Several men lifted Brother Rob onto a makeshift gurney and carried him to the far end of town where the healer worked. Maria wanted to go along, but after examining her own wounds with his sensitive fingers Gaeten asked her to stay, along with Timmy and Sam. "Someone will need to take care of the orphans; they should not stay at the church alone."

Sam nodded, and realizing that only Timmy could tell that, spoke up. "Yes, I agree. I would like to ask Maggie if she could either take them in temporarily or stay over at the church tonight. She has a store to run herself, so that will only work for a day or two. My wife can help out some also, but if Brother Rob is out of commission very long we will have to find some other more permanent arrangements."

"I may be able to help with that," Gaeten said softly. "If they can be looked after for a few days I think we can work out something better. Sam, can you take Timmy back to the church? Please let me help with their food ..." He fished a coin out of a pocket, but Sam refused it.

"No, I should have seen this coming a long time ago and put a stop to it. I will feed them, at least for a few days."

"You are a kind and godly man, baker Sam. Blessings be upon you." Gaeten turned. "Maria, please stay a minute, I want to talk to you."

Chapter 4

Maria makes a new friend

aria remained sitting on the small bench outside of the vegetable shop. She was not crying anymore, but her bruises were turning an ugly purple and were beginning to ache.

"Come, I would like to talk with more privacy." Gaeten stood and Maria did also, though she was still a bit wobbly. He sensed her unsteadiness and let her lean on him as they slowly walked between the shops and out into a small field behind the street. With each step Maria winced, but Gaeten knew the only way to keep her legs from stiffening up was to move about. When they had walked a few minutes Gaeten eased himself down onto a fallen log he had bumped into and helped Maria to sit as well.

"You have been very brave, with all that has happened to you. But then again, you have had to be brave many times in the past, haven't you Maria?"

Maria slumped next to him and began again to cry, but more softly this time. Gaeten wondered how many times she had been abused by the Greely boys or others. Life as a little blind orphan would have been hard enough by itself.

"Maria, I want to give you something." Her crying quieted down and Gaeten pressed a small object into her hand. It was metallic and tubular, with two openings. In fact, it was a duplicate of what he wore on a lanyard around his neck.

"What is it?"

"Put the thick end up to your mouth and blow into the hole."

She did, and a squeaky high pitched sound came out. She stopped immediately.

"Here, hold it like this and blow straight in and somewhat hard." The sound that came out was eerie and extremely high pitched, so high that Maria could barely hear it, and it caused her to wince at its piercing intensity.

"Now this is a rather special whistle, Maria. Very few people can hear it. I rather thought you might be one of them, and by the way you just reacted I presume I was correct?" She confirmed with a squeeze to his hand. "That is not the only reason this is special. I suspect we should shortly hear from the other reason. Sasha should not be very far away." As if on cue, a high pitched screech sounded in the distance, high in the sky. Maria had heard somewhat similar noises before, and had been told that great birds of prey made them.

"If you are in dense woods it usually has to be blown a few more times so she can home in, but out here in the open her sharp eyes will have picked us out from miles away." A rushing fluttering sound came close, and Maria felt a breeze suddenly blow into her upturned face. She became silent and a bit cowed, leaning into Gaeten more closely as she realized *something* else had just entered their presence. The bird — she could tell that much by the smell and small cooing and clucking sounds it was making — had landed a few feet away. Gaeten made a peculiar clucking sound and Maria could hear the bird taking a few short hops over to them.

She did not know how she knew, but she sensed that the bird before them was immense in size, at least compared to the song birds she knew of. "Maria, meet Sasha." Gaeten pressed something small and squishy into Maria's hand. "Hold this up, but don't hold it too tightly. Sasha is pretty careful, but her beak is very sharp and she is not particularly built for gentleness."

Maria gulped and lifted the small piece of meat — she could smell what it was — and made a passably good imitation of the sounds Sasha was cooing. These changed, sounding curious, or at least that is how it seemed to Maria. She held her hand up with the meat dangling out, and felt a hard bony ... beak ... nudge up against her hand. She felt the meat tugged forcefully out of her grasp and she heard impatient swallowing noises. Maria tried to make the sounds again, and this time succeeded to nearly exactly duplicate Sasha's noises. The hard beak again nudged against her hand, but gently this time, and the bird made a series of different clucking sounds. Maria cocked her head to one side, paused, and then repeated the exact sequence back. That seemed to excite Sasha, who hoped up so close to Maria that she nearly sneezed from the feathers brushing against her face. Another string of hoots, clucks and coos rattled out. Maria did her best to imitate it again, and apparently got it pretty close, for Sasha seemed to settle down and cozy up close to her. She tentatively reached out and touched the magnificent bird. She gasped as she realized Sasha must have stood over three and a half feet tall. She wondered how great a wingspan such a bird must have.

Gaeten listened to the interchange and marveled at how well Maria had repeated Sasha's greeting. It had taken him many months to get it even half right, and Sasha had been very patient with him. There was no question though, that the great bird of prey and Maria were bonding at their first meeting. That pleased Gaeten. "Maria, this is Sasha. She is an Alterian Gryph, not normally found away from the northern mountain passes. She is probably the most magnificent bird in all of God's creation — although I fully admit I am heavily biased!"

"Is ... is she yours?" Maria inquired.

"No one "owns" a gryph. She is free to come and go as she pleases. No, we have a kind of friendship, Sasha and I. I provide a place for her to roost when she wants, and extra food and treats — though I think she takes care of her own meals quite well. No, I do not "own" her. However, we have learned to work together at times. And that brings up the whistle. It is at a pitch that Sasha seems to be able to hear for many miles, yet almost no people can. I suppose a few other birds might, I have not really explored that — not many birds stick around long when Sasha appears. She responds to the whistle. If you blow it long and hard she will come to you, at least if she is within earshot. There are a few other things she can do too, but those are not particularly relevant to you right now."

"I am giving you one of the few of these whistles I have — don't worry, I can get more made. And yes, I have one too." Gaeten moved one of Maria's hands to feel his lanyard and whistle. "I have a small chain for yours too. You can call her if you are lonely, she is a pretty good listener — she rarely interrupts! And especially call her if you need help — but use that option only if your situation is rather desperate. Don't expect her to automatically know who is a friend and who is an enemy. Don't misuse the friendship." Gaeten said the last rather solemnly and Maria instantly agreed. "If those Greely brothers or anyone else ever attacks you again, don't hesitate to blow the whistle. There is no guarantee that Sasha will hear it, but if she does you will get help in a hurry."

"How can you give me such a gift? You don't know me, and I do not know anything about you. I am a poor blind orphan and you … what really are you? You like to sound gruff, but I can sense you really are a gentle soul on the inside. You like to act old, but you can move faster and quieter than anyone I have ever heard. You seem so very confident and capable, and I … I am just a poor blind girl."

"Maria, you are much more than that in God's sight! And you have some impressive skills and gifting too, from what I can sense. And besides, we share a few pretty important things in common."

"What do you mean? What could we have in common?"

"Maria, give me your hands." She complied. Gaeten took them to his wrists. She felt the scars. Her hands moved upward, feeling the hardness of his arms and the thick muscles bulging under his shirt. He was much more muscular than she would have thought. Her hands moved upward, feeling his shoulders, then his face. His beard tickled her fingers, and as her delicate fingers moved upward to "see" his face, she suddenly stopped and gasped.

"Mr. Gaeten … you are … your eyelids hardly ever blink!"

"Yes, Maria. I too am blind, have been since a childhood illness clouded my eyes completely. I can sense light levels, but that is about it."

"But … how can you do so much?"

"That is mainly from practice, and learning to listen."

"Listen? I know how to listen!"

"Not just with your ears … with your heart … to God's Spirit."

"Oh. What is that like? I'd like to learn how."

"It can be the most exciting and scary thing you ever do. You have to very literally walk by faith that the directions you get from His Spirit are true, but when you do it is amazing! Perhaps one day you shall be able to also, Maria. Talk to God about it … ask Him to show you how. But for now, I think you should get back to the church to help with the children — they look up to you and will need you all the more now that Brother Rob is hurt."

Maria stood to go. Sasha squawked her disapproval and leapt into the air with a great rushing of air. Gaeten walked her back to the main road. As she turned to go he added "Maria, I suspect a few things will be happening this evening, things that may put a stop to the gang that has been oppressing this area for the last while. Tonight I want you to make sure to lock up the doors and ensure everyone stays inside, you included. Do you understand?"

"I … I think so. Will I meet you again?"

"Oh yes, you can be sure of that. In fact, I would like to meet with you again tomorrow, to let you know if the gang — and the Greely brothers — is done with bothering you and everyone else."

"I'd like that … Mr. Gaeten".

He laughed good naturedly and squeezed her hand. "Tomorrow then."

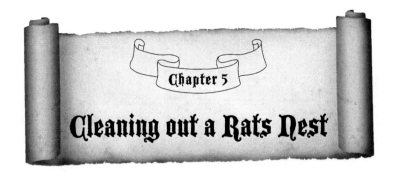

Chapter 5

Cleaning out a Rats Nest

aeten hurried to get back to the inn, but he was later than he wanted. When he arrived he heard the sounds of several more horses tethered outside than had been there that morning, and assumed Quentin had returned. As he entered the hall, his suspicions were confirmed.

"Ho Gaeten, my good friend! We have been waiting for you!" The voice was deep and rich, well fitting the large yet lean body to which it belonged.

"It is good to hear you, James! I appreciate that you came so quickly at my request."

"Well, it was a rather strange request. What is this all about?"

Gaeten found a chair and filled him in, Quentin and the others crowding around to hear the details. After discussing a few minutes James sat back. "It may just work Gaeten, but I don't like the chances you are taking."

"There are risks, yes. But the need is here and now, and I think we have sufficient resources."

"Yes, you are probably right. I do have a real issue though with a certain personnel selection."

Gaeten knew what James the Master Warden was implying. "It's time, James. I feel it in my spirit."

James sighed. "I don't want to admit it, but yes, I agree. When do we start?"

Gaeten was ready for that. "Quentin, let's go outside a minute, and get your horse." In a few minutes Quentin was mounted and ready. Gaeten took out his whistle and blew three short blasts. From experience Quentin knew not to mention that he could not hear anything. A few moments later Sasha's cry sounded overhead. Gaeten sounded the whistle again and Sasha wheeled about and headed out toward the other end of town. Quentin knew the routine, and urged his horse forward to follow as best he could. Sasha had done this with him many times before, and would ensure Quentin could find the intended target. An eye-in-the-sky could be a very handy thing indeed.

Gaeten turned toward James, who had followed him outside. "Before Quentin returns I suggest we get ready to ride. We will need some time to scout out the place ahead of time and be well hidden while we wait until it gets dark. I suspect that is when they will likely meet."

Maria helped to settle the children down after a late dinner. She helped Maggie with the dishes and checked the door latches while Maggie got herself readied for the night in a cot in with the youngest children. Maria was not really sure what Gaeten had been talking about, but she was surely glad he seemed to be on her side!

Jarl was in a very foul mood, having a new black eye and multiple deep bruises. When Ramsey had come to his senses back at the Rat's Nest, the first thing he did once regaining his feet was to give all three Greely boys a thorough thrashing. Jarl got the worst of it, since he was the oldest and hence the leader of the three, and since he had been the one giving the exaggerations and outright lies. Ramsey still did not really know what had happened — his memories of the afternoon were a bit foggy — but he knew at first glance that the priest had not been who Jarl had made him out to be. Then there was that strange old blind man that seemed at first to be immovable and then unstoppable! In any case, Jarl was at fault, no matter what the details. After making an example out of him, Ramsey had assigned Jarl to the lowest duty, keeping watch outside in the nearly moonless night. As though anyone knew where they were or would even think to try to bother them. And worse, the King Rat was visiting tonight. Jarl did not even know who that was, but supposedly there was going to be some announcement tonight and he was going to miss it. The others would surely only tell him dribs and drabs and hold out the best details.

Drat it all, it somehow all boiled down to that stinking blind orphan girl! All their troubles of late seemed to involve her. She was the cause of his problems. She was the reason he and his brothers had been beaten. She was the reason he had this stinking watch duty and had to stay out all stinking night. No one even needed to keep watch anyway, he figured.

Jarl slouched off to the barn. He was supposed to walk around the perimeter once every 30 minutes, but who cared? Everyone had just gone inside when the hooded figure on the horse had shown up and waltzed in. Who would ever know if he did the rounds or not? There were no lights outside, and they had carefully boarded up all the windows and covered the door edges with cloth so that no light could be seen leaking from the house at all. And there was only a tiny sliver of moon out tonight, so with any clouds it would be as close to pitch black as it got. Who would know?

He found a place back behind some straw bales. The straw was not as comfortable as a bed, but was still better than being out in the stinking dark watching for exactly stinking nothing! He had comfortably settled into the straw and was already asleep when a handful of shadows detached from the trees to the south and converged on the dark old house.

⚜

Warden James had compromised. He would have only taken perhaps 3 or 4 men with him for the activities outlined by Gaeten, but with Ethan along he'd have to answer to Chancellor Duncan if anything at all happened, and he was not about to risk his position … or Ethan's welfare. And anyway, his crack Alpha-Red team had been inactive for awhile, and there was nothing like a bit of … adventure … to keep their skills honed. Gaeten did not really need to know that the entire Alpha team was present in Westhaven, and followed them toward the north end of town at a discreet distance. He had selected 4 of the team to directly accompany himself, Ethan and Gaeten — oh, and Quentin too, who should prove quite capable for this mission — while the rest would act as back-up in case something did not go according to plan … and it was a well known axiom that no plan survived intact once a battle started. Gaeten also did not need to know that he had placed seasoned Watchers at each of the main roads leading into and out of Westhaven, and a few others scattered throughout District 17 as well, for that matter. Nor that a small band of apprentice Watchers was due to arrive at daybreak. Master Warden James was nothing if not very, very thorough.

Gaeten had counted on it.

Eight barely discernable shadows flitted across the space between the trees and the house. Gaeten actually led the way, since the darkness was normal for him — he could move at his normal pace and had to slow for the others to make their silent way behind him. Actually, moving about at night was in some ways almost easier — there were less distracting people noises, yet the small sounds of the many active insects and even the night breeze moving through the trees and around objects made an audible map laid out before him.

Ethan came next, followed by Quentin. Ethan was a boy of 15, a bit small for his age perhaps, with rather plain features sporting an often serious expression. He was someone no one would tend to take a second look at, someone easily dismissed and taken for granted. That would be most people's error. He was certainly the youngest member of this expedition, though only a year behind Quentin, and also the far least experienced. Yet Gaeten had requested him, and he was quite excited to be so selected and now about to go into danger. He understood there were risks, but he had no fear whatsoever. He was anxious to see how his special talent would work in a real battle, even if only with third rate hoodlums.

They reached the house and the team split towards the front and back doors. Gaeten, Quentin, Ethan and James went toward the back door and the four others went to the front. They approached the doors slowly without making even the faintest of sounds. James slowly turned the handle of the back door, surprised to find it unlocked. The confidence of their quarry would only make things easier. Gaeten moved up, listened intently at the door, and then pushed it open a tiny fraction of an inch. They could hear sounds coming from an inner room, but none directly in the room before them. The door swung open without a sound. James figured the occupants may have oiled the hinges so they themselves could enter and exit silently. The four entered a small kitchen area with a solitary candle burning in a holder on the far wall, with all of the windows blacked out. The door closed as quietly as it had opened and they glided forward to an inner door.

Gaeten again was in the lead, both because of his skill level and his highly acute hearing and "sense" of what lay before him. Muffled sounds were coming from slightly further inside. Gaeten opened the door a sliver and James peered through the crack. He tapped his fingers on each of the men's arms in a code long ago perfected for the Watchers for communicating when words could not be used. They moved into the adjoining hallway. The hallway had two closed doors along the left side, presumably holding small bedrooms, and appeared to then turn and open into a larger area. The previously muffled voices were now much clearer, though they were all in hushed tones.

Quentin thought the main voice was vaguely familiar. "Westhaven has been good pickings, but I think it is time for our Rats to move." That got a lot of murmuring dissension. "I've heard there may be some attention coming here from the Keep, so we need to stay very low for a few weeks. This is just a temporary setback; we will be able to be back in full operation again very shortly I'm sure. As a reward for how well you have been doing, I have several new swords and bows to give out; some of the best the Keep has to offer!" Movement and sounds indicated the audience was examining some of the proffered items.

"It's Warden Harden!" hissed Quentin in a tiny voice easily drowned out by the small talk now going on in the adjoining room.

The four now crept forward, wary of a telltale floor squeak or other sound that might give them away prematurely. James did not know for sure where the other four men of the team were, or if they had even been able to enter the front of the house as his group had the rear, but that did not matter greatly yet. When needed, the members of the Alpha Red team would find — or make — a way to enter quickly enough.

"You see how well I can take care of you Rats, getting you the things you need? We are just beginning. As we grow stronger we will be able to collect "security" allowances from businesses, and in return we will ensure they are not vandalized or broken into. We will be able to start our own business, like pawn shops where we can sell the various items we "find" from one area in another town far enough away to avoid any suspicion. We will grow so powerful that no one will be able to stop us!" That brought a few delighted cheers.

They were ready. Master Warden James took a step out from the hallway. "Oh, I think we just might have something to say about that!"

Bedlam erupted. There were 15 or so older teens and young men in the room, as well as a hooded figure standing over by the far wall next to a small table. At the sound of James' voice they all jumped with alarm, and then turned with anger. James smiled. They had figured on about a dozen, maybe a few more. This shouldn't be overly difficult.

He had a short truncheon secured in a loop on his belt, but didn't think he would need it. James had figured it was unlikely the group of miscreants would just give up when he announced his presence, and he would have been quite surprised and somewhat annoyed if they had.

As the group started to surge toward him, Gaeten, Quentin and Ethan stepped out beside James. The other members of their team had not shown up so far, but no matter ... there weren't that many of the likely poorly trained youth here. Jake, over near the hooded figure, yelled out "It's him!"

No one seemed particularly to care.

The first older teen Rat moved forward and swung a knife that had quickly appeared in his hand. Warden James sidestepped the swing and returned a powerful chop. The knife clattered to the floor from a now broken arm and an immediate second blow dropped the wielder to the floor out cold. James had wondered if a rapid downing of the first man might unnerve the group and put an immediate halt to the fight, but the hooded man — Warden Harden — shouted "Get them!" and that galvanized the group to rush forward as a mass. Nearly all had pulled out knives, and two near the speaker grabbed at the short swords on the table. The room was too small for effective sword play, but it did change the dynamics of the fight — and the seriousness. With still no sign of their backup, this encounter was not quite playing out as expected.

Of them all, Gaeten was the most calm. He had settled himself into a battle-mind, where every sound conveyed location information. In his mind he could almost "see" each person, and this type of pitched fight was really his specialty. Rather than waiting for anyone to come near him, Gaeten propelled himself forward slightly to the left of James, right into the thick of the assailants. For a few moments the others nearly lost sight of him as the nearest four Rats gave the strange old man their full attention. Quentin, seeing his mentor's lead, immediately followed a step behind.

Ethan paused a moment. James was engaging two men to the right, and Gaeten and Quentin had the attention now of five. He was about to move forward beside James when both doors to the side rooms they had past burst open, disgorging numerous more Rat gang members who had been sleeping off their last shift of duties Hearing all the commotion, they had awakened and all came out armed. Ethan was the only one in direct sight, and he certainly was not a fellow Rat. Sink or swim time, Ethan thought. He wondered where the other Alpha team members were as the first two assailants came at him down the now crowded hallway.

Preoccupied with the melee in front of them, no one noticed Warden Harden grab the bows and two quivers of arrows and race up the stairs to the open loft. The short bows had been strung already to show everyone. They were ready. Harden grinned a wicked sneer. He handed one bow to the Rat who had been coming down the stairs to join the fracas and they both nocked arrows and drew. As he did so he nodded at the three other Rats who had been upstairs and they raced down to join their comrades.

The other members of the Alpha Red team out front were having trouble of their own. The front door had been locked, and apparently reinforced — they could not kick it down as they heard commotion start up inside. Then a basement storm door had burst open, spilling a flood of light into the dark night. In the glare they saw four or five young men leap out and begin to run into the darkness. The Alpha team had been given strict orders — no one was supposed to escape. Torn between helping out inside — where surely there could only be a relatively few present to fight — and the escaping men outside, they made a snap decision and sped out after the fleeing suspects. One was felled with a quick reaction- thrown knife, but then each Watcher split off to chase after their own escaping target and disappeared with them into the dark.

Jarl was woken by crashing sounds coming from the house. He groggily got to his feet and peered out the barn. He saw the basement door flung open, and in the light he saw a fellow Rat fall and four others run off into the night with large figures chasing after them. He gulped, wondering what his fate would be for not performing his guard duty. He figured it might be better not to find out. Jarl swiveled around and raced out the back of the barn, following one of the worn pathways they had made as escape routes, one they all knew quite well and could navigate rapidly even in pitch darkness. As his path diverged from the others, no one ever knew he had been there, or that he was now cleanly escaping.

As the first Rat stepped out of the bedroom with a large knife held at low-ready preceding him, time stopped. Well, not exactly. For Ethan it essentially did, at least regarding everything happening around him. His mind instantly cleared and his vision took on a slight bluish tint. The lighting seemed to suddenly flare to bright sunlight and Ethan could notice the smallest details, and he could even hear the floor begin to creak slightly from the heavy steps of the first men exiting the bedrooms. A part of his mind began to catalog each assailant: what weapons they had, their movements, and a faint reddish hue seemed to color each one. Though they were now moving in very slow motion — at least relative to his sight and speed of thinking — Ethan could tell the direction and likely trajectory of each. With cold calmness he turned his back to the fighting in the main room and blocked the hallway's exit. His movements, in contrast to the others, were at close to normal speeds.

The knife was inching forward toward him, and Ethan easily brushed it aside as he stepped inside the man's guard. A thin hazy bluish ribbon seemed to float in the air before him, though he knew it really was not there. It showed a proposed course of action and his stiffened hand followed it exactly to connect with an unprotected Adam's apple. Even as it contacted Ethan was ducking under the barely moving arm to reach the second man who was just trying to come out of the room directly behind the first. He had a small staff that was just starting to rise. A blow to the side of his head shifted his balance completely and swiveled his whole body sideways. The energy the youth had put toward his forward momentum was redirected … into the doorframe of the room he was just beginning to exit. Ethan had already plotted out his next movements when two arrows were loosed behind him.

Gaeten was in his element, as much as that may have surprised others. His hands and feet were a blur of continual motion and he mowed down the four Rats in moments — they really had not the slightest chance against someone of his skill level. Quentin also readily dispatched his sole antagonist and turned to see how Master Warden James was doing. He hardly needed to have bothered. The last of the men who had come at the Warden was currently flying through the air backwards from a forceful forearm blow and the body crashed into the far fall where the hooded Harden had been. All three paused for a moment as their ears were just beginning to process the twang of bow strings loosed of their projectiles and the heavy steps of more people descending the far staircase.

If time around Ethan had been slowed before, now it was nearly at a dead stop. His mind located the arrows even as they were just leaving their strings and red lines appeared tracing their most probable flight paths. He saw the room as though from distance, a static picture with red lines that ended in cones of likely impact zones. One terminated on Gaeten, the other … on himself.

Even his own movements were slowed now, though not nearly as much as the world around him. Ethan's potential course of action showed as several ribbons in his mind; there were several options. The men before him were now not the immediate concern and Ethan pivoted sharply back toward the main room. Without even looking his hand precisely grabbed at something moving in a slow arc towards him from one of the two remaining nearby assailants. Ethan started to twist his body as fast as his mind could make it move while he began a slow-motion dive forward and slightly sideways toward the general direction of James. That would remove his body from the arrow's flight path. All of this had taken the merest fraction of a second and the arrows had only traversed a few feet from their launching points.

Gaeten could be incredibly fast. He had dispatched the four men — including Brak and Jake who had been in front of him — in just a few seconds. However, a blind man even with his skills is at a very distinct disadvantage with an arrow loosed less than 20 feet away. By the time his mind registered the twang his ears had picked up it was well too late for him to do more than begin to pivot away from the spot he had been, hoping that would be enough. But he did not even know which way to go or even if the shot was aimed at him. There was very little he could do to prevent the arrow from finding its intended target.

The men who had been in closest bedroom heard the commotion, grabbed weapons and came barreling out. Drang was first, having grabbed the large hunting knife that he preferred, and he instantly saw a young boy in front of him that did not belong to the Rats. He did not know who the boy was, but from the sounds coming from the main room he had to be an enemy. Enemies were to be destroyed.

Drang charged forward, bringing up the knife into a ready position with its point held low. He figured he would skewer the runt in front of him and then see what was making all the noise in the main room. Then everything changed. The boy moved faster than should have been humanly possible and Drang felt a sharp pain in his throat. The boy was moving past him in a blur, and then suddenly he was in view again and diving back into the main room. Drang felt a wrenching force in his hand with the knife, and then all his attention was focused on the fact that he no longer could breathe.

Ethan easily ripped the knife from the first man as he swiveled and dived forward, the large hilt guard helping immensely for him to get a fast grip. His hand continued the arc it had started, accelerating with all the speed and force Ethan could put behind it. That arm swung forward even as he continued the process of diving away from the path of the arrow aimed where his body had so recently been. When his hand was most of the way through its arc he released the knife. The blue line was clearly marked in his mind, if only his skill was sufficient to send the knife true to the indicated path. The arrows had already covered half the distance to their targets and the timing was going to be very, very tight.

The knife spun in what looked to Ethan as a very slow, lazy tumbling path almost directly at Gaeten, who was still pivoting in slow motion. Ethan had noticed Gaeten's movement and his mental targeting system had compensated. Now two projectiles were actually both speeding toward the elder man, who was oblivious to being the center of their respective attention. The knife clanged into the arrow no more than a foot in front of Gaeten, and the momentum carried both of the deadly objects past Gaeten's head with only inches to spare. The other arrow, heading Ethan's way, also found a target, just not the one intended. Drang no longer had to be concerned with breathing.

Ethan's dive had carried him well into the main room. He rolled as he hit the floor and sprang upward, angling directly toward the base of the stairs just as the first of the descending men reached it. In slow motion the man swung even as Ethan was just regaining his feet. He dodged to the right, against the wall, and slipped past him. The older teen that followed was also easily passed as Ethan sped up the stairs. He did not want to allow another round of arrows to fly if possible. The third young man was crowding the wall halfway up, making it nearly impossible for Ethan to pass. Instead he ducked down low, going to all fours in a blur of motion. The fellow barely even saw Ethan coming, and could not stop his descent. As he moved forward in slow motion he began to fall over Ethan's bent over form. As that started, Ethan pushed forward and then lifted up. Though he was not large, leverage and gravity were great force multipliers. The man pivoted down and over Ethan's back, and as he stood, the Rat went airborne and became Ethan's own projectile aimed at the men further down the stairs. Ethan zipped upward.

James was also racing for the stairs, though he was at a significant temporal disadvantage. He reached the bottom in time to "assist" the Rats coming down, who were already being propelled by their fellow Rat crashing down on them from above and behind.

Quentin could not keep up with all that was happening; he turned to see a flicker of motion that was Ethan diving and rolling, and saw an arrow embed itself into a choking Rat stumbling out from the hallway. He moved a step in that direction in time to see a second man run head first into the door frame of the first room. Then two other men were emerging from the hallway and he forgot about all else as his years of training took over and he went airborne, lashing out his right foot to catch the first squarely in the chest and send him crashing backwards into his companion.

"That is not possible!" whispered Harden under his breath in shock, standing in the upper balcony area. The arrows he and the Rat at his side had loosed had not struck their intended targets and the situation had gone from tolerably bad to very much worse. And the fourth person who had suddenly appeared with the Master Warden was moving far faster than he had ever imagined possible. He reached for another arrow.

Gaeten sensed rapid movement coming close to him from two different directions, and had time only to begin to snap his head and body back when there was some sort of collision in the air in front of him and two fast moving objects flew past to clang onto the floor beside him to the rear. The one that had come from the general direction of the bedrooms they had past sounded like a knife whistling end over end through the air, and from the timing he figured the other may have been an arrow — but he did not know for sure. But he did know exactly where the bow twang had come from. In his own blur of motion he whipped out a sharp pointed throwing star and launched it with considerable force in a reverse trajectory.

Ethan looked upward as he cleared past the last of the descending figures and saw two men further down the short railing that overlooked the room below, one with a rather large girth and the other a tall skinny younger man closer by. Both had just grabbed fresh arrows and were bring them up to their bows. He also noticed a large wooden knob at the top of the stair railing just within reach, with a blue wispy ribbon in his mind showing a possible course of action. He leapt with as much force as he could muster and as his hands closed around the knob he pulled and twisted with all his might, swinging his body into a tight arc through the air. His feet crashed solidly into the Rat and both of them tumbled backwards.

Harden was bringing the bow up with its new arrow when the bow string suddenly parted in half and he felt a sharp stinging pain in his rather large belly. He looked down to see an inch of metal protruding out from his concealing robe. It hurt considerably, but his layers of fat prevented any real damage.

Quentin landed lightly on his feet after his kick and charged forward toward the fallen men. They were in a sprawled pile and were only slowly untangling themselves. As the first stumbled upright Quentin dropped him with a chop to the base of his neck. The other backed into the corner of the hallway, hands spread out in submission.

Ethan landed, rolling his body to more quickly get upright as he brushed against the back wall. The skinny archer had slammed backwards into the wall, and toppled senselessly to the floor. There was one left. Ethan saw the man's bow string snap as though cut and his mind showed a blue line indicating a friendly projectile originating from below. He saw it strike with no noticeable effect. The man was very large, far heavier than Ethan and far more so than anyone he had sparred with before. He realized his own small body weight would have much less impact on such a massive person, so his options were more limited — but several lay before him in blue ribbons in his mind. He chose one. He lifted one foot up against the wall and pushed off with all his strength.

Harden turned, figuring it was probably a good time to exit. His plans were in shambles, his Rats were defeated, and he would now rather be anywhere else than here. He had not even noticed the loss of his fellow archer, and was just finishing his turn when an airborne Ethan slammed into him at chest level with a shoulder. The impact was not enough to cause damage, but did propel Harden backwards with some force. He crashed heavily into the railing which held for a moment, and then the old wood splintered and his momentum carried him over the edge. Harden's arms pin wheeled once before his huge frame hit the floor below.

And with that the fighting was over, just a few minutes after it had started.

Jarl by this time was well down the path into the woods, and fuming. Another colossal problem! And it probably somehow again could be traced back to that dratted orphan girl! He heard crunching under his feet and realized he had reached the small gravelly road that lead directly into town, just a few blocks away from the old church … where the orphans stayed … with no priest to protect them after the clubbing Jarl had given him earlier that day. SHE would surely be there, like a little mother hen brooding over her clutch of chicks. A little blind hen in the henhouse, with the farmer not home. An evil smile came over his face in the dark. He would now have his revenge.

Chapter 6

Faith is not by sight

aria got the last of the children bedded down. Maggie helped and, after a few other chores, settled into a cot set up near the littlest children. Maria moved over to her mat. It had been a long day and she was quite tired. She laid her head onto her pillow, said her evening prayers, and drifted off to sleep.

It seemed like she had just closed her eyes when the old mare whinnied loudly enough to startle her awake. She rose quietly and went to the door. The mare had probably bumped up against her sore and opened the wound again. She had done that once before, and then had ground straw and dirt into the sore by laying on it. That had caused a worse infection and delayed healing by over a week. Maria had extra bandages out in the barn, and a little bit of the healing poultice was left in a jar out there too. It would only take a few minutes to take care of things, and if she hurried the others might not be woken. She donned a light weight cloak and her sandals, then unlatched the door and eased out into the back yard. It was very dark outside, with clouds that had moved in to let no moon or starlight through, so visibility was extremely limited. Not that this mattered one whit or was even known to Maria. To her, it could have been bright sunlight outside. She knew her way around the church yard and barn very well and carefully avoided the wheelbarrow and various items that formed a sort of simple playground for the younger children.

She opened the barn door and light flooded out, though of course she did not know that. The mare whinnied again and Maria moved toward her, making gentle sounds that normally calmed the horse. She was several steps in when she felt something different. She did not know what it was that was different; something was just not … right. She swiveled about to listen more intently, and as she did the barn door slammed shut.

"I thought you might come to check on that old hag of a horse." Jarl's voice was cruel and he sounded confident.

"What have you done to her?" Maria exclaimed as she stepped over to the mare's stall and opened the latch to go in.

"Oh, not much, just enough to get you to come and check on her".

The mare had been tied with two ropes, each pulling her head tightly in a different direction, enough to be quite uncomfortable. "Oh! You are so cruel Jarl Greely! What has this horse ever done to you for you to treat her so meanly?"

"SHE has not done anything. But YOU sure have!" The last was said with considerable spite and anger and Maria could hear Jarl moving closer. "We had it all under control, all going smoothly until you came along with that strange old man! You have been nothing but trouble for us." Jarl's anger was building as he talked, stoked on by his own harsh words and imagination. "And now the Rats were attacked, our Nest has probably been taken over …" Jarl sputtered a moment and then thought about his brothers who had been inside the house. "And because of you Brak and Jake have likely either been captured or killed! Well, they may not be able to do anything about the cause of all their trouble, but I sure can!" With that he strode forward.

Marie had untied one of the ropes binding the mare and was working on the second. She heard the anger building in Jarl's voice and it made her afraid. She knew he was capable of being very cruel, and when he was angry he could be very, very dangerous. She moved a step further into the dimly lit stall, brushing against the mare. The horse was picking up on her distress and getting even more fidgety. "Oh God, please give me an escape … a way out!" she silently cried.

Jarl was at the stall entrance. "It's time for you to pay for what you have caused, Maria!" She instinctively moved even further into the stall, now at the horse's hindquarters. She heard a slapping sound and knew Jarl had grabbed one of the short whips that had hung unused in the barn since before she had arrived. If he used that in the stall, the mare would surely panic, and even an old horse could do a whole lot of damage to a small girl if it began to buck and thrash about.

She heard the whip being drawn back. "Jarl, NO!" she screamed and without really thinking about it she ducked under the mare, her hands searching for a latch for the door in the stall that led to a small outer corral. Maria tugged at the rope connected to a short wooden peg that held the door shut. They rarely used this door, and the peg was seated quite securely.

The whip flew through the air above the stall and cracked overhead. It had the expected result. The mare whinnied loudly in fear and kicked out. Maria was to the side now, and not in the path of the hooves, but the horse was moving agitatedly around the stall and it would only be moments before she would accidently smash into Maria and crush her against the wall. She yanked at the rope again and the peg sprang free. Marie pushed the door open and ran out from the confines of the small stall into the corral. She raced to the gate and unhooked it, and began running as fast as she could toward the back door of the church.

Jarl saw her escape and dropped the whip, ignoring the frightened horse. He yanked open the main door he had just slammed shut and raced to cut Maria off before she could reach the church. As he started off across the yard he yelled out "Go ahead, Maria. Go inside the church. Do you really think that little old back door can stop me? It looks pretty flimsy. One hard kick or shove and then I can have my revenge not only on you, but on all those snot-nosed runts inside!"

Maria despaired. She had thought if only she could get back inside she would be safe. She always felt safe there. But now she realized she might instead endanger Timmy and the others. And Jarl was right about the door — it was thin and at least one hinge seemed to always be coming loose. Even the latch was loose. If Jarl wanted to get in, it would not stop him. She stopped her wild dash with a cry. "Jesus ... you are my Savior! I NEED HELP!" Jarl wanted to get her, not the others. She just couldn't let him harm them. An idea formed in some quieter part of her mind. She cried out "You will never catch me, Jarl Greely!" and turned and sped off in another direction, through the play yard and off into the open field behind the church.

Jarl sneered. This was not going quite as easily as he expected, but still, how far could a little blind girl get anyway? He could easily run at double her speed. She would not get half way across the field before he would be upon her. He laughed and took off in her direction.

The open barn door spilled some light out into the yard, creating a patch of visibility and long shadows where it met any obstruction. For Maria, it was irrelevant. She picked her way across the yard, sidestepping around each item she knew by heart was there. She cleared the last obstruction and sped full speed into the field.

Jarl thought he had been especially clever to have a lamp lit inside the barn and to have pushed the barn door widely open as he rushed out. The light was not much, but easily showed him the direction Maria was going and the entire layout of the back yard. Or at least he thought it did. He was almost half way across when he stepped into a shadowed and unnoticed sandbox that caught his feet. He tumbled to the ground hard and banged his knee, but rolled and sprang back upright. Maria was entering the field now, but he had cut the distance somewhat. He charged forward with only a slight favoring of one leg. He had almost made it out of the play area when he went down again.

Maria raced forward unhindered, heading for the thick woods at the other end of the field. If she could only make it in time!

Jarl got up again, angrier by far now that he had new bruises atop of his others and an aching knee to show for his activities. That girl was nothing but trouble! Bad trouble! His world would be far better off if she were taken care of … permanently. In the now very faint light from the distant barn he could just make out Maria at the far end of the field, and he grinned again as he broke into as rapid of a run as he could. There were no obstacles in the field, and at his speed he would reach the trees in a very short time. How fast could a blind girl move in thick woods?

Not very. Maria held her hands out in front of her face to shield it from the snagging branches. She had to slow to a walking speed to avoid bumping into trees or tripping over roots and hillocks. She was also becoming more and more frightened. "Oh God," she whispered. "If I ever needed Your help it is now!" There was no direct answer, though her fear seemed to subside somewhat. She kept going, pushing deeper and deeper into the woods. She heard Jarl crashing into the outer trees in roughly her direction. She veered right and tried to pick up her pace. "God, HELP ME!" she yelled into the special place in her mind. At that instant her front foot came down onto thin air and she cried out as she tumbled forward. This did not exactly seem like help.

Jarl charged into the woods, rather expecting to find Maria stopped cold a few feet into the thicket. She was not there. At first he fumed and charged blindly forward, but a few branches slapping him in the face convinced him to go more slowly. In fact … he stopped moving completely to listen. There! Off to the right! He started up again in that direction, going slower now. He realized he was actually at a disadvantage here in some ways. He could see next to nothing, and was very unaccustomed to trying to move about with that handicap. Maria on the other hand, had grown very used to that mode of travel. His anger rose again at the thought that here she may be able to move about as easily as or even more easily than him! It just was not fair! She was causing him more trouble … again!

He stopped once more to listen, and then strode forward, bearing down inexorably toward the sounds from a moving source which was less than 40 yards ahead. He knew he was gaining on her, and he pushed on even faster, wanting to end this as quickly as possible.

Maria pitched forward, pushing out her arms to try to break her fall. Instead of a small dip in the forest's floor that she had expected, she had stepped over the edge of a rather steep hill. She hit the ground hard and tumbled further down the hill, crashing through branches and small undergrowth. It was incredibly frightening for her, as she wondered with every pitch if she would smack hard up against a solid tree. However, none materialized in her path and she tumbled and rolled over and over. The ground leveled off but Maria's momentum carried her further and she felt scratching needles of a spruce tree rake over her just before she did finally hit a solid tree trunk. It stunned her for a moment and she struggled to catch her breath, remaining motionless. Then she reached around her, feeling prickly dry needles all around and above her, and further out the thick growth of a mid-sized evergreen. Maria realized she was under the canopy of a dense spruce tree whose heavy branches stretched out and drooped to the ground. She was in the dry enclosed center. It was as safe of a place as she could hope to find to hide, and she realized that at night in the dark, her hearing would give her ample warning of Jarl's approach even through the muffling expanse of thick evergreen branches surrounding her.

She began to cry softly, but they quickly changed to quiet giggles. God had just hidden her in a sanctuary of His own making. This tree had been in just the perfect spot, as though waiting for her not-so-grand arrival. Did God put it here in part for this purpose, she wondered? Surely not … she was far too insignificant for that! But God had been so good to her, even in the midst of terrible struggles. Could He care that much for her? Even if the tree had another purpose to be right here, still her fall had been at just the perfect angle and speed for her to tumble right into this safe haven. Either way, she thought, it was God's direct help and answer to her cries.

Though deadened by the thick canopy, she could hear Jarl coming her way. She thanked God silently and barely breathed, listening intently.

Jarl was moving slowly enough to hear Maria's cry and her crashing descent down the hill. He laughed cruelly and moved forward in that direction. In a few moments he came to the top of the hill, and Maria's fall gave him good warning to watch for the edge. He did not hear any more movements below. "She probably killed herself with that fall" he said under his breath. But he was going to make sure. He headed down, feeling ahead with his feet for trees … or a body. He made it to the bottom and felt around the base in both directions for 10 or 15 feet. Curious, Jarl thought. She was not making any noises, but where was she? He spread out his search, figuring her tumble may have carried her body out further. He had to work around several evergreen trees, kicking at the lower branches along the way. Nothing. Where was she?

Maria was very, very still. She could hear Jarl moving around, and bit her lip as he kicked at the branches only a few feet from where she huddled. Then he moved off, scuffing the ground all along the way. After a few minutes he stopped and was silent. Maria held herself, unmoving, barely breathing. After what seemed like hours she heard him mutter something and return to right outside of the tree where she was hidden. He did not stop this time, but started off in a direction roughly the same that she had been falling. In a few minutes he was a distance away, crashing through the branches. Then, silence. She sang a song of praise in her heart to her God who never slept and never left her. He had provided for her needs, as He always had. Maria had had many opportunities to grow in faith in her short life. Being blind, she had learned to trust even more in the all-seeing God than most sighted people had.

She crept out through the needles and moved toward where she had fallen. Feeling around, her hands came across a long, thin stick which Maria figured would be just about perfect to swing about so she could avoid obstacles and tap on the ground ahead to avoid tripping hazards. The hill was too steep for her to navigate, so she moved off alongside it, hoping to find a pathway up. Unknowingly, she was heading further and further away from the church.

She wandered forward for over an hour, and some time back had veered away from the hill. In fact, she had circled around her own path several times and now was hopelessly lost. Exhausted, she finally sat down with her back to a large tree. She had not heard Jarl or anyone else since being under the spruce. She knew it must still be dark by how moist the ground felt and by the night sounds around her. She felt oddly at peace, given her circumstances, and in a few minutes she slumped over into the soft undergrowth and fell asleep.

Nearly a mile away — which in the woods is a very long distance indeed, Jarl also stopped. He had been forcefully marching, stopping every so often to listen for sounds of movement. Several times he had thought for sure he had found her, only to be led for who-knows-how-far by a squirrel or opossum or other woodland creature. He was heavily scratched, fed up and tired out. Jarl finally stumbled out onto a small dirt road which he did not recognize in the dark. There was a shallow ditch close to the road and Jarl rounded up some nearby leaves and moss to make a bed of sorts. He settled down and was soon fast asleep.

Back at the Rat's Nest, the other three Watchers had returned with two of the escaping Rats, one returning empty handed. Master Warden James sent one of the men out toward the nearby main road to contact others of the Alpha team. He returned shortly with two others of the team, and the last Rat who had mistakenly thought the road made a great get-away route. They put all the gang members to one side of the large room in the house, with several Watchers standing by with short swords in their hands at the ready. No further high jinks would be tolerated.

Quentin was looking at Ethan with renewed respect. He had seen the boy before a few times, working out with Master Gaeten, and from that knew he must be quite skilled. But Quentin had now seen him move with a speed that was astounding. And he obviously had no fear of a fight. He was staring at Ethan when James stepped in front of him, Gaeten at his side.

"Quentin."

"Yes Master Warden?"

"I have something to ask of you. Ethan has some special talents, most of which are not fully developed yet." At that Quentin gulped, wondering what Ethan would be like when full grown. "You are not to tell anyone about his being here. As far as you are concerned, it was just the three of us inside this house tonight, and the Alpha-Red Watcher team members. Some of the Rats have seen him, but who will believe their story?" James looked Quentin straight in the eyes. "Do you understand?" Quentin nodded. "Now I want you to promise before God that you will do your best not to mention anything about Ethan being here, or what you saw him do." Quentin did not understand the secrecy, but Gaeten had chosen him as a companion in part for his skill and in part because of his loyalty.

"Sure Master Warden. I promise to do my best."

"That is all I can ask of you." James turned away to talk with Gaeten, leaving Quentin to wonder how he would tell the other apprentices of the battle they had had here tonight. They probably would never have believed him about a faster-than-possible Ethan anyway. So, he would need to come up with some alternate story … one in which he of course would need to play a very prominent role.

James took Gaeten aside. "I think we have them all. You were certainly correct — there was a major problem here. I think we had better audit this district, and maybe review our entire way of supervising the outer districts. If it had gotten this bad here, there may be issues elsewhere too. I think we may even set up a schedule for the apprentice Watchers to rotate around — it would do them good to see more of the countryside anyway."

Gaeten nodded agreement, but just couldn't help but thinking he was missing something. They would wait here until morning, alternating shifts to guard the prisoners, and then send someone to get a larger contingent of Watchers to escort the prisoners to the nearest jail. Gaeten figured that sometime mid-morning he and Quentin could head back over to the inn to freshen up, and then he had another errand for Quentin at the Keep. While he was gone, Gaeten planned on visiting over at the church to see Maria.

Maria woke to songbirds singing sweetly. She was cold, but her cloak had been sufficient to ward off most of the night chill. She moved out from the large tree she had slept under and felt the warm sunshine on her skin. It took a few moments for her to realize the predicament she was in, but she was not too frightened. God had protected her this far, and He surely would protect her still. But she had no idea where she was — everything seemed unfamiliar. As she pondered what to do, she thought she heard a noise afar off and she started off slowly in that direction, tapping ahead with the stick which she had retrieved by her side, in hopes it might be someone who could help her.

She traveled perhaps an hour, and this time she did not circle about as she had the night before. Every so often she would hear a noise, and as she got closer she suspected she was nearing a road where an occasional traveler would pass by. She eventually found the trees to thin and came into an opening. The flatness of the ground and texture of its surface informed her it was the road she had suspected. Since she had no idea which way to go, she picked one and started walking.

Jarl woke up later than Maria. He was stiff and sore and in a grumpy mood. Then again, he was nearly always in a grumpy mood. He knew roughly where he was, and wondered where that troublemaker Maria could have gotten too. How could such a nobody cause so much trouble? She would not even let herself be found without making it difficult! Under the bright sunlight, she now should be far easier to find. But which way should he go? As he pondered that a horse and rider rounded a bend in the road before him. Jarl had no time to move out of sight, and so instead stood still. The rider pulled up alongside him, a merchant by the way he was dressed.

"What have we here? A young man out in the middle of no-where?"

Jarl's thoughts moved remarkably quickly. "Sir, have you seen a young girl anywhere nearby? My sister and I went for a walk last night and we got separated. I have been looking and looking for her — she must be lost."

His ruse worked. The merchant did not seem at all suspicious. "Well, as a matter of fact, just a bit up the road around the bend the road forks. As I came down from the north and turned onto this path I did see a young girl along the other road, slowly walking this way. Come to think of it, she did seem like she might have been lost. I waved at her but she did not wave back, so I rode along. Would you like me to take you back to her? It is not very far."

Jarl grinned, but he tried to keep it a pleasant looking one. "No, that's ok. Thank you very kindly for the information. I will go run and fetch her now! Thanks!" With that he took off at a slow run, mindful of his now throbbing knee, toward the bend, and toward Maria.

Maria had just stumbled on an upturned root when she belatedly recognized the sound of a lone horse ahead. As she picked herself up she yelled out and waved in the general direction of the sound, but it had already turned away and was moving off. A bit frustrated, she continued walking. A few minutes later she heard movement again, coming from the direction the horse had taken. "Perhaps the rider is coming back!" she said to herself.

Jarl came around the bend in the road at a medium paced jog and saw a diminutive figure about a quarter mile away. He dropped into a measured pace that he knew would eat up the distance without overly tiring him. Everything was coming together now ... finally.

Maria waved in the direction of the noise and yelled out "Over here!" She noticed now that the sound was different, not from a horse at all ... but from someone running in her direction. Maybe it was help!

Jarl loosened his long and very sharp knife from its sheath as he ran. This was going to be awfully easy, for once.

Maria wavered and slowed her pace. The runner was very rapidly approaching but had not made any verbal response. Then a chill went up her spine. She recognized that running pattern, even with the slight limp … it was Jarl! She screamed a wail of despair and turned sharply off the road, running now through a field beside it angling away from the runner, her walking stick madly waving to ward off trees. She cried out as tall sharp edged ferns cut at her arms as she tried to run through what appeared to be a large patch of them and she tripped on a low bush her stick had not warned her of. Maria crashed down through the leafy fern canopy onto her hands and knees and began to crawl through the tall plants.

Jarl was almost upon her when Maria dashed off sideways into the field full of low bushes and ferns. He altered course and pursued her, and saw her go down. Then he saw fern tops moving and realized she was crawling, trying to hide. He laughed out loud. "There is no-where to go. Hiding just delays the inevitable, and will make me angrier …" Actually, he rather enjoyed the prospects of this dragging out, of terrorizing his victim even more before the kill. He saw the ferns and bushes stop moving a short distance away and he slowed to a leisurely pace. "You know Maria, things might have been different …" he kicked a swath of ferns down with one foot, off to the side of where he figured she was cowering.

"… if only you had not resisted so much. If you had gone along with us …" he kicked another row of ferns down "we could have been friends. Maybe you could even have joined us — collecting money as a poor little orphan girl, while picking the pockets of your oh-so-nice donators." He mowed down another row, edging closer.

Maria had never been more terrified in all her life, not even on the ship after her father had died. She scuttled along the ground, feeling the ferns and small bushes brush aside around and above her. She came across a small dip in the ground to her left, and she sank down into the slight decline, finding a small opening in the stalks. She pressed on. "Oh God", she whispered in her mind, "I have trusted you all my life, and I still trust you now. I know you can save me, but even if you don't, still I will trust in you." Her hand struck an old, low stump and she found an even lower depression in the ground on its far side. She slunk down into the low lying area and ran into a thicker bush that blocked her path. Panic started to set in when without warning a part of her day-dream thrust itself into her conscious mind, commanding all attention.

Maria saw herself dancing along a road. Brightly colored ribbons of living light swirled around her in perfect choreography with her movements. She was singing, and the sounds combined with the lights and dance into a sublime beauty that transcended the physical and thrived in joyous abandon within the spiritual realm. She knew from past experience that this part of the vision usually just preceded the march directly toward certain destruction.

The vision faded and Maria felt a strange calmness descend on her and she thought she heard — or somehow felt — a voice say "Be still." The voice had immense authority and power, yet was soft, as though spoken from far away, and yet very close all at the same time somehow. She sat low to the ground, with her back to the stump and the sharp bush branched at her side. As she settled in, one of the branches poked past her arm and jabbed at her neck, catching on something.

Maria pulled at the branch, untangling it from the small lanyard about her neck. At once she remembered the gift Gaeten had given her for just such a time as this. With a quick prayer of thanks she lifted the whistle to her lips and blew on it with all her might.

Jarl was getting frustrated. It was time to end this little charade. That nuisance had to be right … here! He kicked again and again, mowing down swathes of ferns and catching his foot on small bushes. Maria just had to be close … very close. "Where are you, you little rat?" Jarl laughed at his joke. The thought of Maria as a Rat was hilarious. His tone turned harsher. "Now I am getting really mad. Come out now, and I will make this fairly quick. Otherwise …" he let that hang ominously in the morning air.

Jarl's voice was only a few yards away. Maria took a large breath as quietly as she could and blew again in an extended long, hard blow. Nothing. No screech, no rustling of feathers, nothing. At least it seemed that Jarl could not hear the whistle. She began to despair again, but resolutely told herself she would trust in her Creator, NO MATTER WHAT. She took a breath and blew again.

Gaeten had sent Quentin back to the Keep with some specific instructions while he headed over to the church. He was most of the way there when he heard a high pitched, barely audible whistle from a great distance away. His blood ran ice cold. A moment later the whistle sounded again, a long, drawn out cry for help. "Oh God, protect that little child of yours … and grant me speed!" He turned about suddenly and ran back for the inn, not caring if anyone saw the most unusual sight of a blind man running at full speed unerringly through the street. A block down the road a horse and cart pulled out, blocking the way. In wonderment the merchant looked up to see a strange man racing toward him and leap into the air, soaring over the cart as though he were a gazelle. That would be a sight he would not soon forget. As he neared the inn in his mad flight Gaeten boomed out "J A M E S!"

Maria was nearly out of breath from blowing so hard on the whistle. She was very light headed and had to stop. She thought — she was not sure — that she heard a high, far away screeching sound. Then the light headedness took hold and she slumped into a near-faint. In that condition her blank mind was all the more open to the vision which came to her as though a dream.

The wind was blowing over her fiercely. She blinked and picked up even more speed, searching out the ground below. She could see for miles with incredible clarity, detecting every movement, every shade of color, it seemed like she noticed every single leaf that twitched in the breeze. There! She could see a lone lanky young man stomping about haphazardly in a field about half a mile away. The Summons had come from very near there, but certainly not from that creature kicking about in the ferns. No, it had come from … there … near that old stump barely peaking out between the fern and bush leaves, from that tiny flash of fabric she could just barely see peeking out near the bush. That meant the kicker was an ENEMY. She screeched a fierce hunter's cry as she pushed forward in a rush of speed and started a power dive for which her kind was famous for. She never missed.

Jarl was getting angrier and angrier. Where was that dratted girl? What should have been easy pickings and a quick thrust to end a major thorn in his side was becoming more and more bothersome. He had stomped out a fairly wide area in the ferns, but it had been haphazard, going in one direction and then switching to another. He growled and began a more systematic pattern. He mowed down another clump of ferns on his way toward a funny old stump he could just see jutting out of the greenery.

James was just exiting the lodge to head back to the Keep where his main duties lay, figuring he would escort Ethan back at the same time. At Gaeten's bellow they looked up to see him nearly flying down the street, his face set in a stern grimace.

"James, its Maria — she needs our help!"

"Wait a minute, Gaeten. Who is Maria?"

She was cutting through the air at tremendous speed, and gaining even more velocity with each second. Her eyes were locked on her target, and at just the last moment she extended her claws and flared her immense wings to strike.

Jarl never heard it coming. But then again, intended targets never did, otherwise they would have the chance to get away. He was almost at the stump when something sharp stabbed into his back with incredible force and raked upward even as he was knocked forward off his feet.

Maria startled to her senses violently. Her hands were clenched into claws and she could almost feel the impact force. She heard Jarl scream out in pain and land heavily onto the ground just feet in front of her. What had just happened? It seemed like a dream and yet …. Sasha's screech broke her reverie and she climbed up from her hiding place. The great Gryph was perched on the stump, clucking with great intensity and seriousness. Maria clucked back — she did not know what she was saying, but somehow she knew it was the right thing to "say". She heard Jarl moaning loudly on the ground ahead, and she could smell fresh blood. She had no interest to investigate.

"NOT NOW! GET HORSES!" Gaeten bellowed out. Several Alpha Red members charged out of the inn, and with one look at Gaeten they faced outward, looking for enemies, hands on weapons. James was very curious, but obviously whatever was causing Gaeten's concern and whoever this Maria was, it had to be pretty serious. A high screech sounded in the distance. "FOLLOW SASHA!" James wondered if Gaeten would ever speak again without yelling. They rapidly mounted their already saddled horses and sped off at full gallop.

They traversed the town and turned down a small dirt road. James mentioned they could no longer see Sasha, but that they were headed in the general direction they had last caught glimpse of her, before she disappeared in a steep dive. Gaeten pulled out his whistle and blew a series of short blasts in a particular cadence.

Maria could just barely hear short pipes of the whistle when Sasha suddenly unfurled her wings and launched upwards. She screeched a different note and began to circle high overhead. In a few minutes Maria heard the thunder of horses moving at full speed coming up the trail. She stood, figuring that now, finally, all might be well again.

Chapter 7

The Keep

aria had ridden in wagons before, usually besides bales of straw or baskets of produce, but NEVER in a *carriage*. It was much less bumpy and much, much faster. She had her head partly out the window, letting her long hair billow in the wind and taking in the smells and sounds of the countryside passing by. She partially pulled her head back in. "Gaeten, why do I and the others have to leave?"

In an exasperated tone Gaeten growled "We've been over that already — several times! Brother Rob will need weeks to recover — he received a pretty nasty blow to the head. No one in Westhaven can take care of all of you in the meantime. I have made arrangements for the others to stay at several families at the Keep. After a few days we can determine more permanent arrangements for them."

"Wait a minute! You said 'the others' that time! What about me?"

Gaeten had slipped that time. He had been wondering how he should approach the topic and had been putting it off. That would not be possible anymore. He had also been slipping back into his gruff persona as they neared the Keep. "You are a special case," he said rather roughly.

She slumped. "I know. Not everyone is ready to take on a blind orphan".

"I ... er ... " Gaeten stammered over the words he wanted to say but did not know how to get them out. "Oh bother. I was wondering if you would like to stay with me? There. I said it." While the first part was said somewhat gently, the last was in a harrumph.

"Oh Gaeten! Would you really take me in?" She pulled herself back in from the window and reached over to give him a giant hug. He did not really know what to make of that.

"Well?" Gaeten asked.

"Well what?" Maria answered.

"Do you want to stay with me?" To answer, Maria kissed his cheek.

The carriage wheel noises changed as the road suddenly transitioned from dirt to cobblestone. They were on a main road now, nearing the Keep. The Keep was not really a castle — many, many years ago in the center their once had been something like a castle, and even now there was a large building that had the vague outline of such an edifice. As typical, a town had grown around that, and over many decades and even centuries of peace it had spread wider and wider. The Keep, as such, was really the entire town, the capital of Freelandia. Yes, there was a central area surrounding the old castle-like buildings that had a stout stone wall, within which was the true and proper Keep, but everyone had called the entire town by that name for a very long time.

The town was quite large and sprawled out over the countryside down the sides of a sloping hill. Once it had grown with no real thought of order, but over the last several decades its further growth had been planned. In the new sections of the town the streets were laid out in squares, while in the older sections they were much more haphazard.

Maria was certainly bewildered by the huge variety of unknown sounds and smells that spilled though the open window of the carriage. At first she reveled in the novelty, but after a few minutes she pulled her head back inside — it was quite overwhelming in sensory overload compared to the sleepy small hamlet of Westhaven. But it was the noise of so very many people that began to frighten her. It was all so unfamiliar and alien. She knew it would be very easy to get lost, since she knew exactly zero spatial references or boundaries. The thought of that made her withdraw deeper into the carriage and go very quiet.

Gaeten heard and felt the difference. There was no getting around it; the Keep was not going to be anything like Westhaven. But he knew Maria was tough — she had to be most of her life — and would adapt. Since he really did not know how to offer her comfort, he just sat in stoic silence.

Finally their journey ended. Quentin hopped out and assisted Maria in getting down from the carriage. The smooth stones under her feet felt very odd and a bit harsh compared to the soft earth and planks she was used to. Her dilapidated and thinly soled shoes would not provide nearly as much protection for her feet on these stones. But she knew she was in no position at all to complain — she was very grateful to God and to Gaeten for saving her, and if that meant sore feet, then so be it. Gaeten came down and they all moved forward. Maria gingerly reached out to find and then hold onto Gaeten's hand, even though it dwarfed her own. "It's ok Maria; you will get used to it, and especially to this area. We are now in the Watcher Compound. Consider everyone here your friend." They walked further in silence, with Maria trying to absorb the strange surroundings.

Maria could hear the sounds of people … working, she thought, and it must be rather hard work based on the grunts. She also heard clattering sounds and even an occasional metallic clang. It was all rather confusing. Eventually they reached a door and went into a simple apartment. Quentin showed Maria to a small side room that was to be … hers. She did not know what to say. A room for herself? She never recalled having one. It was rather spartan, only a small cot, a narrow closet and a little table with a chair. It was absolutely wonderful.

Gaeten showed her around the training hall, as he called it. He said it was actually one of many, as there were many Disciplines a Watcher learned as they journeyed through the seven apprentice ranks to become a Master. Maria did not really understand, but dutifully tried to memorize not only what Gaeten was saying, but especially the sounds and smells of the route. Once taken around an area she rarely lost her way.

He led her into one of the lower level rooms, which he explained was where beginners started. Maria heard many young voices, and then a girl's voice that sounded more like her own age. After a few minutes, Gaeten spoke up "Xenia, can you come over here, please?"

"Yes Grand Master Gaeten". Xenia had a very light step, almost like her feet barely touched the floor, which Maria found rather fascinating. In a way it reminded her of the quietness of Gaeten's walk.

"Xenia, this is Maria. She is my guest and will be staying here for awhile."

"Hello, Maria." Xenia's voice was low and measured, as though she carefully weighed out each word.

"Hello, Xenia."

Gaeten continued. "Xenia, I need someone who can show Maria around, both the Watchers compound and a bit of the surrounding areas, at least for a few weeks until she gets herself oriented enough to wander about on her own. I would like you to help. It may take some time away from your other duties, but I will take care of that."

"Yes, Grand Master Gaeten. When would you like me to start?"

"Oh, tomorrow morning should be fine. For now though I think Maria needs some additional clothes. She only owns what she is wearing. I think some of our training uniforms will work for the present."

Xenia made a face that she knew neither Gaeten nor Maria could see. "Alright. Then I will see you tomorrow, Maria, at 0800 hours." Xenia wheeled about and softly padded away.

"Well, that was brief" said Maria quietly. She was not so sure she liked Xenia, at least not yet. Perhaps tomorrow she might warm up and be friendlier. She turned toward Gaeten. "What is 0800 hours?"

Gaeten gave Maria a thin yet tough reed to use as a walking cane and took her on an ever expanding tour, guiding her back to the apartment every so often so she could lock in her bearings to that central location. By late afternoon he was making her find her own way back and she was correct most of the time. By early evening she was exhausted. The two ate a simple and quiet dinner in the apartment and Maria was ready for her first night at the Keep. As she lay down on a real pillow — the first she could ever recall having — she sighed contentedly. The last few days had surely had to be the most unusual and exciting she could ever remember having. Maria wondered what adventures God had in store for her as her eyes fluttered closed.

Xenia met her the next morning with several bundles. "Hi Maria. I brought some of our uniforms — you really do need something different than that … that … torn up shift. Let's see if one of them will fit you." Maria found one that would work, though it hung rather loose on her scrawny frame. Xenia waited the few minutes and when Maria was ready she asked "So where would you like to go?"

"Oh, I really have no idea, I have never been to the Keep before. I am only used to little old Westhaven."

"Westhaven? I have heard of that town — it supposedly really is not much of a place to live." There was an awkward pause. "Oh, I'm sorry. I did not mean to belittle your hometown. So tell me, what did you do in Westhaven?"

"Well, I had several younger orphans to watch after and care for … and clean up after continually! Otherwise I did odd jobs here and there, and sometimes I would sing at the bakery."

"Uh … sing?" That was said without much enthusiasm. Maria though she heard a hint of sarcasm coming through. "Well, did Grand Master Gaeten tell you where he wanted you to start, in which Watcher training hall?"

"No … er … he did not mention anything like that. I don't even really know what a Watcher really is or does."

"You really are a newbie, aren't you? Didn't Westhaven have a Watcher, or at least one that would come through the town every so often?"

"Not that I ever heard of."

"Wow, that must have really been a backwards tiny town. A Watcher is someone who keeps the peace and ensures the laws are obeyed. They are also charged to be the defenders of Freelandia from any enemy."

"Oh — so they are like an army?"

"Well, not really. More like a cross between a Special Forces unit and a highly trained police force than an army. Freelandia does not have a standing army, or even a reserve one at that — since we have never been at war I guess they figure we have never really needed one. The main focus here is more of law enforcement, and outside of Freelandia it is more of elite bodyguards."

"Ok, well that would explain how Gaeten …" Maria realized that here he would likely be addressed more formally. "… how Grand Master Gaeten could so readily dispatch the Greely brothers. But I still don't understand how a blind man like him can accomplish so much."

Xenia shrugged and then realized Maria could not see that gesture. "Grand Master Gaeten is not like any other blind man. He is probably the most skilled Watcher in all Freelandia, with or without sight. I have heard him say he thinks it actually is an advantage in some ways, but I don't really understand that part. Regardless, he is highly respected, and not just within the Watchers. I've heard he regularly is called on for advice — and is even personal friends with — the Chancellor himself! He also is very busy teaching apprentices every day."

Maria was trying to digest all of this. "But, then why did he bring me here?"

"You're not planning on training? I mean, why else would Grand Master Gaeten have brought you here? Everyone in the Watcher Compound is either a teacher or an apprentice Watcher."

"Now that you mention it, I really don't know." Maria was close to tears at the thought that she would not fit in here … that if she did not fit in maybe she could not stay. That was not a thought she wanted to dwell on. "Maybe you could just show me around inside the compound."

"Sure, that is what I am supposed to do, isn't it?" That sounded to Maria like it lacked much enthusiasm. This did not sound like the start of much of a friendship.

The sounds within the Watcher compound were chaotic. After walking around in a near repeat of what Gaeten had done with her yesterday — which helped Maria cement down in her mind the exact placement of the main buildings and pathways — Xenia led Maria through a large set of heavy doors. They exited onto a street that seemed to Maria to be livelier and have more friendly and vibrant sounds. As they passed by little shops and stores Maria smelled a large number of things that were new and foreign to her, some pleasant and some not so much. And there were SO many people! They spent most of the morning wandering around outside the compound in a roughly circular pattern, with Maria always keeping a reference in her mind as to where the gate back in was located. By lunchtime they headed back and Maria unerringly led Xenia back to the compound and right to Gaeten's apartment.

"Wow, you really are pretty good at finding your way, you know, for a blind person."

Maria had already learned that Xenia had very little tact in how she said things. "Thanks for being a tour guide Xenia."

"Do you want me to take you around again later this afternoon?"

"No, I think I really have a pretty good hang of the area already. I think I can manage now. And anyway, if I get lost I can just ask. There are SO many people!"

"Well, alright then." Xenia sounded quite relieved. "If you change your mind let me know".

"That's ok. I will tell Gaeten how helpful you have been. Thanks."

Maria found her way to the cafeteria by herself, led by the smell of fresh cooking. As she pondered how she could obtain and pay for a meal, a kindly elderly woman came up to her. "Can I help you?"

"Yes … maybe … I don't know. I am very hungry, but I don't know anyone other than Xenia and Gaeten, and I can't hear either of them in this noisy area."

The older woman chuckled. "You mean Grand Master Gaeten. You must be Maria. He asked me to keep an eye out for you. Come child, you look like you have not eaten for months. The food here is free for all Watchers, and I think you at least qualify as an "honorary" watcher apprentice." She led Maria over to the serving line and helped her pick up a tray and a simple fork, spoon and table knife. Maria could smell various foods as they passed by and began to salivate at such a variety of savory smells. The woman told her to point at whatever items seemed to smell good to her, and gave her visual cues as to what the items were. They collected some food and sat at a low table.

"Maria, my name is Suevey. This must have been a very big day for you — how has it gone so far?"

"Ok I guess." Maria felt at ease with this gentle sounding person. "It is all a bit overwhelming, and I am not sure how I really fit in here".

"God has given each of us precious gifts and abilities. Yours may or may not be as a Watcher. Some people don't really know what skills they have until they try out a few things. And the things you learn as a Watcher, especially in the early levels, are pretty useful for anyone. Give things a try and don't give up too early because things are hard. That Grand Master Gaeten brought you here speaks loudly that he has confidence that you do indeed belong. He is a very tough one to impress!"

Maria tried some of the items on her plate as she thought about that. "Thanks, I will keep that in mind. By the way, this food is really good! Do you always have such a feast, or is this some special holiday here?"

Suevey laughed heartily. "Maybe this is a feast from where you come from, but for us it is pretty normal fare. If you really want a feast you will need to try out some of the restaurants in the Keep. Some are better than others, but even some of the smaller places around here are quite good. And they have such a variety! You can have food from Alteria or Symbthia or anywhere else in the world!"

That was a bit too much for Maria. She had barely even heard of those far away countries. Besides, compared to what she was used to, this seemed rather heavenly. "You mean … you actually get … you can have as much food as you want? Every day?"

"Yes Maria, though if we eat as much as we might want every day we soon would not fit through the doorways! But to answer your real concern … Maria — you will never go hungry as long as you are here. The Lord knows you look like you have been hungry much of your young life."

"Well … yes, I guess I have. In Westhaven Brother Rob did the best he could to feed us, and Sam the baker was always so generous … but there were a lot of mouths to feed, and the younger ones were often so very hungry."

"Maria." Suevey reached out a kind hand to touch Maria's arm. "Gaeten said you were the oldest. You went without meals sometimes so the younger ones would have more, didn't you?"

Maria stopped eating for a minute and tears started forming. "They needed it more than I did. Sam would often let me clean up after his customers had left. The others only had what Brother Rob or I could bring to them."

Suevey saw the painful memories wash across the young girl's face and knew it was time to change topics. "So Maria, what are your plans for the rest of the day?"

"I am not really sure, but I think I would like to explore on my own — its helps me to lock in my bearings." Maria was indeed glad to switch topics. She marveled at the idea of food … everyday. God's blessings seemed to never stop.

"Alright. If you need anything, or any help, please just ask anyone. And of course you can always ask for me — I would be delighted to spend more time with you."

"I assume Gae …Grand Master Gaeten is quite busy?"

"Oh yes, child. He has a very full schedule here. It would be better not to disturb him if possible."

"Ok, thanks … Suevey. Should I address you as something other than your name? I mean, all morning I kept hearing 'apprentice' or 'master' for everyone we met."

"Maria, you can just call me Suevey. Everyone here will know who you mean."

After lunch Maria wandered first around the Watcher area and then out of the Compound on her own. She really was rather good at directions, keeping a form of a map running in her mind as she walked. And she could not remember when she had felt safer, at least not in a very long time. Instead of revisiting the areas Xenia had taken her to, Maria found herself on a main street that sloped upward and she started off on that. She had to walk slowly, given the newness of the surroundings and the number of people jostling about, but with the walking cane Gaeten had given her most passersby seemed to give her extra space. She pressed on over a small rise and then over a higher hill after that. She was just about ready to turn around when something caught her attention, a sound of some musical instrument being sounded a ways off down the direction of a side street.

She listened intently and carefully made her way tapping along in that direction. As she got closer she could hear other instruments, and then voices singing. It was amazing! As she stood listening someone bumped into her accidentally and nearly sent her sprawling.

"Oh, I am sorry miss, let me help you up"

"I am ok. Tell me, what is this place where all the music is coming from?"

"Oh, you must be really new here, right? That is the Academy of Music. They take in apprentices from all over, at least those who can pass the rigorous entrance exam. There is usually quite a line up and wait to get in. The higher level apprentices and Masters are well known and eagerly sought after all over the world as minstrels and musicians for high courts in many countries."

Maria took that all in. A whole building — or even group of buildings — devoted to music? To an orphan who sang so she could eat, it was astonishing, almost beyond comprehension. She stood soaking it all in, and then began to thread her way back to the Watcher compound, barely making it back in time for the evening meal. She ate again with Suevey, who happened to be there at the same time.

That night, as she lay down on the thin mattress and hard pillow, both of which seemed like royal treatment compared to what she had been sleeping on just two days prior, she wondered about how much more there was to the world — even her little slice of it — that she had never even known existed. God had been so very good to her. Maria said her nightly prayers, and they took quite a bit longer than normal — she had so very much to talk to God about and be thankful for. With a smile on her face she finally drifted off to sleep.

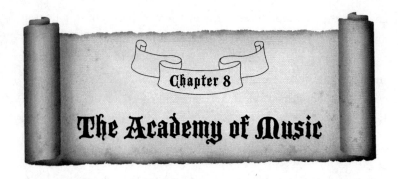

Chapter 8

The Academy of Music

Over the next several days Maria rarely even heard Gaeten, and when she did he seemed rather preoccupied with things he did not want to discuss with her. He mentioned she was free to explore the compound and the city, but that she should talk to Xenia about taking some very basic beginner Watcher apprentice classes. Maria was doubtful about that, but found the first few classes mainly taught you how to fall down — she felt she was pretty good at doing that already — but soon learned ways to lessen the hurt and gain more control in her descent to the ground. There were also several classes that were mainly exercises aimed at building up the strength of various muscles or at becoming more limber with stretches. Her very lean body made many of the stretches and movements fairly easy, but the instructors had to move her manually through the many moves and she could tell it was frustrating several of them. She remembered Suevey's words about not giving up, and so she stayed at it. She knew Gaeten was extremely capable of these movements, and if he could do it, so could she … at least that is what she kept telling herself.

The classes only took up part of the day and while they were rather strenuous for her they did leave plenty of time to pursue her other main interest — exploring the area both inside the compound and in ever widening circles beyond. She was very curious about everything.

In the evenings Maria would try to relate to Gaeten what she had heard and experienced, though she felt he was only really listening halfheartedly. During the day he was very busy teaching classes and he often went up to the main governing offices deep within the Keep. She did not know what he did there, but it seemed to be rather important. Everyone here had a very high respect for him, she could tell that readily enough. Still, the activities within the compound were really not of that much interest to her — though she would never tell that to Gaeten — and so whenever possible she roamed outside.

As she became more and more comfortable and familiar with the area around the Watcher Compound, Maria occasionally heard more of the sounds coming from what must be the Academy of Music. Her curiosity was very definitely piqued and she determined to explore this most intriguing place further. She felt drawn toward it and yet somehow she was also nervous about it too for some reason. She learned it was not one building, but a collection of several buildings next to each other, which was called a "campus". Her courage grew over the course of several days until she finally slipped onto the campus itself. She found she could spend most of a day just sitting between the various buildings in a little grassy area they called "the Commons". She would sit on the grass for hours just listening, cataloging in her mind the great variety of sounds.

It was incredible! It was overwhelming! Maria had never heard such wonderful sounds before and did not know the names of more than just a couple of instruments she thought she recognized. To her highly sensitive ears and innate musical inclinations this place was the closest thing to heaven she could imagine. Singing came so very naturally to her that she barely thought of it as music, it was just a natural part of her that she knew brought pleasure to others, and which she used herself to worship God both out loud and even silently, singing only in that special place in her mind where she could go to worship her Creator. But she had never had an instrument, never even held one before. Several times a day she would get caught up in some tune being played within one of the buildings and all other senses would fade as she focused on just the wonderful sounds that intrigued her beyond measure.

Occasionally an apprentice would practice with an instrument in the Commons, and Maria would try to wander in closer to listen. What was played was often different than what she could hear in the buildings — simpler and more akin to the score for the folk songs she had been singing at Sam's only a few days ago.

During her third visit an apprentice started playing some kind of stringed instrument nearby during an afternoon break from classes. Maria carefully picked her way over the grass and quietly sat nearby. She was thankful to be able to get quite close, and she could hear the small sounds the fingers made as they slid over strings. Maria began to notice a pattern — yes, those specific finger slidings corresponded to specific different notes that were sounding. Though of course she could not see what was happening, Maria could detect quite a lot from her acute hearing and her imagination filled in the rest. The intensity of her attention must have been obvious.

"Hello, you're new here, aren't you?" The girl's voice was melodic and gentle, but nevertheless caught Maria very off guard.

"Ah … yes, I am new to the Keep. I just came from a little town called Westhaven less than a week ago. Were you the one playing so beautifully a few moments ago?"

The girl chuckled good naturedly. "Beautifully? I somehow doubt my instructors would agree with you. They usually want us to play orchestral pieces, and to very exact and demanding standards. They are beautiful, but can be quite complicated. Sometimes I like to just strum something simple — it relaxes me." She lowered her voice "and sometimes I like to just make something up myself, just for fun!"

Maria could hardly believe what she had just heard. "You … you create your own music?" She had made up a few songs to sing to herself, but never thought they were very good, hardly worth even calling them songs.

"Yes, sure — why not? Out here, on my own time, we are free to create whatever we want. Would you like to hear one?"

"Oh yes, please!"

A catchy tune began to be plucked out and within seconds Maria was humming along with it, haltingly at first but then with greater confidence.

"Hey, where did you hear this before? I thought I had made it up all myself, yet here you are humming along as though you know it by heart!"

"No — I have never heard it before! I was just trying to hum along, and I was guessing some as to what would come next — I think I was right most of the time, wasn't I?"

The other girl was silent for a moment. Then she reached out a hand to hold Maria's. "My name is Ariel, Apprentice Ariel. What's yours?"

"My ... my name is Maria."

"Well, hello Maria! Did you like my little song?"

"Oh yes, very much." To show she meant it Maria began to hum it again, start to finish ... perfectly.

Apprentice Ariel had only played this tune to a few other people ...ever. Yet here sat a little blind girl she had never seen before who just repeated it note for note, with perfect cadence and inflection after hearing it exactly once. "How did you do that? I mean, you just heard it once!"

Maria laughed. "I don't know, I guess it is just something God gave me the ability to do. I rarely got a chance to hear a minstrel sing a song more than once, so I learned to memorize them all the first time so I could sing them later myself. Once I have them down I sometimes ..." she lowered her voice in a mimic of the other girl's conspiratorial tone "... even added an extra verse or two of my own, or modify the basic melody a bit as I sing it."

Ariel cocked her head to one side and looked quizzical. "So how would you modify my little tune?"

"Oh, I wouldn't change your song! It's yours and it is perfect!"

"Maria, one thing you learn here at the Academy of Music is that perfection takes years of practice, maybe even decades. Nearly everything can be made better. I am not so proud to not realize that my simple little tune could be made better. So humor me ... I will hum it and you join in — and improvise however you want."

"Improvise ... what does that mean?"

Apprentice Ariel chuckled. "That means change it however you want as we go along."

"Oh — ok, I guess. I am not sure how I would change it though."

Ariel began to hum the tune at about the same speed that she had played it. She would have strummed it again, but she wanted to hear Maria as clearly as possible.

Maria joined in after a moment and the two picked up the pace, blending their tones into a unified whole. Then it was Maria's turn to cock her head to one side in thought, and she began to hum a counter melody, intricately blending her notes in above, below and around the basic melody. Apprentice Ariel's eyes went wide as her simple tune suddenly became considerably more complex ... and more beautiful. She closed her eyes to concentrate and began a second verse while Maria continued to soar and flit about with increasingly elegant and fanciful additions. Within a few minutes both began to smirk and then giggle and soon collapsed into delighted laughter.

"Maria, that was astoundingly pretty! It took me weeks to work out that simple tune and here you go and create a multi-part masterpiece from it! I don't think I can get half of what you hummed down on paper — but I sure am going to try. I have to leave for my next class now — can we meet here again? I have this time slot open most afternoons."

"Uh, sure. I cannot always come at exactly the same time, but I can try to be here around this time again as often as possible. But what do you mean by 'getting it down on paper'? I was just humming — there were no words. I have had people read to me from books, and especially from the Bible. But that is not music."

Ariel looked closely at Maria to see if she was trying to be funny, but then responded in surprise. "Uh ... Maria ... there are other kinds of books, music books, that contain symbols representing notes and timing and everything else needed to re-play musical score."

Maria drew in her breath sharply. "You ... you have whole books about music ... that contain ..." she struggled to find words ... "a written language of music?" Maria sat back in wonder. This was all so new!

"Yes, I guess you could call it that. And it is a good thing we have it too — most of us cannot remember something we hear note-perfect like you seem able to! Anyway, I would love to capture more of your additions on paper ... if it is ok with you, I'd like to use this rendition sometime with one of my instructors."

"I guess so, I mean — do what you want with it ... it is your song, I just had some fun with it."

"You're a gem, Maria! Thanks." Ariel squeezed Maria's hand. "Gotta run — hope to see you again soon".

Maria heard the girl move off, carrying her instrument. She smiled. She had just made a new friend.

The Commons was also a great place to, well, eavesdrop. From listening to the many conversations going on by apprentices who sprawled on the grass during breaks she learned that each building was dedicated to different kinds of instruments and one whole building was mainly for just singers — a whole building! She also learned that just on the other side of one set of buildings was a huge theater, or at least that is what some people called it, which could seat a thousand people and where great concerts were occasionally performed. It was also where advanced classes were held and which housed some of the finest instruments ever produced within Freelandia. It all sounded very interesting, and this theater place sounded especially fascinating ... and Maria was determined to explore it — but how?

She spent most of her free time for the next several days walking around the buildings on the Academy of Music campus, though her class schedule kept her from reaching the Commons until later in the afternoon. People chatted freely with her and they all seemed very friendly. Several were very curious about her Watcher clothing — it seemed that not many Watchers made it over to this area of the Keep. That was going to be a problem — she stood out badly enough being blind, though she thought she could hide that fairly well as long as she acted like she knew where she was going. But the Watcher uniform stood out way too much if she wanted to quietly explore places where she may not have been … exactly … invited. That would have to change.

"Gaeten — can I please get some different clothes?"

"What's the matter," he growled, "those Watcher uniforms are not working well enough for you?"

Maria turned on her sweetest little girl voice. "Oh Gaeten, they are certainly adequate, but not for every day! Can I have one dress, nothing fancy, just something else for variety? After all, when I am walking around in the city I stumble on street corners and run into all kinds of other things — and everyone around must look and see someone in a Watcher uniform bumbling along."

Gaeten knew he was being manipulated, as if knowing really helped all that much. "Why haven't you told me about this before? We can't have the whole Keep thinking the only Watchers we are training are stumbling about little girls!" Coming from Gaeten, there was no sting — she knew he really loved her in his heart. "I'll send Xenia over tomorrow morning and she can take you shopping."

"Uh … I was wondering if Suevey could help me instead — I think she will know more of what I want."

"Suevey? Well, yes, that would be ok. I think she might enjoy that — and almost certainly more than Xenia! How much money do you need?"

"I really don't know. I have never shopped here. Do they have a second hand store nearby?"

Gaeten laughed. "I don't know Maria. Life here in the Keep is quite different than in little Westhaven. I will talk to Suevey. She has a good head on her shoulders and I am sure she will be sensible."

"Oh thank you, Gaeten!" Maria gave him a sincere, if not a bit dramatic, hug.

"Er … that's enough of that! Can't you tell I have more important things to do than dither about with such girly things as dresses?" Gaeten liked to put on his grumpy old man attitude.

Maria was not about to let that one go. "You know, you really are a softy inside — just one sweet lovable he-bear!"

"Argh! I'll get you for that one!" He took a wild swing through the air, totally missing her, which they both knew was certainly on purpose. Gaeten never seemed to miss unless he wanted to.

Maria started laughing, and in a minute Gaeten was chuckling too — her laughter was rather infectious, he had found much to his chagrin. "Go … scoot! It's time for dinner anyway. Go find Suevey and tell her your scheme … I mean plans … and ask her nicely — and say you both have my blessing. But NO frilly nonsensical dandy things, and we are not talking about an entire wardrobe, no siree. I will not have my ward filling her closet with a bunch of …" By that point Maria was already gone.

"New clothes?" Suevey looked puzzled. "Come to think of it, all I have ever seen you in is an old Watcher uniform. What sort of things do you need — what other things do you have that you want it to work with?" Suevey was sitting across from Maria as they both ate dinner.

"Uh … I really don't have anything else — except a second hand old dress from Westhaven that got all ripped up my last day there." Maria shuddered at the memory, though it seemed like such a long time ago.

"You don't have anything else? What has that old goat Gaeten been doing with you? Certainly not shopping! First thing tomorrow I will stop over and we will visit a few shops. I can't believe he has not provided more for you!"

Maria laughed good naturedly. "Suevey, back in Westhaven, before Gaeten came along, all I had was a very beat up shift that was a size or two too small. It was not even that great as a rag. And I felt blessed if I got to eat the scraps left over at the bakery after the lunch crowd. Here I have so much! I do not mind not having other clothes … well, not much anyway. I would like one or two other things, if possible — but I really do not want to impose. Gaeten has been so good to me."

Suevey took her hand. "I know Maria, but he has never raised any children, much less a young girl growing into a young woman. Oh well, let's see what we can find tomorrow."

Maria smiled both at the prospects of shopping for alternative clothes and for one intended special use that was her own little secret.

Maria woke early the next morning in excitement. The only shopping trips she could ever remember was to the second hand shop in Westhaven with Brother Rob, and even there they had to really pinch their pennies to be able to afford anything. The concept of shopping in the Keep, the biggest city in all of Freelandia, was wondrous to Maria. She was certain even the second hand shops here would be fabulously stocked, though she was quite concerned that they may be too expensive as well.

Suevey took her to several shops that were not overly far away, and had Maria try on several dresses. The fabrics and textures were all so … so wonderful. She was without words. She could not find a single rip or button missing either — so these shops must have only really top quality second hand items. They finally settled on two outfits that seemed to fit her quite well, and Suevey assured her they looked great.

"Now, these aren't too expensive, are they? I mean, this place must have only the best used items — I could not even find a flaw in either dress!"

Suevey laughed. "Maria, these are new dresses, not second hand. If you do find any flaws we will simply return them and find replacements."

"But … won't they cost too much then? I … I don't ever remember having something new before." Tears were forming and Maria's voice began to quiver.

"Maria, those days are over now. God is giving you a new start. You are no longer a poor orphan struggling to get enough to eat. In the week or so you have been here you have already begun to fill out — when you first arrived you looked quite emaciated to me! You still have a ways to go yet too, so in another month we may have to either get these dresses altered or get you something else. Gaeten is paying; don't worry, he can easily afford them. And he will not mind you getting a few nice things. Don't be concerned — if need be I will talk to him. Oh, and you certainly need a new pair of shoes."

They found a pair, though they hurt her feet — Maria was far more used to going bare footed or with light sandals — but Suevey insisted that in the Keep it was more proper to wear real shoes, and that they would protect her feet better anyway once she got used to them. The price seemed outrageous, but Suevey assured her it was reasonable for living in the Keep. Maria swallowed hard, wondering what kind of chewing out she would get from Gaeten when he heard about the bill. Nevertheless, she was very excited about it all, and about how she might now be able to blend in with the crowds of people … and perhaps even be able to slip into some of the Academy of Music buildings mostly unnoticed. And then there was the theater. She was extremely curious about that building. Something about it tugged at her, and she was bound and determined to thoroughly discover its secrets.

Suevey had been right. When they returned Gaeten had not said a thing about the clothing. The next day Maria raced through her workout — she was getting better at it as she became more limber — and as she filled out her bony figure with regular and proper eating. She got back to the apartment and changed, then strode out the compound and toward the Academy. She was fairly familiar now with the Commons area, and she knew the main purpose of each of the buildings based on what she had heard from apprentices and from the sounds emanating from each. Several times she started to head into one and then lost her nerve about going in. It seemed everyone here had a purpose and she figured she might stand out as too different — especially since she would have to feel her way around. Then she hit upon an idea.

"Excuse me …" she started up a conversation with some younger sounding people coming out of one of the buildings. "When does this building get shut for the evening?"

"Why, I don't know … I have never seen it closed. There are several apprentices that have rooms in the building — I suppose they keep an eye on things. Come to think of it, I don't think they ever lock up these buildings or the theater either for that matter. But of course, no one is around them after it gets dark unless there is some kind of concert or special event going on. Even with candles it gets pretty dark inside."

"Oh, uh … thanks!" Maria's mind was racing. Nighttime darkness was to her like the brightness of a noonday sun — it did not slow her in the least bit.

Gaeten kept odd hours, and regularly traveled. He had mentioned how much more people would talk in front of a blind person, almost as if they assumed the person could not hear either, which of course was the opposite of the truth. It appeared to Maria that someone in the Keep wanted to get information, and would ask Gaeten to go out and about Freelandia to get it. It was all rather odd, and Gaeten did not talk about, so it seemed rather secretive. In any case, he was out the rest of this week, so she could try to implement her exploration plan this very night.

❦

Maria slipped silently out of the compound late that night, full of excitement. She was a little nervous too, but she headed directly toward the Academy of Music. There were very few people about, and only once did she slide into a closed doorway to avoid being spotted. Shortly she was there.

Maria wondered which building she should try out first. She chose the nearest and indeed found the front door to be unlocked. As far as she could tell she had not been noticed by anyone, and so she entered. Inside it was silent, so different from the rich sounds that came out during the daylight hours. She paused for a few minutes in the entryway, listening. Nothing. She crept along a wall, her hands out before her to feel her way. Down one hallway she entered a room and by carefully feeling around she found many chairs lined up in a semi-circle. In the front there was a small open area, and past that there was a long cabinet with a flat top. And sitting out on that … Maria smiled in the darkness. These had to be instruments! Many wooden shapes lined the cabinet top, all having strings stretched tight along their top surfaces. Maria went along, feeling each one. Finally she picked one of the smaller ones up and held it. She was terribly nervous and excited all at the same time.

Maria slowly and softly plucked one of the strings. She giggled to herself at the discordant note that sounded. She had never played any instrument before — poor orphan girls don't exactly get much chance for that, and Westhaven was not known for having any concerts.

Fascinated, she plucked a few more strings, listening intently to the soft sounds. She had no idea how the instrument was supposed to be held or played, or even what this thing was called. Awkwardly, she tried various ways to hold it and finally settled on one that seemed the most comfortable. Now, how was this thing supposed to be played? She plucked and strummed on the strings, but at best produced only slightly pleasing sounds. After some experimentation, she discovered that by holding her left hand out on the long neck of the instrument and pressing down on the strings the tones could be changed substantially. For the next several hours she totally forgot about further exploration of the building, being fully immersed in concentration on this one instrument. Finally she put it down, her fingers sore and tired, but rather pleased with her findings. This would take a lot more practice … and it was only one room of one building!

As she walked back to the apartment she realized this was easily the most interesting and exciting thing she had done so far in the Keep. Maria knew she had discovered a new-found passion. What more was there to find?

Chapter 9

The song

Over the next few weeks Maria spent several hours of every night she could get away exploring and trying out the various musical instruments that she discovered in the buildings of the Academy of Music. Occasionally she would hear someone in the building moving about, but she could easily avoid them. It was all rather exciting, and though she did not understand why, she was powerfully drawn to the sounds the instruments could produce. She also spent more and more time during daylight hours in the Commons area, soaking in the various sounds of both instruments and people. She found that when she listened to someone play a piece she could readily hear when they made a mistake — it just would not sound "right", and she also began to "hear" possible counter melodies and harmonies whether someone was actually playing them or not. And, more than she could ever remember, she was feeling truly, fully happy. It lifted her spirit, at times she felt like dancing in the street for the sheer joy that filled her and she praised her God for showing her such a beautiful part of His creation.

She now regularly met with Apprentice Ariel in the Commons, and Maria learned a great deal more about the Academy and about being an apprentice there. Yet she did not feel comfortable in confiding with her new friend about her nighttime explorations — Maria did not know what rules there may be, but she was sure the instructors would frown upon such unauthorized visits. Yet Maria also knew she could not just walk into one of the buildings during the day and ask to touch and play the instruments — she was not an apprentice here, did not even know how one could become such an apprentice, and so she would surely be denied. And she just could not now imagine not being allowed to explore as she was doing — it filled her with such delight and joy, and with such praise to her Creator.

It was all so very interesting to her — every sound, every instrument. As she listened to people talking on their breaks in the Commons, she also picked up ideas and tips, and her nighttime playing was steadily improving on several of what had become her favorite instruments. She was a very rapid learner, though she felt so woefully inept. She knew the instruments were far, far more capable of producing beauty than her inexperience could draw out. And that was one of the largest motivators inside her … she so much wanted to draw out the potential of the instrument, to discover what it could do, how it could sound, to recreate some tiny portion of the beauty God had placed all around her and release some of the joy she felt in her heart. And, deep down inside, in her secret special place where she imagined herself stepping into the very presence of God, she now not only sang and danced her worship before Him … now her soul seemed filled with the musical sounds she was being immersed in.

The one thing she could not gain during her nighttime escapades was listening to the singing. She especially enjoyed that part of her daytime visits to the Academy. Most of the singing seemed to come mainly from the theater, down further from the other buildings on the campus. Maria had visited that building only a few times. It was absolutely huge, and she had only begun to explore its many passageways. In the center it held a gargantuan hall, with a raised platform in front she had heard was called a "stage" and seating that gently sloped upward the further you went away. She could only wonder what the hall was used for, but whatever it was it must be glorious, she thought.

One night she passed on playing any of the instruments to more fully explore the theater. It had many side hallways and rooms, and she discovered that behind the stage there were still more small passageways and side rooms, almost in a maze. Some even had small staircases that meandered up to seating areas above and to the sides of the stage, and a few even ended directly above the stage which had strange seams and holes in the floors. She did NOT like those rooms, those floor adornments made her quite nervous for some reason. The theater was easily the largest and most complicated building she had ever been in — making it all the more interesting to investigate.

After an hour or so of exploring, Maria walked out of a passageway and stepped out onto the stage itself. Standing there in front of a vast open and empty space was rather startling at first, and she let out a brief "Oh!" Then she stopped in wonderment. Even with that little sound, she could sense a small part of the superb acoustics engineered into this huge room. She was suddenly intimidated and stood there in silence, not really knowing what she should do next. Then a song came to her mind and she timidly and softly began to sing the beloved anthem "Freelandia". She sang it very quietly, a part of her listening to the marvelous sound the hall produced. She somehow knew she could only hear a part of the effect — the room was designed for the audience to have the best experience, and her voice seemed to exit the stage and get lost in the vastness of the concert hall. Yet even still she had a sense of the grandness, of the potential here. It was almost frightening to her, and spellbinding. She tried singing louder, and then stopped as she realized the room would amplify her voice significantly. This place certainly had interesting potential! She really — REALLY — wanted to hear someone singing from this stage, listening from various spots in this great room to experience the effect. But how could she do that?

Several days later she discovered a way. There were excited whisperings around the Commons when Maria arrived, and she listened intently. People were talking about some concert coming up, and something called "auditions" were going to be held. These sounded like some kind of competition among the apprentices for who would get to play in the theater, and the highest competition was for the honor to accompany some famous guest singer coming to Freelandia for the event. It was going to be a grand concert, and prior to the guest singer there would be several musical arrangements, some which would involve apprentice singers from the Academy. Therefore not only the musicians would compete, but also the singers. It sounded all so very exciting. And she heard that the singers would audition in the great hall of the theater itself, starting in just a few more days. The auditions were not supposed to take time away from the regular studies, and so would be held in the evenings. She knew where she wanted to be!

Later that week Maria enacted her plans. She ate dinner at the Watchers compound, and then slipped out and headed for the theater. By now she was quite familiar with the area and with that building, and knew several back doors that led to the many passageways behind the stage. She nonchalantly strode behind the back of the theater building, where there rarely were any people anyway. When Maria's acute hearing told her no one was around she rapidly opened a door and slipped in. After a momentary pause she heard voices, and silently crept up one of the stairways that connected to several other passageways. Some went up to the highest level balconies, others went to middle tier seats, and a few snaked around to the sides of the theater seating area. By this time she even knew which boards creaked so she could avoid making any noises.

Maria glided along to a middle tier balcony box and crawled to the small parapet that opened out into the vast concert hall. She leaned up against the wood and settled into a comfortable position. She could hear several apprentice singers warming up, and then she heard several new people coming into the recital area. One voice she recognized — it was Master Verniti. Several apprentices in the Commons had identified that commanding voice emanating from one of the buildings as some student was apparently being chastised for being off-key or not knowing their part. Maria had been told Master Verniti was the head of the singing department. She heard another voice too, but did not recognize the older gentleman.

There was a tapping sound and everything went quiet and still. "Apprentices ..." - it was Master Verniti — "... we are now beginning the most important audition we have had in several years. You know that Sir Archibald Reginaldo is coming next week, and the following week we will be having a Grand Concert. We will invite the most important people in all of Freelandia, and you can bet that they will all come too, at least all that can. We must put on our very best performance. Before Sir Reginaldo sings his virtuoso Masterpiece we will have the opportunity to perform several of our own songs. Now, don't any of you expect you might get to sing with Sir Reginaldo, not even as backup singers. And of course no one sings with him for his Masterpiece — no one yet has had a voice to keep up with him, and we all know that that work is a solo-only performance. Sir Reginaldo has decided to do his portion of the concert singing alone, as is his custom.

Now, it is time for the try-outs. We have a special guest who will help me in judging, at least for this evening — Grand Master Vitario."

Maria could hear hushed nervous whispering. Gaeten was the only Grand Master she had ever met or been around, as far as she knew. She was not even sure exactly what a Grand Master was. She had heard that apprentices had to go through seven levels or ranks, after which they had something called an "examination" by a group of Masters. If the apprentice passed, they became a Master themselves. However, she heard that was very, very difficult. Whatever a Grand Master level was, it must be extremely difficult to attain.

The first apprentice began to sing. There were no instruments playing, so all that could be heard was the boy's voice. Maria listened intently. She only knew a few songs herself, and was eager to learn new ones. As she listened she marveled at the acoustics — they were everything and more than what she had imagined. The song was somewhat complicated, and Maria hummed very, very softly to herself, repeating the tune. After a few minutes the boy was asked to step down and a girl took his place. She started in on the same song. She sang to same tune and with the same words, but she added her own flair. Her notes were clear, though Maria could tell in a few places where she was not quite … right. She was very close, but to Maria's highly sensitive ears it was not exactly spot on right.

The next apprentice stepped forward, shoes scraping slightly on the wooden floor of the stage. Maria realized everyone tonight must be auditioning for the same song, as they all did the same piece. She would have preferred learning additional songs, but she did hear many subtle differences between the various singers. She did not know yet who was judged best, though she knew which one she would have chosen. And by the end of the audition that night she knew another song quite well. When the last apprentice was done and everyone had left, Maria slowly retraced her steps and made it back to the apartment, and far earlier then what had become her normal late night wanderings.

Over the coming evenings Maria tried out several other sitting locations, and learned several new songs. She felt that while everyone sang fairly well, there were a few exceptional apprentices who to her ears stood out from the others. As the week ended, the energy level of everyone around the Academy rose higher and higher. The excitement was contagious and Maria found herself wondering just who this supposedly world famous singer Sir Reginaldo really was. She did not have to wait very long to find out.

The excitement level in the Commons was the highest Maria had heard. Everyone was talking about the arrival of Sir Archibald Reginaldo, the most famous singer in the entire world, and of his forthcoming singing of his signature song called his Masterpiece. There was considerable speculation spoken about that song, which Maria found fascinating. She did not know how much was exaggeration or folklore, but apparently this song was mysterious as well as famous. Supposedly only Sir Reginaldo could sing it with any justice, as the song was highly complicated and required a voice with incredible range, power and skill. Another mystery was that supposedly no one ever sang this other than as a solo — a blend of voices was said to nearly ruin the song, and, even more mysterious, no one had ever sung a harmony that could last more than a few chords. Maria was horribly, terribly curious. However, she also heard from more than one conversation she had eavesdropped on that Sir Reginaldo allowed no one in on his practices; all Academy apprentices were hereby banned from the theater after hours. However, of course, Maria was not an Academy apprentice!

The next day Sir Reginaldo arrived. Maria heard it being discussed, how there was great commotion at his appearance and that Grand Master Vitario himself had been there to meet him … and had been forced to wait because Sir Reginaldo had refused to exit his carriage unless a special carpet was laid out so that his new shoes would not get dirty! He sounded to Maria like a bit of a pompous oaf. Still, he was supposed to be able to sing like none other. And that evening he would begin practicing for the concert that was scheduled for only 4 days hence.

Maria arrived extra early to the theater and she found it was just as good she did. There were many apprentices milling about outside, and she hurried to the rear door and entered just before she heard an older apprentice step up to the door on the outside to block it. She would have to come even earlier the next day.

Maria was especially cautious and quiet as she moved about inside. She could detect a few people moving around in the back rooms and corridors, but her superb hearing and the many interconnecting passageways allowed her to easily evade detection. She chose a balcony further back than usual and crawled to her normal position leaning against the small outer ledge. She had to wait nearly an hour, but then heard some loud voices coming down the central walkway in the great hall.

"Well, this theater appears adequate … I guess." Maria figured the rich, deep voice must be from the illustrious Sir Reginaldo. "I suppose this is the stage? It will do. Now, let's see my dressing room." The people — it sounded to Maria like three or four others were accompanying the famous singer — walked into a back corridor and the voices became muffled. A short time later they came back. "This is preposterous! Outrageous! Those rooms are much too small, too dingy. They are totally unacceptable. Either they are fixed up or …"

"Don't be so upset, Sir Reginaldo — we will certainly fix the rooms up to whatever specifications you desire". Maria did not recognize the voice, but it sounded like a fairly senior person. "Please make a list of whatever you want and we will take care of it by tomorrow evening".

"Well, it had better! Now, I want everyone out! I need absolute silence and focus for my practice."

"Yes … yes Sir Reginaldo!"

"Have you remembered to remove everyone? Guards posted at all doors? You HAVE remembered that, haven't you?"

"Yes Sir Reginaldo, everyone is out, the theater is exclusively for your own use."

Maria stifled a snicker, everyone that is, except her.

Once everyone left Maria could hear Sir Reginaldo move to the stage and begin to make the odd noises she had heard called "warming up your voice". Then he began to sing. Maria held herself very still, straining to catch every sound, every nuance, to soak it in as completely and thoroughly as possible. His voice was incredible, filling the great hall powerfully and yet not overwhelmingly. It was the richest voice she had ever heard. And the song — oh the song! She had never heard anything like it. It soared high, and then sank low. It rolled out and around in such a complicated melody that Maria thought for sure she could never remember half of it — but she surely would try.

Sir Reginaldo went through several renditions of the song, varying a few notes here and there, as though he were seasoning a soup and deciding if it needed a pinch more of some aromatic herb. By the time he was part way through his third practice, Maria was silently humming along. Her mind was racing along with the song, cataloging it, examining it, enjoying it. All too soon it seemed to be over and Sir Reginaldo walked off the stage, muttering to himself the whole way as he strode out.

Maria went home, with the song running through her mind. It was absolutely beautiful, and terribly difficult. And yet ... something was stirring in the back of her mind, a mere wisp of a breeze of ... of a haunting counter-tune that drifted in and out of her consciousness. It was not something she could grasp; it was almost as if she could hear just bits and pieces of something playing in the back recesses of her brain. It continued in her sleep, and Maria was eager to try to sneak back in — earlier — to hear that glorious song and voice again.

The next morning Gaeten was back from a longer trip.

"Well, Maria, I hear you have been quite the wanderer around the Keep while I was gone."

"Er ... yes, I guess I have been. It is all so very interesting. Have you heard about the concert coming up in three days?"

"Yes," — this was said in his characteristic growl — "So what? I don't have time for such nonsense. Is listening to such babble what you have been doing out so late at night?"

Maria gulped. Someone must have spotted her returning some evening ... or early morning. "I have been spending some time near the Academy of Music. Have you been invited to the concert? I heard that only the really important people in Freelandia were ... so I suppose maybe you were not ..." She said that with a steady voice, not letting a laugh leak out even though she had to hold it in hard.

"WHAT? Of course I was invited, you ungrateful wisp. But ... I do NOT plan on going. That is just sissy stuff anyway!" He said that a bit churlishly, baiting her.

"Now Gaeten, I know for a fact that you seemed to like it when I was singing at Sam's bakery!" She had him there, and they both knew it. Now if you don't want to go, I certainly do. Maybe Suevey can take me ... besides, you surely don't have anything decent to wear to such a gala event and I doubt they would let you in with those old smelly workout uniforms you normally wear."

"Hmph — you really are getting irritating!" His voice said otherwise. "If you would like to go, I suppose we can."

"Oh thank you, thank you Gaeten. You are the sweetest ... the sweetest Grand Master I know!"

"Ha! As though you know any others!"

Maria left, realizing she had neatly steered the conversation away from the late nights she had been keeping. She didn't think she was doing anything wrong, but she did not really want to tell Gaeten about her discoveries, at least not quite yet.

This time, to avoid being possibly locked out, Maria arrived to the theater quite early and snuck up to a balcony nearer the stage to hear how Sir Reginaldo would sound up closer. She had a longer wait, but used the time to try to catch that tune that was flitting in and out of her mind. Maria tried to listen to it inside her brain, but it did not seem to want to be captured just yet. After awhile she heard Sir Reginaldo enter and fuss everyone out of the hall again.

As he again warmed up Maria sat up to hear better, staying well back from the edge in what she hoped was in the shadows. Then he started to sing the song and Maria was enraptured once more in it. She pictured herself in the special quiet place in her mind where she went to talk to God. There she began to dance to the tune and where the flowing sounds began to take form and shape and a corporeal life of their own.

This time she knew quite a lot of the song already, and so could anticipate where it was going. The harmonious tune in her mind grew stronger, weaving in and around Sir Reginaldo's voice over a wide range of octaves. As beautiful as his Masterpiece was, and as marvelous as his voice sang it, the tune Maria started to hum was yet more beautiful, superbly complimenting the strong voice she was listening to, and it seemed to somehow bring out even more richness and depth. She was lost in the song now, totally focused to the point she no longer noticed her surroundings but only the scene playing out in her mind's special place where both melody and counter melody were weaving about in an impossible rainbow of colors and shapes that swirled around her graceful and athletic dancing form. Somehow the harmony she was softly singing seemed to amplify Sir Reginaldo's voice, creating something new that soared and flitted about with an energetic life all its own. Maria was so enthralled by what she was experiencing as she sang along that she did not notice immediately that Sir Reginaldo … had stopped.

Maria's voice faltered to a halt. The harmony in her mind ceased as she realized what had happened. The complex and beautiful song that she had been dancing to … and singing along with in her special place in her mind … she had also begun to sing out loud. Terribly frightened, she began to creep out of the balcony box, only to stop suddenly as to her astonishment she heard … sobbing.

Confusion overcame her fear. The crying was coming from the stage, and while it had started rather softly it was increasing into great sobs. Then she heard Sir Reginaldo move and she scampered off down the hallway, through the maze of corridors, and out the back door onto the side street. "Hey!" a voice shouted out after her but she did not stop, half-running as fast as she could down the street, through the Commons and back to the Watcher compound. She crashed into the apartment, out of breath, and sank to the floor panting.

"M a r i a!" Gaeten's voice had strung out her name, pronouncing each syllable in a way that she knew spelled trouble. "Exactly what have you been up to?"

Maria was about to say something incredibly lame like "Oh, nothing", but she couldn't do that to Gaeten — she owed him way more than that. "I ... I was in a building down at the Academy, just exploring, and I ... I almost got caught". That got most of the things right, sort of.

"Is that all, child?" Gaeten's voice had grown soft ... a worrisome sign.

"Well ... not ... exactly." Then she blurted out everything, from her midnight treks to her listening in on Sir Reginaldo. "Oh Gaeten! I knew he wanted everyone out of the theater, but I just had to hear that song! And then I started singing a harmony to it, and ... and I think no one is supposed to do that ... and I think I terribly upset Sir Reginaldo! What if he refuses to sing now? What if I have ruined the whole concert? What should I do?" The last was said in a desperate wail as the thought of the biggest and most important concert in Freelandia in years might be put off due to her curiosity came crashing down onto her. The tears started and she buried her face into Gaeten's chest, clinging to his sturdy frame.

For his part, Gaeten did not really know what to do with this, but whatever had happened could not possibly have been that serious, could it?

Sir Archibald Reginaldo, singer to high courts around the world, the most famous singer on the planet, was a broken man. He slumped in Grand Master Vitario's office. "I am ruined I tell you! An angel was singing with me last evening, it had to be. And that harmony! That is it. I can never sing my Masterpiece again. I just cannot."

Grand Master Vitario, head of the entire Academy and himself a very talented musician, doubted the part about an angel, though he could not totally discount it. It had been quite a few years since anyone had reported an angelic visitation. But this talk of not singing for the concert, now less than two days away, was preposterous.

"You must, Archibald. The High Council will be present, expecting your performance. I don't really think you would want to disappoint the High Council of Freelandia, would you?"

"But you don't understand! How can I sing that song again by myself? Now that I have heard such a harmony, such a pure voice, I sound flat and dull without it. Done alone it is now horribly incomplete! It is ruined! I cannot focus, I keep hearing bits and pieces of that angel's voice flitting in and out and around. I strain my ears to hear it again, but it is gone. My song ... my Masterpiece ... my signature song is ruined for me!"

"Archibald. Archibald! Come to the theater again tonight. I will come with you. Perhaps you will hear your angel again! Come now, let's go have some lunch. Maybe you can tell me more about what you heard ... a harmony to your Masterpiece? Is that even possible?"

Reginaldo was only mollified to a slight degree, but remained quite flustered and totally out of his normal aloof and disdaining character. The two got up and slowly walked out to a restaurant, but not one too close so they would have more privacy. And Sir Reginaldo now did not seem to mind if his shoes might get soiled.

Gaeten had suggested to Maria a course of action. She was to go to the theater this evening, early enough to get in before the doors were sealed. When Sir Reginaldo entered she was to walk out to him, apologize, and ask his forgiveness. That would be what God would want her to do. She knew he was right, but the thought was incredibly frightening. Gaeten had said though that the most important things in life required great courage, but when you were doing what God wanted He would supply the grace and strength needed to accomplish His work. Resignedly she had agreed.

Maria walked much more slowly this time to the theater, nearly dragging one foot ahead of the other and slipped in the back door as usual. She was later than the day before, and she took a longer passageway that ended at a narrow entrance into the great hall at the ground level about half way back from the stage.

Grand Master Vitario and Sir Reginaldo entered the theater early themselves, and slowly walked to the stage. "Now where was this voice from?" Archibald pointed upward. "I tell you, it was an angel!"

Maria was just about to exit the passageway into the theater proper when she heard Sir Reginaldo's voice, spoken rather softly. She did not catch exactly what he has said, but he did sound agitated, though not at all angry. She held back a moment.

"Archibald, why not try again — try singing your Masterpiece again?"

Maria shrank back ... It was Grand Master Vitario!

Sir Reginaldo mounted the stage. He warmed his voice up as normal and then launched into his song.

Maria held silent, though immediately the harmony began to flow in her mind. She was NOT going to get caught singing again!

Sir Reginaldo stopped part way through and literally sat down on the stage floor with a sob. "It's no use. I can't. It just isn't the same."

Maria's heart nearly stopped and she gasped silently. It was true! She had ruined everything! She was about to turn and run back to the apartment, back to safety, when the next words stopped her in her tracks.

"I just can't do it without that harmony. Last night it was so beautiful ... I MUST hear it again. The song ... it is just worthless now without that harmony sung with it. I cannot get it or that angelic voice out of my mind! Without that, I can't go on. Cancel the concert!"

As Grand Master Vitario tried to console Sir Reginaldo, Maria was dumbstruck. Now what? Obviously Sir Reginaldo had heard her … but he LIKED it? Could he be possibly speaking about her?

"God, I know you can hear me. I just must hear that harmony again — please send your angel to sing it once more! I will try it once more myself. If I don't hear it again, I swear I will stop … and never sing the Masterpiece again!"

Reginaldo slowly stood, looking downcast. He took a few deep breaths, shook his large frame as though trying to shake off heavy burdens, and began to sing again, in a rather hushed quiet voice. Maria did not know what she should do. She just couldn't be the cause of stopping the concert, yet she was mortified to open her mouth. Yet even with this quieter, gentler version the counter melody sprang unbidden into her mind powerfully and insistently, drawing her in. Maria stayed back in the passageway, and softly began to sing the notes that soared and danced and seemed to captivate her mind.

As Sir Reginaldo strained to listen for a heavenly voice, a small grin began to spread over his face. He heard the soft strains, barely discernable, and he picked up his own singing, growing more vibrant and confident. Maria followed suit without any conscious thought, her clear and perfect tones exactly following his. Before she had purposely sung very quietly, but as the song went on both of their voices grew, intimately blending together, whose combination was far greater than either individual voice. It was exhilarating, bursting with energy. Maria was caught up in the beauty of creation, of life. In her mind she danced with wild abandon in graceful gravity-defying leaps and pirouettes among the colored ribbons in her mind, worshiping in dance as she did in song to her Maker.

Chapter 10

Caught!

rand Master Vitario was dumbfounded. At first he began to look around for the source of that perfect voice, but quickly did not care — he was swept up into the intricacies of the singing. The Masterpiece was an epic story of the founding of Freelandia, with multiple stanzas, each sung slightly differently that built on one another, growing in intensity and rising to a nearly impossible crescendo, followed by a few more lines sung in a near whisper. Reginaldo was now fully in his element, putting both his great vocal strength and his heart into the rendition. Maria, amazingly, kept up, and if anything her voice seemed to pull the world renowned singer's voice along to even greater heights. As they reached the highest notes of the crescendo Maria's voice soared to notes so high the Grand Master Vitario could barely make them out –as perfect as they were — and somehow even if he did not quite hear it he knew it was being sung anyway. Then their voices fell to the whisper, a sung whisper that anyone in the hall would have still heard, one that begged for contemplative silence and yet craved the last few notes for fulfillment. The air hung heavy when they finished. No one spoke or moved for several full minutes as the enormity of their performance sunk in and seemed to satisfy a portion of their being, their very soul in some strange new way.

Now it was Grand Master Vitario's turn for weeping. Tears coursed down his cheeks unashamedly. In a moment, the same happened for Reginaldo and then Maria, still back in the shadows of the back passageway. Vitario found his voice, quaking as it was. "That was … was … breathtaking. I … I don't have words for it."

"You see my friend? How can it ever be sung again without that accompaniment?" Sir Reginaldo turned to face Maria's direction. "Please … please — whoever you are, please come out. I want to thank you."

Maria was still in awed shock over the song, and barely felt herself move. Then fear again took hold, but by this time she was well out into the open hall. She froze in a panic.

Both older men looked in amazement at the diminutive form standing before them. Grand Master Vitario even began to peer past Maria, wondering if perhaps someone else may still be back in the shadows. Reginaldo did his own double-take, and then he peered down from the stage on the young girl. "Don't be afraid, little one. Your singing was marvelous. I have never, ever heard anything like it." Sir Reginaldo paused, thoughtful. "You must sing it with me tomorrow night, you simply must!"

Maria could barely register his words. It was far too overwhelming, and she fought the impulse to run even as her body trembled. "Oh — I could not possibly do that! I am not … I'm not a real singer."

Sir Reginaldo laughed heartily. "Oh really? You sure can pretend to be one rather well! I insist. I really don't think I can sing that again without you. I was up most of last night, hearing your singing over and over. The song seems empty now without it. I really cannot sing my Masterpiece tomorrow without you!"

"But … but … I can't! Certainly not in front of all those people! I could never do that. No, I can't!"

"What do you mean? A singer must perform in front of others!"

"But I'm not really a singer!"

"Nonsense. What is your name?"

"Uh … Maria."

"Alright then Maria, I want you here by noon tomorrow. No excuses. We will have lunch and get to know one another, and we will get ourselves prepared. We must be in tip-top shape for the concert."

"But … but …" it was all happening much too fast for Maria to process. That made her a little ornery. "No. I won't go out in front of everyone. I …" She had taken a few steps backwards unconsciously and now she stumbled, throwing out her arms and hands wildly trying to catch herself from hitting the unseen floor. She stood, groping about awkwardly to orient herself again to the surrounding chairs.

"Maria, you MUST!" Reginaldo was certainly not used to be told no to … and NEVER from a little girl.

Maria just stood there silently, her face a defiant mask. She almost stomped her foot.

Grand Master Vitario put a hand onto Reginaldo's shoulder. "Perhaps we can work something out, Maria. If you are so nervous, what if you stood in the back of the stage? Or maybe behind a small screen?"

"Preposterous!" Reginaldo was turning livid. He was NOT used to being refused. He almost stomped *his* foot.

"It would add to the mystery," soothed Grand Master Vitario. "The first ever rendition of the Masterpiece sung as a duet — and that by a mystery singer! Think of the drama, Archibald!"

That got his attention rather forcefully. "It would be rather dramatic, wouldn't it?"

Maria was wondering what Gaeten would think … if he would even allow it. "I don't know if I can … I mean, I have never done something like that before … I have never even been to a concert. The most I have ever done was just sing in Sam's bakery!"

Reginaldo looked scornfully toward Grand Master Vitario. "You don't even let your students practice at concerts — they have to panhandle at restaurants and bakeries? Tsk Tsk. Really, Vitario!"

Grand Master Vitario had an odd puzzled look on his face. "Of course we do, even at early apprentice levels." He did not recognize Maria, but then again he only worked with the most advanced level students. "Maria, this is very important. Of course you can perform tomorrow. I will personally speak to your instructors and whichever apprentices you report to."

Maria was not sure she liked the way this was going. "I … I can try, but I will have to ask first."

"Ask who, child? Reginaldo spoke in a imperial tone, wondering who would even think to DARE turn down his request, and such an opportunity.

"Gaeten, I will have to ask Gaeten. I will try to be here tomorrow — if he lets me."

"Gaeten? I do not know of any apprentices in the Academy by that name." Vitario was now very puzzled. He thought he knew every upper level apprentice who would have charge over the younger and lesser experienced apprentices. And which of his apprentices or even Masters would even think to refuse him?

Maria tried to laugh, though it came out rather awkwardly. "Oh, he is NOT in your Academy, nor am I."

If the two men had been confused before, they were doubly so now. "Maria, try VERY hard." Reginaldo said that almost as a command. Then he softened. "I really do need you, my dear. Really. I would be honored if you would sing with me at the concert. If you do not show up, I don't know if I could even sing the Masterpiece. All of Freelandia would be disappointed."

That helped — right! Now she felt a large weight of responsibility settle down on her. She seemed to have no choice. What had begun as joyous worship had suddenly turned oppressive. While she had been happily singing and dancing along, now there was a dark gloom directly ahead. Her daydream sprang into her mind. Was this the ominous doom she had dreamt about? Glumly she turned back around. "I'll ask. That is all I can promise." She slumped back out the small passageway she had been in, rather than walk out the back of the auditorium.

The two men watched her go. Vitario was deep in thought. Who was this little blind girl (he had noticed her recovery from the near fall and guessed at her condition), and who was this "Gaeten" that she felt beholden to for permission? There was absolutely no way the only Gaeten he knew could be involved! And this Maria … she was not even in the Academy of Music? How was that possible, with a voice that could have been easily mistaken for an angel's?

Maria staggered her way back. She was very confused and not a little frightened. She wandered over to the eating area, not really wanting to face Gaeten back at the apartment. She was not particularly hungry, though there were a few pastries available for late snackers. Suevey was there, sipping a cup of tea.

She glanced up. "Oh, hello Maria. Say, are you alright?"

"I guess so. Maybe. Not really. I just am faced with being told I am supposed to do something that I really don't want to do. Others are depending on me, but the weight of that is crushing me down. I don't know what to do. I tried to do what Gaeten had told me was what God would desire, but it did not go at all in the way I expected. I am kinda scared."

"Wow. Sound's like a lot for such a little girl."

"It is …" Maria was almost crying.

"Maria …" Suevey sounded a bit mother-ish, which is exactly what Maria could use right now. "Don't ever run away from something just because it is hard or scary. If it's what God wants you to do, He will give you the strength to accomplish it, and you usually will know when it is His will. Do it with all your strength and heart, and then watch how God will use it for His glory."

Maria pondered this. "That's close to what Gaeten said too. I think this might be God's will. It certainly feels right, and it is to help others. But I am still scared! I've never had to do anything like this, not ever!

I … I don't know how to start, and I certainly don't know how to tell Gaeten about it."

Suevey held Maria's hand. "It is normal to feel afraid of things that are hard. Feeling afraid is not the problem. Letting fear control you is. Never let fear stop you from doing good."

Maria had to ponder that one. Fear had always been a part of her, but so had faith. "Thanks Suevey. That sounds right. I think I know what God wants me to do now. And the first thing is to go and try to talk to Gaeten."

Suevey gave a little laugh. "Don't let his gruffness get to you — he really is a very caring man inside who loves His Lord and God … and from what I can tell, I think he loves his little ward too."

Maria sat upright, startled. "Do you really think so? I mean, I know he likes to pretend to be grumpy, and I think he does like me, at least a little — even if I am not much of a Watcher apprentice."

"Maria, you are one of the easiest people I know of to like … and to love!" Suevey leaned over the table and gave her a big hug. "Now go tell Gaeten what you need to. Don't be coy or beat around the bush — he likes straight shooting and when he sees how serious you are he will stop whatever he's up to and listen … and if he doesn't you just tell him I told him to!"

Maria laughed, some of the tension inside her easing out. "I'm sure that would put the fear of God in him!"

Suevey began to laugh too. "It had better!"

Maria stood to go, but first came around the table and held onto Suevey for a moment. "Thanks, Suevey. You have been such a dear friend to me. And you have reminded me of God and His ways … that makes you the best kind of friend!" Maria turned and began walking out of the cafeteria. She turned back as she was walking out. "Are you going to the concert to hear Sir Reginaldo?"

"Oh my, dear! I would love to, but the tickets for inside seating only go to the most important of people … not for a simple person such as me! I do hope to picnic on the grassy area outside of the theater, where I suspect I may be able to hear at least a little. Still, it would be so grand to be inside!" She sighed at the thought. "Maybe you can sit with me Maria ... unless Gaeten plans on going and finds a way to get you inside!" Suevey began to laugh again at the thought. "Gaeten, going to a concert? My, oh my, wouldn't that be a hoot!"

Maria turned back to leave, wondering again just how important her mentor Gaeten really was.

As she left, Suevey wondered just what kind of trouble — or responsibility — Maria had gotten herself into. Or just what God had planned for this special child of His

Maria did not find Gaeten in the apartment, but knew at this time of the day he might be walking in a fragrant garden nearby and so she carefully felt her way there.

"Well, Maria. Are you ready to talk about it?"

"But ... how did you know I wanted to talk to you?"

"I don't know if I should tell you all my secrets! I'll tell you this one, anyway. I can tell when you need to talk when you get quiet. You walked over here and just went along with me for several steps, silently. That is not at all normal for you."

"Oh Gaeten!" The storm of emotions began to break. " I went to apologize and it did not go at all like I expected!"

"What, did someone yell at you for apologizing?" Gaeten's voice had been quite gentle until now, but with this his tone became much sharper. "What did they do to you?"

"No, it's not ... Sir Reginaldo said I must come back tomorrow, and then Grand Master Vitario agreed and said I just had to show up ... and I was scared ... and they were being quite forceful ..."

Gaeten interrupted. "They were bullying you? Scaring you?" He was getting angry, though Maria could not see his face turning red.

His words were sharp, but spoken quietly ... deadly quietly. She normally would have had warning bells ringing at that, but she was rather distracted. "And just when and where were you *ordered* to appear?" He said that in a rather sickly sweet voice, which should have stopped her dead in her tracks before the Grand Master Watcher stopped something else ... dead in its tracks.

Maria however was crying by now; this was not going well with Gaeten either. She was frustrated and tired and was getting a bit angry, which did not help the situation much. "They ... they said I had to meet them ... at the theater ... at noon to ... tomorrow" she said between soft sobs.

"Then tomorrow," Gaeten was speaking through clenched teeth now, though again his voice remained rather saccharine, "we will pay a visit to this 'Sir Reginaldo' whomever he is, and the Grand Master of the Academy of Music. I do not recall having ever spoken to Vitario. Let them present their *demands* to me!"

Maria just sobbed again and went off to bed, shaking her head.

The night was long for Maria. She was so nervous and frustrated that she wasn't sure if she had slept at all, and in the morning her stomach was much too fluttery to even think about food. Gaeten was not in the apartment when she finally ended her restless tossing, and so she did not have the opportunity to try to correct any misunderstandings.

Resignedly, she wandered around the compound, going down a set of stairs into an area she had not explored yet. Maria heard what sounded like metal hitting metal through one partially closed door, and she quietly slipped in. She could hear there were two people in an adjoining side room, and from the grunts it sounded like one was Gaeten. She did not recognize the other person, nor could she really tell what was happening, other than it seemed to involve a great deal of fast movement.

Ethan was in good form this morning, sparing with Grand Master Gaeten. But he was just not fast enough, not in such friendly competition. He really had little control over the "time slowing" that occurred when he was in danger — he could not turn it on or off at will. A foot slammed into him especially hard, sending him tumbling. For some reason Gaeten seemed particularly rough today. Ethan picked himself back up, and without warning grabbed a stubby wooden peg off a rack and threw it at the older man.

Gaeten was itching for a good workout … really for a good fight, but this would have to do. He liked sparring with Ethan — the boy was pretty good and was a quick learner. He regularly practiced with senior apprentices, but those were mainly training sessions since few could hold their own very long if Gaeten really tried hard. Several Masters could give him a much better workout, at least within their specialty. The half-dozen other Grand Masters within the Watchers could at least make him work up a sweat, though if they did it in the dark or blindfolded Gaeten could still prevail with ease. But they had very busy schedules and rarely had time for a full practice session with him. But Ethan was usually available and wanted the practice — and on rare occasions when he pushed particularly hard he got a workout that only the most skilled could offer him. He was definitely in the mood for that now. The peg flying at him was good, but he heard the movement and easily caught it, reactively spinning it around in his hands and sending it around for a return flight.

Ethan had not counted on that … Gaeten was particularly fast today and while he had expected the peg to get deflected, he had not expected such a rapidly returning projectile. He began to move, but was too slow, he would not be able to avoid the impact or even really deflect it well … but then the peg seemed suspended in the air, lazily moving toward him on a trajectory with his forehead. Ethan now moved aside with ease and flicked the peg right back, following it as he leapt at Gaeten. In a quirk of his talent, Ethan was actually moving quite a bit faster than the thrown peg, and so overtook it in flight and reached Gaeten first. He rained a series of blows at Gaeten, who somehow kept up, even though he seemed to be moving in slow motion. It was as though Gaeten somehow knew what Ethan's next several strikes would be, and moved to counter them even as Ethan was making his more-rapid-than-life movements. Even the returning peg did not faze him, but was casually swatted away.

This went on for several minutes, going faster and faster until Ethan kicked at a seemingly unprotected spot while it appeared Gaeten was still following through on a previous move. It had been a trap, and even with time slowed down Ethan could not recover in time to avoid several strikes that knocked him to the floor and would have seriously incapacitated him had Gaeten really been trying. Time returned to normal as Ethan laid there on the floor an extra minute, catching his breath.

"You are getting quite a bit better, Ethan. I was barely able to keep up with you."

Ethan picked himself up gingerly from the floor. "Let me know when "barely" means I might be able to beat you, even once!"

Gaeten laughed good-naturedly. "It is not just speed that wins a match. That certainly helps a lot, especially when it's your kind of speed! But you also need to out-think your opponent, to know what he is going to do before even he does, and know what he will do in reaction to what you do."

"You set me up ... you tricked me!"

"Yes, of course! And when you learn to successfully trick me, you will begin to win our little bouts. I also realize that if you were truly in mortal danger you can move even faster, and I am not sure if I could keep up with you then or not. Now, do you want to try it again, but this time blindfolded ... to be fair?"

It was Ethan's turn to chuckle. "Fair? I think it might be fairer if you had both hands tied behind your back, and even then I am not sure I could win."

"Ha — you might be right, at least for now! You know, we all have handicaps that God gives us. Some are more obvious, like my sight. Some are much less visible. And some are not from God at all ... instead they are of our own making. And blindness is not limited to one's sight."

Ethan looked puzzled. "I'm not sure I understand."

Gaeten smiled. "You will, over time. For now, consider what your weaknesses are, and what truly limits you. It usually is only partly physical. Remember that only God can truly set you free from those limitations, free to fully be the instrument of His purpose."

Maria, who had been silently listening to this exchange, gave a little gasp. 'An instrument of God's purpose' Gaeten had said. Wasn't that exactly what she was supposed to do? Wasn't fear her limitation? And being an instrument fit her pretty well indeed.

"Ah Maria, it is about time for our little ... visit, isn't it?" Gaeten sounded relaxed, though there was a distinct edge to his voice at the end.

"Gaeten ... I ... I think what they want is part of me being 'the instrument of God's purpose' like you just said. I think I am supposed to sing in the concert tonight with Sir Reginaldo."

"WHAT?!" Two voices sounded that out simultaneously.

"YOU are singing tonight at the concert?" Ethan sounded incredulous. He had been with the Watchers when they had found Maria along a small side road a mile or so out from Westhaven. She was a torn and tattered little blind girl standing in a field of partially mowed down ferns with a very badly mauled young man nearby — a Rat he learned who had not been at the Nest when they had cleaned it out. Ethan had never seen those kinds of wounds before, caused by the great gryph Sasha. And, incredibly, afterwards the huge bird of prey had landed on a small stump near the girl and it had seemed like the two of them carried on some sort of communication. It had been obvious the gryph was fond of her. He had heard that Maria had come to the Keep with

Gaeten, and was staying with him in his apartment, but he had not seen her around the compound area, and certainly never down in these lesser used training rooms which he and Gaeten preferred for their more private bouts.

"Now Maria," Gaeten began, "What is this all about? You were supposed to apologize for spying on the practice sessions — how did that transform into singing in the concert … and with the guest singer? I don't think you can just waltz into the concert tonight, climb up on the stage, and expect them to invite you to sing! You might be able to manipulate me with your sweet-little-girl ways, but I doubt that would happen with the head of the Music Academy."

"But Gaeten, they ASKED me to sing with Sir Reginaldo … he said the show could not go on unless I sang with him. In fact …" a bit of fear crept into her voice again …" in fact they said the whole concert would be ruined and all of Freelandia would be disappointed if I didn't … that it would all be my fault …" Tears were forming and her voice was catching and wavering. "I don't know if I can even do it! They expect ME to sing in front of everyone, and I have never done that … but it will be my fault if the whole concert is ruined … Oh Gaeten!" The fear had gotten the better of her again and she ran to her large friend and clung to him as she sobbed.

"There, there Maria. You do not HAVE to do anything you do not want to … not as long as I am around!" The last was growled out in a low yet very distinct warning. "Let's go meet these two who are scaring you so. I want to have a few words with them."

"Can I come along?" Ethan had been standing there listening, and while rather confused, he was also highly curious. This little girl appeared to have more to her than, well, than met the eye.

"No Ethan, I think this is for Maria and me to take care of. I presume you will be at the concert tonight with your parents — you can find out the results then."

"Yes, of course I will be there. We have front row seats. If there is anything I can do to help, let me know".

It was Maria's turn to be surprised. She did not know who this Ethan person was, but his parents must be awfully important if they had front row seats. Maybe they were special bodyguards for someone really important, like the Chancellor or something, she thought. Remembering her prior conversation Maria piped up "Well, there may be one thing I know of you could help with ..."

Chapter 11

The Masterpiece

aeten and Maria stopped by at the apartment so he could change out of his work-out clothes and they both headed toward the theater. This was the first time the two had gone out into the town together, and Maria noticed a considerable difference in how people were treating them ... really in how they were treating Gaeten. Where she often had to weave in and out among people and even get off to the side when it was really busy — people did not seem to give much room or second thought to a small blind girl — now the crowds cleared a wide berth for them and she often heard things like "Oh, excuse me Grand Master" as they strode along at a much faster pace than Maria was used to. She had one arm in Gaeten's as much to keep up as anything, and she noticed the cloth of whatever he was wearing was different — finer, silkier than normal. "Gaeten, you DO have nice clothes to wear!"

"Yes of course, Maria. I do sometimes get invited — and go — to more formal affairs," he said with a bit of a sniff.

In a few minutes they were at the Theater. It had a garden area outside with a restaurant, and today it was particularly busy. The whole area was buzzing with excited voices — all atwitter about the concert that evening.

Someone must have been watching for them, for immediately a teen-sounding girl ushered them over to an empty table. They sat and the young lady asked if they wanted anything to drink. Maria had never been to a restaurant before; the closest thing had been Sam's bakery. She had no clue what to ask for. Gaeten ordered something called "lemonade" for both of them and in a minute a cold glass was placed before her. In other circumstances, this might have been rather fun.

Maria was trembling, partly from excitement and partly from timidity. Her throat was dry and her palms sweaty. She lifted the glass and took a large drink … only to nearly sputter it back out over the table. "Oh my! That is very tart! What was it called again?" she partially choked out through puckered lips.

"It is called 'lemonade' my dear, have you not had it before?" The voice was from Sir Reginaldo.

Maria heard chairs being bumped and slid aside and several people say "Excuse me" as he finished his way to them. From the amount of chair movements Maria formed an opinion that Sir Reginaldo was not only a very important person, but also a rather large one too.

"No, never. I was not expecting so much flavor and … tartness!"

In the bright sunlight both Sir Reginaldo and Grand Master Vitario had their first real look at Maria. The previous night in the theater it had been quite dim, and they had only known she was a slight, young girl whom Vitario had guessed was blind. Now they could see that she was very slender and petite. Reginaldo thought she looked rather emaciated, though from his perspective most people looked a tad under what he considered a healthy size and weight.

"I hope you have had a good night's sleep in preparation for the big event tonight," offered Grand Master Vitario.

"No, not really. I am much too nervous."

Reginaldo frowned. "You look rather pale, Maria. Perhaps some of the food here will help that. I, for one, am starved to the point of exhaustion. Vitario here has been touring me all over the Academy. You really should try to eat more too — you are all skin and bones. It just wouldn't do for you to collapse in front of the High Council and the rest of Freelandia, now would it? Has no one been feeding you?"

Gaeten had been silent to this point, but at that last remark he could not hold back any longer. "Now just wait one minute there mister. Maria has been quite well cared for."

"And who, pray tell, are you? Her father? You don't look anything like her."

"No I am NOT her father," Gaeten growled. "But I am her … her guardian. And I do NOT like the way she is being forced into this … this concert singing thing! She is very young, and has had a quite traumatic childhood. Unless you convince me otherwise, I am not sure I will allow her to be bullied into singing tonight."

Sir Reginaldo was NOT used to being talked to in this way. He pushed back his chair loudly. "And just WHO ARE YOU to make that decision for such a talented young lady?"

Gaeten bristled, but tried to calm himself — first by unclenching the fist that had formed. It would be so very easy to … no, that would not be right. It would ruin their meal. This pompous … person … was getting to him. Gaeten felt quite protective of Maria, and he was not about to let someone whose ego seemed to outsize even his own very large body begin to tell her what to do. He was idly considering how he might artfully embed his fork somewhere in very close and personal proximity to the person across the table from him when Vitario interrupted his train of thought — pity about that, he mused. It could have been rather entertaining.

"Archibald, if I am not mistaken this is Grand Master Gaeten, one of the most esteemed trainers of Watchers in all Freelandia and personal consultant to Chancellor Duncan."

Reginaldo backed down, or at least tactically regrouped. He knew the reputation of Watchers. They were one of the top exports of Freelandia, leased out under tight conditions as personal body guards to people of high importance all over the world, as well as for training and security and, he suspected, other more covert activities. He himself of course was important enough to have one, but had not wanted to pay the steep fees they commanded — nor did he really want one trailing around like a groupie. However, it was quite a status symbol to have a Freelandian Watcher of high rank in your retinue, and if you could afford a Master … well, you were sure to be both rich and important.

The Grand Master sitting in front of him did not particularly look threatening — though with more careful observation Reginaldo did notice the scars and evidence of taut muscles — but nevertheless, prudence dictated a less confrontational approach. After all, if legends and rumors had it right a Grand Master Watcher was one of the most talented and dangerous fighters in existence — not a good person to make an enemy with … especially with pointed silverware in easy reach.

"Oh, well then! I do apologize for my rude remarks," he said with a hint of dramatic flair. "She is obviously in extremely capable hands." Reginaldo glanced down at Gaeten's hands, which were casually toying with his fork in a rather mesmerizing and yet somehow threatening manner. Prudence was needed indeed! Those hands did look like lethal weapons, and he had no intention of seeing them in any action.

"My most esteemed Grand Master, your little ward there is perhaps the most gifted singer I have ever heard. Last night she sang with me in practice, and I decided on the spot that she just must sing with me tonight." When he saw Gaeten bristle again at his use of the word 'must', Reginaldo continued a bit hurriedly, "What I really mean is, I need her. When I first heard her sing I thought I was hearing an angel — Grand Master Vitario can attest to that. No one has ever come up with an acceptable harmony for my Masterpiece song, no one! Yet Maria here heard it once or twice and just sang out a perfect accompaniment for it. I would have said it was impossible, and I still can barely believe it. She has such an incredible talent! I do not know where she has been hiding. Vitario here has told me she is not in the Academy of Music. I simply must know where she learned to sing like that — I want to compliment her vocal teacher, maybe even hire him or her!"

Gaeten snorted. "Maria is — was — an orphan from a small rural town a day's journey from here. She sang for a few small coins of charity and whatever leftovers remained on the tables. I sincerely doubt she has ever had any singing lessons!"

Maria felt her cheeks become warm and she hung her head dejectedly. It was all so true. She was a nobody from a no-where town. What was she even doing here? A tear formed and trickled down her cheek, unnoticed by Gaeten.

But not by Reginaldo. For all his outward pomposity, on the inside he had a heart of warmth and gentleness. He reached across the table and took Maria's hand. "No formal training, and yet I'd wager the angels are hushed just to listen in when you sing! Amazing! Incredible! I am truly honored to have met you, Maria!"

Maria lifted her head and smiled, buoyed by the kind and sincere sounding words.

Vitario picked up the conversation. "This is designed to be the biggest and best concert we have had in Freelandia for many years, with the High Council and many others attending. We want to give them our best. Your Maria," he emphasized 'your', "has one of the best voices Reginaldo and I have ever heard. Such a voice is given by God to share with others, to help others give glory to God. It would be a shame to hide it."

Gaeten was contemplating all of this. He certainly agreed that Maria's voice was unlike anyone's he had ever heard before. That talent should indeed be shared, he reasoned. Regardless of what he might feel toward this 'Sir' Reginaldo — and at the moment it was not very good — if he felt Maria had enough God-given talent for this concert, then it would be an honor to God to use it for His glory. Satisfied with his thinking, he turned. "Maria, what do you think?"

Maria was in a dilemma. She realized that she could say no, plead with Gaeten not to let them make her do it, and he would back her up in no uncertain terms. She had an "out". Yet she too had experienced the duet, and it had been … "right". She really couldn't define what that meant, only that deep down inside her she knew it was fitting, filled her with peace and joy, and left her heart praising God. And when she was singing, Maria felt 'right', like she was in her own element, where she belonged. She had not felt that way since she was very little.

"I … I think I should … and I think I want to … but it terrifies me at the same time."

Reginaldo reached his massive hand over to hold Maria's. "Don't worry, child. I myself will help you!" Maria figured that was supposed to help somehow.

They ate their meal, although Maria only picked at hers. She felt guilty about not eating what was likely one of the fanciest meals ever presented before her, but the butterflies in her stomach were back in force.

"So Grand Master Gaeten, what do you think about the gathering strength of The Dominion? I was traveling in Alteria last month, and people there were getting nervous about how rapidly that kingdom was spreading, taking over surrounding countries by the sword and growing stronger and bolder." Reginaldo was a world traveler, welcomed in most countries — even in those whose politics he disliked.

Gaeten cleared his throat. "Well …" his voice was softer, more private "The Dominion leaders seem to be in direct opposition to God's ways. They take by force and brutally suppress both the newly conquered and even their own people. From what we hear they demand worship of their 'gods' and none other — on penalty of torture and death. And their proclaimed 'gods' demand blood sacrifice. They really worship demons, and the leader of demons, those that don't really worship gold and power. They have been growing very strong, dangerously so. There are few free countries left that could put up real resistance to their plans for global domination. At some point they will have to be stopped."

Reginaldo nodded, but then realized it would not be noticed. "I see you do keep up on world events. Yes, the Dominion is becoming quite the blight. I have heard it rumored they have quite an appetite for Freelandian steel — known for being the very best in the world, and especially for sillarium — you of course realize that Freelandia is the exclusive source for that particularly unique metal. They supposedly are building quite a hoard of metals, and it is well known they are substantially bolstering their production of war materials ... and of warships."

That last perked Gaeten up considerably. "What have you heard about the ships?" That was of particular importance to Freelandia, since it was nearly inaccessible by any means other than the ocean, and its shipwrights were considered some of the most advanced anywhere.

"I don't know what is rumor or fact, but I have heard they have dozens of shipbuilding sites now, and are rapidly expanding their fleet with ships they have captured and are re-fitting. I was on a ship that neared one of those ports recently, and one area had an immense new building. I asked the Captain about it. He said it was shrouded in secrecy, but that there have been sightings of immense new ships — the Dominion is calling them "Dreadnaughts" — that dwarf any other ship in the world. They are supposed to be unstoppable and nearly impervious to even the largest other warship."

"That could be very useful information, Reginaldo. Before you leave would you mind speaking with a few people here in the Ministry of Defense? Your observations from your wide ranging travels may be of great use to us."

"Well now, you must realize I am absolutely neutral, politically speaking. I have never taken sides, and don't plan to now."

Gaeten was taken aback. "Not take sides? There is "right" and "wrong"! If you are not for God, you are against Him."

Reginaldo leaned forward and said conspiratorially, "And there are positions one takes openly that allow you to see and hear far more than if you are known to take sides — even if you actually do privately."

Gaeten chuckled. "Sir Reginaldo, I think there is more to you than I had given credit for."

Grand Master Vitario and Maria had been listening in on all of this, without making too much sense of it, although Vitario had been briefed on the Dominion. Since lunch was now over, he suggested "Perhaps it is time to head into the theater to check on preparations?"

The four walked up to the front doors. Maria had never been in that area before, and it had been quite awhile since Gaeten had either. They were led to some of the back rooms.

"So Vitario, do we have a room where Maria can prepare?" Reginaldo wanted to ensure Maria had all that she needed before he went to his room.

"Yes, this morning we cleared out one of the side rooms for her. Here it is. I must really be on my way; I have many arrangements to finalize before the concert. I'm sure everything will be in order — but just ask for anything else you may need." With that Vitario left them standing before a plain unmarked door. Reginaldo opened it and went into a small, unadorned room with a few chairs and a table, and though Maria and Gaeten did not know it, there was a large mirror on one wall.

Reginaldo clearly was not impressed. "Well, I suppose it will do. But you certainly will need an assistant to help you get fixed up. Maria, it does not seem like you brought your clothes?"

For a moment Maria wondered if she had forgotten to get dressed that morning. "Um ... what other clothes? This is by far the best that I have."

Reginaldo stopped dead in his tracks. "You ... don't ... have other ... nicer ... far nicer ... clothes?" he asked incredulously.

Maria felt her face go hot in embarrassment. She felt tears coming close to the surface. Did that mean she would not be allowed to sing? She clutched at Gaeten's hand. "I don't own anything else."

"I don't understand …" Reginaldo was bewildered — didn't everyone have a wardrobe to choose from?

"A few weeks ago Maria was an orphan in a little village called Westhaven. She has had a very difficult life, up to this point." Gaeten too felt some embarrassment — he had never considered that Maria needed anything else, and he himself lived very simply. He certainly had never anticipated the current events. "She has not had any need for fancier clothes."

Maria piped up. "I had nothing back in Westhaven. Gaeten brought me here, gave me a place to live — with my very own room all to myself and even a bed and pillow! He paid for these clothes … and I have had three meals a day, every single day I have been here! Mr. Gaeten has been so very kind to me." She leaned close and gave her benefactor a hug.

Reginaldo was stumped. He and Grand Master Vitario had discussed Maria the night before, wondering who she was. But it was sinking in that she really was an orphan … from a small village … and had only been at the Keep for a few weeks. As an orphan from some backward hayseed hamlet, of course she would have nothing. That explained her so simple, even poor appearance. Her hair did not look like it had been brushed in days, though it was at least clean. It did not look like it had been cut — at least not professionally — in years … or maybe ever. Unconsciously he ran a hand through his pampered and stylish silver streaked hair.

"This will not do, will not do at all."

He went to the open door and stood just outside.

"V I T A R I O!" he bellowed. Being a large man with a very well developed and exercised voice, Reginaldo certainly knew how to bellow.

Several people came running toward the room. "What … what do you need Sir Reginaldo?" Maria recognized the voice from the first night she had heard Reginaldo sing, and guessed it must be from a highly ranked assistant to Grand Master Vitario. She also heard the breathing of someone smaller and younger.

"First, I need a personal assistant for Maria immediately — if not sooner!"

"Certainly, Sir Reginaldo. Kory — you are assigned to that immediately."

"But … but I was supposed to ..."

"Immediately! You heard Sir Reginaldo. Get whatever he needs and do whatever he desires."

"Next, I need your best wardrobe assistant here immediately! You DO have a wardrobe assistant, don't you?"

"Well, yes. But she is very busy working on the other performers. I am certain I can find …"

Reginaldo did not wait. "V I T A R I O!"

"Alright, alright! Stop yelling like that! I will get Doreen right now."

"Go man, GO!"

The man sped off. Kory remained and timidly asked "Is … is there anything I can do to help?"

"Yes, child." Reginaldo's voice had become soft and gentle. "Maria will need a guide while here — you can see that she is blind. She is quite new to the Keep also, and so is not even familiar with what she might need. She will be singing with me at the concert" — Kory gasped loudly — "and so needs to be totally prepped for that event. You can start on her hair. I will come back periodically to check on your work. If you need any — and I mean ANY — help, you are to instantly demand it from the first person you see. If you have ANY trouble, come and get me. I personally find that people seem to just jump to my requests. Do you understand?"

Kory was in shock and answered numbly "I guess so."

"No guessing my dear — just get it done. Oh, and I will make it very well worth your time and full attention." Maria heard what sounded like a coin purse being opened. Again she heard Kory gasp.

"Now get going, get a brush or something and start on those tangles. Better yet, get your very best hairdresser here immediately!"

"But sir, I don't even know where she is and I am certain she is completely booked right before the concert like this!"

Reginaldo shook his head "Tsk, tsk my dear. You have a lot to learn about getting things done. Now tell me, who is the most important performer for the concert?"

"Well sir, I expect that is you."

"Correct. Now I want you to consider Maria here as equal to me — just as important, but far less ready. It is up to you to ensure she is completely prepared to be upon the stage with me at the concert. She must look as good as me up there." With that statement he stood straight and stared down at the girl with all his royal airs.

Kory's face drained of color. "Me?"

Reginaldo looked upon her patiently while inwardly he roiled at being left with what appeared to be an incompetent young Academy of Music apprentice. "Yes child, you. Now watch and learn. I have to leave shortly and it will be up to you to do this." He stepped to the door that opened to the hallway. He drew in a prodigious breath. "Hairdresser! I need your very best hairdresser immediately!" He waited a few moments, and when nothing happened … "VITARIO!"

Moments later a frazzled looking older woman came scurrying up. She eyed Reginaldo's foppish hair styling and frowned, reaching into a small satchel she carried.

"Not me woman! You will never touch MY hair!" He pointed over to Maria. "She will be on the stage with me tonight. Make her beautiful — that's an order!"

Reginaldo thought this was going fairly well, so far. "Now Maria, Gaeten — if you need a single little thing, don't hesitate to ask for it. This is going to be a concert to remember, I am personally going to see to that!" He strode out of the room and began storming down the hallway. "WHERE IS THAT WARDROBE ASSISTANT! V I T A R I O!"

Kory and the hairdresser excused themselves for a few minutes to get supplies, leaving Maria and Gaeten in the unfamiliar surroundings. They were silent for a moment; the last few minutes had been rather confusing and a blur. Then Maria giggled, slowly at first, then growing and growing until she was laughing heartily, if not bordering hysterically. Gaeten did not particularly see the humor, but he was very much out of his element and unsure of what to do. "Maria! Maria! Get hold of yourself!"

"Oh Gaeten, it is just all so overwhelming and unreal. And in just a few hours …" her laughter suddenly ceased and Gaeten heard a quivering in her voice.

"Maria! Have you brought yourself to this point, or has God? If it is not in your control, whose is it? Will He not provide you what you need to do His will … every time … no exceptions? Is this situation bigger than God?"

Maria was silent for a few moments. Gaeten was right, of course, but the emotions were not totally out of her system yet. She shook herself and settled down just as Kory returned.

"Hi … it is Maria, right? You are about the age of my sister, I think. I used to help her brush out her hair too. Let me get started — ok? I don't want Sir Reginaldo to return without my having gotten at least a good start! Are you really singing tonight? And with him? That must be so very awesome, I mean, singing with the great Sir Archibald Reginaldo, the greatest singer of all time the …."

As she prattled on Maria found herself listening with only half an ear, thinking about the Masterpiece. Soon the haunting counter melody came to her and she began to practice it silently, following the rolling melody that seemed to spiral and twist along a course in her mind. There, she 'saw' herself dancing before a throne where a Being of bright light sat. As the song went on she threw herself into great leaps and spins, moving faster and faster, singing and dancing before He-who-sat-on-the-throne. Somehow, she knew it was God, and that He was pleased.

Maria was broken out of her reverie by the arrival of Sir Reginaldo and an older woman who must have been the head wardrobe assistant — she must have been, or else Maria figured he would be out in the hallway bellowing for Grand Master Vitario again.

"Here she is, Doreen. She needs a total wardrobe replacement, something fit for a star role in tonight's concert."

Doreen looked back at Reginaldo, doubtful. "I can see what we have, but I cannot promise much. We don't get many in here that are so … so very thin."

"W O M A N!" You will not "just see what you can do". You WILL outfit Maria in the most beautiful dress possible, the best in Freelandia that you can get. Spare NO expense. No excuses either. Take the whole staff of the Academy if you have to. If it is not PERFECT I will personally inform Grand Master Vitario of your … your incompetence."

At that Doreen sputtered in anger. Reginaldo changed tactics. "Wait, I did not mean that. I want you do your very best. Here …" he fumbled again in his coin purse and finally poured out a small handful of gold coins. "Use whatever you need. Keep one for yourself for your trouble."

Doreen gaped at the pile of coins that amounted to well over what she made in several months … and maybe all year. "Oh my, thank you Sir! But even with all this money, I only have a few hours! In some of our best shops you may have to wait for nearly that long just to get noticed, much less be waited upon!"

"Hmm." Reginaldo did not like the sounds of that. "That could be a real problem. What can we do?" He drummed his fingers on the table. Looking down at them, he had an inspiration. "Here, take this." He removed his signet ring, gold encrusted with gem stones and with a very prominent "AR" on its face. "This may help."

"I'm sorry Sir Reginaldo, but not every shopkeeper in the Keep will know who you are".

Reginaldo's face started to turn red and a low animal growl began in his throat. He stood up rapidly, sending the chair he had been sitting on slamming backwards with great force and considerable velocity. The chair made it the several feet on its flight directly toward Gaeten before it suddenly splintered in half, each severed piece parting outward in a "V" shape. At the point of the V was a scarred fist. Gaeten smiled rather smugly. He had rather desperately wanted to break something for awhile now.

Reginaldo turned at the sound, and a sly smile crept onto his face. "Grand Master Gaeten, you really are not needed here for the next while — Maria is going to have to get bathed with scented soaps, and I am sorry Kory, but that hair is just going to have to be washed and made up proper — did that hairdresser wander off? Find her. Now Gaeten, I somehow doubt you will really enjoy all that fuss and womanly bother stuff. Perhaps you could assist Doreen here — it sounds like some shopkeepers may need a bit of … persuading … to make this their absolutely top priority. It really would be a great help, and get you out and about for awhile. How about lending a hand?"

It did not sound at all very enjoyable, though the thought of terrorizing some high-faluting dress shop owner had its own rather interesting possibilities. And staying here sounded worse. "Alright, if it is ok with Maria."

"Gaeten" — she grabbed and found his hand. "I don't want you to leave, but it sounds like maybe your special … talents … might be more useful with Doreen. It's ok with me."

The next several hours were a whirlwind of activity. Maria indeed was bathed with the help of Kory — and apparently perfumes had been added to the water, with lavender being the strongest. This was all entirely new to Maria, but Kory seemed to take over and help her immensely, saying it was not all that much different than helping her little sister at home.

Maria's hair was washed several times with buckets of warm water, and when that was finished she donned a robe and the hair dresser immediately went to work on her hair. She had never been fussed over like this and it was quite embarrassing. Kory and the hairdresser both worked non-stop on Maria's hair for nearly an hour. She did not know of course what it finally looked like, but she could feel complex braids and loops with ribbons and some kind of smooth small comb. She was having the time of her life.

Gaeten was not, but it had its moments. Doreen had led him to a shopping district he had never been to — no surprise there! — and into a specific shop. She had waltzed right up to a salesperson and demanded to speak to the owner himself immediately. The clerk had balked, even after Doreen had explained the situation and shown the signet ring. However, when Gaeten had taken a metal rod they used to hang items up on tall hooks and easily bent it into a pretzel shape the clerk had rapidly located the proprietor and they had then received excellent service. Doreen also hired their best alteration specialist on the spot and after purchasing a few other items they had all trouped back to the theater and Maria's dressing room.

Gaeten excused himself as the women went into high gear with their "fuss and bother" on Maria, and he found a somewhat comfortable chair to sit on out in the hallway.

As Maria was preparing — or more accurately being prepared — Grand Master Vitario was in his office, taking care of some last minute details. One of his chief assistants knocked and then entered.

"Sir - I have asked all the section heads, and they have asked all the senior apprentices and sub- leaders. There are two other Maria's in the Academy, but both are accounted for. It does not appear that this Maria you requested checking on is part of our Academy."

"Yes, I just learned she was from some small village nearby … let's see … what was the name again? Westenburg? Westivilla? Westharbour?"

"Westhaven sir? That is a tiny little hamlet about half a day's hard ride away. I do not recall having ever heard of anything good coming out of that place."

"Well, you have now. We have perhaps the greatest new singer to be found in all of Freelandia, and we don't have a clue who she really is or what her background has been — other than she is an orphan who was living in … Westbury did you say? And that she somehow caught the interest of a Grand Master Watcher, of all people."

"Westhaven, sir. If she is from Westhaven, then for sure she has no formal training in singing or music in general. That town is not even on our regular route of tours across Freelandia. Is she really that good?"

Vitario looked out his window at the late afternoon sunshine. "She came up with a perfect duet part for Reginaldo's Masterpiece the second or third time she heard him practice it. And her voice could easily be mistaken for that of an angel. It was probably the most beautiful singing I have ever heard. And when she sings it stirs you down to your innermost being. It is like being ushered into the very presence of God! Go. Find out more about this unknown virtuoso."

Sir Reginaldo had dressed in his finest, with plenty of jewels and gold chains, with many of his honorary ranks and badges festooning his chest. He had inspected the stage, and the small screen in back that would hide Maria, at least at first. He had no intention of keeping her back there the entire performance. Well, maybe until after the Masterpiece, then he would bring her out. Certainly she needed to be presented before the audience, where he could personally introduce "his find" to the world, whom he very well intended to take along when he left in two days to travel to his next performance. The two of them would make a marvelous team, and he could train her up to be a proper world-leading singer. Well, world quality backup singer to him, of course. He began to plan the short speech which he would give after he dramatically removed the screen and escorted Maria out to the front of the stage. It was going to be stupendous!

They were finally done primping Maria, and just in time too. Kory had tried in vain to trim Gaeten's beard, though she had managed to brush his hair a stroke or two before he could shoo her away. Now she hurriedly led them through the back passageways to the rear of the stage. Maria realized they were really only a short distance from the back door she had used as her secret entrance for many night explorations, and that familiarity helped to settle her just a little. Every little bit helped right now. She was the most nervous she ever remembered being.

Kory found a small stool for Gaeten to sit on, and another one for Maria right behind the screen, out just a few feet from a wall. That gave Maria some comfort — at least there was a solid, non-moving fixture in a world that had seemed to have gone topsy-turvy in the last few hours. Everything was happening so very fast. The concert was ready to begin.

Grand Master Vitario stood before the packed crowd. Before he began to speak he nodded at several guests seated up front, noticing and acknowledging of course Chancellor Duncan, Lydia his wife, his son and ... and who was that older woman sitting with them in the rather simple Watcher uniform? He shrugged and began. "Gentlefolk of Freelandia, welcome to our most special concert tonight. We have an arrangement of musical pieces for you from the best apprentices the Academy of Music has to offer, culminating with our very special guest, Sir Archibald Reginaldo, the most acclaimed singer in the world. He will perform his Masterpiece, and I can assure you that it will be a one-of-a-kind rendition, never before attempted." At that there was a stir in the audience. The Academy of Music Masters scattered about in the audience sat up straight, shaking their heads at one another in puzzlement at this unexpected and odd statement. "And now, we shall begin."

Vitario left the stage and went to his chair on the left of Chancellor Duncan. A group of level seven apprentices came onto the stage with stringed instruments and began to play. Maria sat on the edge of her seat, so eager to soak in the sounds that she temporarily forgot about her nervousness. Gaeten was rather interested too — he had never paid that much attention to music before, especially since he couldn't carry a tune, but since it was obviously so important to Maria, well then, it was important to him too.

Ethan was enjoying the concert as well. He did not play any instruments, but he appreciated precision playing. And front row seating couldn't be beat!

After an hour and a half there was a short break. Kory brought Maria and Gaeten glasses of water. She was obviously quite excited by the concert and also that she was allowed to be up so very close to the stage itself, even if it was actually behind the main stage — with her lowly rank, she would have had to fight for a place to stand or maybe even sit outside on the ground.

There were several songs performed by very talented apprentices — Maria recognized a few of voices as ones she would have chosen from the auditions — and then all too soon ...

Reginaldo stopped at Maria's chair and gave her a light hug. "You look beautiful, Maria," he whispered. "We will have the greatest rendition of the Masterpiece the world has ever heard! And you, my dear, will be seen" — it seemed to Maria that she detected the slightest of chuckles — "as the second greatest voice on the planet. We will make a team such as the world has never known!" He said the last with a great dramatic flair, made even more dramatic since it was said in a hushed whisper. She heard him fumble a moment with something, and then she felt him press a weight into her hair atop her head. With that done he stepped out onto the stage.

Maria wondered what he really meant by all that. She reached up to feel what had been placed on her head, and felt a small semi-circle of smooth metal with what felt like little pieces of glass embedded in several places. It felt heavy, far heavier than she thought something of that size should be, but she had no time to ponder it now as the nervousness returned in full strength and she began to shake. Then Gaeten's hand was on her shoulder, steadying her and she soaked up a portion of his strength. She stood in preparation, keeping the stool in front of her to lean on just in case. Gaeten stepped back and sat on his stool, off to the side but within close reach in case she needed support. He was so proud of his little Maria.

Sir Reginaldo was dressed in his finest arraignment. To some it seemed considerably ostentatious, but he claimed it allowed people in the far back of concert halls to still recognize him up on the stage. As though his girth was easily missed. He strode out strongly to the center of the stage and beamed at the audience. He recognized a few, and nodded at Chancellor Duncan and his family. "Gentle people, I cannot tell you how pleased I am to be here tonight. My visit to Freelandia has been more profitable than I could have ever imagined. You are in for what will simply be the greatest performance of your lives." Reginaldo was beaming. This was going to be SO grand! He was already thinking about how much he could charge for his next performance, once word got out of the Masterpiece sung in a DUET. A very, very profitable trip indeed!

"And now, I present to you … my very own … the Masterpiece." He bowed and stepped back as the subdued instrumental prelude began.

Maria took several deep breaths and said her thousandth prayer. She paused for a moment as Reginaldo began, waiting for her entrance as he had instructed. The harmony was coursing through her mind now, a vibrant bright rainbow that seemed to beg her to join in on a fantastic journey. She held out to the exact moment, and then gave herself freely, joyfully, exuberantly into what was for her a veritable song of life itself.

The audience had perked up, and an electric energy seemed to build as Sir Reginaldo finished his introduction and began to sing. When Maria's voice — full and incredibly pure — began to blend with the rich voice of Reginaldo, there was a collective cry of astonishment that rippled through the crowd and then fell silent as it seemed there was no longer room in the hall for any other sound, not even a whisper. Their voices blended to one and then parted again, weaving in and out and around in a whirl of auditory beauty. In the one and only practice the previous night Maria had sung well, but she had also held back at least a little, given the circumstances. Now she put her all into singing, every fiber of her being seemed to stretch out to add their component to her voice.

The effect was incredible, considerably more so than before, if that were possible. Reginaldo noticed it immediately, and as they continued it only became even better, more vibrant, almost taking on a life of its own as the impact transcended the physical and breached into the spiritual. He was amazed all over again, astounded in its beauty. Maria's addition made his song a whole new entity. It was … Reginaldo's voice quavered for the briefest moment as an entirely new feeling came over him … it was HUMBLING. Tears began to form in his eyes, slowly at first but rapidly growing into little rivulets that flowed down his cheeks. His voice began to falter.

Maria heard the first quaver and it worried her. She pressed on, but then heard Sir Reginaldo, owner of 'the greatest voice in the world' warble off key. She had no idea what was happening, but Maria realized he needed help. But for her, outward existence seemed dim and far away. In her 'special place', before her audience of One, she was so much more alive and freed from physical limitations. There, she danced and sang unencumbered by lack of sight or by gravity, and the sounds were indeed living pulsating ribbons of colored energy flowing around her. The ribbon representing Sir Reginaldo's rich voice had been intertwined perfectly with hers and glowed with its own energy and power. But with the discordant tone it began to dim and slow in its movement, faltering. It needed assistance, and quickly. But what could she do?

In her mind, Maria looked to her sole audience. An idea formed and she altered her dance, reaching out to touch and manipulate the ribbons of musical energy. She altered her singing, carrying his faltering voice, building it up and supporting it while still trying to weave in the counter melody notes. In her mind, she poured some of her own energy into Reginaldo's colored ribbon and used her own to carry it along and bolster it up. Her whole body was rigid with the effort, and sweat was pouring down her back. She strained with all her might to keep up.

To Ethan's ears, something was going wrong … or was it? This was unlike any singing rendition he certainly had ever heard before. He had nothing even to really compare it to. The voices seemed to reach right out into the theater hall, wafting through the air to touch every person, intertwine with some part of them, and pull them along in its journey. Sir Reginaldo certainly appeared to be losing his composure. He had turned pale and Ethan could see the tears falling from his face. Then to his and everyone else's utter astonishment, Reginaldo dropped to one knee and his mighty voice … ceased.

Maria heard it coming, but they had a full stanza yet to finish. Her face formed a grim smile of determination. She would not … she could not … stop now. The song had to go on. It could not be allowed to falter and die. It just HAD to be completed. She sang as she had never sung before, as she had never done ANYTHING before. Her voice lowered as she — somehow — picked up Reginaldo's part, but at an octave more conducive to her vocal chords. She could not of course sing both parts — that was not physically possible. But she was far less limited physically within her 'special place'.

Her face turned white with the effort, but the Masterpiece continued — changed for sure, but it still went on. And somehow, even though she could not now sing it, the counter melody seemed to persist on its own, as she and the audience could nearly hear it soaring along at the outer edges of their consciousness. It did exist in her mind, mingling in among the standard notes and somehow it seemed to peek in and out of her voice. Maria was shaking with the effort and strain, but sensing the audience's attention she gained strength both from them and from her most special audience in her mind.

Reginaldo was unabashedly weeping on the stage, in stark wonderment listening to Maria's Masterpiece. She reached the crescendo and raw power seemed to ripple invisibly in the room. Then came her nearly whispered ending, eerily quiet and haunting, which trailed down and down until the finale of utter silence.

Maria finished, her face lifted up toward God in worship. Her voice faded to perfect silence and then she collapsed. The outpouring of energy and the strain had been too much for her frail body. Her knees buckled and almost in slow motion she toppled backwards. The only sound behind the stage was of her head colliding solidly with the wall behind her.

Chapter 12

Grand Master Mesha

ven before she hit Gaeten was moving. He could be incredibly fast when needed. However, he too had been caught up in the most stirring song he had ever experienced, and he was at an awkward angle and could not reach her body fast enough as it crumpled backwards. He winced as he heard her head strike the wall and as he bent to pick her up he smelled fresh blood. His face went ashen and he spun toward Kory, who was sitting just off the stage in the back and who had not even noticed Maria's collapse, still enthralled by the performance.

Ethan had been mesmerized by the performance and especially the ending. It indeed had been the best singing he had ever heard. Like everyone else in the theater, he had been touched at some much deeper level than from the mere vibrations in his auditory ear channels. But then he somehow knew something had gone terribly wrong. Before he even realized what he was doing he was up out of his chair and most of way toward the small door leading to the back, his body automatically following a blue lit pathway formed in his mind. As he passed, he noticed an oh-so-slowly falling tear dropping from Sir Reginaldo's stooped face.

Gaeten could speak with a command voice that could stop a charging bull pachyderm, even when spoken at fairly normal levels. " KORY! Lead us to the Ministry of Healing RIGHT NOW!" Kory had been immersed in the song like everyone else, but at that command voice her head snapped down and her eyes went wide. Surprisingly, she didn't just stare in shock. She seized on the situation with one look and leapt from her seat. "This way!"

'That girl may have some potential' thought Gaeten. He had already picked Maria up and he brushed the thought aside and charged forward carrying her totally limp form with as great of care as he could manage while moving so fast while trying to determine exactly where he and everything in front of him was located. His sense of spatial location and surroundings was astounding — and even supernatural. He had long contended that he walked as much by faith as by sight, and that God had never let him down or misdirected his steps.

Kory reached the back exit and was blocked by Xenia, who had been requisitioned to guard the door. She took one glance at Grand Master's Gaeten's face and the unconscious small girl in his arms and threw open the door, barely getting out of the way herself from the juggernaut heading her direction. As they stepped out Kory suddenly halted. "I … I don't know the way from here!"

Ethan was through the doorway behind the stage and raced to the spot the blue line ended and where he could sense the trouble had come from. He saw the blood stain on the wall and rocketed toward the open back door.

Ethan saw his mentor exit seemingly in slow motion. He flew through the door right behind them.

Xenia had heard Gaeten's command and spoke up. "I know the way, I think. It is up this street, then down the next, over a hill, and ..."

Ethan came to a near collision with the stopped trio — no, there were four people ... Gaeten was carrying an unconscious Maria. Since the world around him was moving at a snail's pace, he knew he had to try to speak very slowly or he knew from experience that his words would not be understood. "No!Followme". He knew Gaeten could hold a pretty fast pace if the pathway was relatively clear of obstructions, though his burden would hamper his movements both in speed and dexterity. Gaeten had told him once that all of the sounds around him bounced off everything else, and that gave him a pretty good idea of his surroundings. Ethan did not wait, but sped off at a slightly slower pace than he had been moving at, trusting Gaeten to keep up, burden or not.

Gaeten yelled over his shoulder "Kory, Xenia — follow us to the Healing Ministry as fast as you can!" Kory and the teen Watcher apprentice looked at each other, shrugged, and began running in pursuit, though at a decidedly slower pace.

Gaeten was fast, but his burden did slow him considerably. He was mortified to cause any further hurt, and he was doing everything within his power to minimize the jostles. He also wanted to get her to Grand Master Mesha, head of the Ministry of Healing, as fast as humanly possible. He prayed for speed ... and for his dear Maria for whom he now felt he could do so very little.

Ethan sped forward. Another blue path lay before him in his mind, curving up the street and around all obstacles. He knew the city quite well, but the blue path seemed to take into consideration the people, horses, carts and other obstructions along the way too. He had to restrain his speed enough for Gaeten to keep up, but the two of them were still moving at a considerably fast pace, zigging and zagging through the crowded streets.

Gaeten's entire focus was on the sounds pouring in from every side and especially from in front. He was only a couple of paces behind Ethan and concentrated mainly on following the exact same footsteps just ahead of his own pounding feet.

In just a few minutes they reached the large complex of buildings that collectively made up the Ministry of Healing. They raced for the lobby of the main building.

Back at the theater the long silence was finally broken by thunderous applause. Reginaldo had totally lost his pompous composure. He bowed politely toward the audience and then turned his back on the standing ovation and attention as he walked to the rear of the stage, back in the shadows toward the small screen they had set up.

Grand Master Vitario had noticed the flash of Ethan's movement, hardly realizing it was the boy who was streaking away at such an incredible speed. He stood as if to go with him, wondering what this could mean. He glanced down at Chancellor Duncan and was very startled to see his stricken face.

Reginaldo pushed the screen aside, with no mind to force Maria to do anything. He just wanted to thank her. He saw the toppled chairs and empty space. Then he saw the blood on the wall and splattered onto the gem encrusted gold tiara now lying on the floor. The applause was still deafening, but even so those in the front could hear an enormous panicked bellow

"V I T A R I O!"

❦

Gaeten was having some trouble keeping up with Ethan. It wasn't all that easy to not see where you were going and just follow the rapidly moving sounds ahead of you while also keeping track of all the surrounding sounds and carry a fragile burden. He usually had a picture in his mind of where he was, based on the various sounds he heard, textures under his feet, the feel of the breeze, even of the many smells wafting around him. But in a mad dash like this it was a blur and he had to fully trust in the abilities God had given him, coupled with the faith that his God would guide his path. As they neared the main building Ethan slowed and began to call out some obstacles, such as the step leading up to the lobby entrance.

As they burst through the double doors a young woman looked up from behind a desk. She did not need to be asked what to do next. She immediately jumped up and pointed to a low bed. Ethan turned and both guided and assisted Gaeten to deposit the totally limp Maria. She called out for one of the senior apprentices on duty to come and look her over.

Gaeten set his shoulders and fluffed out his formal attire. "I need to speak with Grand Master Mesha."

"Oh, I'm sorry," the attendant demurred, "he is out on his evening rounds checking on patients. I am sure he will come by as soon as he can." People always wanted the top healer, it seemed like every patient brought in just had to have Grand Master Mesha himself at their beck and call. And the people who felt that THEY were particularly important were the worst. Her eyes fell onto Gaeten's collar which showed the markings of both the Watchers and of his status. So, this one really was a somebody!

"Perhaps you can ask someone to track him down. Tell *Meshaken* that Gaeten needs to urgently see him."

That got her attention. Few knew of Grand Master Mesha's given name — he always used the shorter form. He had standing orders for his full name NEVER to be given out — on penalty of dismissal from the Ministry — but that whenever someone asked for him using that name he was to be told about is as soon as possible. Her demeanor changed, actually becoming more business-like. "Yes sir, I will send someone immediately." She walked to a back room and returned in a few moments. "We are tracking him down now, but there is no guarantee he can come immediately — we have several very urgent and serious patients here tonight."

Gaeten was not particularly good at waiting at times like this.

Vitario hurriedly assigned a senior Academy Master to dismiss the crowd and raced to the back where Reginaldo stood. Meanwhile several Master Watchers were alertly scanning about for what might have caused the sudden commotion. Suevey, from her honored front row seat that Ethan had procured next to him at Maria's request, had noticed the flash of Ethan's faster-than-possible flight and looked over at Chancellor Duncan. When she noticed the pallor of his face she snapped to attention and to action. Duncan had done away with a personal guard that was not only due his station, but which Master Warden James had only felt prudent — but that just meant every Watcher had standing orders that whenever they were in proximity to the Chancellor or his family they were to assume that unofficial duty.

Something right now seemed very, very wrong. The Watchers had numerous codes for getting attention and immediate action, but when unknown imminent danger seemed to threaten someone they were guarding, the simplest was deemed the best.

It only took a fraction of a second for Suevey to go from thought to action. In a very controlled and yet urgent voice she yelled out "PROTECT!" Even as it was voiced she pulled out a thin but surprisingly strong metal chain that had been wrapped inside her clothing. It had a rounded weight on one end and that instantly began swinging in a quick arc as Suevey's eyes darted over each of those seated nearby and began to sweep out in wider circles, looking for the source of any danger.

The effect was nearly as electric and dynamic as had been Maria's singing, at least for a small subset of the audience. Every Watcher in the building went on instant high alert and leapt over seats and dodged among the slowly moving, standing and seated audience to gather and form a human shield around Duncan and Lydia … a shield that was just as capable offensively as it was defensively. The most senior Watcher present spoke up. "Sir, is everything all right?"

"Yes … maybe … I am not really sure. I need to get over to the Keep Museum, and I need the head curator, and a Master Theologian, preferably who specializes in prophecy." Just then something else clicked in Duncan's mind and he jumped up with a gasp. His eyes darted down the row of seats, just realizing that Ethan's was empty. "Could it be … yes!" His eyes were shifting back and forth rapidly as his mind was churning through possibilities. "If it is …" He focused on the nearest Master Watcher. "FIND ETHAN AND THAT SINGER!"

Duncan paused for just a moment. "Until I tell you to stand down this is a Red-4 Alert!" The Watchers had also long ago developed a system of codes that allowed instant communication of various levels and types of danger. Red was the top level, reserved for matters of utmost urgency. Red-4 meant that a life may be in imminent danger, someone who was considered of utmost importance to the High Council of Freelandia. A Red-level alert had not been called in the memory of anyone present.

The Master Watcher's eyes grew large, but to his credit he did not falter or hesitate in the least. He pointed to several other Master Watchers and without a word they peeled off after Vitario, since he was heading in the same general direction that they had seen the somewhat blurry form of Ethan speed toward. He then scanned the theater — the crowds were now only slowly beginning to leave, totally blocking the normal exits. He had to get word to the Master Warden immediately! Suevey saw the dilemma, caught his attention, nodded in acceptance, and spun about and ran toward the back of the theater to find a faster way out.

Vitario reached Reginaldo just as the large man, stunned by what he had discovered, was turning back toward the stage and ready to bellow out once again. "What is wrong, Archibald?" Reginaldo just pointed mutely. Vitario saw the blood and absence of Maria, Gaeten and Kory. "What … where have they gone?" he asked in bewilderment. Before he could grasp the situation further, several Master Watchers stormed into the area, their body language speaking of a high level of alert. They took in the surroundings, glanced at the wall, and then raced out the nearby back door of the theater.

"I don't understand," Reginaldo whispered as he and Vitario stood at the back of the theater. What could have happened? Did … did someone come and take my Maria?" His eyes began to fill with tears and a sniffle sounded.

"Archibald, it will do no good to speculate. God will take care of her … and of you. Besides, I hardly think anyone with ill intent could possibly get past her benefactor — I surely would not want to attempt it, even with a dozen of my largest apprentices!"

"Yes, God always has taken care of me. Still, I worry - I can't seem to help it." He turned and picked up the fallen golden tiara, seeing bits of darkening blood flecking its polished surface. He shuddered. "She will be ok … she just has to be … I know it …" Reginaldo turned to look imploringly at Vitario. "She is going to be ok, right? RIGHT?"

Vitario saw the 'greatest singer on earth' about to go into belligerent shock and knew he had to redirect the situation at once. He grabbed the big man's arm. "Yes, yes of course she will be, Archibald. In fact

I am sure that whatever happened, she is already being attended to with top care! Come — there is nothing for us to do here. I don't know about you, but I think I could use a bite to eat. Did you recall that we had a special VIP room at the Theater Restaurant? I understand they prepared some real specialties for tonight …"

Reginaldo forcefully regained his composure, pulling away from the fear that had threatened to engulf him. Then what Vitario had said registered as much to his stomach as to his ears. "Why yes, now that you mention it, I think I do recall there was a place for me to mingle with the most important guests … and I do get terribly hungry after a performance … and WHAT a performance it was! Maria was … was spectacular!"

Grand Master Vitario wondered silently about what was just said. 'Maria was spectacular', not 'I was spectacular' or even 'We were spectacular'. It seemed like Sir Reginaldo may have been affected by the song like everyone else! This would be interesting to watch as it panned out!

"Archibald, I will be sure to send word to you as soon as I hear anything. I will have several of my Master teachers trying to figure out who was back there with Maria and Gaeten, and I will send word to the Watchers that I wish to speak with Gaeten as soon as he is found. The Watchers in the theater seem to be very agitated right now though" — even as he spoke those words the older female Watcher who had been sitting next to Ethan raced by them with surprising speed — "and I fear we may have to wait until morning before we will learn much else."

The two made their way out of the auditorium and to the small but well stocked Theater Restaurant. Several of the guests were already there mingling and discussing in awe and near reverence the performance they had just experienced, and the mystery of the ending. Reginaldo puffed out his massive chest and strode in, instantly becoming the center of attention as was his usual desire. Within a few minutes Vitario excused himself, seeing that his absence would likely not even be noticed by most. Even so, several Masters of the Music Academy tried to pull him aside to discuss what this most singular happening within the Academy any could remember might mean. He demurred, telling all he would call a meeting of senior Masters the next day. Then he begged off all further questions and hurriedly departed.

Vitario walked quickly to his office. He sent assistants to track down the head wardrobe manager, but one mentioned that she had left right after the performance and would not be quickly found. Someone said it appeared that some young Academy apprentice had been assigned to work with Maria, but no one seemed to know who it had been. Frustrated with the lack of information, he instead began to replay the rendition of the Masterpiece in his mind. He had a superb memory for music, and even in recall he felt caught up in the majesty. He grabbed a pencil and a sheaf of bound paper and began to transcribe the never-before-heard amazing counter melody Maria had sung. He would assign several others to do the same, and then they would compare notes. As he began to inscribe he marveled anew. This was going to take a lot of paper. He was not even sure he had all the symbols needed — he was pretty sure some of the notes went beyond even what his finely tuned ears could hear.

Shortly after the assistant had sent for Grand Master Mesha, Kory and Xenia raced through the doorway, panting heavily. "Good, you are finally here" Gaeten growled. "You … Kory … I am charging you with staying with Maria no matter what, no matter where she is taken. She needs a female companion who has a good head on her shoulders, and you are it." Kory thought about arguing that she had other Academy responsibilities, but only for a split second. The look on Gaeten's face precluded any other actions and she figured she could much more likely survive a scolding by anyone at the Music Academy far better than by crossing this Watcher.

He turned toward Xenia. "I want you to go to my apartment and get a few things" he listed off a few personal items of Maria's. "Get them and bring them back here. Go!"

Even as he said that, Grand Master Mesha entered the lobby, quickly assessed the situation and immediately went to the still form of Maria. Her face was gravely white and her breathing shallow. He looked up worriedly. "Gaeten."

"Yes Meshakan?"

"This does not look like the normal apprentice Watcher you bring in here. This girl is so thin and frail! Who is she and what happened?" Mesha was very gently probing the back of Maria's head and his hands came up bloody.

"She ... she is Maria. She is not really a Watcher ... she is more of a ... of a ..." he stumbled over how to best describe her. "She is my Ward. She sang tonight at the concert. She was straining pretty hard there at end, when Reginaldo stopped singing, and then she collapsed. On her way down she hit a wall."

"Gaeten, this is a very ill young woman. Her head wound may be serious — I really can't tell yet. She appears very, very weak." He motioned for two of his assistants who had accompanied him to lift her. "We will take her to our trauma area. We will do what we can."

Gaeten had gone quite pale himself and his body was quivering slightly. Mesha noticed and put a hand onto Gatean's arm. "Old friend, I will do the best I can. The rest is, and always has been, in God's hands."

"Meshakan ... she is very important to me. And after her singing tonight, I have a feeling she perhaps may be more important to more than just me."

"Alright, Gatean. I will take personal care of her; she will be my personal patient. Now I really need to see exactly what must be done." Mesha turned to leave with the two assistants carrying Maria. Kory turned to follow.

"Meshaken, I asked this young lady to stay with Maria — I presume that is ok?"

"Yes, as long as she stays completely out of the way and does not faint or get hysterical".

Kory gulped. "I have helped deliver cows and sheep on the farm, and some have been breach."

Gaeten motioned for her to come over. He pulled out some gold coins from an inner pocket. "Here. If you need anything, get it — for you or Maria. And take these too." He removed his signet ring and handed it to her, then retrieved the small metal whistle on a cord that Maria had taken off for the concert. "Make sure Maria has the whistle nearby, it will comfort her".

Gaeten knew he would only be in the way if he stayed, and besides, sitting and waiting was never his greatest strength. Waiting with nothing productive to do — that was not so good. He needed to keep his hands busy ... like in breaking things.

He heard them all leave, and then departed himself, back to the Watcher Compound.

Grand Master Mesha strode along, with Kory trailing behind. They past several doorways leading to other wings and were about to enter the trauma area when he called a stop. "You know," he said to no one in particular, "I must be near another patient upstairs tonight. We can bring her to my personal care ward near my office. I think that would be better." The group turned right down a hall and went up a flight of stairs and around a corner. On the third floor they brought Maria to Mesha's personal ward, a few very well stocked private patient rooms. The assistants gently lowered Maria onto the clean white bed. "I think her head wound is only superficial, though she has lost some blood from it." He turned to the older of the two assistants. "Get Head Nurse Abigail. Tell her I want Maria washed up and given a very thorough look over."

He glanced at a rather nervous looking Kory. "Don't worry; Nurse Abigail is our very best. She has a true gift from God in discerning injuries and the best healing techniques. I frankly don't know how I could do my job without her. You can sit on the chair beside the bed, and when you get tired there is a sleeping roll you can pull out from the cabinet over there. Grand Master Gaeten must have quite a lot of confidence in you ... especially since it appears you are an apprentice musician ... level 1 from your insignia?"

"Yes, Grand Master Mesha. Sir — she really was wonderful tonight. When she sang it made my heart stir, my soul soar ... I ... I have never been affected like that before. I felt closer to God than I can ever remember. It has to be one of the greatest gifts I have ever experienced. You have just ... just got to heal her!"

Mesha looked at her in puzzlement, then over at Maria's form. This was certainly turning out to be an unusual night, and an unusual patient. It was not often you had two Grand Masters attending one unconscious little girl.

Chapter 13

Prophecy

rand Master Vitario was steaming. No one seemed to know anything! Well, that was not quite right. The head wardrobe seamstress had finally been located, and she relayed that an apprentice named Kory was assisting The Singer — that was what everyone seemed to refer to Maria as, since she was a total mystery to all but a few people — and he had a dozen apprentices racing around the Academy trying to locate this Kory, or anything about her. Even the entire Keep was not THAT large ... one would think it should not be too terribly difficult to find such people. He had even dispatched an apprentice to the Healing Ministry, but there were no young girls fitting Maria's description in the trauma or any other ward where she might have been taken. Where could they be?

Master Warden James had immediately implemented the Red-4 alert. It called for doubling of the Watchers at the Keep entrances, and closing of the main gate at the inner Keep. He also sent a contingent of Watchers to the High Council building. He had only gotten the sketchiest of descriptions of what Chancellor Duncan had ordered, and so he was heading toward the Museum to try to find the Chancellor, along with several of the Alpha-Blue team who were on call that evening. He had an Alpha team always on call. As best he could make out, Ethan may be in danger, and maybe someone else … but no one seemed to know who. How could he protect someone if he did not even have a name, description, location … anything? The best he could hope for is that whoever it was, they were with Ethan.

As he left the compound a young female apprentice came running up and was immediately ordered to report to her squad leader. The girl began to protest, but before she could explain she was cut off and ordered in no uncertain terms that a Red-4 Alert overruled any errand she may be on.

Gaeten and Ethan were just exiting the lobby when two Master Watchers came sprinting up. "Grand Master Gaeten! Chancellor Duncan has just ordered a Red-4 Alert on Ethan! Oh, and I think we are supposed to watch over whoever it was that was singing with Sir Reginaldo too. Chancellor Duncan is heading over to the Museum, and he seemed really upset over something." The elder of the two Masters picked up the conversation. "Master Gaeten, I think we should get Ethan to a …" he glanced around " … to a more secure location immediately."

Gaeten had snapped to full attention at the mention of the Alert. He had duties to perform and he would have to put Maria's needs to the side — besides she was in the best of hands. But why was a Master Watcher assigned to Maria? He wondered if it was a mistake. Perhaps Duncan has assumed Maria was with Ethan and sent the Watchers after both. Regardless, his duty was to be near Duncan. He turned to the senior Watcher. "Right. Take us to the Chancellor immediately." To the other he added: "she is inside, in the trauma area." With that he turned to go, flanking Ethan with the senior Master Watcher and they jogged off into the darkening night.

The junior Master Watcher — junior in age by only a few years — darted into the lobby. "Where is the trauma center?" he asked the attendant. She was startled — two high level Watchers in just a few minutes, this was a strange night. "Down this hall, take the second left and go through the first set of doors." She had no clue as to why he was here, or who he was looking for, and she really did not care — her shift was ending now, she was quite tired, and just wanted to go home to bed.

He strode rapidly to the described location. He saw a nurse station and walked over to it. "I understand you recently took in a ..." he paused. Gaeten had not described who the singer was, only that it was a "she". He knew that already from the concert. The voice had undoubtedly been feminine, and could not have been too old, but the volume and energy must have been from someone well practiced in the singing arts. "... that you took in a young woman in the last, say, thirty minutes?"

The nurse looked at him with a very puzzled expression. "Well ... yes, we did. She is in the bed over to the left. A healer has just looked her over. She is asleep now, but that is fairly normal. We will be moving her over to a more private room when she wakes up." The Watcher wheeled around and went over near the indicated bed. A twenty-ish year old woman was asleep. To him, she seemed rather ... puffy and overly chubby, but knew that was none of his business.

The nurse looked over at him. What would a Master Watcher want with someone who would shortly be a first time mother?

Nurse Abigail entered Maria's room quietly. She had learned to walk silently to not disturb patients. She glided up to Maria and went to place her hand onto the girl's forehead. Abigail paused for a moment. My, she thought, the Spirit seemed strong in this one! She prayed for healing discernment and began to examine Maria's still form. No, the head wound was not overly serious, it was mainly a flesh wound and head injuries always involved a lot of blood. She would clean that up shortly. The young girl was wearing a beautiful dress, though now it was stained with her blood. Abigail noted that the fancily done up hair had probably deflected a large part of the force from whatever Maria had fallen into — the angle of the wound indicated a likely tumble. But the girl's breathing was rather shallow and her color was not good at all. Her heart also seemed to be weak. If anything, little Maria appeared to be utterly exhausted, so over-exerted that her body could not keep going and had just begun to shut down. Abigail frowned. It was now her responsibility to ensure that shut down did not go any further and then to reverse it.She laid her hand again on Maria and began to pray. Healing, she knew, came only partly from healers.

Chancellor Duncan and his escort reached the Museum. He had sent runners ahead to rouse up the head curator. "Uh, Chancellor Duncan … what is it you need to see?" Duncan had several very alert looking Master Watchers around him, and that alone was quite noteworthy.

"I need to see the Book of Prophecy."

"You roused me out of bed for that? I am an early riser and so get to bed early as well. Can't it wait until tomorrow?"

"Now, Master Curator, this is important. Volume Three please."

"You know that was written over three hundred years ago, by the so-called school of prophets. The tome you requested is the last volume, written as the school was closing down. The number of students had declined, and finally there was just the old schoolmaster who remained. You know," the curator said snidely, "it is widely held among many of my peers that he was quite senile, especially at the end. His writings seemed to wander around haphazardly … it was a lot of nonsense. Of course, all that "prophecy" is just interesting historical literature. What do want that for?"

Chancellor Duncan looked oddly at the curator. "So you don't believe in prophecy? You don't believe God has spoken to some in dreams and visions, that He has put His Spirit in some to be His prophets?"

The curator chortled. "Hardly! I certainly wouldn't expect any highly educated person would!" He looked suspiciously at Chancellor Duncan. "You certainly do not, do you?"

Duncan pitied the oh-so-proper curator. "I don't suppose you have ever felt guided or directly by God then, either?"

"Most certainly not! I would never trust something so based on 'feelings'. I expect such would more than likely really just reflect one's own personal wishes, or maybe what one had to eat the night before!" The older gentleman chuckled derisively. No sir! Give me the facts, just the facts and I will decide my life from that. I have no need of 'leadings'! And if anyone under my leadership dares bring up such a thing, I would instantly dismiss him."

Duncan sadly shook his head. The man may be good at what he did, but ignoring contact with the source of all knowledge? It appeared the curator was rather puffed up with his own intelligence and his pride had blinded him to God's ways.

It was a shame — and a considerable limitation. Duncan was a gifted administrator, and a historian. He knew Freelandia had been founded by solidly godly men who sought a place where they could worship and live freely, and they heavily relied on God's guidance and gifts to find and establish a settlement that flourished into the country it was today. What's more, one of the founders had a vision from God where he saw them sailing on a ship, and he was convinced that a specific prophecy —

And I will go before my people and prepare a place. To the north I hollowed out from the mountains a shelter, a land between mountain and sea. If they look for my face and listen to my voice, if they will love my Son and hold to my ways and honor my gifts, then I will grant them a land of freedom. Do not fear the winds of storm nor crashing of waves on rock, for I will be with you. I will protect you from the left and from the right.'

— was literally true and meant for them. The band of twelve families outfitted a ship and sailed north with all their earthly possessions with the blessing of the church where their families had been for tens of generations.

The voyage had gone well enough at the start, but then a fierce gale had come up from the south and their ship had been tossed to and fro for over a week. A few had begun to lose hope, but their leader had urged them to continue to trust in their Creator. In the midst of the storm they began to sing hymns of thanksgiving as each testified of the greatness of their God. Then they lifted up prayers for mercy and direction. They did this for three days and three nights, and as dawn came on the fourth day of prayer a lookout shouted that land was ahead. The waves were crashing roughly on the rocky cliffs as far as they could see, yet the wind was too strong to counter and was driving them straight ahead. Again they feared, and again they turned to their Maker. They reminded themselves again of the words of the prophecy and in great faith did not try to steer away.

Closer and closer they were driven towards the looming cliffs, when suddenly a narrow inlet was noticed. The captain believed it to be river, and feared grounding the ship on a shallow bottom or on outer sandbars. He desired to drop sea anchors to slow their progress, but the founders stayed his hand. Their ship was propelled directly for the inlet, which had steep rock cliffs to the right and to the left. The cliffs acted as baffles for the wind, and they passed through into a much calmer and huge bay. They were in awe of the miracle of deliverance. The bay was really more of an inland sea, with only one opening to the ocean. After they negotiated around dangerous rocky reefs and stone spires that rose right out of the water, they found a beach inside two rocky points that jutted out into deeper water, with a fresh water river nearby, and it was here that they anchored, came ashore, and eventually formed their first settlement. They called it "The Keep" because it reminded them that God had kept them in the palm of His hand and had guided them so surely to this new 'land of freedom' that they christened "Freelandia".

God had blessed them on their journey, and blessed them even more in this unexplored and previously uninhabited new land. The families had prospered as they worked the fertile soil, and had found exceptionally rich natural resources all around them. They had grown and prospered, and had welcomed others to join them in "God's country". Not everyone believed exactly as they did, nor did they force such belief. But the leadership remained firmly rooted in and true to God and encouraged all to believe and to seek ever more of God and His goodness, and to trust in His guidance and gifts. Over the next several hundred years they grew into one of the most prosperous countries, remaining safe from aggressive neighbors by their easily protected bay and by the grace of God. Freelandia became world-known for its open policies of learning, and the very many breakthroughs discovered in science, engineering, medicine and other fields. Not everyone who came to Freelandia trusted in God, though few could deny the incredible blessings that seemed to surround them. Several times in their history other jealous countries had tried to acquire Freelandia's resources by force, but they had been thwarted every time.

God's provisions were undeniable, certainly to Duncan. He made a mental note to himself. The curator may be talented in his office, and his own personal lack of acknowledgement of God was his own choice, but his policy of forbidding his subordinates to take guidance from God … that was not right. He may not be the best candidate for the level of authority he had.

"Well regardless, get Volume 3 of the Book of Prophecy. I need to refresh my memory on a portion of it."

The curator scurried off with a scowl. He returned about the same time that Gaeten and Ethan arrived from one direction and Master Warden James from another.

"Gaeten! James! I am surely glad you both are here. And Ethan!" Duncan went over and hugged his son. "James, could you please have some Watchers escort Ethan to a secure location — either my residence or perhaps the Watchers Compound?"

"Father, can't I stay?"

"No, not until I understand a few things better."

"Alright — but I really want to hear all about it!"

"Oh, I have a feeling you will be in the middle of it all!"

Ethan left with two senior Watchers. The rest crowded around a small table as Duncan opened the book to the passage he was seeking, save two who stood watch at the entrance to the room.

"I may have been overly hasty in calling the Alert, James. But as the concert was ending I felt a stirring in me, and a memory of parts of this prophecy reverberated in my mind. Things started connecting … the latest update on the Dominion and this new singer, and then when I saw Ethan gone even more came together. Gentlemen, I think we are entering a time of the fulfillment of some of the last prophecies made by the school of prophets."

Another person came up to the table, having been vetted by the Watcher guards that were now here in force. "Uh, good evening gentlemen, Chancellor Duncan. I am Master theologian Mordecai. How can I be of help?"

"Let me get to the passage." Duncan flipped through the pages rapidly, oblivious to the concerned glances and sighs from the curator. "Here".

Dark days will come to my people, as an enemy arises with fear in its wings. They will set themselves against my chosen people and against My name. In those days I will pour out my Spirit on my people, and once again the old men will dream dreams and the young see visions. If you will listen again to my words, if you will not neglect the ways of your fathers, I will save you with my mighty hand and all the world will know that you are mine. And I will raise up a worshiper who will stir my people to renew their hearts toward me and my only begotten Son, one with a voice like an angel — but will anyone listen? I will bring my wind-runner, but will anyone see? I do not choose my messengers as would the world. I choose my own vessels, and out of weakness I will be made strong, so the world will know it is by my power that I save.

In those days the darkness will come against my chosen vessels, their enemy will try to strike fear in the hearts of my people. Yet the arrow will not pierce, the sword will not strike until My glory is shown. The darkness will try to kill, try to take, try to behead my people, but they will not prevail. Yet still they will not stop, they will not repent; they will come against my people with might, they will gather their strength to come against my people on mountains of the sea. But without seeing my people will know, though scattered they will hear, and with my provisions they will prepare. The darkness will crash against my people; will send their tendrils within and their force without. And if my people listen to my words and trust upon my gifts they will not fear, and their enemy will not prevail but be crushed. Instead of piercing they will be pierced by their own swords, out of the darkness will come my light. The world will see and hear, and rejoice in my deliverance.'

Duncan stopped reading aloud. He looked over at Master Mordecai.

"Well, sir, this passage has had many interpretations over the years, and many feel it was meant as a figurative interpretation of the founder's voyage through the dark dangers of the storm, driven like a runner before the wind. But their singing overcame their fear and they found themselves cast ashore on the beach of Freelandia after passing through the mountain cliffs of the sea and into Freelandia Bay." A barely suppressed chortle was coughed out by the curator, whose eyes were rolling upwards.

Duncan looked at the theologian with exasperation. "So you are saying this was just 'figurative speech' of events that had already happened?"

"Chancellor Duncan, you must know that the latest research on prophecy holds that most was actually written after the supposed events, with figurative and poetic language that disguises the meaning enough so that it can sound like it may be speaking of events in some possible far future. This passage in particular was written by a largely discredited semi-hermit who lived about a hundred years after the founding of Freelandia, yet he uses phrases that clearly are very thinly disguised as being borrowed from the mythology of the founder's voyage."

Gaetan blew out a loud snort. "And, pray tell, this is what is being taught at the School of Theology?"

"Well, of course! Over the last several decades we have thoroughly dissected this and all of the other so-called prophecies in these volumes. Our best minds have analyzed the text, delved into the nuances of the older dialects to understand the real meanings of the words they used, cross referenced the allusions to discover the sources they borrowed from, and have even constructed biographical sketches of most of the authors. You must know that not a single one had any formal education or university degrees — can you imagine trying to claim some sort of literary authority by, well, uneducated unknowns? And we have found that most were highly, shall we say, shady characters — one might even say 'kooks' who at times acted and lived very strangely. Of course, they all to a person claimed they were doing what their so-called God told them to." He laughed dryly. "We in academia don't fall for that crutch — we need far better proof than a 'God told me so.'"

Master Warden James's eyes were wide in astonishment, but he held his tongue. Gaeten was not so reserved. "WHAT?" He was about to launch what likely would have been a lengthy diatribe when Duncan cut him off.

"I see. Thank you Master Mordecai, you have been very … enlightening. I had no idea that much … analytical research … had occurred regarding these prophecies."

Master Mordecai puffed out his chest in pride. "No problem, Chancellor. Now, is there anything else I or my esteemed and learned fellow academics can do for you?"

While Gaeten sputtered and the curator beamed, Duncan nodded thoughtfully. "Yes, I think there actually is. I may need additional help with some interpretations. I have found some people … well … some seem to have rather active imaginations with regards to these old writings."

Mordecai preened himself even further. "Oh my, yes. Some — if you would believe it — try to make the softer-brained uneducated crowds think that they should … believe that these writings are somehow true. They beguile the low-brows into churches, where they can fill their untrained heads with stories and myths and promises of either eternal bliss or everlasting damnation, all the time mainly working to fleece them of the few coins they can make at their labor."

"Yes, yes … I have heard of that myself." Duncan gave a somewhat strained smile. "You can help me, Master Mordecai — perhaps even help all of Freelandia. I am appointing you to form a commission of sorts to look into this … problem. I would like this to be a very, very thorough commission, to include all of the … academics … that you find have a similar view to yours. I'd like you to first prepare a complete list of who should be on this commission. But be very careful! I do not want anyone to slip in who might be of that other … persuasion say we say?"

"Oh very good, Chancellor! And I must add, you seem to be far more intellectual than many of my peers have thought. They will be so very pleased to hear of your true stand. Now I, of course, have always thought that your public statements were largely worded to please the masses, to gently guide them toward the greater truth. So many people have to be herded about like sheep; they really have no training in how to discern fact from fiction. It is a wonder how they survive at all. I suppose most wouldn't, if it were not for the gentle guiding of the enlightened intellectuals like us."

"See that you do. I want a draft of the list in, say, two weeks. I very much want to know who I can really trust to know the real truth." The last was said with a wry smile playing over his face. Turning to the curator, Duncan continued. "I am sure you, sir, would be on that special list!" The curator beamed with pleasure at the distinction. "Now, from you I want an exact copy of this prophecy to my office by morning — I fear there are some that may soon try to use this passage out of its purely ancient literature context and I need to prepare ways to combat incorrect and potentially dangerous use. I want you personally to prepare this, someone I can trust to exactly copy it with literal accuracy and without concern of injecting any personal bias into the work. That is, if you think you can do this very important task, and in secret so as not to arouse any suspicions from the 'commoners'?"

The curator nearly stumbled over himself as he pushed his way forward to gently lift the volume. "Oh yes, Chancellor. You really had me going for a moment there at the start! I suppose you were actually testing me?" Duncan just smiled. "Of course! I should have recognized that immediately! Yes, I will personally prepare a precise copy for you, even if it takes all night. I will not sleep until it is accomplished to my very high standards — and no one else need know about it." He glanced around the room. "Does this project need special security? I mean, you did come here with quite the protective detail."

"Oh yes, this is Top Secret work, no doubt. I don't think we will need to leave you a Watcher though … that might cause too much attention … what do you think?"

"Hmm. I think you are right, Chancellor. That could jeopardize the secrecy. Far too many of the younger staff even here seem to be at least somewhat, well, religious." The curator almost spat out that word as though it was a particularly egregious derogatory description.

"Really? That surprises me, given the strength of your convictions."

"Yes, it is sad, really. It is so very hard to get good and proper help these days. It seems many of the younger crowd have been getting more religious lately … we really must look into our schooling and training system."

"That is an excellent idea, Master Curator! Perhaps we should reexamine what is being taught to our young people. We would not want to lose the next generation to dangerously wrong and incomplete instruction."

The curator was positively glowing now. "I will get right on it!"

"I'm counting on you to" Duncan said gravely, though inside he was ready to laugh out loud. Then he motioned for his retinue to exit. Once they were clearly out of earshot he continued to Gaeten and James. "I want to call a meeting of the High Council in three days hence — that should be time enough to convene."

Gaeten was barely holding his thoughts in. "Duncan — did you hear? Well of course you did, you called us all in. That bit about the darkness — surely that refers to the Dominion. And the wind-runner — who could that be other than Ethan? But the worshiper … that could be … that must be MARIA!"

"Who is Maria?"

Gaeten explained as they walked over to the Council chambers. "You heard her — could she be the worshiper mentioned?"

"That is entirely possible, and what I concluded after the concert. I have never felt so stirred in my spirit by such singing. It was as though God was hovering right there in the theater, just out of physical sight, ministering to our souls. And I agree, the wind-runner would certainly seem to fit with Ethan. But other things don't seem to have fallen in place yet." Duncan thought for a few seconds. "But if this prophecy is indeed being fulfilled now, then that means the Dominion is surely preparing to come against us — and soon. We have been suspecting that for awhile, but we have no solid proof, and we do not know the extent of their preparations nor their anticipated timing. We will need to discuss this all with the High Council, behind well closed doors. James, our best strategists have worked on the protection of Freelandia for centuries — how recent was the last full review and update of our defenses?"

"It is due, it has been many years. We continue to drill, but there has not been a really serious overview in too long — and no real strategic updates for several decades. I think we have become complacent."

"Time to change that James. We will need Council approval, but I think you can get a draft review prepared for the meeting — right?"

"Yes sir, I will get right on it. And I am immediately placing two senior Watchers on duty to be with you at all times."

"Oh, I don't think I am in any particular danger!"

"I don't like that part of the prophecy that talked about 'beheading my people'. It is my duty as Master Warden to ensure your protection — and I will take nothing short of a full Council decision to change my mind!"

"Alright, James — I will not push it … for now. Go ahead, get started. We need a decent review in just a few days." As James left, Duncan addressed another key issue. "The thing we really do not have is solid information on the Dominion or its intentions toward us. Gaeten, your thoughts?"

"I have just been thinking about that. We should enact the Watcher's Eyes." That was an old plan that had never been used. Freelandia had sent out hundreds, maybe thousands of military advisors and highly talented guards to many friendly countries, kingdoms and individual people. They technically were under lease — money was sent to the Watcher Compound here in Freelandia, where in turn it was disbursed back out to the various Watchers all over the world as wages. It was thought this would encourage stronger ties to Freelandia, and it also provided a network of highly trained operatives in many scattered locations. These Watchers regularly sent reports back, but under this plan they could also report on special topics of interest when called on. They could effectively become a network of eyes and ears whose first loyalty was to Freelandia.

"I was rather wondering if that was part of the "though scattered they will hear" part of the prophecy." Gaeten paused. "And I am thinking about something else too, but I want to check out some details before discussing it."

"Alright old friend. But now I think we should all work on getting some sleep — except perhaps for the museum curator!"

"Oh Duncan — that was brilliant work on your part! I would have been much more ... direct! But now you have that other peacock theologian collating an entire list of people who probably should have been cleared out long ago!"

"Now Gaeten, we don't force people to believe, nor is that a requirement for working or living in Freelandia. But you are correct — if this lack of belief, this lack of faith is rampant in some of our academies we need to root it out. We cannot allow our youth to be indoctrinated in unbelief! We have been woefully ignorant about what heresy was creeping in, and we have to put a stop to it being spread by those who are in positions of authority, as though such rubbish were condoned by the Council. We ..." Duncan's voice dropped and he stopped walking. "We must first repent. The fault is as much ours for not keeping a better eye on things."

With that the two men dropped to their knees in earnest prayer.

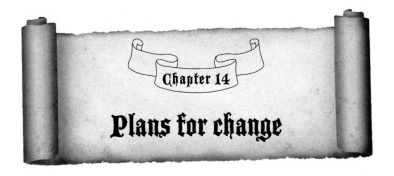

Chapter 14

Plans for change

aria was floating on something incredibly soft. She slowly drifted up from sleep, not understanding what she could be atop of. Her fingers splayed out and she realized it was a bed — a big fluffy bed softer than anything she had ever experienced before. And her head was on what must have been a real feather pillow! She had heard of those, but had never had anything more than a rolled up towel or relatively hard pillow for her head. Even though Gaeten's apartment was luxurious by the standards of the orphanage, it was still very utilitarian. Was she in heaven? That thought wandered about her sleepy mind for a few minutes, but then she felt the dull ache from the back of her head and she knew her location must be much more terrestrial. But if not heaven, then where was she? She could hear very little, even with her keen ears.

Maria pushed back covers — my, were they nice! — and swung her feet to the floor. It was cool and very smooth, not the rough bare wood of Gaeten's apartment. For a moment she panicked, reaching wildly to feel around the bed. She discovered a small table close by, on which was her whistle for Sasha. She clutched that tightly, her only reminder so far in this strange room of her past reality.

As she more fully woke up, she did hear something — the regular deep breathing of someone sleeping. It reminded her of being back at the orphanage and she wondered how the others were doing. Her head ached, and she gingerly felt bandages covering the back of her head. What had happened?

Then it all rushed back: the concert, Sir Reginaldo, the song, his faltering voice, her immense effort to keep going, to make it a glorious offering to God. She recalled the finale and then … falling … she cried out at the sharp memory which ended in blackness. The breathing across the room abruptly changed. "Maria?"

She recognized Kory's voice and in a relieved voice answered "Oh, Kory! I'm sorry if I woke you … I just remembered finishing the song and falling … Where are we?"

"We are in the main building of the Ministry of Healing, in a recovery room I think they called it. You had a nasty fall. Grand Master Healer Mesha checked you over, and Nurse Abigail cleaned you up and bandaged your head. She said I was to get her immediately whenever you woke up." Maria heard Kory get up and take a few tentative steps, then she seemed to stumble. "It is really dark in here!" Kory felt her way gingerly across the room. Maria smiled — for her it was always dark, though it did not bother her at all. God had given her other abilities to compensate. Maria lay back down on the incredibly luxurious pillow. It was amazingly soft. She closed her eyes to revel in the sensation.

A door nearly silently swung open, and now Maria could hear distant noises of people moving and talking in hushed tones. Kory was gone for a few minutes and then returned to stand just outside the door, with a second set of nearly silent footsteps following closely.

"Hello Maria! I am Nurse Abigail, and you are in the personal recovery rooms of Grand Master Healer Mesha — but I presume Kory already told you that. Kory, could you please open the window drapes? I want to take a look at the bandages."

Kory began working on something over on the far wall, and seemed to be having trouble with it. Nurse Abigail tsked softly and addressed Maria again. "And how do we feel this morning dear?"

Maria smiled. How many times had she ever had someone really ask how she was doing, especially the first thing when she woke up?

She turned toward the sound of the voice and sat up. "I am ok, I guess. I don't recall what happened very well."

"Well now, that part is not all that important. It seems you had a rather hard knock on your head, but the wound was only slight."

"Kory, do you need help with those drapes?"

Maria tracked their voices. "Do either of you know what happened at the concert … after the last song?"

Kory and Abigail finally loosened the stuck drapes and Kory threw them open in a rush.

Maria gasped and in her weakened state, she fainted.

At a considerable distance from any village, down a long abandoned trail an old dilapidated shack stood which once was used by lumberjacks when this area had been logged of its large pines. Now the area was densely overgrown with saplings and other trees, nearly impassable for anything but small animals and deer. There was nothing special about the shack, nothing to indicate from the exterior that anyone had been near it in decades. Yet exterior looks could belie what might happen inside.

Three men sat around a rough hewn table. They were large, with darkly tanned skin and thick arm muscles befitting their token profession of lumber men. They even had large axes and other tools of that trade, and indeed could use them proficiently. The leader had a scar alongside his cheek, dark eyes and a very unpleasant smile. Murdrock spoke "We will have to be more careful, now that those blasted Watchers have stepped up their patrols in this area. That fool Harden was too greedy."

Another spoke. "Will this set back our schedule?"

"Only slightly. The time is becoming ripe for our first action, which should strike fear in the populace and cause chaos in their High Council." He chuckled evilly. "Without a leader they will surely fall into confused bickering that will derail any cohesive actions for months … and by then in will be too late."

"When will we be ready to strike?"

"The rest of the team is coming over the next two weeks, no more than a single man per any given ship. There is a need up north for skilled woodsmen and lumbermen, and our people will come in as we did, laborers looking for good jobs. When they arrive, we will prepare for the first strike. We have a contact within the Keep who will set up supplies and any preparations needed there. All that really remains will be an appropriate venue, a good opportunity. Meanwhile, we need to check on how our other cells are doing, and make sure there are no more like Harden. The loss of every Rat cost us the time and money it took to recruit and train them. We don't want to lose the other groups, and we are about to start more intense training sessions. There is not a lot of time left. We have many plans for our indigenous recruits!"

The other man now spoke up. "I learned that the Rats that were not killed outright were taken to the prison in Chesterfield, about 10 miles from here."

Murdrock grimaced. "We may want to break them out. Harden was a fool, but he had recruited a few men with potential. I don't want to lose them. And we could use the others too. Also, anyone wanted by the Watchers will be more desperate to please us."

"I also heard that there was one other of Harden's Rats, not in the prison"

"What! A traitor who betrayed his brothers? I was told the Watchers captured or killed everyone!"

"That I do not know, but apparently one was not at the Nest when it was attacked, though supposedly two of this brothers were, and neither survived. However, he was gravely wounded by the Watchers the next day, so if he was a traitor he was justly repaid for it. I hear he is at a healer in Chesterfield, under light guard. He is nearly healed enough to be dismissed, and is supposed to be delivered to the prison immediately."

"Hmm. Not likely a traitor then. His two brothers were killed you say? He must have a great deal of hatred for the Watchers, and therefore for the Freelandian High Council. He sounds like a good candidate to ... expropriate. What is his name?"

"I heard it was ... Jarl."

Grand Master Vitario was really beside himself. He had scouts all over the Keep, and the only thing he knew was that The Singer — Maria — had been taken to the Ministry of Healing, but it seemed no one knew where she had gone from there. And that gruff old Watcher Gaeten was also missing, though it was reported that he might be at the High Council chambers. For some reason there seemed to be a great deal of fuss going on around that place this morning. The young apprentice Kory had been identified, but her bed had not been slept in last night. He had wanted to ask the Watchers to check on that, but they too were in a flurry of activity — some sort of Alert had gone out last night for an unknown reason. And then there was Reginaldo. The man was ... was ... was just not himself! He actually had toured one of the Academy buildings, introducing himself to several classes to listen and compliment many on their skills. That was NOT like the Reginaldo he knew, not one little bit. Vitario wondered if he were ill.

Master Warden James was nothing if he was not thorough. He had assigned a dozen of his best inspectors to the task of setting up a complete review, audit and analysis of both the defenses of the Keep and of Freelandia itself. He had made it known in no uncertain terms that this was not a random drill and that they essentially had an unlimited budget and could appropriate any Watchers needed to complete the task … in ten days. That had met with huge resistance. James knew it was too short to do a really thorough check, but he demanded the best possible results. He also sent an urgent message to the Defense Ministry to gather their section heads for an emergency meeting later that afternoon. He had further sent out riders to every District in Freelandia, to get an assessment of the conditions in each. Finally, he called a meeting of all the Master Watchers for that evening. If the Dominion was planning to come against Freelandia, they would NOT find them unprepared!

Gaeten was sitting in the chapel of the High Council. He had been there now for several hours, praying. The Council Chaplain Mikael had watched him for awhile, noticing that Gaeten was struggling with something, seemingly struggling with God himself.

"Gaeten, my friend, my fellow servant of the Most High God … what is troubling you?"

"Mikael, I am torn between two good things, two good choices. I see benefits to both and am not sure which I should do."

"Ah, my friend … that is a somewhat common situation to be in!"

"Yes, but the stakes are quite high. It is one of the most important choices I have been faced with in many years."

"Hmm … and so you were seeking God's guidance?"

"Yes, but I just don't seem to be getting an answer. Usually when I take such things to God in prayer I can tell what He wants, He stirs my heart and mind in a way that I know what I am supposed to do. But this time … God is strangely silent."

Mikael frowned. Gaeten had always been quite sensitive to God's leadings in the past. Then he asked "Gaeten, God sometimes doesn't give an answer in the timeframe we expect. Or … there could be another reason."

"Huh? What are you getting at?"

"Sometimes God does not answer ... because you already know the right answer, but you really want something different. Let me ask you a question: is one of the answers doing something that is mainly for you — for what you really want?"

"Well ... it really would help out Maria — my ward. I think it would be best for her ..."

"Or would it really be best for *you*, my friend?"

Gaeten sagged. "You have a great gift of knowing what to ask, Mikael. It can be most annoying at times!" The last was said with a wry chuckle. "You seem particularly adept at not telling someone an answer, but leading them to the right question."

It was Mikael's turn to chuckle. "And you, my dear friend, seem particularly adept at knowing things even without seeing them."

Gaeten suddenly stopped short. "Say that again?"

Gaeten's mind was whirling, going down multiple pathways all at once. And yet one pathway in particular, one course of action seemed clear. He had his answer, and God had confirmed it several hundred years ago. Now he had to get back to Maria; he did not think he had much time to spare!

One of the Academy apprentices Vitario had sent back to the Ministry of Healing came crashing into his office. Vitario looked up in surprise. The lad panted out "Grand .... Master ....Vitario" between gulps of air, "the receptionist who was at the lobby last night ... she just came back on duty ... she said a young girl came in ... with a Grand Master Watcher and several others ... and that Grand Master Mesha had taken her up to his personal care rooms on the third floor. She — the receptionist — had heard the girl was still up there recovering, but that she may be doing better. The receptionist said if that was the case, the girl could be released anytime now!"

"Great God Almighty! I must go to her at once!" Vitario leapt up and nearly ran into Reginaldo who was just entering the room.

"Archibald, I think we have found her — come on!" The two men raced down the hall and out the nearest exit. For such a rotund man, Reginaldo could move quite quickly when he had a mind for it.

A runner found Master Warden James. "Sir! I have a message from Grand Master Gaeten!"

"Go ahead, out with it. I have a great deal to do!"

"Sir, he said you would know what this meant, and he made me repeat it twice to get it correct: 'James, God has just shown me my place in the prophecy. I must hurry, but I will first see Maria with Meshaken. Come as soon as you are able."

James stopped what he was doing, eyes rather wide. Gaeten? In the prophecy? And in a hurry? What did that have to do with Maria? He knew Maria was in Grand Master Mesha's personal rooms, the Master Watcher he had sent had finally figured that out. This must be MIGHTY important. James was extremely busy, but this sounded like something he needed to know personally, perhaps immediately. Without further thought he grabbed the nearest horse and galloped off toward the Ministry of Healing buildings.

Meshaken was hurrying himself. He was in the far end of the building when word came that his special patient Maria had collapsed again. She had seemed to be doing quite well when he last checked on her while she slept. What could have gone wrong?

Maria heard voices calling her name. It took her a few minutes to recognize them as Kory and Nurse Abigail. At first they sounded like they were coming from quite a distance away, but then they gradually seemed to be getting closer. There was concern in their voices. They seemed to be asking her something. She struggled, trying to move toward them. Then she woke up more fully. She was trying to get to the voices, and she actually sat bolt upright in bed even as the last strands of sleep brushed off her face. She opened her eyes, and immediately cried out loudly.

Gaeten was half way up the stairs toward the third floor and Maria's room when he heard her loud cry. His face went pale as memories of a few weeks past stabbed into his mind. He was not sure his feet even touched the steps of the last flight of stairs.

Grand Master Mesha heard the cry too, as he walked up the long hallway that led to his office and the private rooms nearby. He picked up his pace to a run.

Vitario and Reginaldo were just entering the lobby when they heard the cry from the open window above. Highly concerned, they raced on, Vitario in the lead. He had been to Meshaken's office before and knew the way. They started up the stairs in quick bounds even as Master Warden James pulled up his horse and dismounted. He had not heard the cry, and so did not rush in, but even so his tall body ate up distance quickly even in a normal stride.

Abigail was very concerned. "Maria! What's wrong? Maybe you had better lie back down." She was trying to ease Maria backwards, almost pushing her sleepily resisting body when Gaeten burst into the room.

Gaeten's memory was superb about locations. He remembered the number of steps from the stairs to the room, and knew the distance to Maria's bed from when he had come very early that morning to check on her and had been shown to her private room. As he entered the room he could discern the breathing of three people. One was Maria on the bed, another was Kory, off to one side and a few paces away. The third was from someone much larger, an adult, who was standing right next to, probably even over Maria. He had no idea what was happening, but he could sense considerable tension in the room. In a leap he was to the bed, arms sweeping out to block any moves against either himself or his ward. He did not swing his arms hard, but he was moving very fast. One hand connected with Abigail's shoulder and sent her spinning backward away from Maria.

"Maria!"

"Gaeten! I am so glad you're here! But you seem to be in a rush — what's wrong?"

That caught him completely by surprise. He was just re-configuring his thoughts when Nurse Abigail spun back.

She was NOT used to being pushed around, figuratively nor literally. "And just who are you? What are you doing here?" She paused a moment, "Get AWAY from my patient!"

Gaeten had just calmed himself with the knowledge that Maria was ok — her voice was calm and normal, she was obviously just fine. But the woman was ordering HIM away from Maria? He bristled and was about to loudly retort ... and get rather physical if necessary ... when Mesha's voice thundered out "GAETEN!"

Mesha had observed Gaeten stiffen up at Nurse Abigail's words and saw he was gearing himself up for a response. He knew it would not have been pleasant or gentle. As a healer, he usually spoke very gently. However, he could put a Master Watcher to shame with the authority he could put into his voice when he wanted to.

Gaeten caught hold of himself again and began to back down. At that moment Vitario and Reginaldo burst into the room. Reginaldo was normally a rather high strung person, and the rapid run and race up the stairs had stressed him considerably. He had been nearly constantly replaying Maria's Masterpiece rendition in his mind ever since the concert and not being able to find her had made him especially agitated. "MARIA!" When Sir Reginaldo bellowed, it was really something spectacular to hear, especially in a small room which had become quite crowded with tense people.

It was all too much. Everyone started yelling at once, even Kory seemed to join in. For Maria it was quite frightening. She edged backwards on her bed as far as she could go as the tension escalated higher. What could she do to stop all this? She remembered when she was last very frightened, and reached around to find the bed stand. On it was the whistle. She blew it hard, though even Gaeten did not seem hear it amidst the tumultuous quarrel that was erupting in the room.

Sasha must not have been too far away, for almost immediately Maria heard flapping noises from outside, and then a very loud screeching squawk as the great bird landed at the open window and voiced its disapproval of the commotion happening inside the small room. That screech got everyone's immediate attention. Into the startled silence that followed, Master Warden James came to the door. He had heard the ruckus coming up the stairs, and was appreciative of the momentary quiet after Gaeten's Sasha cried out.

James took charge, which was also something he was very good at. "Alright! Everyone! Quiet!" His voice boomed out and everyone was indeed quiet for a moment. James glanced around and assessed that Grand Master Mesha had priority — this was after all his private hospital rooms "Mesha, what would you like to do?"

"I and my nurse need to look Maria over — in private."

James nodded. "Everyone, out into the hallway."

Gaeten frowned deeply, but nevertheless made a few cooing noises that seemed to satisfy the gryph, who settled down on the window sill and began to preen herself, oblivious now to everyone in the room. Then he followed the others as they retreated out of the room. In just a few minutes Mesha and Abigail exited. "She is doing very well, even unexpectedly well. I really do not want to overtire her though. Gaeten, she is asking for you."

As Mesha turned to go, Vitario spoke up "Perhaps we can have a few words with you, Mesha?" He nodded and led Vitario and Reginaldo to his office. When they had walked the few steps and entered, Vitario continued. "Mesha, when will she be fully recovered … how long before you will release her?"

"Well, she is doing quite well, but she is still very weak. I want her to get total rest for several more days, and then only mild activities for several more weeks."

Reginaldo deflated. He had hoped to ask Maria if she would consider traveling with him. But if this Master Healer said she needed rest, then he would not try to pressure that to change. He certainly could not be her nursemaid, and his next concert required him to be on a ship heading south within two days. Maybe that would be for the best anyway — he could hype up the mystery of the Masterpiece Duet for several more months, then return to see if Maria was available for a world tour.

Vitario had another question. "And what about her voice? Mesha, you should have heard her sing … I have never heard the likes of it before."

"Her voice? I really do not know, but there should be no issues there. The bump on her head did not affect … that. I understand she is Gaeten's ward. But if she can sing as you say, I presume you will want her into your Academy?"

"Yes, of course, if that is possible … as soon as that is possible."

"You may want to work that topic up slowly — I doubt Gaeten will be all that open to her leaving him at the Watcher Compound."

Back in Maria's room, Gaeten was awkwardly holding an exuberant Maria. "Gaeten! When they opened the window drapes … I could 'see' the light — well, at least I could kind of sense it!"

"Maria! That is … that is absolutely wonderful! I am so very happy for you — and thankful to God. That in a way makes what I need to tell you easier."

Maria quieted down immediately. "What do you need to tell me? You sound so serious!"

"Maria, I was so very proud of you as you sang. It filled my heart with wonder and awe. I have been told that everyone who heard you is giving glory to God. That gift should not be hidden or bottled up within the Watcher Compound. God gives those gifts to share, and to be nourished and grown. I want you to be the best you can possibly be — but I do not have the skills to do that. Maria, you are not a Watcher — you are a Singer!

Secondly, it appears difficult times are coming upon Freelandia. An enemy is gathering strength, and we believe we are living out the time spoken of in prophecy. I believe God has shown me a role I am to play. Maria, it will require me to leave Freelandia for a time, at least several months but it could be longer. I do not want to leave you, and I will ensure you are well cared for. If nothing else, you can stay in my apartment, and I can leave you all the money I have. But I must leave — it is a duty to Freelandia, and I believe it is what God has planned for me."

Maria was silently quivering at the totally unexpected news. "But … but who will help me? I can now see a bit of light, but I am still blind. I hardly know anyone else in the whole Keep! And …" she began to sob quietly, "I don't know what I would do without you."

"I think perhaps I can help with some of that." Vitario had entered the room. "Grand Master Gaeten, Maria … I would like to make you both an offer. I would like to take Maria on as my ward. She would be both my apprentice — really an Academy apprentice — and also my junior assistant. As my assistant she would earn an income, and I would provide both a place for her to live and a helper … I am thinking perhaps Kory might fill that role nicely.

Maria, as an Academy apprentice you would get training in all forms of music, and in your case specialized training in singing. You have a very special gift from God, Maria. I want you to be able to enhance that, and provide many more opportunities for its use, to bring the greatest praise and glory to God.

We can start this as soon as you would like — I will make all of the arrangements today if you agree."

Gaeten offered up a prayer of thanksgiving at how God had orchestrated all of this. "Thank you Master Vitario. I would be highly relieved to know Maria was so well cared for … she is incredibly special to me. Maria — what do you think?"

"It is all so much to grasp, so much change! But I do want to be an Academy apprentice, I think. And Kory has been very nice to me ever since we started preparing for the concert. Gaeten, how soon do you need to leave?"

"Very soon, Maria, within a day or two anyway. You may well need to stay here a few more days to recover fully. By that time we should be able to have all the transition details covered. I need to make arrangements now, so I will leave you to rest. I promise you not to leave Freelandia without saying goodbye."

Maria sniffed back her tears, but was not totally successful. She turned toward the voice of Grand Master Vitario. "I … I think I would like what you are offering, sir. But … could I still occasionally go to the Watcher Compound to visit with Suevey? She is my only other real friend. And … I have been occasionally visiting several of the orphans that also came from Westhaven — will I still be able to see them now and then?"

Vitario chuckled. "Yes, of course Maria! You will have as much freedom to see others as you want! I would be very pleased to take you on as my own personal ward. But I also meant what I said — you have an incredible gift from God, and I expect that to be nourished and worked on to bring it to its fullest bloom. That will entail hard work on your part, believe me."

"Oh, I am not afraid of hard work, sir. I guess I am rather used to that." Maria turned and found Gaeten's hand. She traced it up and as he bent over she framed his rough face with her soft and tiny hands. He reached up and very gently traced his fingers over her face.

"Don't worry little one. I will not forget you — ever. And I promise you what by God's will and power I will return to be with you again."

Sasha had been rather quiet, not knowing why she was called. She had finished her preening and was now impatient not to have received any attention. She let out a string of insistent clucks and coos, bobbing her head up and down rapidly and bouncing back and forth on her massive legs.

Maria turned toward the sound and responded with a quite good facsimile of the gryph's vocalizations. Sasha bobbed a few more times, but seemed satisfied and settled on the window sill, watching them all with great avian intensity.

Vitario looked on in astonishment. "Uh … can someone explain what this … bird … is doing here?"

Chapter 15

New duties

Sir Archibald Reginaldo strolled into Grand Master Vitario's office. "So, I hear that Maria is coming to your Academy?" It was said more as a statement than a question. "Now don't you go ruining that pure voice with all your voice lessons and fanciness! She has more raw talent than anyone I have ever met."

Vitario was not about to be baited. He was in a rather good mood, all in all. "A raw diamond, no matter how large, is only a pretty rock until it is sculpted and polished. I have no intention of ruining anything ... but I've every intention of fine tuning and channeling that talent, of buffing and polishing until it is the very best it can be!" Vitario had grown agitated, his eyes burning bright. "Just think of what it might yet be, Archibald, with further training? And ..." he paused suddenly, a far-away look glazing over his eyes for a moment. "Yes, Lord ... yes."

Reginaldo looked at his friend quizzically. Vitario was the best music trainer he knew, and an excellent musician in his own right. He was also a man of God, who seemed particularly tuned to God, as though when God's voice spoke, Vitario's heart vibrated in resonance. Reginaldo had seen that look on Vitario's face before. "What is it, my friend?" he asked softly.

"Reginaldo, I have just seen ... I am not sure what it was exactly ... I was looking down from above and saw Maria was leading ... she was leading a procession of musicians. They were all playing instruments and were worshiping. Then I turned and looked to where she was going. Archibald! There was an army facing her — she was heading directly for them! I tried to yell and warn her, she surely could not see them — she is blind after all, how could she know — but she could not hear me. The enemy was in darkness, like a great black shadow spread out over ... Freelandia! It was over a part of Freelandia! Yet where she was a bright light was shining, and it was like they were pushing back the blackness." Vitario was shaking, and his eyes were still glazed. He shook his head a few times. "I am not a dream interpreter, Archibald, but certainly God has some special purpose for that little girl! I want her to get started as soon as possible!

Reginaldo pondered this. It made him even surer of his decision. "Vitario, I leave tomorrow morning on a ship to Moldavitor."

"Moldavitor! But that is Dominion controlled! Archibald — are you sure it is safe?"

"Well, the ship has several stops along the way, and I don't intend to announce my prior itinerary. I have several concerts planned all within Dominion controlled areas. They have promised my safety, and I suspect they will keep that promise — they want to show to the world that they remain "civilized" and no one else need worry about their intentions. Of course, no one believes that part, but regardless, they pay well. And who knows, I may pick up a tidbit of conversation here or there as I schmooze it up with their uppity ups and such." Reginaldo snickered knowingly. "And if later, at some other stop I happen to meet some Watcher or another, who knows what might spill out? Even so, there always is some level of danger traveling to the Dominion territory. That brings me to my main point of this visit."

Reginaldo removed a large pouch from a carry bag he had draped over a shoulder of the rather plain coat he was wearing. He opened it and poured out its contents — gems, gold coins, a wide assortment of jewelry, a treasure easily worth the fortune of a nobleman's estate. Vitario's eyes went wide. "And there is more. I have several large bank accounts here in Freelandia — you do realize that Freelandia's

banks are considered the safest in the world? Here are documents I prepared this morning at each of them." Reginaldo pushed several sealed documents over to Vitario. He watched with amusement as the Grand Master spread out the greatest wealth he had likely ever seen in his lifetime.

"But Archibald! I don't understand. I am sure I saw you wearing many of these at the concert! What do you want me to do with this trove?"

"Vitario, my friend — my very trusted friend! I replaced them with costume glass jewelry — from any distance you really cannot tell anyway. I do need to maintain my stage presence! These are for Maria. And the documents give her full co-ownership of the bank accounts — a very sizable sum spread out between several of your most prominent banks. I am putting them into your custodial care, with copies at the banks and with my lawyers. I hear she is now your ward … and now you have a stewardship role as well. Use it however you need to, but only for Maria. And by all means, don't spoil her!" He pointed a long finger into Vitario's face. "Don't you dare let her get uppity! It would be best, I think, for her not to know about all of this, not for quite some time. Protect her innocence, her sweetness! I will hold you personally responsible!"

Grand Master Vitario sat back, stunned. "Archibald … are you sure? This is a fortune! She could buy a sizeable estate … several estates I think. What should I do with this?"

"Now don't go buying her a villa or gaudy things … though she desperately needs a full and complete new wardrobe! Use the bank accounts for what you need. Keep the jewelry for now; you could store it at a bank if you want. Let her use some of it now and then, maybe? Make sure you pay her bills at the Ministry of Healing too. And … even that gruff old Gaeten — see if she owes him anything. She is a very, very special young lady. And I am …" A tear trickled out. "I have become very fond of her."

Vitario smiled. "She does seem to have that way with us, doesn't she? I am becoming quite fond of her too. If this is what you want, Archibald, then yes, I will accept the responsibility. But two things first: One, it is my decision on what to spend — no letters from you showing up telling me to do this or that. If I am her guardian, then I need full control of the money until I deem she is of age to take it on herself. Second, and even more important — Maria will not owe you anything — she will not have to pay you back, and you may NEVER use this to exert control or influence over her."

Reginaldo was aghast. "Never, Vitario — of course I would not do that! And yes, you have total control over the finances. I am not much of a money manager anyway. Now, one thing more for you — don't tell her who her benefactor is. It would ruin our budding friendship, she would never treat me the same again."

"Done! You are very generous, Archibald. She must have really affected you."

"Maybe, Vitario — or maybe it was not Maria. Maybe it was that for the first time I can remember I felt actually close to God, and that He was close to me. I have amassed great wealth, and have typically only spent it on myself. I think that should change. Oh — and come to think of it, let her pick a charity or two if she wants to support something. It would be good for her to be able to help others in that way."

Grand Master Vitario pondered that for a second. "Well, Maria did mention she visits some other orphans that came to the Keep about the same time as she did. I could look into their status as well."

"Excellent idea! Maybe even an orphanage in her name? Well, I guess she would not really want it named after her, now would she?" Reginaldo stood. "I have a few other things to wrap up before I leave. This has been life-changing, Vitario."

Reginaldo waggled a thick finger. "Now you take care of my Maria … and of all this treasure!" He smiled broadly. "Goodbye my dear friend!" He turned to leave, paused, then turned back and embraced Vitario in a massive bear hug. Then he swiveled and walked off, leaving a somewhat bewildered Vitario who now had much more to think about.

The first was what to do with all this jewelry lying on top of his desk.

Chancellor Duncan was the busiest he had been in ages. He had sent out the call for an emergency meeting of the High Council and had hoped to present them with more than just the prophecy — though all by itself that was rather compelling. He had sent urgent requests to the head of every university, academy and ministry for an immediate assessment of activities, and had asked each to report of anything unusual too … he was not sure, but he had a feeling that if prophecy was involved, it may well be that other singular events could be occurring also. In addition, he sent for updates on the agriculture, shipping and mining — of all of the main economic activities within Freelandia. Next he asked for reports on the status of the allies of Freelandia.

Most importantly, he had asked Master Warden James on how the Watchers were doing. Freelandia had not had a standing army for nearly two centuries, though the Watchers acted like a loosely run military and could fairly rapidly reorganize into fighting units rather than the more individualistic training that was more common. Given their nearly exclusive importance and reliance on ocean travel, Freelandia did have a navy, with a fleet of vessels that guarded the main shipping routes to and from Freelandia as well as the large inland bay and harbors, and they did have an active Coastal Defense network that usually was more active in rescuing ships that had difficulty negotiating the narrow inlet that was the only entrance through the rocky outer coastline.

The navy was constituted of smaller but very fast and agile lightly armed sloops. 'Lightly armed' however was a bit of a misnomer. Compared to the warships of other countries — and especially compared to the reports he had been getting on the new Dominion ships — the Freelandian sloops seemed indeed to be more fitting for policing the inland waterways and coastal areas than for any real sea battles. Modern warships of the day were typically quite large vessels fitted with multiple large catapults and heavy arrow arbalests, and many had a formidable ram prominently on their bows. All that armament and especially the rams required a relatively massive ship to support them, and in turn large rams were often needed to punch through the thick and heavy hull construction of those kinds of ships. Conventional naval wisdom said that such small vessels would be no match against these titans of the sea, and most of the world seemed bent on creating ever larger and stronger behemoths that would be impervious to the previously best constructions of the year before.

While Freelandia had not been involved with a sea battle in over 100 years, their sloops did occasionally go up against pirate vessels that while of intermediate size compared to full warships, were still usually larger and stronger. What the Freelandian vessels lacked in size they more than made up for in agility and in somewhat unconventional tactics and weaponry. Long ago a School of Engineering had been established and well funded, and a goodly portion of their funding was always directed toward ship design and armament. Over the decades the innovations had finely honed the design, materials and construction of every portion of the sloops to make them the fastest and most maneuverable ships in the world — and some of the deadliest in battle against ships even several times their size. Innovation prospered in Freelandia across all walks of life and interests, and inventors were well esteemed and compensated for their improvements. And most importantly, it seemed that when God was given the credit as the source of the creativity and abilities, then even more ideas and advances were made.

Still, they had never gone head to head with a truly modern warship, and certainly not with a fleet of them intent on destruction. It was one thing to battle pirates, quite another contemplation to come up against a flotilla of the latest and biggest warships the Dominion might send their way. And as he pondered that, Duncan realized he had not heard of any upgrades for the Watchers or the navy out of the School of Engineering for quite some time ... he would have to question Master Warden James about that ... he could not even remember the last time James mentioned any such occurrence. It was just another item to track and manage.

As Duncan was sending out his latest list of requests, Gaeten knocked on the open outer door. "Do you have a minute you can spare?"

"For you my friend, nearly always. What is on your mind?"

"Oh, nothing much, just how I see something God wants me to be doing from the prophecy you read."

Duncan put down the paper he was glancing at. "You either have a very dry sense of humor this morning or you are about to tell me something rather important! Should I ask Lydia to come in?" Lydia was his wife, and she had a strong gift of discernment — of understanding the truthfulness of a statement or action, of knowing clearly if it was something of God or not. It was an invaluable aid to him and was one of the reasons he had been chosen by the High Council for the top administrative position within Freelandia. Well, truly they had been chosen, it was a team effort even though he held the titular title.

"I suppose that might be a good idea, though I am quite sure I know at least the 'big-picture' part of what I am to be doing is indeed from God."

Duncan pulled a small cord that hung on the wall behind him, just beside a large window overlooking a well kept flower garden. He had several cords of different colors strung on the wall there, each connected via pulleys to the offices of his top assistants and officials. A short pull would raise a small bright ribbon in the other person's office elsewhere in the building to indicate they were wanted sometime soon. A longer pull would raise a second, larger ribbon to indicate some urgency. A very hard long pull would ring a small bell, indicating their immediate presence was requested. If the person was in their office, they simply responded with a short return pull which returned the bell or ribbon to its place and in turn raised a small flag below the cord on Duncan's wall to indicate they had received and were responding to the summons. It had saved a lot of running for the errand boys and was quite a lot faster. One of the students in the School of Engineers had thought that up last year and Duncan had agreed to have it installed, and had awarded a prize for the practicality and inventiveness of the idea.

The answering flag popped up, and a few moments after Duncan had reset the cord Lydia made her entrance. Even Gaeten, though blind, thought of it as 'an entrance'. Lydia did not just walk into a room. She swept in with regal flair. This was not the pomp and haughtiness of self-imposed grandeur; rather it was a natural outcome of her serene uplifted countenance, stunning beauty, and her preference of colorful and stylish clothing that leaned toward the formal side without being pretentious or overly expensive. And somehow, even with the aura that seemed to drape around her wherever she went, Lydia always put everyone immediately at ease with her open personality and overt kindness.

"Yes, dear? Oh, Grand Master Gaeten, how nice it is to see you!" Lydia had a very pleasant voice that exuded charm and sincerity.

"And I dear lady, can only wish I could in return see you!"

Lydia giggled and swept over to give him a hug. She and Gaeten had had this routine for many years and were old friends.

"Lydia, Gaeten feels God has shown him a role he must play in the prophecy, and I thought you should hear it too." Her smile faded into a serious look, though her eyes still showed a hint of merriment.

"Yes. I have been praying over this, and it was Chaplain Mikael who actually gave me the confirmation to the role I believe I am being called to. Do you recall the part in the prophecy about 'But without seeing my people will know'? Mikael actually said something quite similar referring to me. It fit with what I had been thinking too. We need some direct intelligence about what is going on in the Dominion. Yet just about anyone we could send as a spy would almost certainly be caught — our pale skin tends to give us away in those southerly countries. Even with good make-up the chances of capture are high — and the Dominion would dearly love to know the specifics of our defenses. We need someone who can gather information, yet not be suspected — and yet if caught cannot be forced to divulge sensitive information."

Gaeten stopped for a moment. He stooped over and seemed to shrink in on himself. He shuffled a few steps over to the wall, hands outstretched to find something that might support his suddenly feeble looking old body. With a crackled, weak voice he continued "Who … would ever suspect …" he hacked out a deep, rough cough "… an old blind beggar … who wanders around the docks and back alleys … perhaps doing a few odd jobs here and there … propped up against tavern walls … to shield himself from the night cold? And if … that beggar occasionally talked … to particular passing merchant seaman … or left a coded message in a merchant captain's quarters … who would notice?"

Duncan laughed out-loud at the sudden transformation, and Lydia clapped her hands in appreciation. "Gaeten dear, you must have had some of the Music Academy's theatrical talent rub off on you during your brief visit! Few would give you a second glance."

Duncan turned pensive. "And your keen hearing would pick up quite a few conversations, and in most cities the beggar community can actually be quite well informed about comings and goings and such. But, would you really be safe? The dockyards in Dominion held lands are supposedly very rough areas indeed, and not just from Dominion soldiers. They allow considerable lawlessness, and merchants have told us of rumored magical power being deployed as well to control their territories."

"Magic, Duncan? You know there is no such thing!" Gaeten had stood again and dropped his beggar pretense.

"Yes of course, but demonic activity would appear as magic to the uninformed — and would be just as dangerous."

"No more danger than anywhere else, not with God providing the protection. I lived my life for a very long time under the principle that I am immortal up to the very second until God is finished with me here, and then I get promoted!"

That brought another laugh. "Lydia, what do you think? Is our friend Gaeten setting out on fulfilling God's will for him, or does he just want a vacation down in southern latitudes and want us to pay for it?"

Lydia smiled and closed her eyes for a moment, asking God silently for discernment of His will. It did not take long. "I believe he is right in this endeavor, and he indeed does have a place in the prophecy. I cannot say I personally like the idea, but what I like or dislike is not terribly important." She looked over to Duncan, who nodded with understanding. "Go with our blessing, Gaeten. Go with the blessing of all of Freelandia. You will be … in our prayers daily." She was tearing up and her voice faltered. Then she swept over and held Gaeten tightly. "And you take care of yourself, you old goat … I … I would never forgive you if you allowed yourself to get hurt! And you HAD BETTER come back quickly too!"

Duncan's eyes were also moist. Gaeten had been their close friend and confidant for decades. "I heard there is a ship from Moltavitor at the docks here now, dropping off cargo and a few lumbermen heading to the northern forests. It sails tomorrow on a round-about route back to Dominion waters."

"Yes, I heard about it too, and figured it would make a nearly ideal vessel for my departure. I have already booked passage, 'spending my last copper to visit my dying sister'. I have a small trunk, which I fully expect to be stolen — it is filled with old, worn out clothes suitable for a poor old blind man, and a few pieces of silver coin on the bottom. When I arrive at a port I will be destitute, with my only worldly belongings on my back. Of course, inside my clothes will be some real money, and a few other … items … I may find useful. Duncan, we need to work out a way for me to communicate back to you. I was thinking that perhaps Alterian merchant captains could be requested to set up a message box in their staterooms. Anything addressed to, say, the Alterian Minister of Falconry would be delivered at best speed, for a reasonable fee of course."

"But Gaeten, there is no Minister of Falconry in Alteria ... is there?"

"No, not exactly. But there is Falcon Master who runs a small shop near the palace who is reasonable well known — certainly anyone asking for the Minister would be sent to him. He and I have known each other for quite some time ... and we have a mutual interest in Alterian gryphs. I have a running joke with him about having a 'Ministry'. He will know the note is from me, and if someone happened to tell him to send it along here, he would be a willing conduit for messages. I would encode them in the latest High Watcher codex, which to our best knowledge has never been broken."

"That could work! I will make the arrangements. But in a hurry I think you could trust the Alterians with a direct message — they are our closest ally, even though they have always claimed political neutrality. Do you need anything from us Gaeten?" Duncan's voice showed his concern for his friend.

"I don't think so, but thanks. I will miss you both. Now I need to speak with Warden James." He turned to go.

Lydia called out after him "Gaeten, don't forget to say goodbye to Ethan — he would not readily forgive you if you just left without telling him!"

Warden James had requested an audience with Reginaldo before he departed. It was held in the Watcher Compound for privacy, but in deference to the singer, it was held in a room where private lunch meetings were often served.

"Sir Reginaldo, I understand that you widely travel, both in the 'free' world and within the Dominion held lands. I have also been told that you hold no particular political or religious views and therefore do not take sides: you claim total neutrality as though you were an Alterian. Yet, it seems you are at least somewhat friendly to Freelandia. I would like to ask you some questions about the Dominion, but first I must know: whose side are you on? I don't believe in 'neutrality' when it comes to those who represent evil like the Dominion."

Reginaldo leaned back from his mostly finished lunch. "If we were having this conversation a week ago I would have argued with you at length that a true artist like myself not only can be neutral, but in fact must not take sides. I would have argued that music does not have 'sides' — it cannot be evil itself, or inherently good either. That the only 'good' or 'bad' music concerned the skill by which it was played." He sighed loudly. "But that was before Maria. Her singing was not just 'good', meaning skilled. There is no question in my mind at all that it must be a gift from God — not just skill. Skill would come with training, building upon some level of starting talent. Gifting is another matter. That little orphan girl came from nowhere and *touched* everyone who heard her. And no one could have mistaken who the source of the gifting was. You could not help but worship God while she sang, and it was the purest form of worship I have ever heard … that … I have ever experienced. I cannot imagine her performing music that did not point you toward God. That music was GOOD, it defined GOOD. That has fundamentally changed me."

James nodded. Everyone seemed to have felt it during the concert. It was as though a portion of God's very presence had been there while she sang.

"I have looked back over my career, over what I have seen and heard, and now that I know what truly is GOOD, I can more clearly see the absence of good — and isn't that really what evil is? Now there are degrees of 'goodness', but I have seen places where there is very, very little goodness present. I have been at concerts where the crowds were not pointed toward God, but toward utter hedonism, even violence. The outcomes of some concerts — not ones I accept mind you — are drunken and drugged revelries and vandalism. Did the music *cause* it? No. Did it strongly contribute? I must say yes.

Master Warden, I am no longer neutral. I cannot be. Yet I think I can accomplish more by at least *acting* neutral. You asked me whose side I was on. I am … I am on your God's side. That is not necessarily meaning yours! But, I must say, Freelandia seems to be on that same side."

James smiled. "I am pleased. Now, what can you tell me about the Dominion — about what they may be planning against Freelandia?"

"Well, I can only make observations of what I see and hear. However, it can be rather amazing how some Dominion leaders want to try to impress 'the world's greatest singer'. Make no mistake; they are committed to attacking Freelandia. So far they have been taking over neighboring countries, mostly easy targets without strong armies or allies. They are strongest on land offenses, at least historically. But lately they have greatly stepped up their naval forces, especially with all of the vessels they have seized by conquest. Most of the smaller countries they overwhelmed had relatively small navies, but combined they make quite a force. It seems the Dominion leadership is paying particular attention to integrating the ships, and they appear to be building some much, much larger ships — the largest I have ever seen. I saw one a few months ago as I was leaving a Dominion port — it was colossal, easily the largest ship I can recall ever laying eyes on. It was rather frightening, really, like a small mountain. I cannot imagine your little sloops to be able to do much more than pester it like a flea on a hound.

And disturbingly, piracy in some of the sea lanes has been rapidly rising — but somehow it always seems the ships that are attacked and taken are from non-Dominion countries. I have heard that some of the newer ships in the Dominion navy have been remarkably similar to those lost to piracy. The Dominion is aggressively expanding its fleet. Soon — if not already — it will have no equal and they will rule the sea."

James looked glum. "That pretty well confirms what we have been hearing ourselves. It may seem daunting, but we have plans to at least try to counter such a fleet, should it come against us — at least if we have enough time. That brings us to the most important topic. We have had no overt hostility with the Dominion, though of course our beliefs and values are diametrically opposed. They seem to have a bent for conquering and expanding, but so far have isolated their attacks to their surrounding neighbors. Yet we cannot help but wonder about their true ambitions. Freelandia is perhaps the most blessed country in the world, and when the Dominion Overlords look northward we have grave concerns. There have been a few very minor incidences where Dominion warships have interfered with our policing of the main merchant sea lanes in northern waters — you know our navy is highly respected and usually given pretty wide berth. So far I have not heard of any confrontations that led to overt hostility, but we too have seen an increase in piracy in the far south that seems to be spreading, and the pirate ships are becoming much better outfitted and larger. We still normally win those encounters, but our captains have taken to traveling in groups of two or three, and even so they report more aggressive — and competent — pirates."

Reginaldo nodded with a serious look in his eyes. "I have noticed that some of the small island nations north of the Dominion have had particularly frequent uprisings and social unrest. Several have recently fallen to dictators who seem especially friendly to the Dominion leadership, rapidly agreeing to allow Dominion ships dockyard access. In return, they seem to have shifted much of their trade to Dominion controlled territories. On my trip here I noticed that several of these islands appeared to be adding fortifications in their harbor areas in particular.

There are a couple of other things. I have noticed the presence of Basher warriors in Dominion ports. They are from the far south-eastern regions of the Dominion and have many strange ways. They are very unpleasant looking — they pierce themselves rather profusely with small bones as a show of fearlessness, and it is said they are steeped in deep magic that makes them nearly unstoppable. I heard some sailors mention the Bashers seem to not feel pain — they can be severely wounded and yet never stop until they are totally incapacitated or killed. This talk of magic — they call it Blood Magic and Dark Magic — is really picking up within the Dominion territories lately. They seem preoccupied with it, even obsessed with it — and many seem in fear of this magic and the magicians who supposedly wield it. Perhaps that is what I have noticed the most among the people. The regular people and especially those in the more newly captive territories are living in greater and greater fear.

I think the Dominion leadership is using fear to hold everyone in line. In some of the cities there are roving squads of armed men who apparently are looking for excuses to make very public examples out of anyone who disagrees with them– public torture and killings are becoming more common. But even worse are the ritualistic killings that are rumored about in whispers, never openly. Every major city is now getting a contingent of what they call the Dark Order, led by a Dark Magician, someone outside of the local governor who supposedly reports up to one of the Overlords. They seem to hold absolute sway, and even the highest local government officials must obey them — and all fear them.

During my last visit in a Dominion city I was introduced to a Dark Magician." Reginaldo shuddered. He was probably the scariest person I have ever met. Just being near him made the hair on my neck stand on end and gave me the chills. He was the closest thing to evil personified that I have ever met — or would ever want to meet. Yet I hear that they report to the Dominion Overlords — now that is a super-scary bunch from what I have heard whispered. They rule with absolute power over the Dominion, but from what I can gather few have ever seen them. No one seems to know how many Overlords there are, just that they stay in the deep south in a fortress temple.

There are wild rumors about them, like they stand 10 feet tall, have eyes of fire, and can kill with just a glance. Surely of course these must be fairytales, but assuredly I would never, EVER want to meet one."

Reginaldo shuddered again. "The Dominion leadership is evil, Master Warden. I have felt some of it first hand, like there was a cloud of evilness surrounding them and they seem to hold great power.

There are also rumors of new weapons. Something called "Hellfire" was mentioned — it sounds like some sort of sulfurous burning material launched from catapults that creates magic fire that cannot be quenched. Hellhounds have been seen in some cities ... extremely large, long furred savage beasts used during attacks that have fiery red eyes and are said to be invulnerable to nearly all weapons. Only the Bashers can control them.

As to timing, I do not know. I am no military man. I can only say that they seem to be building strength. There is a sense of urgency and purpose among them. I do not think you have very long; they seem to be preparing and planning something soon."

That was sobering, but was the assessment others had made also. James grimaced. "Thank you Sir Reginaldo. I would hope that, in your travels, you may have opportunity to give us any updates you can — but do not endanger yourself unnecessarily."

"Thank you for your concern, Master Warden. My concert schedule roves from Dominion to free territories and back regularly, so I can likely send messages through your leased Watcher network at least occasionally."

"Watcher network? Whatever do you mean?" James had a blank face but was very attentive.

Reginaldo chuckled. "Come now Master Warden! If I leased out Watchers all over the free world I would certainly use them to keep tabs on activities deemed hostile to Freelandia's interests." His face then frowned. "Oh, I forgot to mention — when the Dominion takes over a country, any Freelandia Watchers that are found are immediately rounded up ... and executed. I have heard that few actually are captured; they usually die along with a significant body count of Dominion forces. But there are now standing orders for any captured Freelandia Watchers to be held and turned over to the Dark Magicians." Reginaldo was shaking his massive frame at that thought.

Gaeten caught up with Ethan later that afternoon. "Ethan, I must leave Freelandia for a time. God is leading me to do this, to go into the Dominion to learn what I can about their plans against us. I leave tomorrow morning."

Ethan nodded slowly. "Gaeten, for some reason that does not surprise me. I don't know why, but it just doesn't. It somehow seems to 'fit'. Is there anything I can do to help?"

"As a matter of fact, yes. You do still have that whistle for Sahsa, right? Good. While I am gone, please take care of her. Not that she really needs much caring for, but I try to feed her a bit of sweetmeat from the cafeteria every few days and she seems to like it."

"Sure Master Gaeten. I like Sasha."

"I know, Ethan. And she seems to like you too. Now, there are a few more things. Ethan, you have a very special gift from God. I want to charge you to use it for His glory. Protect yourself, but more importantly protect Freelandia. Do not trust in yourself, but DO trust in God. Put His ways, His goals far above your own. Be self-less in your serving Him. Perilous times are coming upon Freelandia, I fear. We all need to prepare — and you certainly are part of that. It would be easy for you to become complacent with your gifting. Yet you still have much to learn, and as good as you are, you could be better still. Be diligent in your Watcher studies. When I get back I expect you to be able to beat me in sparing … at least every once in awhile!

Another thing. Please watch out for Maria — she is starting over at the Academy of Music when she is released from the Healers, and she only has a couple of friends in the Keep. I would appreciate it if you could check up on her now and again and see if she has any needs. Grand Master Vitario said he would give her an assistant job and a place to stay, but she is just a poor orphan blind girl from a tiny little hamlet dropped into the largest city of Freelandia — she may need greater help. I don't have much in the way of possessions, but I do have an account at the Bank of Freelandia. I have instructed them that your father and mother are to have full access to the funds I have salted away. If Maria needs anything, you can help."

"Sure Gaeten, I can do that."

"Good. That relieves me quite a lot. I will have enough to worry about with adding Maria to the list."

After a brief meeting with James that included all that Reginaldo had reported, Gaeten headed for the Ministry of Healing. Of all the stops he needed to make before departing in the early morning, this was the most difficult. He slowly climbed the stairs, in some ways dreading saying this goodbye. He silently moved to the door of Maria's room. He sensed it was open, and he was just about to knock when he heard "Oh! Gaeten!" It was a welcome-come-in-here sort of cheerful greeting that made his knees weak.

"Now how did you know it was me? Are you starting to see things now?"

"No, nothing like that. I can make out bright light, maybe a shadow moving in front of sunlight. It is really rather exciting! I don't know if the Lord has any more in store for me, but I am thankful for what He has given. I heard someone lean on the door frame, though I did not hear them walk up — you are the only person I know who can walk so silently I cannot hear them."

"I am very pleased for you, Maria! I wanted to stop by to see how you are doing, and see if Vitario has made the arrangements for you in the Academy."

"I guess I am doing fine — though I am still rather tired. Kory stopped by today and said we get to be roommates! And Sir Reginaldo stopped by and … and he said I had dropped something … and that was no way to treat a gift he had given me … Gaeten, he GAVE me the tiara he had put on my head the night of the concert … Kory said it was solid gold! What …∴ what should I DO with it? It's not like I can wear it!"

Gaeten rocked back on his heels a minute. "Hmm. That is really … something. I would not have expected that of him, though from what James said there may be quite a bit more to Reginaldo than I thought. I guess you should give it to Vitario for safekeeping — you never know, maybe you will have another concert and need something heavy to keep your puffed up head from lifting you off the ground!"

"Oh-argh!" She threw her pillow at the sound of his voice and he laughingly caught it. Then unexpectedly she began to cry softly. "Gaeten, I know the other reason you stopped by, to tell me your leaving all by yourself to spy on the Dominion … to say goodbye."

"Yes, Maria. I leave at dawn tomorrow. But God goes with me, so who can be against me?" He walked over, and held her close. For some reason that was getting easier with practice.

"I dreamed about you last night. You were somewhere hot, yet it seemed like a cool mist was constantly falling on you, shielding you from the heat. I was worried about you at first, but for some reason when I saw the cool water I knew you were alright, that you were being protected."

"Thank you, Maria — that is comforting. I believe God gave you that dream to comfort both of us. In dreams and visions from God, moving water often symbolizes His Spirit. So it would seem that God was showing you that I was being protected by His Spirit on my journey. It is all the more confirmation that I am doing what He wants me to. It is still not easy. I am really going to miss you."

Maria held him close, then backed up to arms length. "I have so much to learn, Gaeten. I will miss you terribly. I think … I think I will make a song about it."

"I would like that, Maria. I can't wait to hear it when I get back."

"You had better Mr. Grand Master Sir Gaeten!" Maria laughed, and it was infections. Gaeten joined in.

The next day dawned bright and clear. A full tide was beginning to wane when passengers and cargo finished loading onto the Midnight Star, a trading vessel registered to the Dominion territory of Makrenda. Reginaldo swept on board, arriving no earlier that absolutely necessary. He had the best stateroom on board, second only to the captain's (which he would have preferred, but it was not available for any sum he was willing to pay for). Reginaldo was just a tad nervous — travelling into Dominion waters was not a trivial thing, and their highly aggressive behavior was not particularly appealing to most international-level artists. Still, they had extended a handsome invitation, and gold was gold, regardless of whose hands it came by. Still, he would keep his eyes and ears open for whatever intelligence he could gather without seeming overtly friendly to Freelandia. Reginaldo was a consummate singer, and actually was a pretty decent actor as well.

Totally unnoticed, an old beggarly hooded figure shuffled awkwardly aboard just before the gangplank was lifted. A dark skinned scared arm shown as he fumbled and then proffered his ticket to the ship's steward, who rather distastefully took it with a sneer. The cowled figure, seemingly bent over with many years, shambled over to the lowest cost shared stateroom, tightly clutching a small chest as though it were especially dear to him. That, along with the long white cane with which he tapped his way along, caught the attention of several of the swarthy crew. Easy pickings were always watched out for — especially after leaving a port known for wealth but not for tolerating the economically challenged from appropriating what they deemed as excess income from unsuspecting citizens. Freelandia was well known for being particularly good at enforcing their laws at the port ... they seemed almost supernaturally adept at spotting pick pockets and petty thieves, and no one wanted a stint at the mines or forest work-camps or prisons that were strangely sparse and under populated for such a sizeable country.

And besides, all were under very strict orders — on penalty of a very painful death — of being detained ashore for any reason whatsoever. Only a few knew why, but several had noticed the small kayak that had mysteriously disappeared the night before they laid anchor at the Keep's port. They all felt the absence of the dark evilness that had been present on their voyage to Freelandia. Whoever or whatever had left, they were glad for its absence. With lifted spirits they raised sail and departed.

Chapter 16

Assessments

To say that Chancellor Duncan was busy would have been the understatement of several years. The High Council was meeting the next day in emergency session. That alone required incredible planning and arrangements that was keeping his entire staff working late into the evening. And it also was having the predictable effect of stirring up the entire Keep. Rumors were rampant of imminent invasion, of horrible calamities and of anything the ripe imaginations of the populace could conjecture. That in turn was causing so much commotion in the city that most real work was at a standstill — and that was exactly the opposite of what was needed.

There was only one thing to do, and Duncan had sent out the announcements that he and Master Warden James would speak to the city at the large public square in the center of the Keep. Several thousand people could fill the open square and surrounding areas to hear important announcements, and that made it an ideal venue to tell the citizens of the threat the Dominion posed, and what the High Council of Freelandia was doing to meet it. It was perhaps the most important speech he ever had to give, and Duncan was worrying about it ahead of time, especially since he would not have much time to finalize some of the points until the Council had heard and agreed to the proposals he would make to them. And to be very fair — for which Duncan was well known — riders had been sent out to deliver notices of the public announcement to all the surrounding districts, with the promise that details would be read in each township and city throughout the country within a few days.

Duncan sure hoped James had time to prepare some level of assessment of where the defenses of Freelandia stood.

Master Warden James was not in a good mood, not in the least. Few of the summons he has sent out had been answered yet — he only had a very high level look at many of the defenses, and he had sent out additional messengers with a message threatening to call each of the Directors up before the High Council itself to give an impromptu report in person if he did not have a report from them before the meeting started early the next morning. He was only slightly mollified by hearing that several new defensive ideas had very recently had quite successful early trials.

The Director of Engineers knocked on his door. "Master James, you wanted to see me?"

"Yes, yes Master Brentwood! Please come in … and close the door behind you."

"Do we really need all this secrecy? We have several Watchers assigned at the exits of our compound now, and several roving teams of them wandering around each of our main test facilities. It is almost like you are expecting the Dominion to come sailing into our safe harbor and take up residence at our School!"

"Master Brentwood, you will hear this at the High Council tomorrow, so it probably will not do any harm to tell you now. We have strong reason to believe the Dominion is planning a full assault against Freelandia, likely within a year, maybe much sooner. I suspect when that happens they will likely commit a very large percent of their forces in a massive all out attack. We also have growing evidence that they have spies and maybe even special forces already being positioned among us."

That really got Brentwood's attention. He had heard some rumors floating around, but to hear it from the Master Warden himself meant it was very, very serious indeed. "Well ... that changes things. I see the reason for the recently added security. Can you tell me what sort of evidence you have?"

"Not all of it, there are some things that do not relate to you specifically. I do not know for sure how much will be spoken of at the High Council tomorrow, nor how much Chancellor Duncan will want me to make public in our joint speech at the town square tomorrow evening. But consider this: Duncan himself had a revelation regarding one of the last prophecies, and it has since been independently confirmed by several trusted advisors with prophetic giftings. The prophecy spoke of a great war coming upon us, and events seem to be falling into place according to what was foretold."

"Wow ... I had no idea. But maybe it explains a few things."

James sat up straighter. "What things?"

"Well, a few strange things. We recently had a promising young engineer disappear. He was relatively new, coming from ... I think he said Alteria, though come to think of it he did not particularly look or sound like an Alterian. He was a rather inquisitive apprentice — a trait we generally look for. He seemed particularly interested in metallurgy and wanted to be part of one of our projects on a new alloy of sillarium that has some quite interesting properties. He was much too junior of an apprentice to be on that project, or on any of the really advanced stuff. Still, he seemed to be always asking, always trying to befriend some of the senior apprentices on those projects. I had received several complaints and was just planning on a stern talk with him when he just up and vanished one day. We sent inquires around, but no one seems to have seen him."

"When was that?" James wanted to know.

"Oh, about a month ago. He seemed to have extensively toured our compound grounds and buildings. I figured maybe he ran off with some young lady ..." Brentwood suddenly got a rather suspicious look on his face. "You don't suppose he might have been kidnapped, taken prisoner by Dominion forces? ... or ...he couldn't have been a spy himself ... could he? Who would want to spy on our engineers?"

"I think the Dominion would be very, very interested to know what war preparations and weapons we might have, Master Brentwood. Before you leave I will want a thorough description of the lad, and one of my people will work with you to develop a sketch of what he looked like so we can do a thorough search. Now what else — you mentioned several strange things."

"Oh, I did, didn't I? Well, you know we have a very wide range of things we study, evaluate, test and tinker on within the School of Engineering. Why, just the other day we were working on an enhanced irrigation system for the farmers in the western growing zone where we piped in water from ..."

"Master Brentwood! Keep to the topic, please! I have many more assessments to get before I must speak to the High Council ... unless you were planning on giving the engineering assessment yourself?"

"Oh ... oh my ... well, no ...you are sure you don't want to hear about the new irrigation system? No? Well, alright. I was going to say that over the last six months or so we have had an abnormally high number of insights and ideas for new inventions, mostly around defensive technologies. I really cannot explain it. We typically have a few new ideas in that area each year, but it really has not been a very high priority area for us to work on ... oh, I suppose that will change now, eh? Anyway, the sheer volume of new idea activity there has been highly unusual ... yes, highly unusual! Just the other day one of the level 7 apprentices demolished a test building with some confounded device she was working on — nearly blew herself up in the process. I put an immediate stop to it of course; I mean the danger and all ..."

Seeing the wide eyes of Master James, Brentwood stopped to reconsider. "Hmm, maybe I should check on what she was up to? There have just been so many newfangled ideas that sound so, well, so outlandish that I have not wanted to put much time toward them unless I see a more practical use! Now that barn leveling … I suppose it might be useful for the miners, or for farmers to remove tree stumps. But it was just too dangerous and should have been thoroughly reviewed before anything like that was ever worked on. I do NOT allow such shenanigans at my school!"

James had a deep scowl on his face. He admitted to himself that he had not been following up on the engineers for the last several years, perhaps in part because no reports had been coming from them. He had hoped work was going merrily on without his supervision, but that apparently may have been a considerable blunder. "Master Brentwood, immediately after the High Council meetings I want to visit your School. I will bring along a few others. I want a review of every project, every idea that has been coming out of your apprentices and Masters that has the slightest potential for defensive use. Wait … make it a review of everything — let us determine if it has defensive utility. I will spend an entire day with you — more if needed — and I want your brightest thinkers, those who are particularly good at spawning new ideas, even whacky, wild ideas, sitting in with us."

"But Master Warden, that will take time to prepare, to get drawings and schematics made up, to prepare formal documents and presentations …"

"No, it will not. Have the inventors come and just talk to us about their ideas. If any have prototypes or have taken their ideas to some level of practice, have them show us."

"But the time, Master Warden! I only have limited resources and I cannot take everyone off their jobs to do a show-and-tell presentation! And besides, we don't do impromptu presentations or present half-baked ideas. I demand full formal presentations once an approved idea has been thoroughly tested out."

"Master Brentwood! The future of Freelandia may be at stake! And as for resources, any project we select for further development will be funded by the High Council itself … I have access to the very coffers of Freelandia as resources for worthy projects!"

Now THAT got the Director of Engineering's attention like nothing else had!

Taleena nervously glanced behind her. She was already 'on report' this month for being late several times, and a few more of those and she would lose her job as a cleaning servant in the High Council chambers. It had taken her months to get the job, along with a large payment to the previous girl to recommend Taleena when she had to leave suddenly to help her poor sick mother in one of the small towns to the far west. Taleena looked to be fifteen or sixteen years old, but actually was twenty four — her people were generally rather small and were often mistaken as being much younger. A bit of make-up and clothing more common to young girls and hair often in a youthful ponytail completed the disguise. She was quite good at hiding where she could listen in on Council meetings, though it had become much more difficult after she had been put on report and watched more closely. And it was all the fault of that Lydia! She just had to be a witch! Taleena had been ever so carefully pilfering food here and there, never enough to be really noticed, and she had begun to snitch items from some of the offices to supplement her income.

That is, she had. When someone noticed an item missing, Lydia had the entire staff line up. She had moved down the line, looking into each face and asking them each a question with a smile that was supposed to look kindly. Taleena knew better. Where she came from, witches were readily recognized, and their powers were respected … and feared. When Lydia had come to her, Taleena had put on her best innocent-little-girl smile and answered with a voice long crafted to deflect any suspicion. She was quite talented at the act, honed over long practice and use. Taleena was quite good at what she did, though very few people knew exactly what that truly was.

And it had seemed to work again, until Lydia paused after moving on and came back to look into her eyes, seemingly to read her mind behind them. She had been put on report and her pay docked until she could pay to replace the item — which she had already sold in a local pawn shop — and her access to the offices had been restricted until she had proven herself reformed. Oh, that witch! Every time Taleena was near Lydia she felt strange, like her hidden past was being reviewed. She rapidly avoided being near her at all, and had been on extra good behavior for awhile, at least on the job. Even so, she was not allowed back to the offices and it seemed her supervisor was keeping a much closer eye on her. It was awful.

Taleena was not sure how much longer she could stay at the job, with such strong magic being used against her. Every day she recited protective incantations and re-inked the magical runes on her skin kept hidden by clothing. Yet she still felt under 'the evil eye' of a witch and had to strongly restrain looking over her shoulder while accomplishing her tasks. The feeling was especially strong when she was in bright light, and so she had taken to staying away from windows on sunny days and staying in the shadows inside. She was taking quite a large risk now, saying she was running an errand for Chancellor Duncan himself. She had commandeered a horse from the Council stables under that guise. Her master would need to know about the unexpected High Council meeting, and the public announcements being given the next evening. That was enough reason to risk exposure. Certainly Murdrock would want to know immediately. Perhaps her departure would not be noticed — there certainly was a great deal going on, far more than normal in preparation for the Council meeting. Taleena would have dearly loved to stash herself away in the little cubbyhole she had found to listen in, but there was no easy exit and she doubted she could have remained there for an all day session. She had to choose, and the easy choice was to leave now to tell Murdrock. It was a half day's ride to the old lumberjack hovel, and she needed plenty of time to ensure she had no followers.

As her horse picked its way down the overgrown trail she felt she was being watched and so she moved even more carefully. Surely there would be a guard or two in the woods, and she was certain she would never spot them — they seemed to be highly skilled professionals. That actually put her more at ease … professionals were much less likely to put an arrow in your back by mistake. When she arrived she slowly and very deliberately dismounted. The horse seemed nervous, as though it were sensing something that made it uncomfortable. Taleena tied the reins and waited. A few minutes later she saw a burly man in lumberjack clothing coming down the path she had just taken. He looked at her coolly, then went to the door and gave four quiet raps. The door opened a crack. The man motioned for Taleena to come, but just as she was reaching to push open the door he grabbed her roughly, one hand over her mouth and another over her eyes. The suddenness startled her and she would have cried out but for the gagging hand clamped tightly over her small mouth. She was lifted right off the ground, the man pulling her diminutive body cruelly into his by the force of the grab and he pushed into the small cabin.

She heard a few noises of other bodies moving, and then she was dumped down to the floor. Before she could adjust her eyes to the darkened interior a handkerchief was whipped over her head and eyes and very tightly bound. This time she did cry out slightly, and a hand slapped over her mouth hard enough to bring tears to her eyes under the rough cloth.

"Quiet wench! Another outburst like that and I may quiet you … permanently." A hand grabbed her ponytail and pulled her head back sharply, and she felt something cold and very sharp press against her bare neck.

She whimpered very, very quietly and tried not to move. Taleena swallowed hard and felt a tiny trickle of warm liquid drip down her skin from where the blade rested.

"Good. Now you had better have an extremely good reason to come here during the day! You risk our exposure and you have left your post! It is a good thing no one was following you, or ...." Murdrock left that hanging in the silence, letting Taleena's imagination finish the thought. He saw her shudder ever so slightly, trying hard not to cause any movement to her throat.

"Perhaps I should ask the questions?" The voice she heard was somewhat high pitched, even when spoken in a whisper, and sounded positively venomous. Taleena went utterly cold and her face drained of all color. She feared Murdrock, but he was a professional ... soldier? ... and so was rather predictable. He had taken her arrival a bit more aggressively than she had expected, but she knew well enough how to work with him. But this voice was from someone far different, far more ... sinister.

"Now, little girl ... or should I say, young woman ... tell us why you came. Leave nothing out — I will instantly know if you are even the least little bit lying." The voice was cold and dark and Taleena could feel creeping tendrils of evil reaching out to her. She felt a sharp fingernail trace a path from her left ear down to her mouth. "Such a lovely face, with skin so soft and smooth." The knife had left her throat and now Taleena shuddered much harder. She was vain, and always thought her face was particularly pretty and innocent looking. The magician had somehow known this and was giving her a very real warning. And it was very effective.

"Chancellor Duncan has called an emergency meeting of the High Council. No one seems to know what it's all about, but the whole Keep is buzzing with rumors — mostly around an imminent attack from the Dominion. Many people seem rather panicked by that, and there was even a minor run on a few of the banks and talk of moving out into the farthest outposts of Freelandia."

"Good ..." the voice dripped with sweet scorn — "fear is something we want, something we can use ... and maybe something we can stoke up, hmmm? Continue."

"The Chancellor has also proclaimed that he and the Master Warden will give a public announcement tomorrow early evening;

it is being scheduled for six o'clock in the central square of the Keep. Builders were erecting a tall stage on one side in the square as I left. I knew you would want to hear of this immediately."

"Yes, child. This is useful news. But what of the Council meeting? What will be discussed? Surely you have heard or seen things in the offices of the administrators that give you more detail?"

"Well, it all came about very, very quickly — just in the last day or two. I know most of the Academy and Ministry leaders will be present, and all the talk has been about the Dominion. They really seem afraid of … us."

"I wonder what caused the sudden concern, hmm? Never mind, it is not terribly important. The ostrich may be finally taking its head out of the sand. It will not like what it sees. This was bound to come soon or later, and in the end it should not really matter much anyway. But my dear, you did not fully answer my question — you are holding back something, now aren't you?" The fingernail returned and dug into her skin painfully now, just below her right ear.

"I … I have not been able to get into the offices recently. I have been made to work in the lower levels and have not been allowed elsewhere."

The fingernail edged downward and forward, and Taleena was certain it was beginning to draw blood and would leave an ugly mark. "And why is that, my smooth skinned little girl?" The voice had grown even colder and more dangerous.

Taleena thought quickly. She was in a very tricky situation right now. "It was the WITCH! Chancellor Duncan's wife Lydia — she is powerful witch! I have had to avoid her, not even allow her to get near me — she seems to be able to read my mind, and my best disguises do nothing around her. Only with my strongest magic have I been able to counter her treacherous powers. I have seen her do strange mystical things … she says incantations under her breath frequently, often with her eyes closed even as she walks along. And the Chancellor himself seems afraid of her — he brings her into meetings to cast truth spells on people, and at times she looks like she is listening to some demon or spirit. One day I could not escape being near her, and from that point on she forbade everyone from letting me work in the offices. She can read minds, I tell you! She is a powerful witch!"

The fingernail stopped its slow movement. "Hmm, now that is indeed interesting. We have had reports of magic here in Freelandia before, and it would explain many things we have suspected. We will have to prepare for this, but we anticipated we might have to. We have our own magic, and it should be far more powerful than these simpletons can muster up. Now as to the Chancellor's wife … she sounds like she must be a powerful witch indeed! We may have to take care of her, or find a way to circumvent or compromise her power. You have done well, child."

"Murdrock, we are being given a wonderful opportunity here. It sounds as though the Keep is already in a panic. Let's see what we can do to accelerate this terror, and cause maximum confusion and indecision. Even a month or two would give us an even larger advantage when we launch our inva …" he stopped abruptly, having already said more than he had wanted to. "Child, tell us more about the platform they are making and the layout of the square."

"Well, it was just being constructed when I left. I think we can easily get a good look at it though — almost a bird's eye view for that matter."

"Why is that?"

"They were building it just a short distance away from the apartment I am leasing. You should be able to look down from my window nearly directly onto the platform. If we leave soon we could arrive just after dark."

Chapter 17

High Council Meeting

"Members of the High Council of Freelandia, thank you for coming to this very necessary but hastily convened meeting." Chancellor Duncan stood before the several dozen members of the Council and other invitees, most of whom he counted as friends. "We have grave news, but also great hope. You recall the many briefings we have had about the Dominion and the growing threat they are to the southern countries. Several here have wondered out loud if Freelandia itself might sometime find itself in danger as well from this foe. I am here to tell you that we no longer need to wonder. It is a sure outcome." That brought several startled gasps and unsettled commentary swept through the room. Duncan allowed the hubbub to die down and then continued. "You are right to wonder how I can be so sure of this. I have questioned it a few times myself over the last two days. A few of you have heard about this already, but many of you probably have not. I have asked Chaplain Mikael to read something to you, a prophecy we believe is being played out right before our eyes. But first, friends, I think we should pray — pray that God grants us wisdom to discern His directions for us, grace for any actions we decide to take, and mercy for the future of Freelandia."

The construction work was going strong, after taking a break for the night. The workers had built a platform the height of about two men, with a set of stairs on both sides. They were erecting a narrow podium as a curtain shifted slightly in a third floor window perhaps 150 feet away and a set of dark eyes assessed their progress. There were only two men in the room — any more might have raised suspicions, and really only one was absolutely necessary. The second could have been considered "over-kill", and both would have laughed out loud at the ironic description. Other team members were elsewhere in the square making their own preparations. Murdrock had insisted on doubling up everything, and their magician 'guest' was busily preparing his own counter spells … no Freelandia magic was going to interfere with their mission.

The men in Taleena's apartment had been carrying in various items for the last several hours, dressed as delivery men. Several recently purchased pieces of furniture were stacked over against a wall, and a large rolled carpet and a nearly equally large tapestry were laid out on the floor back away from the window. Food and drink had been brought in, and at irregular intervals one or another of the men had strolled around the building, looking at the roof and all entrances. They still needed to further explore and map out in their minds the surrounding buildings and alleys, just to be completely comfortable with the area. But that could wait. They now began to unroll the bulky carpet and tapestry, removing the hidden contents.

Master Warden James addressed the Council. "You have heard the words of the prophecy, and the interpretations of Chancellor Duncan, Chaplain Mikael and several esteemed theologians. You have heard the words of confirmation from several of our trusted and proven discerners, that the words and interpretations are true. We have a grave duty before us. In Freelandia's history, only a few threats have ever grown into a magnitude to endanger our very existence. The last time was over two hundred years ago, when Freelandia was far smaller in population. The Dominion represents the greatest challenge our country has ever faced. God protected us in the past, with miracles that made the nations of the world acknowledge that our God was great. I have no doubt He will do the same again. Yet we should not sit on our hands and wait for His deliverance. He expects us to resist evil with all our strength."

James watched the faces before him. Most were nodding in approval, though some seemed not totally convinced. That was to be expected, but the largely positive response encouraged him to continue. "And what is resisting with all our strength? I am here to give you a high level assessment of what our strengths are. Given the short preparation time, I can only give a broad overview. If we had to fight tomorrow, frankly we would be in very serious trouble. During the long centuries of peace we have largely neglected our physical defenses — and perhaps even allowed some of our spiritual armor to get rusty. And truthfully, no physical defenses we can possibly develop are nearly as important as our spiritual defense.

I have the duty and honor of being the Master Warden for Freelandia. It is my responsibility for the state of affairs of our defenses and security and I give you no excuses, other than I was only appointed to this position fairly recently. I will now give you a picture of where we are defensively, and where I think we can be with many months of intense preparation. I will follow that with a sober review of what we might expect from the Dominion, a few likely scenarios of how they will launch an attack and my current expectations of how we will fare against them, barring miraculous intervention from God. Finally, I will wind up with my recommendations. There are some things we can accomplish within current funding and resources, but there is much more we could and should do."

❦

Taleena made her way back to the large building that housed the Council chambers. There was an extra compliment of Watchers present, but no one challenged her and she passed through unhindered, carrying a large bag she said was the result of an errand she had been sent on.

The Dominion assassins had completed setting up Taleena's apartment. The now empty tapestry had been hung over the window as a thick drape, with one end held out a few inches by a short block of wood they had attached to the top frame. They each wore several amulet charms the magician had said would make them invisible to Freelandia magic. Each also had a few good luck charms of their own. They had drawn a series of runes on the walls and floor that were supposed to make them invincible. There were a few more rituals to perform, but they were best done later, closer to when they were to make their strike. For now, each would take a turn cautiously walking the area to circumspectly inspect the final stages of the construction activity and their planned escape routes. One remained in the apartment at all times, alert to any suspicious noises. Both knew a second team was somewhere else near the square, but they did not see them nor know their objectives — and so could never be tortured into betraying them and compromising the entire mission.

"Council members and guests, we all are aware of the outer God-given defenses that have served well to limit enemies in the past from plundering Freelandia. Anyone trying to reach us via land has nearly impassible mountains to cope with. There are no routes through the mountains beyond adventuresome hiking paths. It is very unlikely that any sizable force would choose that means to come upon us.

Even so, we are evaluating ways to block the few passes that do lead into Freelandia. Our most prominent defense of course cannot be missed by any ship visiting us — the small channel that leads through the ocean cliffs into Freelandia Bay. That channel is too wide to be blocked, but every ship passing through comes within range of our largest catapults on either the east or west cliffs. We can rain down a deadly barrage, but the machines are quite old, and there has been little practice with them. I fear if we tried to press them into battle in their current state they might snap after the first few shots. Even with the needed maintenance and diligent practice, I think at best we may be able to hit one out of every four or five ships coming through — maybe a few more if the wind is low and the tide against them.

Before even reaching the channel our own navy may be able to take out a number of enemy ships, but they may be better utilized within the Bay, where they know the waters and rocky shoals far better than any enemy pilot. But we must expect determined warships and troops to reach our shores. You know we have several good ports, and many fine sandy beaches that would be rather inviting spots to land. The best and most important port is here at the Keep, but there are other worthy spots close by. So even if we somehow could keep Dominion ships from landing directly at the Keep, it would be only a partial day's march from a number of other beaches for their troops to reach our city. And bear in mind, the Keep would be their main goal — it is the center of our government and commerce.

The Inner Keep still has its old walls, and they can and will be heavily fortified. We believe our Watchers can hold at bay a considerable ground force, and if necessary make a final and decisive victory at that inner rampart.

That, my friends, is where we are today. It is not where we can be in even a few months! I have yet to get all reports in, but from what I have learned there are considerable activities within many of the Ministries that have direct utility for our defensive efforts. Several Directors have mentioned that God has apparently already been at work, inspiring many new ideas and inventions. I plan on an immediate assessment of every idea, and see what may be employed for our benefit — and to the unpleasant surprise of the Dominion!"

James had their full attention, and some members were jotting down notes. He would give them more details and include some of the things he had already initiated before getting to the much more somber section of his report — on how very strong the Dominion forces really were, far stronger than most feared — and the depth of evil they truly represented. That would come right after lunch — no sense spoiling their appetite beforehand.

Taleena took a circuitous route through the Council building. She did not want to be spotted by her supervisor or other staff just yet, maybe not at all if she could manage that. She had no idea if she would be fired on the spot, or even taken captive. It may be that no one had even noticed she had been gone for a day. Caution seemed the wisest course. Taleena furtively darted into a back room that she knew from experience had not been used for quite some time — that is, not by anyone other than herself.

As she opened the door a tiny piece of feather floated down. Taleena smiled — her simple precaution of placing a piece of feather in the door jam as she closed it acted as an effective tell-tale sign that no one had entered the room since she last left. She scurried inside and reclosed the door quietly. There were several pieces of old furniture in the room, a few with large cloths draped over them to keep the dust off. She ducked under one and came to her private stash of stolen goodies — nonperishable foods, a few office odds and ends, some cord, sewing supplies, and several knives she had snuck out of the kitchen. She opened her satchel and removed several items. The first one looked remarkably like a rag doll, with long flowing hair and a reasonably well made dress. The name "Lydia" was inked onto the front of the cloth. Over every other square inch of the dolls surface there were blood-red runes and magical symbols. She began to recite the incantations taught to her and removed several large sewing needles and pins from her collection. As she finished each spell she savagely pierced the doll with one of the pins. Once that was accomplished, she removed a few more items from the satchel and began mixing a few powders, taking great care not to spill any and certainly not to get any on her fingers or clothes. Once done she scooped the mixture aside into a small vial which she carefully sealed. That would wait until later in the afternoon, when she would make her cautious way to the kitchen.

Lydia had woken up that morning with quite a headache, after a restless night. Her dreams had been dark and very troublesome. Duncan had already left — he had a very busy day and wanted to get several final preparations taken care of before the High Council meeting. She should still have plenty of time to get to the meeting herself in the afternoon as planned, but the dreams and headache did not seem right, not just normal happenstance. She felt like a cloud was surrounding her, making her thinking foggy and God seemed far away. At that thought her eyes snapped open fully and she shook her head as if to clear it. Even as she did so a feeling of dark dread enveloped her, cutting her off from the light of morning. A coldness crept up, freezing her body and confusing her mind.

Yet deep within a bright light shone, a light the cold and darkness and confusion could not extinguish. It flared brighter and Lydia's spirit within her fled to it, embraced it, and clung to it. Fear raged all around, but the light burned brighter still. Lydia knew the source, God's Spirit within her. She began to pray, simply, defiantly. The darkness swirled about, but began to retreat as the bright light advanced. Lydia began to sing inside, worshiping her God, and the light blazed far brighter, washing away the feelings of dread. In a few moments the attack was over. Lydia panted, exhausted by the ordeal, but more determined than ever. The enemy obviously had wanted to stop her from attending the Council meeting, and though the main attack seemed over she still felt a sharp headache. Gritting her teeth she dressed and prepared for the meeting, praying both under her breath and occasionally out-loud.

As soon as she exited her bedchambers, she called one of the servants and sent out an urgent message to all her many friends to pray for protection, especially for the Council meeting. Then she went to the Council building and gathered the staff — they too could be praying — anything the enemy wanted to disrupt was likely an important activity to be praying for.

Lydia had many things to take care of before she would join the meeting, and the first order of business was ensuring a good lunch was prepared. No one noticed the absence of the young cleaning girl Taleena.

Ethan wandered across the public square, noting the tall platform with many rows of chairs. He sat down to eat lunch at one of the small cafés which opened out to the square. Something did not seem quite right to him, but he could not pinpoint what it was. Everything looked like it was coming together well for the public announcement later.

After lunch James continued. "Council members, friends — you have been briefed this morning on the state of readiness of our defenses, and of a few of the activities we have already started. We are not in bad shape, but there is much we could do — will do — to be far better prepared. More on that later. Now I must turn to a less pleasant topic: the state of readiness, if you will, of our enemy.

The Dominion was created when a band of rebels appeared in the deep southern areas across the sea with strange new beliefs that were very much in opposition to the true God. One of them claimed to be a prophet who had a vision from a dark Power. He is said to have performed miracles and created quite a following which grew rapidly. One of the main reasons for the spread of this new religion was force — you became a convert by the edge of the sword, and members zealously enforced their new beliefs. This violent sect staged a revolution in one of the poorer southern countries and managed to convince the army there that their might made right. The Dominion grew, engulfing other poor surrounding countries, often with mysterious "powers" that wrought superstitious fear throughout their enemies.

We have long figured that much of the rumors of strange evil power were just highly exaggerated superstition. We now know there is more to it than we had thought. Just recently, the Dominion has forcibly expelled most missionaries from their territories. Many have stayed, going underground, but more have been made to leave — and quite a few have been horrifically murdered. I have interviewed several who escaped, and have brought Minister Polonos here today to give you an update from someone who has dedicated the last 20 years to delivering the message of the true God to those within the territories of what are now parts of the Dominion."

James stepped away from the short podium and ushered an older, very sun-tanned and very lean figure to the front. "Ladies and gentlemen, please give a royal High Council of Freelandia welcome to Minister Polonos."

Every chair was swept back as the entire Council and all guests rose to their feet in a thundering ovation. Missionaries were held in extremely high opinion in Freelandia, and all felt it was their honor to give a royal welcome to the servant of God standing before them.

Tears came to Minister Polonos's eyes. Striving 20 years in an often thankless and dangerous situation could easily embitter a person, but in humility and thanks Polonos bowed deeply and waved the rather exuberantly clapping crowd to be seated. "Kind people of Freelandia, I do not deserve such applause. I am just a fellow servant, doing what God has appointed me to do, much like you. Even so, I thank you on behalf of Him whom I serve.

Master James asked me to give you a brief report on the Dominion. I understand you anticipate them coming against you shortly. I am saddened at this news, but not disheartened or afraid — our God is SO very much bigger than the Dominion!

I know little about their war preparations, but I can tell you what I have observed. First and foremost you must understand that those from the far southern regions where I lived are a very superstitious lot. They live every day in real fear of witches, magicians and demons. Their leaders capitalize on this, even as they too fear "the dark magic" as they call it. Those who rise to higher leadership positions are typically steeped in demon-worship. I do not believe in magic like they do, but I certainly do believe in demons and demonic power & influence. I have seen truly amazing supernatural things occur, which I directly attribute to demonic actions. And I tell you, the power of God is so very, very greater! I and my fellow ministers have repeatedly stood in direct opposition to their shamans and witches, and their incantations and magic have not been able to stop us. Yes, we do fight, but not against the people — against the demonic power behind them.

In battle, they threaten their warriors with the horrors of the Darkness, as well as physically, to drive them on. The Bashers, you should know about them. They are mainly from a fierce nomadic tribe that claims ingesting the roots of certain desert plants makes them invincible in battle. I have learned about them. They are very large, nearly giants. Some of the missionaries believe their frequent eating of those roots causes such large bodily growth, as well as their other very distinctive feature — blood red eyes. It is common for them to take a large dose of these roots just before going to war, and it puts them into a nearly drunken state — but with extreme strength, fearlessness, and almost no noticeable pain. They feed some of the root to their ... well I suppose you would call them dogs or wolves, though they are nearly the size of small bears. The root given to these beasts likewise causes their eyes to be blood-red and they become almost uncontrollable ... indeed, only the largest Bashers have any ability to control these beasts when they are in a root-crazed deranged attack. They keep the hellhounds bound with chains, always holding one end or having it attached around their waists. If a handler somehow is killed, the beast sometimes goes berserk in a killing frenzy.

Now, not all those within the Dominion are like this. They have overtaken many much more civilized countries, and forcibly integrated the defeated armies into their massive war machine. Those fighters though are typically semi-slaves, at least those that have not proven themselves to be more trusted. Others have more readily taken to the evil nature of the Dominion, as depraved men will. So the army consists of a wide range of people, motivated by fear, by greed of plunder, by power, and by evil.

That is really all I have to offer you, my friends. Well, perhaps not all ... I will be praying for you, and for God's mercy and grace."

Minister Polonos stepped away and was ushered out of the chamber. He was heartily thanked by many, though others were obviously so shaken at the report that they hardly saw him exit. Lydia had been listening from the antechamber, and now entered. She spent a moment whispering something to her husband as she took her appointed seat, and his face went from shock to consternation with a hint of anger. He did not take well to the enemy's spiritual attack on his beloved wife.

James stepped back to the podium. "I hope that gave you a feel for what we are facing, from a very personal perspective. Now I will update you on what we know of the Dominion's army and navy and the tactics others have observed — usually before being taken over. Don't get the idea from Minister Polonos that the Dominion is led by superstitious savages. They have shown great cunning and they have amassed the largest land and sea forces that the world has ever seen, and more, they appear to be backed by strong demonic powers. Indeed, several witnesses to major battles report strange darkness, noises, and engulfing fear that would sweep over the defenders before the Dominion advance, demoralizing even the most stalwart fighter before the ruthless attack. It has also been common for political and military leaders to suddenly disappear, die or become very ill days or months before major battles, and for surprise civil uprisings among the populace to break out in anticipation of Dominion attack.

I need to report to you that we too have noticed strange happenings within Freelandia. Just two months ago I requested Grand Master Gaeten to visit outlying areas to assess reports we had been having of gangs arising in some districts. I had not wanted to believe it, but I was personally involved with the break up and capture of one of those gangs in Westhaven. It is likely there are more. And they are becoming much bolder too. Last week there was an audacious prison break, which freed many of the captured "Rats" — that what they called themselves — as well as other prisoners. Several good men were killed in the attack and I am afraid we were not able to get any witnesses to what actually happened. It appeared the action was quite well coordinated, far better planned and executed than I would have expected possible from the likes of the Rats we encountered. I think we must conclude that Dominion spies are already among us."

That got the room worked up. Everyone was glancing around nervously and James could sense fear building. "Now wait, good people — this should be expected, and from what we can gather few gangs have developed beyond a roomful of disgruntled and disaffected youth — hardly fuel for an uprising. We can assume the people of Freelandia will likely be much more resistant to this sort of thing than what the Dominion may have encountered elsewhere, and we do not consider them much of a threat — but nonetheless they may be acting as agents of the Dominion, and I take that very, very seriously. We expect these agents to try to foment fear in the populace — which is a major reason Chancellor Duncan and I will be giving a speech out in the square in a few hours. We need to combat fear with facts — and with faith.

Now, on to the makeup of the Dominion army and navy. From what we have heard …"

Taleena stealthily worked her way toward the kitchen. She knew of several back ways, since the kitchen was a frequent site of her pilfering hands. From a shadowy doorway she peered at the preparations being made for the Council dinner. Several large pots were boiling away, and a pig was being roasted over a large fire, with a bowl of marinade nearby that was being brushed on regularly. She slipped back into the shadows and made her way around to the stairs leading out of the kitchen which the servants would use to carry platters up to the meeting room. Taleena cautiously made her way up the flagstone staircase and then paused where the stairs curved around near the mid-point for a few moments and stooped over, her hands busily moving about. Satisfied with her handiwork, she carefully made her way back to the shadowy doorway. Now she just had to wait for the opportune moment.

Jarl and the other Rats who had been helped to escape from the prison had traveled to a number of the outlying cities. They had instructions to keep a low profile, but cozy up to tavern regulars for a few days, befriending one and all with the occasional free drink. No one had to know the gold paying for it was from the Dominion. They were to make as many "friends" as possible, all while speaking of the conquests of the Dominion, and how for sure the leadership of Freelandia had to be terrified of what was inevitably coming. In particular, they were to speak of the Dominion magic, and how the leaders of every country they ever attacked always seemed to suddenly die ... that no one could resist that Dark Magic, that it was far better to negotiate, far better to join with the Dominion instead of trying to fight it. They were to work up the local populace, and then when Freelandia's top leaders were indeed assassinated, they were to agitate the people even more, stirring up as much fear and confusion as possible — and maybe even a riot or two. And all they had to do was eat and drink, spending an almost unlimited amount of Dominion gold. All had been sure any such assassinations would be months away, but word had just come to them that it would be much more imminent.

The assassins were both in the apartment now, their time was coming closer. They were beginning their final preparations, spewing magical incantations and performing their good luck rituals. In the midst of this each removed a small vial that hung on a cord around their necks. They gingerly poured a small amount of powder from the vial onto a porcelain plate, taking extreme care to ensure none was spilled. A few drops of oil were drizzled onto the contents on the plate and a little wooden spatula used to slowly smear the mixture together. It turned into a sickly red-green color as it was worked back and forth into a thick paste. Each man lifted up an arrow and began to slowly apply the vile paste to the razor sharp bladed head. Once completed, the arrows were ever so carefully stood, point down, against the wall and both men began the process again with a second arrow.

Once four arrows each were finished they sat back and just waited ... with the patience of hunters waiting for their prey.

Murdrock and the magician Turlock were casually wandering about the Keep. Turlock felt oppressed and very uneasy — even in his disguise he felt like he stood out, and occasionally passerbies would turn to look at him with an odd expression on their faces, almost as if he had some strange unpleasant odor. Therefore the two of them did not linger anywhere, but kept moving. They still had an hour or so before they needed to ensure they had a prime spot in the square up close to the platform.

James went to the last section of his presentation. "Now, on to what we can do. That of course is largely dependent on how much time we have — on how long God gives us — before the Dominion attacks. At this point we think we have at least 3 or 4 months, maybe longer — but almost certainly not a year. Therefore, we need to divert the entire country of Freelandia over to the war effort. We will need to raise and train a citizen army, stockpile food and weapons, build additional fortifications — the list is long. But I think it is fair to say that if Freelandia falls, the Dominion will sweep over the entire world. We are the last hope."

James laid out some of the details of what he had been doing over the last several days, and a tentative plan for moving forward.

"It would be tempting to request martial law powers. I do not want to do that. I do, however, need a small group of leaders — no more than five to seven, to be the voice of the Council in decision making. We will need to delegate considerable authority to those most qualified to make preparations. And we need financing — and lots of it. We know Freelandia is a rich country — blessed immensely by God. We will need to spend whatever it takes to prepare.

So first, Council members, I need authority to do whatever it takes to make those preparations — but I want to be under the guidance of the Council, or some smaller subset of it. I will make mistakes, but if others can help with the major decisions there should be less of those. If for some reason you wish someone else to take on this role, by all means appoint them — but do it very soon! We must start right away."

Duncan stood. "Council members: I would like to commend Master Warden James for his efforts past and present in defending our beloved country! And I would like to strongly recommend that we appoint him as War Preparation Director, with authority only short of mine until the crisis has past. Does anyone have objections?"

There was a general murmur of consent. Duncan continued. "There is one thing James left out of his discussion of what we need to do to prepare, the most important thing." James sat up straight, looking hard at Duncan.

Taleena did not have to wait very long for her handiwork to bear fruit. A kitchen maid who had been taken a load of plates up to the dining hall came hurrying back down for another load. She stepped on the nearly invisible soap Taleena had spread out on several of the steps and with no warning completely lost her footing. She screamed as her arm broke upon hitting the hard rock and she tumbled badly down the remaining steps. Everyone in the vicinity hurried over to see what they could do. Meanwhile Taleena immediately slipped out of her hiding spot. She dumped about half of the contents of the powder into the marinade, giving it a quick stir to hide it, and the rest went into the soup pot with another stir. It was all done in less than a minute, and no one had noticed. She glanced over at the stricken kitchen maid and then scurried out without another look.

A few minutes later the head cook came back to attend to the food. She stirred the soup, wrinkling her nose at a slightly odd smell in the pot. She walked over to the fire and brushed more marinade on the roasting pig. The strong aromatic spices hid any odd smell there. That done, she went back to the soup … something did not seem quite right about it. The smell was definitely off — it must have burned on the bottom while she and the others tended to the poor girl who had so very badly fallen. She hesitated with indecision and reached for a spoon to taste the contents to see if it could be salvaged. With a sigh she stopped and put the spoon back down. This was a meal for the High Council of Freelandia ... one did not serve even slightly burned soup to the most important group of people in the entire country. If it did not smell right, it was not right. She reluctantly hauled the pot out the back door. Perhaps the pigs would like it.

"I am too well enough to go out! I have never even seen the Chancellor, much less hear him give a speech! Pl ...ea... se?"

"Now Maria," Grand Master Mesha tried to speak sternly to her, but after spending a couple of days now with her as his "special" patient it was getting rather difficult to hold the act for long. After trying a moment longer — rather unsuccessfully — he gave up entirely and allowed a small wry smile. "You have recovered considerably, far better than I would have expected. But you are still too thin, and you are still weak. Yes, I know ... you walked the length of the building this morning with Kory — but you were quite tired out afterwards!"

"Of course I was — I have not been allowed to do more than sit up in bed these last two days ... I need some fresh air, to get out into the open, to move around! You said yourself in another day or two I can leave here and start classes over at the Music Academy. Now wouldn't going out and listening to the announcement be a great test ... to see if I truly am strong enough to leave? And if I get too tired out I may just have to stay an extra day or two, laying here on this so soft bed and asking for you to come check on me every hour or two, day and night!"

Mesha knew when he was being played, and this surely was it — so why did it seem to work anyway? "Well, alright, Maria. But only if I go with you ... and if I say we leave early, then that is exactly what we will do, with zero complaints or wheedling by you! Deal?"

"Oh, Master Mesha, I would NEVER do such a thing as "wheedle"! You are such a dear — and a blessing. Thank you." She reached up and gave the old man a giant hug — not something many of his patients ever did. He found he rather liked it.

Duncan continued. "Master James does indeed have the responsibility to make preparations for Freelandia — for the physical defenses of our country. But we have an even greater responsibility for the spiritual preparations. We need to pray. We must pray. It is God who will win this war. We must pray for His grace and mercy. I recommend, my friends, that we call an immediate day of mourning where we repent of our lax ways. Perhaps had we been more vigilant to start with the Dominion would never have gotten so powerful. As I found out for myself a few days ago, many holding positions of importance in our schools and elsewhere have drifted away from God, not even believing in our spiritual founding, heritage and ongoing dependence on His spiritual power and guidance. It shocked and sickened me. I have made plans to replace those in high positions of leadership who do not actively seek God and His spiritual directions.

We have been too tolerant; we have allowed sin and unbelief to flourish. It is not God's way to force belief and trust in Him, but we certainly cannot allow leadership that lacks the power and source of real truth and justice. We need to clean house, we need a spiritual revival back to the true God.

Revival needs to start here … it needs to start now. I suggest we start immediately, with a 24 hour fast and seek God's forgiveness and mercy, and His ongoing grace to help us prepare and to stop the Dominion and the evil behind it. I believe we should announce this to everyone, starting here at the Keep and spreading all throughout Freelandia.

Gentlemen, ladies of the High Council … you have your positions based on the skills, talents and abilities God has given you, and even more importantly on the deep personal love, trust and dependence you have in our God. You have heard our situation. You now know what we face. Will you join me on your knees in prayer?"

All over the room chairs were scraped back and everyone in the chamber dropped to their knees. Many began to vocally cry out to God, others wept unashamedly and repented of their own sins. All felt the presence of the Most High.

After half an hour Duncan stood and the council members returned to their seats. "We have your approval on what was requested. I am certain we will need further meetings over the next few weeks and months, and we should convene a subset of our larger group that can meet daily as needed for timely decisions. We have an incredible amount of work before us, and we have an incredible God who will enable us to complete His will!

Members of the Council, pray for me now, that I may give this news to the people, and that it does not rouse fear, but rather turns hearts to God. Let the revival that has started here in this chamber spread out to the Keep and to all of Freelandia!"

Duncan turned to go. "James, Lydia — let us go out to the square — it is time for the public address."

The head cook rolled her eyes at the news. A fast had been called? Now what will she do with all that food?

Chapter 18

Assassins Strike

he square was now quite crowded, waiting for the address by Chancellor Duncan. He sat on the stage, with Lydia on one side and James on the other. There was a distinct nervousness in the air, and Lydia looked pale — she said she felt very troubled, but was not sure what about — but that they should go on as planned. Chaplain Mikael was also on the stage, eyes mostly closed as he prayed. He had sent out the word, and many clergy were doing the same. There was a spiritual oppression present, the likes of which he had rarely felt — and many ministers who similarly felt it were fervently praying for protection. Something seemed to be going on that they could sense, like a battle that was brewing in the heavenlies, and they were not about to sit it out on the sidelines. Prayer was their weapon and faith their shield. With determination they joined the fight.

Duncan looked out and recognized many faces, including Ethan who was sitting right up front. Duncan smiled at his son, and at several others. Then he stood and stepped up to the podium.

"Gentle people of Freelandia! I come before you this day humbled by the responsibility God has entrusted to me. I have always spoken to you simply and straight, and so will do so again. You have heard of the Dominion, and the menace they have become. I come to tell you more — they have become a menace directly to Freelandia. We have just learned the Dominion appears to be intent on the conquest of Freelandia. They are building a massive war machine to hurl against us. They likely expect that we are soft and weak, and that an unexpected strike can take us out quickly. Once we are out of the way, the rest of the world would fall like dominoes."

The crowd was silent, caught up in Duncan's words. Then they began to look about and nervous comments began, rippling through the crowd.

"The Dominion would want us to fear them, to be terrified of their might and power. But God is far, far more powerful! Is God worried about the Dominion? NO!"

That caught the crowd's attention again, and they settled down slightly.

A tapestry hung over a window overlooking the square briefly fluttered as though in a breeze.

Ethan had a dull headache. He rarely had those. Even odder, it seemed located in a very specific part of his head, on the back upper left side that made him want to turn and scratch at it. And now it seemed to be growing stronger.

Gaeten woke from a light nap. Something was wrong. He did not know what it was, but Duncan came to mind. He began to pray.

Maria was very excited, sitting in the far back of the square. The acoustics here were not theater quality for certain, but nevertheless Chancellor Duncan's voice was clear. She was frightened about what he had said about the Dominion, but secure in her trust both of the leadership of Freelandia, and even more in her God. At that thought she smiled and felt a warmth flush through her, comforting and filling her with strength. The anthem of Freelandia began in her mind, and it buoyed her up with even more energy. In her mind's eye she pictured the Chancellor up on the stage that Mesha had described to her, and the anthem took on shape and form and began to swirl around him.

"People of Freelandia! The Dominion is indeed strong, and we have much to do to prepare. We do not believe we have much time, not nearly enough under ordinary circumstances to be as ready as we should be. These are not ordinary circumstances. We have as much time as God will give us, and with His help and direction we will achieve what is necessary. We are one people, and we need to be united in this one over-arching cause. The High Council and I are calling on each one of you — every person in the nation of Freelandia — to join together in the preparation for war."

The crowd began murmuring more loudly and Duncan let his words sink in for a few moments. "There will be hardships ahead for all of us — but we can endure much hardship as free citizens of a God-fearing nation versus the hardships the Dominion tyranny would impose on us if they win. You likely have heard much about the Dominion, and perhaps you have assumed much was exaggeration or speculation. I am here before you to say that without question the Dominion is bent on destruction and driven by evil intent. They do not acknowledge God's sovereignty or justice. They are completely opposed to what we believe in; indeed to the very God we serve. The master they serve has set himself up against God and rules by fear. The Dominion wants to crush Freelandia and extinguish the worship of the true God. We will fight — not just for Freelandia, but for our God.

I mentioned hardship. We must unite all our energies toward defending our nation. Each one of you needs to take inventory of your skills, abilities and possessions and determine how you personally can contribute to the war effort. Given the very short time we believe we have, what is most needed is your time — we need workers by the thousands, by the tens or hundreds of thousands to build, to repair, to train. Effective immediately we will be opening up recruitment centers throughout all of Freelandia. We will need miners, lumbermen, ship builders, masonry workers … and a whole host of others. It may take some time for us to be fully organized to know where the needs are greatest, but we need people with a will to work wherever that need may be. Ask God to show you what you can do, and then do it with all your might!

Master Warden James here has already begun, and we are highly confident of his ability. However, we will not be saved by our own might and strength. We will only be saved by God's mercy. Therefore I call on the entire country to enter into a day of fasting and prayer while we seek God's grace. I and the Council have already begun. We …"

Ethan had not heard anything unusual, nor seen any movement, and he had no idea why he was up out of his chair and moving forward — his body seemed to be reacting without any clear conscious thought. Then Ethan recognized a bright red line shown in his mind's vision, terminating in the middle of his father's chest.

Time stopped. Or nearly did. All sound collapsed into a hushed monotone and the world became almost like an ethereal high definition three dimensional painting. Ethan did not try to turn his head to trace the red line back to its origin; he focused instead on the blue ribbon he could clearly see in the air before him. With all his might he strained, his limbs resisting his will. While his mind raced it seemed like his body was sluggish, like the air around him had thickened to the consistency of pudding. He was he heading for the stairs when a second red line appeared, ending up on the platform, but he could only see it went behind his father. The first line was brighter, and began to pulse in urgency. Ethan's heart sank — in the past that had always meant one thing — that he could not intercept it in time.

The first poison tipped arrow was halfway to its target and was flying true, straight toward Duncan's chest. The second arrow, loosed a moment later, was aimed at a target behind him. Both assassins reached for a second arrow, not even noticing the blur of motion to the side of the stage — their focus had narrowed down to their targets to the extent that little else was even visible.

Maria did not know what was happening, could not know what had transpired in last fraction of a second. But the anthem swirling around Chancellor Duncan suddenly became much more solid and vibrant and the tune much more strident and loud and somehow urgent. She began to rise from her chair, caught up in whatever was happening in her mind which now seemed far more real than her actual surroundings.

Ethan was nearing the stairs. It had only been a fraction of a second in real time. As he did, the blue line shifted and became brighter. Without hesitation Ethan leapt forward and upward, his left foot thrusting out against the thick, resistant air. It connected with the central rail in the middle of the wide stairs and provided leverage, launching Ethan further forward and upward. His right foot caught the top of the railing perfectly and provided the final solid surface to push off against. The two blue ribbons and two red lines nearly intersected, but in his mind there was a way … just barely. He had never attempted anything so acrobatic like this before. He was not sure he could do it.

His body was airborne now; he was fully committed to his course of action. Time, if anything, seemed to go even slower. The first arrow was just entering his periphery vision, slowly slicing through the air, and its poisoned tip was like a brightly glowing red ember in his vision. That complicated things and his timing would have to be perfect. Timing, for Ethan, was something easier to work on.

Ethan began to twist his body along the arc he was traveling. One hand was stretching out in the path of the arrow, and for a moment the red line intersected with his body. The arrows were traveling at an incredible speed in real time, though to Ethan they seemed to be only inching along. His hand began to close on empty air, the first arrow entering his encircling fingers at the last moment before they closed, the tip fractions of an inch ahead of his hand. The friction burned his skin as his hand clenched, and the arrow's momentum propelled him off his original flight path, jerking first his arm and then his body left toward the podium. Ethan's face was now turning toward his father, and he saw a look of shock just beginning to wash over it in slow motion. Ethan could not see the second arrow, but he was swinging his foot in a path of intersection as indicated by the second blue ribbon in his mind, twisting his torso and flinging out one leg and foot. It was going to be very, very close.

The assassins had lifted up their second arrows, nocked them, and were refocusing on their targets. In astonishment they saw a blurred young man's body flinging through the air in front of their targets at an astounding speed. Where had he come from?

James was not the Master Warden for being good at sitting or giving speeches. He saw the flicker of movement from the window as the arrows were launched. Like the true professional he was, his first thought was of protecting Duncan, and he launched himself forward to get the Chancellor down and out of harm's way.

Ethan could not see that movement, he was totally focused on contorting his body along the blue pathway he could see in his mind and of the red line he was trying to intersect at just the right moment. The red lines remained perfectly straight, but the blue lines were dynamic, changing as events altered — and the second blue line was now moving. He tried to twist his body even harder, and the heel of his boot connected with the arrow. The best he could do was try to deflect it. Then his airborne body was past the podium and Ethan started to relax as the immediate danger seemed over … and then realized that with all the twisting and contortions he had put his body through, and with the momentum change from grabbing one arrow and then deflecting another, he had no idea where or how he was going to land. He also was still clutching the arrow, with its tip an angry burning red in his mind that warned him of its continuing danger, and he had to take great care to ensure its tip never got near his own skin even as his body gyrated. His face was turned away from the direction of his trajectory; he actually found himself facing back onto the stage. His mother was sitting with eyes wide and mouth open, likely in some kind of a scream — though Ethan could not really hear anything coherent with the slowed time. He saw James slowly grab his father's shoulders and begin to drag him down behind the small podium. The arrow that now seemed likely to have been intended for the Master Warden's chest instead sliced along his right leg and buried itself in the wood of the stage.

People in the crowd at first did not know what was happening and most were rooted to their spots by the shock of sudden movement. Whatever had happened was certainly not planned.

In a moment there would be chaos and pandemonium as people would panic and try to escape what was about to become a killing ground. A few arrows sent into thick knots of people would assist with the confusion significantly. Then Murdrock and Turlock would make their move. It was an often stated maxim in the Dominion that chaos in an enemy offered many opportunities.

Ethan's trajectory carried his body clear of the stage entirely. He had been traveling nearly directly across it, and his side struck something hard. But instead of crashing into an immovable object — coupled with the high likelihood of severe injury, instead Ethan felt himself begin to skid. He rolled to his back and then over to his other side before realizing he had landed almost perfectly on the opposite stair railing and was now sliding and tumbling down its length toward the ground below. Time was still slow, though now that the immediate worst danger seemed to be over it was moving faster. Having time now to think through all his movements, Ethan had already slowed his gyrating limbs and as he rolled he saw he would crash into a couple of ceremonially dressed Watchers who were just starting up the stairs, their pikes held in a ready stance. Their astonished looks were somewhat comical. As he rolled again he released the arrow in hand, letting the momentum carry it off toward an empty spot on the ground, just before careening into the Watchers, thankfully at lower position than the points of their pikes. All in all, it was a rather soft landing.

The Dominion assassins were just as astonished. The magic of Freelandia was indeed strong! Both blinked a few times and paused, and then their training kicked in. They had a mission to finish. Both drew and released at the same moment. It was convenient that both primary targets were now entwined. The small podium did provide some cover for their prey, but one of the benefits of poisoned arrow heads is that you did not need a solid body mass impact. All it took was a scratch, and there was plenty of available flesh to target.

Grand Master Mesha had not noticed Maria's movement, but stood up himself, along with most of the crowd. Something was terribly wrong. Even as the crowd began to panic and surge away, he began to charge forward. He totally forgot about his patient — he figured he may well be needed more urgently up front.

James was straddling over Duncan, and he saw a few Watchers coming up the stairway to the right. He realized the blur of motion in front of them must have been Ethan, but he had no time to look. He was just pulling Duncan down and engulfing as much of the Chancellor's body as possible when he felt a sharp sting running down his lower leg. He smirked — the archers would have to do much better than that!

Ethan's forward momentum was effectively stopped as he bowled over the Watchers starting to come up the stairs, and he was still falling in a tangle of arms and bodies when a new set of red lines appeared in his mind, again ending near the podium. It was not over yet. He pulled his legs in as his last roll left him facing toward the stage and he pumped them strongly against whatever resistance they could find — which happened to be one of the burly Watchers. He was slower to get started this time, though he was closer to the stage. One of the pikes was ever so slowly falling through the air next to him, torn from the grasp of the Watcher who had been holding it. Ethan grabbed it, not really even knowing for sure why.

The crowd was now beginning to fully panic, still not sure what was really going on, but sure that danger was present. It would not take much to start a veritable stampede. The assassins had clear instructions — their third and forth arrows were to be into the crowds to accelerate the chaos. That took less aiming, and they very rapidly reached for their next arrows without waiting to see the outcome of those just loosed, eyes scanning the crowd below to select likely targets.

Lydia had been frozen in shock as she realized it was Ethan's young body flying through the air across her field of vision, and as James somehow had seemed to appear behind Duncan and pull him down behind the podium. She was just beginning to rise from her own chair when the second arrow thwacked hard into the wooden deck and splintered. She turned and saw a few drops of blood on the decking too. She spun back in time to see Ethan tumbling down the railing on her side of the stage and she took several steps in that direction.

Murdrock was pushing and bumping people aside as if they were rag dolls as he and the magician began to make their way forward to the base of the stage. As each person passed Turlock they felt a tiny prick from some unknown source. Most grimaced in annoyance that quickly passed as they surged away from the stage. Turlock himself was smiling a wickedly evil dark grin. He glanced up and saw Ethan tumbling into the Watchers. Where had that boy come from? What magic was this? He had not felt any disturbance in the spirit realm, aside from the nearly constant oppression present in this awful country. From his angle he could not really see Duncan, though he imagined the sight of a feathered shaft protruding out of that proud chest. Then he noticed Lydia rise and head toward the stairs which he and Murdrock were themselves approaching. That would make their mission all the easier, he thought.

Ethan propelled his body forward, back up the stairs. The blue pathway in his mind was confusing, but he did see several possible intercept vectors. However, this time he would not be able to grab the arrow, there was no time and no way to get both. He was holding the pike near its center, and he began to spin it in a great circle as he had been taught by Gaeten in practice sessions. He was just reaching the podium when the first arrow struck the lower portion of the long wooden pike shaft where the tip stuck fast while the rest shattered, sending splinters deflecting upwards. Nearly simultaneously the second arrow glanced off the other half of the pike shaft, slamming downward into the deck planks. The force nearly wrenched the pike from his hands, but he held firm, coming to a fast stop and planting both feet spread apart in a well balanced form that Gaeten would have been proud of. He angled one end of the pike staff at the window from where he noticed the red lines had originated from this last volley, almost in defiance that he was now ready for any more attempts.

Even as he stopped two screams sounded from different parts of the crowd as arrow shafts suddenly seemed to have grown out of two of the milling people. Two more terrified shrieks sounded and now the crowd went wild with fear. People were pushing and shoving to reach an exit, any exit from the death that was appearing around them.

As several Watchers leapt to the stage Ethan pointed to the covered window. "There!" Unfortunately, there was nothing they could do to effectively move in that direction against the panicked crowd, though several immediately tried to make headway. James stood and took several steps toward the stairs before he suddenly crashed to the floor, his bloodied leg giving out on him. He stared at the wound in amazement — it was only a light scratch, and then his eyes turned upward in their sockets and he collapsed unconscious.

Lydia was at the top step when an Ethan-shape blurred past her going in the opposite direction and a moment later she heard the sound of splintering wood. The Watchers had picked themselves up from the tangled mess Ethan had left them in and were rushing up the stairs on the outer side of the railing, while Lydia's momentum carried her down on the inner side several steps before her mind could tell her to stop. She turned back to look at Duncan, not noticing two men from the crowd who were forcefully moving toward the stage while everyone else was desperately trying to escape in the other direction.

The Dominion archers glanced back at the platform after they launched their last arrows. The both paused in shock — somehow that boy now appeared in the center of the stage, this time with a large staff. Duncan was standing, but they did notice with grim satisfaction that the Warden had just fallen. The poison was designed to be fast acting. They also noticed the boy pointing directly at them. Not that it mattered much. It was time for them to leave anyway, and the wild melee below should provide more than enough distraction and confusion to make good their escape. Each dropped his weapon and threw on their worker-men coveralls, heading out the door toward the back staircase.

The crowd was in a mindless panic and people were getting hurt as they wildly pressed against one another to escape. It was a dreadful, deadly chaos. Maria was in the back, alone in the center of the arranged row of chairs. She did not know exactly what was happening, though she heard the screams and terrified cries of the people around her. A part of her said she should also be trying to escape to safety, from whatever calamity had befallen. However, in her mind the anthem of Freelandia swelled to a roar, drowning out all other noise. It was so loud, so powerful, and it swept her up in its consuming strength. Even without realizing it, she began to sing.

Turlock was at the bottom of the stairs now, only a few feet down from Lydia. He pulled out a fresh needle that he had in a vial of poison, ready for a quick prick, and stepped upward.

Ethan was rather angry. Assassins had just tried to murder his father, and it appeared that Warden James had been hit, even though he had done his utmost to defeat the arrows. He was almost hoping another arrow would come, just so he could swat it away. Instead, just as time was coming back to normal, it slowed yet again, but this time with no red arrows leading toward the stage. Ethan felt a dull ache off to his left and he swiveled his head — as fast as it would turn in the thick soup the air seemed to become, to see a dark red haze enveloping a rather strange looking man on the stairs. The redness was a dark cloud, almost hiding his features, but there was a bright red dot on his ever so slowly rising hand. Ethan could not see what was there, nor tell what the man was trying to do — but the only person within his reach was … his mother.

If he had been angry before, now he felt cold, with almost a touch of fear. Then a blue ribbon snapped into place. Even at his speed he could not reach his mother in time. There was only one alternative. He gave the pike he was slowly spinning a mighty twist and heave. If he had at all miscalculated he realized the pike might just as easily lethally strike his mother. He only had time for a quick prayer.

The problem with slowed time is that once anything left his hands it seemed to travel in excruciating slow motion. The pike lazily swung end over end, completing a full revolution before it traversed the distance to the stairs. The bottom of the shaft was just torquing upward as the man's arm extended in what appeared to be an upward stabbing motion. The butt end caught his arm just below the wrist, snapping it upwards … and backwards. Even as it struck Ethan was himself halfway across the intervening distance. He saw the man's hand smack backwards into his own shoulder, propelled by the momentum of the pike collision. The man's eyes widened in disbelief and he began to mouth a curse in slow motion. Then Ethan was upon him, knocking the small man backwards, one hand striking the arm that had been stabbing toward his mother and was now just starting to lower. They both careened down the stairs, Ethan's momentum propelling them backwards.

Maria was standing on her chair, without ever realizing how she had gotten there. She was caught up in the anthem, and her voice swelled out with far more power than one might think possible from such a small body. The sound reached out palpably. Those near her stopped in their tracks, fear dissipating like fog when struck forcefully by the sun's rays. The song rolled out further, washing over the panicked crowd. Within a few seconds, really as soon as the sound registered on their ears, everyone slowed and then stood still. Maria sang with all her heart and her normally quiet voice resounded mightily throughout the square.

What magic was this? Murdrock was two steps back from Turlock, just far enough so that the tumbling pike missed him as it struck Turlock and it nearly hit him as it fell to the stairs. Where had that come from? Then a young man suddenly appeared, and he and Turlock were crashing backwards off the stairs just to his side. Murdrock only had time to see the poisoned needle sink into Turlock's own shoulder, before both the boy and the magician were falling in a tangled mass on the ground. Murdrock looked up at the stage and saw a shaken but standing Chancellor Duncan hunkered down behind the podium, surrounded now with Watchers who looked like they could kill just with the fierce looks they were casting about at the crowd. Things were going very badly. The mission was a loss. It was time to leave.

Murdrock turned to escape. Now what magic was going on? The stampeding crowd had … had stopped! He heard a powerful female voice singing … SINGING! … some drivel about Freelandia and their god. Murdrock was no magician, but even he felt some of the power emanating from that voice. But he needed to leave NOW. Several Watchers were looking his way, and one was starting to move toward the commotion. The few Watchers at the base of the stairs were now reacting to the boy's actions, and had drawn swords and other weapons. There was no way to escape back through the crowd. The only way out was … back behind the stage, into the open door leading into the Council building. Murdrock tried to be unobtrusive as he slipped sideways, disassociating himself from the fallen and stricken Turlock. No one seemed to notice as he backed into the doorway. There were people in the hallway, trying to see what the tumult was all about. An empty stairway winded upward, and so that route of retreat looked most promising.

The assassins went along their predetermined escape route, down the back stairway and out into the side street, where a few people were still hurrying to get away from the square. They mingled in, affecting a look of fear like the rest, and rushed along with them away. No one ever noticed the two more men leaving the area as fast as they could.

Master Healer Mesha was affected by the singing too, but not so much as to stop his forward progress. As the people around him rather suddenly went still he pushed on, now making much better time. The Watchers let him through, and he climbed the right stairway and rushed to the fallen Warden James. Mesha grimaced at what he saw. There was an angry redness to the skin around the flesh wound, and a dark red patch was spreading up the leg. Mesha whipped out a small and extremely sharp knife and cut off the lower hem of his Master's tunic. He bound the leg above the red patch rather tightly to slow the spread of the poison, and with the help of a few Watchers he had James propped up on a chair, keeping the leg low compared to the rest of his body. He pulled out a small vial of alcohol and poured it on the wound to sterilize and hopefully slow or neutralize at least some of the poison. He would need to get the Master Warden to the Ministry of Healing as quickly as possible, but even so, without knowing what kind of poison was involved — and he was hardly an expert on Dominion poisons — he had very limited options for helping. He next took the most important option — he prayed, laying his hand on the Warden's leg.

Watchers were pulling Ethan up and glowering at the small fallen man underneath him. They did not need to restrain the man — he was curled up into a fetal position with eyes rolled back in his head and a long needle protruding from his shoulder. They stayed several steps back. Lydia came to Ethan's side, wondering just what had happened. Ethan, after assuring himself there was no further danger, wrapped her in his arms in a giant, protective hug.

Maria neared the end of the song, and then was done. The paralysis on the crowd slowly ebbed, but the fear had now passed. They looked around nervously, and moved to help the fallen and hurt. Maria felt exhausted, but the rest and meals she had been partaking of the last few days had strengthened her considerably. Even so, she gingerly stepped down from the chair — when had she gotten up there? — and, not knowing what else to do, sat down. It now seemed frightening to be alone and blind in a very large crowd of people she did not know, in a place she was not familiar with.

Murdrock hurried up the last few steps and down a hallway. The Council meeting chambers appeared to be off to one side, and a few tables were set up in the hallway with eating utensils but no food on them. He looked for more stairs that might lead him back down and hopefully away from the square, and spied a smaller set that looked like what the servants might use. By the smells coming up, it likely led to the kitchen. He sped down the empty staircase and was just rounding a corner at the midpoint at full speed when with no warning his feet went completely out from under him. Murdrock was a very athletic man, but even so the best he could do was land heavily on his seat, with one leg bent awkwardly underneath. He stood and nearly fell again as that leg would not bear any weight. It was either sprained or broken. He tried to take another step and found his shoe nearly slipping again. Cursing, he sat down for a moment and felt the bottom of the shoe — it was slick with some slippery substance — what idiot would drop … soap? … on the stairs and not clean it up? Cursed Freelandia magic! He wiped his shoes and hobbled slowly and painfully down the rest of the stairs and out the back kitchen exit. As he passed a small fenced area he noticed six or seven pigs, all lying dead. Even the pigs were cursed here!

Chapter 19

Aftermath

The Ministry of Healing was normally a very busy place. In the hours after the public announcement it was especially so. Mesha had cordoned off one wing of the second floor just for those who seemed to have contacted the Dominion poison. It appeared the poison was very quick acting, but did not kill right away. Several people were in very serious condition, Warden James being one of them — though he seemed to be reacting slower than most — perhaps from the wound being so superficial and far down on one leg. Still, he was unconscious like all the others, barely breathing, and turning a ghastly black color.

One patient seemed to be in considerable worse shape than all the rest. He was a short fellow, and from Ethan's description it very well may be that this was the Dominion poisoner himself. He apparently had gotten the largest dosage, and in the shoulder — that was not far away from his heart. He was barely alive now, taking breaths so very shallow that Mesha could barely tell he was breathing at all.

Grand Master Mesha, the most skilled healer in all Freelandia, felt helpless. He had tried every antidote he knew, but this poison appeared to be something he had never experienced before, probably originating somewhere down in the far south of the Dominion and reserved for their most evil uses. How would he ever find a way to stop this thing?

After the very real scare of having a large pike miss her by inches, seeing Ethan crashing to the ground and then finding that she had been the target of this last assassination attempt, Lydia had felt a bit of panic rise in her — but she promptly suppressed that. God had just miraculously saved her, and she WAS NOT going to turn into a blubbering mess, especially in front of all the people who needed leadership and direction now more than ever. And then she had heard the singing, and looked out over the fear-filled crowds to see a little girl standing on a chair, singing her heart out. Lydia watched as a wave swept over the crowd, ending their panic and restoring calm order. She herself felt the spiritual dimensions of the song washing over the entire square, and was astonished at the source. Then the song ended and the young girl seemed to crumple down onto her chair, all alone and not moving. As Lydia surveyed the situation on the stage she noticed no one coming to the girl, and from her vantage point it appeared she could use a friend. There was nothing on the stage Lydia could work on or do, so rather than just stand there she filtered down through the crowd to reach the singer.

As she neared, Maria turned her head toward Lydia, hearing the footsteps approaching her. At first she felt worried, but then felt a peacefulness about the new person, a gentleness and godliness that seemed to accompany the footfalls.

"Hello, little one. My name is Lydia."

Maria did not know any Lydia's, and the only one by that name she had ever heard of was the Chancellor's wife — which of course this could not be, why would such an important person as that come to greet her? The voice was full of gentle and genuine sounding concern. "Ah … hello. My name … my name is Maria."

"You seem all alone."

"Yes …" The weight of that was feeling heavier, and Maria's voice quavered. "I was with … I mean, before the commotion … then people were screaming and I could not tell what was happening … and the anthem was playing in my mind so very loudly. Then I was standing on the chair and singing, I don't really even know why. But the people stopped yelling and it seemed things quieted down. I was … scared." The last was said in a way that made it obvious that this was not just in past tense.

"I heard you sing, and it was amazing. God is surely working in you mightily. Say, Maria … are you The Singer from Reginaldo's concert?" Lydia was thinking back, and the affect that night had been different, but had distinct similarities in how it touched everyone who heard it.

"I … I … guess …so". This almost came out as a sob as Maria's control began to slip. She was very tired, felt a bit abandoned by Grand Master Mesha, and just wanted to go back to her room at the Ministry of Healing.

Lydia looked intently at the young wisp of a girl in front of her, marveling at God's grace to put such a powerful gift into such a frail looking vessel. Then she gathered Maria up in a hug and held her close. All pretense of composure left Maria and she did begin to cry as emotions overwhelmed her. It did not last more than a few minutes — growing up as an orphan made her seal up many of her emotions; it was the only way she could survive. Yet somehow she felt incredibly safe with this Lydia, whoever she was, and her defenses wavered.

"There now … it seems to me that was not just about feeling lost and alone right now. That's ok, perhaps we can talk more about …" Lydia paused, cocking her head to one side as though listening to something. "… about how hard it has been for you since your father died."

Maria gasped. "But how did you know …" She stopped, feeling it somehow did not really matter. "I really should try to find Grand Master Mesha — he may be worried about me."

It was Lydia's turn to be startled. How did this little one know Mesha? "Maria, Master Mesha is very busy right now — quite a few people were hurt in the square and he is tending to them. Tell you what; I will let him know that you are with me right now. Perhaps we can get away from all these people and get a cool drink. I would offer you some food, but Chancellor Duncan has called a day of fasting — you heard about the Dominion?"

"Yes, but I am not sure I understand. And what happened here — I was listening to the speech and then there was screaming and yelling all around, and people were pushing and shoving to get away?"

"Come, let's walk by the stage and I will let Mesha know you are in good hands, and then I will explain."

Lydia took Maria by the arm, steering her through the chairs and milling people. As they neared one of the dead, fallen by an assassin's arrow, Maria crinkled up her nose and veered further away. Lydia observed this and asked "What is the matter, Maria?"

"I smell something awful! It is faint, but very pungent. What did the person die of?"

"How did you know someone was dead?"

"Oh, I have been around farms enough to know the smell of death. It is not very pleasant either, though not too bad for the first day or so. But there is something else present too, something I have never smelled before … and it is awful."

Lydia sniffed several times, but could not detect anything amiss. "I can't seem to smell anything unusual. Perhaps your sense of smell is keener than mine. I suppose that might happen to help you compensate for the loss of sight."

"Maybe. But what happened — why is there a dead person here?"

"Well Maria, it is really part of the whole story of what happened. Let me explain." Lydia gave an abbreviated account of what she had deduced about the assassin archers, Ethan's heroic actions, and the final attempt on her own life. "And then I saw you standing out in the back all alone, and it seemed you could use a friend. I'd like to be that … a friend that is, Maria. I can sense God has great things in store for you, even beyond what it appears He has already been doing."

Maria was trembling. "But … but that means … but you're THAT Lydia … Chancellor Duncan's wife … THE Lydia!"

Lydia chuckled and pulled Maria in close. "Yes Maria. But I am just a fellow servant — and worshiper — of the Most High God like you are. Well, perhaps you are in a whole different class of worshiper, from what God has shown me!"

"I don't understand what you mean. But why … why would you come to talk with me? Why would you want to be my friend? I'm just …"

"Just a poor orphan girl? I think in God's sight you are far more than that, Maria. You are His chosen vessel of a great and powerful gift. And why would I want to be your friend?" Lydia laughed in a good natured, kind sort of way that invited you in to share whatever it was she found humorous. "Well, the most important reason is because it seemed like you needed one just now. I also sense part of God's workings in you, and find it … delightful!" She did not add that she felt that somehow Maria was going to play a vitally important role in the upcoming war with the Dominion … but only if the fear rooted in her past could be overcome.

The two had walked up near the stage. Mesha glanced up. "Hey Maria! I had forgotten about you for a few minutes. Don't worry, I have never forgotten a patient for very long!" His eyes took in the way Maria and Lydia were walking close together, and the motherly concern showing on Lydia's face. "It looks like you are in very capable hands. Good — I am going to be extremely busy, and am heading back to the Ministry now. Lydia, I would appreciate it if you could bring Maria back … she has a room near my office, at least for a few more days of recovery." He eyed the wilted look of Maria. "Maybe more than just a couple of days. We'll tend to that later. Lydia — she really does need rest, she has been through a very taxing ordeal and concussion, and she is quite weak. It looks like today really did her in. Please make sure she rests." With that he dismissed them from his attention to work with the victims.

Lydia led Maria into the Council building. "Come, let's get some fruit juice — that should still fall within the boundaries of the fast, at least for patients of the Ministry of Healing." They walked along the lower corridor, past various servants who seemed decidedly uncertain about what they should be doing next. As they neared the kitchen Maria's nose started twitching and she had a grimace on her face. "What is it Maria?"

"That smell — can't you smell it?"

"Smell what, Maria? I smell the remains of cooking dinner…"

Maria was stepping into the kitchen now, letting her nose direct her feet. She wandered over to the dirty dishes area, which were being attacked by several kitchen maids. Lydia guided her around tables and the like as they went along. Lydia wore a concerned expression, though she did not yet know what Maria was talking about.

Maria led her to a large soup pot that had not yet been scrubbed out. As she neared it, Maria became more agitated and her face was crinkled up into a serious frown. "It's very similar … maybe the same … as I smelled out in the square where the de … the people had fallen. There are other spice odors overlaying it, but I think it is the same." One of the maids, intent on her work, reached out to grab the pot as the next item to be scrubbed. Lydia did not hesitate. Her hand flashed out and caught the maid's wrist in an iron grip just as she was grabbing the pot. The poor girl shrieked in surprise, and then cowered when she saw the dire look on Lydia's face.

In a moment two Watchers ran in — they were on extremely high alert and a dropped utensil might have caused one of them to come running with drawn weapon. They saw Lydia's stance and expression and immediately positioned themselves next to the maid, as though she might have been a Dominion assassin.

"The pot — I think it may have been poisoned!" The maid, terrified enough of the attention from Lydia and the Watchers, fainted right away. One of the Watcher's grabbed a towel and wrapped the pot with it, then removed it from the counter. They had cordoned off an area outside where the poisoned arrows and fragments were being carefully gathered, and this would be added to the collection.

Maria was still troubled. She turned her head this way and that, puzzled. Lydia watched her. "Show us what else, Maria!"

She led them through the kitchen, stopping half way across and led those following to the roasting pig. Maria screwed up her face into a wrinkled scowl and pointed. "There! Whatever is hanging there … it has the same odor." She turned to go, then tilted her head again and moved quickly out the back door. A few steps out she began to gag, pointing toward the pigpen. The Watcher took one look, spun around and ran back through the kitchen to get assistance. He returned in a moment with over a dozen senior men. Several took up guard around the pen, others began to remove the roasting pig from over the fire in the kitchen, and the rest began to form up search groups. The most senior came over to Lydia. "Ma'am, I am sorry, but you need to leave the building immediately. If someone poisoned the food, that person or persons may still be present — and still be a very real threat. From what I can gather, you already were the target of one assassination attempt. You will NOT be for any others, if we have anything to say about it!"

"Quentin!" Immediately a younger man came up, moving with cat-like fluidity. Lydia recognized him as a promising protégé of Gaeten's.

"Yes sir?"

"I am assigning you to be the personal bodyguard of Chancellor Duncan's wife, effective immediately. You are only relieved when I personally ask you to step down. Your particular skills may fit in well with your assignment — and I understand you are friends with their son Ethan? Good. He will be busy awhile debriefing us on what happened — it seems he may be about the only one who really knows anything. I am sure he will be more at ease knowing you are watching his mother and her … young friend. Once he is debriefed I am sure Ethan will come to assist you. For now, I am taking Chancellor Duncan over to the Watcher Compound — there is no safer place in all of Freelandia as far as I am concerned. Lydia can go there too, but that is not an order. The Compound is very well guarded now, and we have rustled up a contingent of gifted Discerners to scan everyone coming and going. Lydia is pretty well known among them of course, but if you come in alone be sure to follow the instructions of the guards — everyone is rather short of temper and patience just now."

"Yes sir. I presume under the circumstances that lethal force rules are in affect?"

"Oh, most certainly, Quentin. Use your head, and listen to your charge — but her safety is paramount and you are hereby authorized to use whatever actions you deem necessary to fulfill that mission."

"YES SIR!" "Ma-am, and I think it is Maria, correct? I heard about you and we actually have met a few times during your stay at the Watcher Compound. We need to leave right now. I think the square may be the best route — most of the crowd is dispersed now and the place is teeming with Watchers — so it should be a pretty safe direction."

Maria was shaking — this was all just about too much for her, and now the energy she had was draining rapidly. She took a stumbling step forward and Lydia caught her, holding her close so she had someone to lean on. Quentin wanted to lead the way, but instead came to the other side of Maria to help give support.

Lydia saw how drained Maria appeared. She knew Duncan and Ethan would be busy for quite some time, and so made a decision. "Maria, I can take you back to the Ministry of Healing — I understand you have a room there now — or we could go over to my house for awhile. I have a feeling Duncan and Ethan will be out for quite some time, and I really did not have anything else planned for the evening … and I would enjoy getting to know you better. I can pretty much guarantee our hospitality may be a notch or two better, and if you get sleepy we have several spare bedrooms with big soft beds and fluffy pillows. It is up to you, but I would very much like to spend some time with you — and I think our house qualifies as a pretty secure place!"

Maria was flabbergasted. She was being invited to the home of the Chancellor of Freelandia? How could this be happening? She was half tempted to turn down the offer as not being real, or since she did not at all feel worthy of such an honor. And after all, the room at the Ministry of Healing was very nice — far better than anything she had ever had in Westhaven. The food too was far better than table scraps, though she did not have the choices available at the Watcher Compound. She felt she should say no … but this Lydia seemed to be a very nice person, and she really should not turn down the Chancellor's wife, should she? "I … I think that would be wonderful! But Kory will be worried, wondering where I am."

"And who is Kory?"

"She is my new friend. Grand Master Vitario — of the Music Academy — asked her to be my helper."

Lydia smiled. "My, Maria — you seem to be collecting Grand Master acquaintances — both Vitario and Mesha?"

Maria gave a tired chuckle. "Oh, one more too — Gaeten. He is a Grand Master Watcher."

Lydia's eyes widened. "You know Gaeten as well? There seems to be quite a lot more to you that first appears! I have a feeling you have a few stories I truly would like to hear!

Maria, I think we will have a grand time. Let's have a little tea party, just the three of us girls. How would that be?"

"Oh Miss Lydia, I … I don't know what to say! You are being so very kind! I really am nobody important!"

Lydia laughed gently. "Maria, in God's sight we are all important. And now I am very curious about you! I can sense some of God's work within you … and I think I would like to be your friend, if I can."

Maria marveled again. She wondered if she should pinch herself to see if she was dreaming or awake. It was all too wonderful.

Lydia turned toward Quentin. "Let's stop over at the Ministry of Healing first to find Kory and pick up anything Maria may need or want — would that be ok with you?"

"Yes ma'am — it is not likely any Dominion folk will be wandering about there!"

Actually, there was one Dominion person at the Ministry of Healing, though he was hardly wandering anywhere. Turlock's body was curled up in a tight ball, his skin nearly black from the affects of the poison and his breath was an occasional soft rasp. Mesha figured the Dominion poisoner would be dead within an hour or at most two.

Lydia, Maria and Quentin shuffled into the main Healing building. Maria was being half-carried, she was so exhausted. They had to pass by the special area where Mesha had arrived with all the patients and was trying anything and everything to try to stop the poison — and failing. He glanced up with a very stricken look at Lydia as they passed by. "I just can't stop it! They are all dying, even Warden James. This cursed Dominion poison! He held up the vial found in Turlock's coat pocket. I have never run across it before. I think it is from the deep south of the Dominion, and unless we somehow find someone who just happens to be familiar with that area and this poison ..." his voice had taken a sarcastic tone in his frustration.

Lydia stopped in her tracks. "But Mesha ... at the Council meeting we did have just such a person, a missionary who just escaped out of Dominion persecution — Minister Polonos!"

Mesha stood up very straight, his eyes going wide. He turned to one of his assistants. "FIND HIM AT ALL COSTS RIGHT NOW!" The young man raced out the door. Quentin helped Maria to sit down with her back to a wall for support.

The assistant could not have gotten more than half way down the hall when all in the room heard what sounded like a loud collision. There were several thuds, scuffling sounds and low voices, and Quentin positioned himself between the others and the exit, one hand straying inside a side pocket of his coat. Then the assistant returned leading a thin, older man who seemed as if the years hung on him rather heavily.

Lydia spoke up. "Minister Polonos! We … we were just sending for you! How … why did you come here?"

The vigorous voice offset the somewhat frail weathered appearance. Polonos smiled. "Ah, that is simple. God told me to. I have learned to listen, and to obey, regardless of the directions. I have been given two tasks." He smiled again at their somewhat bewildered expressions. He looked over at Mesha, evaluating who he might be. "I presume you are the healer? Good. First, I am to give you these. He removed a small satchel he was carrying over one shoulder. "I really don't know why you need my herbal tea that I brought back with me from the mission field, but perhaps you can find some good use for it." Polonos peered around the room for the first time since entering. "Oh, my Father in Heaven! Black Rubous poisoning!"

Mesha could not constrain himself. "You recognize this?"

Polonos shuddered and lowered his eyes. "All too well. It was one of the favorite poisons of the local witch doctors where I ministered. They would put an evil spell on someone — perhaps they really thought they were hexing someone — and then if nothing bad happened soon enough they would secretly slip some Black Rubous poison into a drink or food, or into any open sore or scratch on their victim. A small enough dose would make the person very, very sick for many days, and a slightly higher dose would kill them over the course of hours or days. A victim's skin would turn black, which the witch doctors would say indicated their dark magic spells were working.

Several of our missionaries died that way, until a converted witch doctor introduced us to the leaves of the small shrub whose roots are used to make the poison. It seems the leaves make a natural antidote — and I might add a fairly decent tasting tea for that matter. Most of the missionaries in that region learned to like it — and no more died with black skin either."

"Quick man, let's get some made. Some of these people are in no shape to drink — can a poultice of the tea help as well?"

"Oh yes, we found it absorbs through the skin readily, and that method works nearly as well. Just brew a strong dark tea with some hot water, cool it down and apply."

Mesha grabbed a handful of leaves and ran down to the kitchen area for hot water. As he left, Polonos began moving from bed to bed, peering at each inhabitant. He would study each one, shake his head, and then move down to the next. He was only half way through this strange procession when Mesha came running back in with a pot of hot water with small pointed leaves sticking out. He had his assistant begin pouring this back and forth between several pots to help the steeping go faster, and to begin the cooling process of the hot liquid. As that was being done, he looked over at Minister Polonos. "Excuse me, sir ... what are you doing?"

"I have a second job to do. God sent me to give you my tea leaves, and also to lay my hands on someone and pray for a healing. I just don't know yet who it is God wants to work His healing power on."

"Well, I have no doubt — it surely is for Master Warden James!" Mesha steered the old Minister over to the large still frame of the Warden. Polonos peered down at him for a moment, and then shook his head.

"Nope, he is not the one." He moved on down the line and then stopped abruptly over the small dark Dominion man.

"Surely not THAT one, good Minister!" Mesha was indignant. "No! He is the one who poisoned all these people ... and as I understand it, he even tried to poison Lydia!"

Polonos peered down at the shrunken person before him, clearly very close to death. He reached out a weathered, somewhat shaky hand and placed it over the hot, dry forehead. He closed his eyes a moment. "Father in heaven, in Your infinite wisdom you have chosen mercy for this poor sinner who is so very lost and set against Your ways." He squared his shoulders. "In the name and power of the great High God, and through the name of His Son, Jesus, I command you to BE HEALED." The last was said with surprising strength and conviction.

Even Maria, as exhausted as she was, pulled herself upright. At first nothing seemed to have happened, but then the folded up body began to straighten out and the horribly black skin began to noticeably lighten. The man's breathing became stronger, and then with a cough he opened his eyes. Lydia gasped, and Quentin drew his dagger. The bright red eyes that glared malevolently out did not seem even human. The man's lower jaw dropped open, and though he did not mouth words, yet a deep, dark voice spoke out.

"What isss thisss?" The voice was thunderous and full of violent evil. The man's head swiveled to look out over the room. "This one is MINE and you cannot have him! He has been mine for years, and it is now time for him to pay us back with his life and soul. Who has loosed my death grip upon him?"

Maria was frightened beyond words and Lydia had all color drained from her face. Mesha was looking on in shock, even as he continued to apply the tea poultice to his other blackened patients. Quentin had his blade held at ready, and had moved to stand between Lydia and the Dominion assassin. Only Polonos seemed rather nonplussed. The Minister stared into the demon controlled eyes. "The Lord God has intervened. It is His will and power to heal. The body has been set free of the poison, and now it will be set free of you as well." In the same powerful voice he intoned "In the name and power of the One and Only God and of His Son Jesus, I command you to come out of this man!"

The demon shrieked a horrific, blood curdling roar. "Noooooo! He is MINE! The man's hand curled into a fist and his arm cocked as if to strike Polonos, but as the head turned to look at the Minister squarely another shriek came howling out. "You servant of the Most High God … you have caused this!"

"No, demon. I am just the messenger, just the vessel God has chosen to use. Now, I COMMAND YOU TO DEPART!" Polonos reached over and grabbed the man's hand and the demon gave another dreadful howl. Then the body before them slumped back onto the bed.

Minister Polonos sighed. "It is not uncommon for their magicians and witch doctors to be possessed like that. God gives us the power to command the demons to leave, and they will. But they leave an empty spiritual "hole" behind. It is an empty spot just waiting to be filled. If it is not filled with God's Spirit, soon the evil spirit will return. If he finds the spot empty, he will try to fill it again, maybe invite a few of his demon friends to come along too, and the state of the poor victim will be far worse than it had been before. Yet for at least a few days their minds will be clear. God gives them a second chance, so to speak."

The small man's eyes fluttered and then opened. Everyone in the room was watching him intently, wondering if the demon had truly gone. When he had become fully awake he tried to sit up, looking rather dazed and wobbly. Polonos quickly grabbed his shoulders to hold him upright. Quentin looked nervous again, and still had a knife drawn and ready.

Turlock looked about. He had no idea where he was, or for that matter, truly who he was.

Polonos looked into his eyes, and saw no trace of the demonic influence. "Brother, how are you feeling?" he spoke in a gentle voice.

Turlock looked at the weather scarred man helping him. "I am ok … I guess … I don't really know. Where am I and who are you?"

"My name is Polonos, a simple servant of God. You are in the country of Freelandia, in a House of Healing. You have been very, very sick. I expect you are feeling rather tired, but shortly you will feel incredibly alive, more alive that you can remember."

"Yes … I do feel … alive — like a weight has somehow been lifted off that was crushing me. But I don't know what it was or what happened to change it." Turlock tried to smile. At least it looked like he was trying — it was almost as though the muscles of his face were not used to moving that way. He did give it a valiant effort. "I seem to be at a disadvantage. I really do not know who you are … and I am even not very sure who I am." He said this rather sheepishly, and then looked down at his hands and arms as if he hoped to recognize something.

Minister Polonos was watching him most carefully. Turlock stared at his highly tattooed arms, turning his wrists to trace the strange symbols. His mouth twitched several times, and he noticed the black patches that were slowly fading to more normal skin tones. Then he looked out over the other patients in the room.

Mesha had not stopped, rapidly applying bandages soaked in the strong tea to every wound and to nearly every available patch of bare skin on every patient in the room. It was clearly already having an effect, as several people including Warden James were beginning to moan now, whereas before they had gone scarily silent. The smell of the tea was strong in the room.

Turlock crinkled his nose at the smell, then cocked his head sideways as though the smell were registering in some distant place in his memory. He slid off his bed, standing shakily with support from Polonos. He was now staring at Quentin. The young Watcher had a deadly serious look in his eyes, and the dagger in his hand pointed unerringly at Turlock. Lydia had moved to Maria's side and had one arm on her shoulder protectively, watching the drama unfold.

"I don't understand … my name is Turlock, but I don't recall where I am from or why I am here … but …"

"Brother Turlock. This is going to be difficult for you, and as your memories return it is going to be even more difficult." Polonos turned the smaller man to look at him directly. "You are feeling more alive because God has set you free — He has given you a remarkable gift of freedom. You were under control of an evil spirit — a demon. God sent me to cast off that demon. All of us here in this room watched it leave you. Before that you were largely under its control. Under that influence you likely have done many truly evil and horrible things. As your memory returns, you will realize this. But you MUST understand — even with what you had been, God still loves you — He loves you enough to give you this gift of freedom. And He loves you enough to have ahead of time sent His Son Jesus to take the penalty of your sins and die for them. The penalty was paid in full, and God raised Jesus back from the dead and He has gone to heaven to sit at the right hand of God to prepare a place for us. Because of that payment, God has adopted those of us who accept Jesus as Lord into His family and inheritance. And, if God can love you that much … so can I." With truly remarkable grace Polonos very deliberately drew the smaller man into a fatherly hug.

"But … Mr. Polonos … I don't …" Suddenly Turlock stiffened and he violently drew back several feet. His face took on a horror stricken look and his eyes bulged. "NOOOOO! It can't be … I couldn't have … I have done …" His words dropped off to silence and his eyes were rapidly darting side to side. Quentin, wondering if the demon had returned, took a step forward, dagger at the ready.

Turlock let loose a curdling scream of despair. He looked at the Watcher and his knife and without warning ran forward, arms spread wide. Just in time Quentin turned the blade aside to avoid impaling the man, and he shoved Turlock roughly away from the women.

"Nooooo! You don't understand! You don't know what I have done! You cannot know what it was like living with that … that … hideous demon! I do not deserve to live!" With amazing speed Turlock wheeled about and dashed out the door.

Polonos was only a few steps behind him, and Quentin shouted for additional help. Several other Watchers had been assigned to the Ministry building, and Quentin was in no way going to leave his assigned duty of guarding Lydia. Two mid-level apprentice Watchers dashed by, following the retreating footsteps of the crazed Turlock.

Turlock raced out of the building and turned toward a small path that led into a little park garden. He was very weak, but even so he ran with all his strength, trying to find some escape from the memories that were flooding into his brain. He saw a small pond and ran to it, hoping to throw himself in.

Polonos was just a bit faster. As the small man slowed to approach the pond's edge, he reached out and grasped him and they tumbled to the ground together.

"Let me go … let me finish this! I do not deserve to live! And I would rather die than allow that demon to come back into me!"

Polonos wrapped his long arms around the smaller man, surrounding him in a protective bear hug. "No, my son. None of us deserve God's mercy. Not you, not me. He gives it as a gift that you cannot possibly earn. But to try to kill yourself would be rejecting the gift He gave you. Turlock! He gave you this freedom from the demon … because He loves you!"

Turlock stopped struggling and collapsed inwardly, even as the Watchers arrived and stood to the side, not sure what was happening. Turlock began to sob uncontrollably, and the two men rocked in their embrace on the ground. After a few minutes of racking sobs Turlock pushed back and, still weeping asked the most important question of his life. "Mr. Polonos … what must I do to know this Jesus? What must I do to be saved?"

Chapter 20

Tea Party

Maria was sitting in what must have been the softest chair she had ever been on in all her life. When she first sat on it she sank down so low she wondered if she would ever be able to get back out without help. She had to learn to sit somewhat on the edge to avoid being trapped. That made it easier to reach the little table which held an elegant shaped teapot, cups and saucers.

This was all so preposterously wonderful that she still could not really believe it. Kory saw the giggle forming and tried to frown to hold her own in control, but it was a lopsided fight and in a moment she began to giggle too. In a minute both girls had to put their cups down so as not to spill as they were caught up in the oddity of sitting in the home of the Chancellor of Freelandia, sipping chamomile tea with the Chancellor's wife in their parlor.

Lydia smiled at their merriment. "Now that you have rested Maria, could you tell me everything about you?"

"Everything? I am sorry that I don't think there is really very much to tell, and it is not all that interesting."

Lydia laughed out loud. "Well, it may not be interesting to you, but I am sure it will be to me … and to Kory too!" Kory nodded encouragingly and quickly realized she needed to add words to her actions. "Yes, Maria — I am interested too!

"Well, let's see … my family was from Morgania, a little country close to Alteria. My mother was the most beautiful woman in the whole country ... at least that is what my father used to tell me. I ... I only remember her a little, and I don't recall at all what she looked like. I lost my sight when I was very young after some kind of accident — I don't remember it, but my father said I had a fall and hit my head pretty hard. Anyway, my mother died not long after that from a sickness that was sweeping through our country. After awhile my father could not find enough work, and said that he and my mother had always dreamed of moving to Freelandia where they could worship the true God freely and wholeheartedly. So he saved and saved and we sold everything but what we could carry in a few trunks. Father booked passage on a ship heading to Freelandia. Since he was an animal healer, the captain of the ship figured he could help look after the crew and other passengers during the ride, and therefore he promised us nearly free passage."

Maria had been smiling while she talked about her father, but now her face grew grim and her voice faltered. "But then father became ill during the voyage. We don't know what it was from, but the crew said another bout of bad sickness was spreading in Morgania. I suppose it may have been — many people had been getting sick in our town, but father never really told me much about it. Anyway, he grew very ill and I tried ... I tried to help ... but I did not really know what to do ... I did not know which herbs to use and ..." Maria's upper lip began to tremble violently and tears came pouring down her cheeks.

Lydia immediately got up from her chair and pulled Maria in close, and Kory came alongside and held her hand. "I didn't know the medicines my father had brought, I was just learning. No one else on the ship knew how to help either. Father just got sicker and weaker ... and then ..." Maria burst into great racking sobs of sorrow. Lydia hugged her even closer and began to speak words of prayer over her, and the sobs began to quiet as all three rocked together in shared pain.

It took several minutes before Maria could continue. "The captain said he had to ... bury father at sea. When we arrived here, the Captain told me we had not fulfilled our part of the deal, and said I needed to pay for passage. He confiscated all our belongings except what I was wearing and one change of clothes. I was given over to a small orphanage at the port, but they really did not know what to do with a destitute blind girl. No one really wanted me."

"Oh, that is terrible!" Kory was aghast.

"But then Brother Rob heard about me and brought me to Westhaven to join with the small group of orphans living with him in his old parsonage. I was the oldest, and eventually was able to help out with the younger children. I guess Brother Rob had a heart for orphans who had special needs, as each of us had some handicap or another. Timmy has a hunched back, for instance. He took us all in as though we were his own children … all the misfits that … that no else wanted." Maria's hold on her emotions broke again and the years of suppressing the pain began to loosen.

Lydia just held on tightly, rocking gently and letting the sobs and tears come out unhindered. She had sensed something like this was underneath the brave exterior Maria showed to the world. Lydia and Kory were caught up in the emotions too and were sniffling along with Maria.

When things had quieted down Lydia sat back and pulled Maria onto her lap. She held her face with both hands, saying "Maria, don't ever feel you are not wanted! The Creator of the universe ALWAYS wants you, and will NEVER forsake you."

"I know … I have come to learn that. But sometimes I think I forget."

"Yes, we often do. Sometimes God seems so very close, and sometimes farther away — and yet He has not moved — only we have."

"Sometimes I wish God were right here, where He could wrap me up in His big arms of love and hold me close."

"Sometimes, Maria, that is what He uses us for." With that Lydia pulled Maria in closer for a very motherly … and needed … hug.

"Yes, but sometimes I still wish He was right here, physically, rather than just in the 'special place' in my mind."

Kory looked quizzical. "Special place? What is that?"

Maria smiled. "Oh, you know — that place in your mind where you go when you sing and worship God, where He is present and watching."

Kory looked over at Lydia, perplexed, and shrugged her shoulders. Lydia had arched her eyebrows and also had a questioning expression, which she verbalized. "No, Maria … we don't know what you mean."

Now it was Maria's turn to look puzzled. "Well … when you sing, don't you have a special place in your mind where He is, and where you picture yourself going and worshiping before Him?"

Lydia answered. "I cannot speak for Kory, but no, Maria. When I sing a spiritual song or hymn I try to think of God as I am singing, but sometimes my mind wanders. And if I am singing something else I usually am not thinking of God at all. And I don't think I really picture anyplace in particular in my mind."

"Me neither. I don't sing a whole lot, but when I play music I am normally fully concentrating on the score in front of me or where my fingers are supposed to go," Kory agreed.

"You don't? But then … when you sing you are not always singing to God?" Maria sounded surprised.

"Not always", Lydia conceded. "Are you saying that every time you sing you imagine yourself standing before God and singing to Him?"

Maria thought about that for a moment. "I don't really think I am imagining it — it seems so very real. It is like I see myself in a big open space, somewhat like a big theater. I am on a stage, and God is my audience … but it is not like He is a man sitting by himself in a big empty chamber. He fills the entire foreground, and it is like He is there in front of me, but also all around me and behind me too. And I can … don't laugh, but there I can see! I can see a brightness that I know is Him, and it is like I can feel God too, all around me. There I have no limitations like my blindness or clumsiness. I can see and I can dance — all before God, all to worship and praise Him. Even when the song is not specifically about Him, I am still giving Him glory for being able to sing, to dance, to enjoy being near Him. And I think … I think He likes it!"

Both Kory and Lydia were amazed. Kory was the first to speak. "You mean … you actually see God?"

"Well, not exactly. I mainly see a pure white brightness that is all around, but seems to have a focal point just outside of sight. And I can sense His presence. I am always accepted there, always wanted, always enjoyed and cherished for being just me."

Lydia spoke up. "That sounds so wonderful, Maria. And I am sure you are totally accepted and loved — God created you as you are, and loves you just as you are. Even with our faults, even though He is still working on purifying us in His image, yet still He fully loves each of us too. It really is a great mystery! Our love is often so shallow — based on how a person looks or acts. God looks at us and sees everything, even our very thoughts and intentions … and yet still somehow loves us fully.

So, Maria … in your 'special place' you can see, you can obviously worship — but you dance as well?"

"Yes. When I sing I am usually dancing before God with the music, doing leaps and things I could never really do with my body! It is like I am soaring without my physical restrictions, just God and me. And sometimes it seems like God amplifies the music somehow — the songs become more powerful, more alive. I can feel power flowing from God into the music and then, sometimes, I can even start to feel and even see the notes. I realize that sounds really strange. I don't understand it either. But it is like when I sang Sir Reginaldo's Masterpiece. I could start to see the music … it flowed in a colorful rainbow around me."

Kory looked misty eyed. "Wow! That is so awesome, Maria! I wish I had a 'special place' like that! How did you get that?"

"I don't really know, Kory. When my father died I had no one — no relatives here, no friends, no one to take care of me or help me. I just had God until Brother Rob came along … was sent by God. Maybe being blind is part of it, at least for me. I asked God if He would give me somewhere to go to talk just to Him, somewhere I could feel His presence. I figured it might be someplace near where I was living, maybe inside a church or some other real physical location. I cried out that prayer to God for quite awhile and kept trying to find where it might be. Then one day I tried to be quiet just where I was and … well I guess the best way to describe it is that I looked inward. I had heard that a part of God actually lives inside us — spiritually speaking. When I thought about that I wondered where such a mighty and beautiful God could reside within me? I mean, I knew I had lots of problems and faults — would God want to live in my ugliness?

What was inside of me anyway? I mean physically there is my body, and when I think about myself I also have my mind — I am not sure where that really resides … in my head I guess … but that part of me that is really ME — my mental image and thoughts of myself — that seems to be more than just some physical location. Brother Rob gave a sermon about our souls. That seemed to be it! If we have a soul, surely it is not physical or mental, but it must be a spiritual part of us that God created. If it is spiritual, and somehow is a part of me or 'in' me, then it seemed that might be where God Himself would dwell.

What would His dwelling place be like? It must be marvelous! A place where God would choose to dwell must be incredibly beautiful — if nothing else, it would become that once God arrived there!"

Kory spoke up again. "This is getting pretty deep. I am not sure I am tracking you totally here. I believe I have a soul, and I too have heard that God dwells in us … but I never connected the two. It does kinda make sense though. Then, what you are saying is that our souls are a beautiful place, fit for the God of the universe to hang out in?"

Maria laughed. "Yes, I do think God 'hangs out' in our souls! Therefore within us — spiritually — there is a place of absolute wonder and majesty that God created as a place for part of Him to reside. We are walking around with God inside us all the time!"

It was Lydia's turn to question. "But if God is in our souls, and with us all the time, then when we pray why do we tend to look toward heaven? I often look up, or assume I am talking to God who is far away … who is still listening attentively and loves me dearly, but who is far away in heaven?"

"I think He somehow is both … up there in heaven, and here within each of us. I don't understand that, but I think it is so."

Lydia spoke up again. "That is called 'omnipresent', where God can be everywhere all at the same time."

"Oh, I did not know there was a word for it. Omnipresent? Ok. So God is in each of our souls within us, all the time. When I thought about that I realized that I could pray to Him in heaven … but that seemed so very far away. If He is inside me, it seemed easier to pray and talk to Him there. So I tried to picture my own soul. I don't think that worked all that well at first, but I tried. I pictured a bright spot with pure white light. I could stand before that and somehow even within it, and God would be there. I asked God to make that real for me — to make it as real as anything else in my life — and I began to always go there to talk to Him. Over time it became more and more real and grew into a stage, and it became easier and easier to go to. After awhile I just thought of it as my 'special place' where I could always go whenever I wanted to talk to God. Eventually I was going there so often that it began to seem just as real as any other place."

Kory was certainly perplexed by all of this — but excited too. Yet she was still not satisfied. "But what about how you sing? I mean, I have heard other good singers at the Academy before; some apprentices and Masters are really, really skilled. But no one sings like you, Maria. It is like your singing is so much more, has entirely different dimensions to it. It somehow seems to connect me to God, as though it is a demonstration of God's Spirit and power, building up people's faith."

"Well, I don't know about that. I used to sing with my father — I remember his deep voice. We would sing to each other, and sometimes even sing duets in our church to the parishioners. When he died it was hard to sing. But then one day when I was talking to God in my special place I did not have any other words to say, but I just wanted to worship Him — so I started singing. I was not sure if anyone else could hear, but it did not really matter. It was great! It brought a whole new depth to my time with God. As I began to do that more and more, I started singing always to God instead of singing to people. Even simple songs. If I sing just to people now, it seems so flat and empty — it's almost like I am singing a sad song unless I am also singing in my special place to God too.

When I am singing to God the song comes alive … and somehow I am more alive too. I guess when I am in my special place I am more alive — I can see, I can dance, I can leap through the air … I can do flips and spins and twirls, I can sometimes even feel and see the music itself, interacting with it in ways I never could in the physical world. And lately it seems to me I am interacting even more with the music that ever before … ever since coming to the Keep it has been more intense each time."

Lydia was thoughtful. "You have a very special gift, Maria. God has given you a phenomenal ability to sing. You have a beautiful voice with incredible range and tone, and yet there is more. Somehow there is power in your singing … Godly spiritual power that interacts with the rest of us. Through your singing we start feeling God's power and presence. It is almost like we are joining you in your 'special place', at least in spirit. I for one have never felt anything else quite like it. It is a gift, an extraordinarily beautiful gift."

"I guess so, if you say it is. I am just worshiping God as He seems to direct. At the announcement today I did not even realize what I was doing, I was just following the direction I seemed to be given, and again I was just singing before God in my special place — I guess I must have been doing it out loud as well."

"That is the best way, Maria. Don't try to force it — don't use this for your desires or to bring honor to yourself."

"Oh my, no! It is not me … it is all God."

"Yes, Maria, it is. But He has packaged it in your small frame."

"It seems daunting. What if I mess it up? What if I use it wrong? What if …"

"Maria!" Lydia interrupted. "Keep trusting God and relying on His directions and guidance. Learn all the more to listen to Him. And, from what I have learned in my own personal experience, especially in my current role — have close trusted friends who love you enough to remind you to stay humble — and listen to them! Learn to ask for other's opinions; learn to think of others much more highly than yourself. Yes, sometimes God will tell you to do something and others may steer you wrong ... but those will be rare. Keep godly counsel, keep communicating with God — both talking and listening! — and keep going along the path He has shown you unless He tells you otherwise."

Maria thought about that a minute. "I sure would like to have friends like that."

Lydia looked over at Kory. "Maria, I think you have two right here."

Maria smiled and Kory helped her back to her chair. "Well, friends ... how about if we have some more tea?"

The three talked well into the evening. Lydia invited Kory and Maria to stay the night — the Chancellor's home was well outfitted for guests, and sent word to Mesha that the girls would be cared for and watched most closely. Each girl had her own sumptuous bedroom with a huge bed and the softest pillows Maria could ever imagine. As she sank into the warm comfort Maria marveled at the events of the last few days, and she danced a silent song of praise as she drifted off to sleep.

Kory was very tired, but also excited. She had never been in a discussion like this before, and she felt especially close to God. But what about Maria's 'special place'? Was it just for Maria? Kory knew she too had a soul, and she believed God did dwell within her ... could she too have a place of infinite beauty inside her? Did she too have a 'special place'? What about praying to God inside of her? What about playing music or singing with God as her audience instead of the Academy instructors or a room full of apprentices? Her sleepy mind was awhirl with possibilities. It was too much for her, at least tonight. Still, before her mind shut down entirely with slumber she tried to picture God inside her. "God … I know you listen when I talk to you. If possible, can I too have a 'special place' like Maria? Can you help me to find it? Can I … would it be alright to … talk to you there, and maybe play music and sing?"

Lydia had a harder time falling asleep. She kept going over and over the conversation with Maria. How had God chosen such a small little blind girl to be so spiritually mature? And what about this concept of a 'special place'? Lydia already felt pretty close to God most of the time. Yet this intrigued her — what if she felt God's presence all the time … had only to instantly visit with Him in her own 'special place' to get direction and guidance, and where she too could worship with ultimate freedom, focus and total sincerity? Was such a place truly available for all? Lydia felt it was very 'right'. "Oh God, open my mind to your dwelling place within me. I want such a place. I want that kind of closeness with Your Presence. I want that kind of worship before you." A peacefulness came over her, and as she settled down into her pillow she began to try to form a picture of such a place, where she too could dance and sing before her Maker.

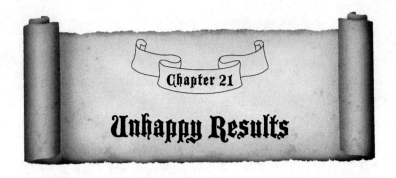

Chapter 21

Unhappy Results

The next day dawned clear over all of Freelandia. Jarl would have preferred dark and dreary, since it would have been more fitting for his and the other Rat's mission. However, this would have to do. Last night he and the others had stepped up their complaining and fear mongering, and some of the tavern patrons were becoming rather receptive to their gloomy message of impending doom. Word had come to him and the others about the planned assassination timing, so they were all to stir up as much trouble as possible when the news from the Keep filtered out, though none had actually made it to Jarl yet. Nevertheless, he and the others were to start the rumors now of the assassination of Chancellor Duncan and his wife, of Master Warden James, and of random people in the crowd who had gathered to hear them. Jarl smiled wickedly. This was going to be fun.

He ambled down to the tavern mid-morning for a late breakfast. Jarl had established a regular spot, and a reputation as a successful — and very generous — traveling salesman who regularly stopped over for a few days. Right outside the door Jarl put on a harried and very worried look and then ran the last few steps to burst into the tavern, panting heavily as though he had been running for blocks.

"I … I just heard! At the Keep!" He panted and wheezed, seemingly needing to catch his breath. "Dominion assassins! And they had their evil magic at work!"

"Hey, what is that, friend?" The owner of the tavern hurried over and every conversation stopped and every ear turned to listen.

"A rider just passed through — I was the only one on the street. He said Chancellor Duncan and Warden James had been assassinated yesterday as they gave announcements, and that many others were stricken with some terrible magic that turned their whole bodies black before they shriveled up like dried prunes and died a horrible death! Then he rode off to spread the news. I am telling you, this is JUST what I have been talking about! The Dominion is coming, and anyone who resists them is going to be the focus of their wrath and black magic. Our leaders here in Freelandia have just been struck because they would not listen, they would not see the facts and take the right action. We are all doomed unless we compromise and negotiate with the Dominion right away!"

The face of the proprietor and everyone else had gone ashen. "It can't be! Has God abandoned us? Have we come under His wrath? Why would He let that happen? Is it … is it our fault? Is He punishing us for our selfish ways?" He turned to his customers. "Everyone, hurry! We must go immediately! Forget your food — I will not accept money for it. We need to go!"

Jarl smiled. This was going even better than he had expected. They were ready to revolt right now! All he had to do was lead them out, rouse the whole town, and march on the Keep. Oh, this was going to be fun! "Right! Everyone, let's go! We must warn the rest of the town. Get your families, get your neighbors! Bring them all to the town center — I have a cart full of weapons I have been trying to sell, and we will take them and march … Huh?"

The tavern owner was looking at Jarl very strangely, as though he had concocted a nasty contagion, even taking a step back away from him. "We do need to tell everyone, I agree. But not to go to the town center! And why would we need weapons? Everyone, hurry, we must go to the church to repent and to pray!"

The customers rushed out following the proprietor, surging wide around a dumbfounded Jarl who was rooted to his spot in amazement, his mouth hanging open, wondering what had just happened.

Murdrock had made it back to the forest hovel on one of the horses that he had put in place for that purpose. The riding was marginally better on his ankle than walking, but every jostle sent waves of pain shooting up his leg. He was glad for the few opiate seeds he kept in a pocket for just such emergencies. As he slid off his horse in the dark wee hours of the morning his leg gave way completely and he cursed vehemently. The two archers half carried him into the cabin and helped to tightly wrap the sprained ankle to immobilize it. Then they compared notes. After an hour in which they went over every detail of preparation and operation, they could only reach one conclusion.

"That boy — who is he? And where did he come from — he seemed to just "appear" to block our mission objectives! That must be Freelandian magic — and a powerful one at that. We are going to have to work out how to "neutralize" him next time. We now need to regroup, set up some meetings with the Rats — let's see if at least that part of the plan bore fruit! And we need to get a message back to our Masters — they are NOT going to be pleased at all. And especially they are not going to like the loss of Turlock … and to his own poison filled hand! We have highly underestimated Freelandia's magic that is protecting them. Our dark lords must take that into their calculations and prepare countermeasures. And we need to begin planning something big — something to lessen the failure of the last 24 hours. Otherwise, I expect this will be our last report. And I don't need to tell you how we might be greeted if we are called home to report in person …" All three shuddered severely. They would far rather be captured by Freelandia than face the sure foul torture reserved for failure. "Maybe something concerning that boy … if he is the focus of that much Freelandian magic, he might be a rather valuable commodity to our Masters, maybe even a key for them to discover a way around the magic of this place. But first, we need to leave this hideout. Turlock was captured. He should be long dead by now, but we will not take any chances. Gather all our things. I have another safe house a half day's ride from here that Turlock did not know about." The others nodded in agreement and they began to pack their few belongings.

The Watchers were most annoyed with Chancellor Duncan. They wanted to keep him buttoned up within the safety of the Watcher Compound for the next several days ... or weeks ... or months ... but he would have none of that, believing now more than ever the people needed to see him and know for a certainty that the leadership of Freelandia was still strong — and now even more opposed to the Dominion. In fact, Duncan wanted more than ever to rally the people of Freelandia to that cause, and now he had an event to galvanize the people to rally support ... and action.

He was standing now outside of the largest church in the Keep, an hour after the bells inside its tall steeple peeled out to alert all nearby of a special proclamation. He stood atop a load of hay bales on a large cart — it was the most expedient stage he could find on the spot — and addressed the few hundred or so of citizens gathered around.

"Friends, you surely by now have heard of the treachery the Dominion planned against us yesterday. Their assassins tried to cowardly poison the leadership of Freelandia, and they indiscriminately murdered several innocent citizens in the public square. A dozen others are in serious condition at the Ministry of Healing, including Master Warden James, who surely would have died from the Dominion poison were it not for a miraculous intervention from God. Good people of Freelandia: these are acts of war committed against us by the Dominion! For what purpose? They wanted us to be in fear! They wanted us to be in confusion! They thought they could frighten us into submission. They thought their demon "magic" would prevail against the Most High God. This fight they have taken on is NOT against Freelandia. It is against our God. They have set themselves against God; they have challenged Him to a fight! And yet it is not the Dominion that has really made this challenge — it is the evil behind them who has always been against Truth and Holiness and Righteousness.

We must prepare for war. You will be hearing a lot more about that in the coming weeks and months. You will all be called on to help, to sacrifice — and many of you will be called on to take up arms and be ready to fight. The Dominion is indeed coming. We expect them to reach our shores. They want that to paralyze you with fear. But I want you to know … God IS NOT AFRAID! God is not the god of fear! God is the god of faith! Therefore be of good cheer — and of determination.

I have called a day of fasting and prayer. Pray for God's mercy and grace. Inventory your own heart and mind. Clean house! Repent of unrighteousness, ungodliness and faithlessness. Turn again to your God and Creator not with your heart left-overs, but with your WHOLE heart. God will win this war for His glory; He will save those who turn to Him, who run to Him. Do not rely on yourself … certainly do not rely on me or the High Council. Rely on God. Listen to Him and His Spirit. You all have gifts and skills from the creative God of the Universe. We will need those! We will be setting up community groups to review ideas, suggestions and anything else you believe God would want you to bring to our attention. Representatives of these groups will then meet with Council members and others regularly. We need you. When the Dominion comes against us, they will be met with the best of what God prepares!

Now, will you join me in a prayer of thanksgiving, and of petition before God that He will go before us and protect us?"

A few minutes later Duncan clambered down from his high perch. He would repeat this message all throughout the Keep today, and the members of the High Council were taking it out to every major city of Freelandia over the next few days.

Gaeten felt a peace settle over him, distinct from the past few days of worried concern that something was happening back in Freelandia, and he could do nothing about it. Well, not exactly nothing. He had prayed and fasted. He had several more days of sailing until the first stop at a small island port. His small trunk had already been … misplaced … during the night. Gaeten had sorely wanted to do something to the deck hand as he tried to "stealthily" creep up to steal the chest. Maybe just to tweak his nose or snap a finger on his ear. He had restrained himself, and almost lost his composure holding in a chuckle at the mental picture of that action. All was so far going as planned ….

An assistant of Master Warden James had just reported that an advance scouting party of crack Watchers had found the burning ruins of the forest shack that Turlock had directed them to. There was no evidence of any useful kind. The news was expected, but nonetheless not well received and the assistant was just leaving as Master Healer Mesha strode into the not-so-patient patient's room.

"See, I am perfectly well enough to assume my duties!" James was not accustomed to lying down for more hours than absolutely necessary for sleep. He scowled darkly. "Now get out of my way, and GIVE ME BACK MY CLOTHES!" The last was said with an impatient roar.

"No you are NOT!" Master Mesha was not particularly used to patients talking back when he gave firm commands to rest. "And if you do not lay back down I will personally ask Chancellor Duncan to relieve you of all your duties for at least a month or two … and you KNOW he will if I tell him it is essential for your complete healing! Now lie back down immediately, or I will have my nurse slip something into your next meal that will keep you next to the bathroom for the following 24 hours straight!"

"YOU WOULDN'T DARE, you overstuffed tyrant! If I felt any better you would see some terrible tyrant trouncing, that's for sure! I could take you on with both hands tied behind my back and one leg locked in irons, I would …"

"Oh hush up you wounded windbag of unworthiness! Tying up both your hands behind your back may just be a pretty good idea, and maybe stuff something in your big mouth to boot. You will get your clothes back when I am good and ready to give them to you, and not a moment before. And furthermore, I have sworn all the Watchers assigned here to obey my commands, even over yours. I told them if I catch any of them trying to assist you in leaving early that I will see to it that the only healers who will ever be available to help them will be the lowest assistants who have barely any practice in setting bones and no training yet in pain relief. Now SIT, SHUSH and SLEEP!"

James slumped back down on his bed. Actually, he knew he was quite weak — but the work on Freelandia's defenses just could not wait, and he was the person the Council had put in charge, and even more, without undue pride he knew also he was the best person for the job. He grimaced and his bravado disappeared. "But … but Freelandia needs me!"

Mesha had watched the play of emotions work their way across the Warden's face and toned down his own rhetoric. "James — you will be far more valuable to Freelandia if you are in good health. I understand your situation. Perhaps we can work out a compromise. I think we could set you up in a larger room, one with a desk perhaps, and allow an hour of visitors two times a day starting tomorrow. That can increase as you grow stronger. But no travel — people will just have to come here to see you." As he saw the bluster starting to return he added "That is not negotiable. If needed I can readily revoke it. James — you are just going to have to delegate, there is no way around that. You have good people under you. Chose some of them, or choose entirely new people — but delegate and organize."

James knew this was good advice. "Alright healer. You are right — I have many talented and capable people under me. But are they the RIGHT people? — we can't afford to be wrong, we don't have time to do things over."

Mesha looked on rather gravely. "Since we cannot afford to be wrong, perhaps we should not be the ones doing the picking. James, there are many spiritually gifted people in the Keep — perhaps it would be best to bring in your top candidates and ask God to show who He wants in charge of each of the major tasks."

James looked up. "Hmmm — sounds like a great idea for several of the leadership positions! For some my choice is obvious, but for others I have hesitations. Oh, and then there are the Engineers. I really am not sure what to do with them. Could you send in one of my assistants? I think I should get started on this right away."

Mesha smiled as he left the room. Now James had something to wrap his mind and energy around while seeming to accept his ordered rest. That was its own little miracle!

Duncan looked up from his reports as Lydia glided in. She seemed to be in a cheerful mood — somewhat surprising for someone who had survived an assassination attempt on herself and her husband. "I see you are finally up?"

"Humph! Just because you felt you had to be up and out at the crack of dawn to give those speeches does not mean the rest of us had to be!"

"Say, what was all the chattering last evening about anyway? I saw two young girls with you in the parlor. I came back home late, and yet the three of you were in there talking and giggling even after I went to bed!"

"Yes, dear — that was Maria and Kory. Maria is The Singer. The one from Sir Reginaldo's concert. She is a most remarkable young lady with a most singular gifting. God has something big in store for her, something very important for Freelandia."

"What is that? What do you mean?"

"I don't know for sure. I just sense from God that Maria is to play a vital role in the conflict between Freelandia and the Dominion. As such, I thought it pretty important to get to know her … and to be a friend. She is such a sweet girl, too. Kory is a friend of hers that Grand Master Vitario assigned to help her out over at the Academy of Music."

"Okay. I am not sure how a singing little girl will be used by God against the Dominion, but I surely have seen stranger things."

"How did your talks across the Keep go, dear?"

Duncan smiled himself. "Quite well I think. Everyone seemed to rally around the need to put preparations into high gear, and I did not see any panic. The attempt by the Dominion to strike fear has instead struck steel — it has had the opposite effect they desired."

Lydia laughed. "What the Dominion has purposed for evil God has used for good! I think we are going to see a rekindling of spiritual dynamics, a revival of calling on the living God and dependence on Him. Such refining is not pleasant — but the end result of purity is worth it!"

"Yes, I agree. To refine a precious metal our smiths have to heat the metal to melt it — a lot of heat! The dross floats to the top and is skimmed off. They do this multiple times, increasing the heat with each cycle to get the metal purer. One of our smiths once told me he continues this process until he can look down on the surface of the molten metal and see his perfect reflection. I think God does that with us too. To make us pure we seem to have to go through many steps where the heat is on in the form of various troubles. The dross in our own lives — selfishness, pride, whatever — seems to come out more when life is not going as smoothly as we want. If we keep taking our troubles to God, keep coming to Him for answers and keep doing things His way, that dross gets removed bit by bit. I don't know if we can every truly get perfected here on earth, but more and more we can reflect our Maker's image to the world around us."

Lydia nodded. "I think the heat is being turned up several notches for us now. The next few months could get rather scorching!"

It was Duncan's turn to nod in agreement. "Indeed … and we have already seen some of the dross of unbelief coming up. At the same time, the events of the past few weeks have all the more shown God's mercy and love over us. The prophecy was given hundreds of years ago, and yet is valid right now. Ethan's gifting is phenomenal … and I expect we are just starting to see it in action. We have been told that the sheer inventiveness of the population appears to be abounding, and the gifts of the Spirit seem to be on the rise and growing more powerful. God is preparing us. Preparing us for something big."

Lydia looked pale, yet determined. "And out of the blue comes along this singer — Maria — who has a gifting to bring us into the worshipful presence of God like we have never experienced or even ever heard of.

I only hope and pray we will be ready…"

The end of Book 1 of the Freelandia Trilogy.